THE PRINCE OF DARKNESS
(*The fourth in the Plantagenet Saga*)

With the untimely death of Richard Coeur de Lion there were two contenders for the throne—one was Richard's nephew Arthur and the other was his youngest brother, John.

With misgivings the leading barons chose John, for although already his reputation was not one to recommend him, Arthur had never lived in England and was regarded there as a foreigner.

John's unpleasant character was soon revealed and his unbridled sensuality, his fierce and terrible temper, his cruelty, his slothfulness and indifference to duty, his injustice and cynical methods of taxation were, in time, to drive the barons to revolt.

John's passion for the beautiful and voluptuous Isabella of Angoulême and his abduction of her when she was a girl of twelve and betrothed to the powerful Hugh de Lusignan was to prove one of the factors which led to the loss of his overseas dominions.

When it became obvious that Arthur was a real menace to his position, John devised the cruellest means of preventing his nephew's taking the crown, and although he was foiled in this by the noble Hubert de Burgh, Arthur later disappeared mysteriously and John was suspected of his murder—a suspicion from which he was never allowed to escape and which proved to be a rallying cry for his enemies.

These were some of the darkest days of England's history when the country was under the Interdict and the King excommunicated, when John all but lost his crown and there were foreign invaders on English soil.

At the heart of the tragedy was John—the King whom all his subjects feared until they defied him, exposed his weakness and forced him to Runnymede where he had no choice but to sign the famous Magna Carta.

His cruelty, the callous manner in which he inflicted suffering on his enemies caused people to believe the legend that the House of Anjou had been infected by the Devil's blood. In John the satanic characteristics were intensified, and many of those who suffered at his hands believed that he was the Prince of Darkness, the Devil himself.

See pages 318 and 319 for a complete list of books by
Jean Plaidy

THE PRINCE OF DARKNESS

JEAN PLAIDY

ROBERT HALE · LONDON

© *Jean Plaidy 1978*
First published in Great Britain 1978
Reprinted 1979

ISBN 0 7091 5404 6

Robert Hale Limited
Clerkenwell House
Clerkenwell Green
London EC1R 0HT

Text decorations by
B. S. Biro

Printed in Great Britain by
Richard Clay (The Chaucer Press) Ltd, Bungay, Suffolk

CONTENTS

BIBLIOGRAPHY

Appleby, John T.	*John, King of England*
Ashley, Maurice	*The Life and Times of King John*
Aubrey, William Hickman Smith	*National and Domestic History of England*
d'Auvergne, Edmund B.	*John, King of England*
Barlow, F.	*The Feudal Kingdom of England*
Brooke, F. W.	*From Alfred to Henry III*
Bryant, Arthur	*The Medieval Foundation*
Davis, H. W. C.	*England Under the Angevins*
Guizot, M. (translated by Robert Black)	*History of France*
Hume, David	*History of England from the Invasion of Julius Caesar to the Revolution*
Lloyd, Alan	*King John*
Norgate, Kate	*John Lackland*
Norgate, Kate	*England under the Angevin Kings*
Poole, A. L.	*From Domesday Book to Magna Carta*
Stenton, D. M.	*English Society in the Early Middle Ages*
Strickland, Agnes	*Lives of the Queens of England*
Stevens, Sir Leslie and Lee, Sir Sidney (Edited by)	*The Dictionary of National Biography*
Wade, John	*British History*
Warren, W. I.	*King John*

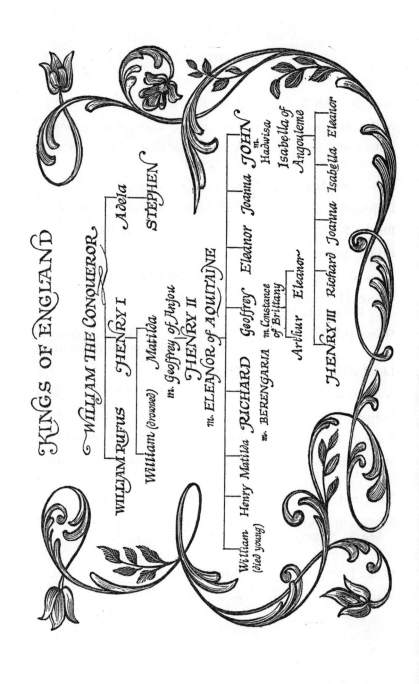

KINGS OF ENGLAND

WILLIAM THE CONQUEROR

WILLIAM RUFUS   HENRY I   Adela

William (drowned)   Matilda   STEPHEN
                     m. Geoffrey of Anjou
                     HENRY II
                     m. ELEANOR of AQUITAINE

William   Henry Matilda RICHARD   Geoffrey Eleanor Joanna JOHN
(died young)   m. BERENGARIA m. Constance   m.
                                         of Brittany   Hadwisa
                                         Arthur Eleanor   Isabella of
                                                                  Angouleme

                                         HENRY III Richard Joanna Isabella Eleanor

Death of a King

In a quiet room in the Château of Vaudreuil William Marshal, the most respected of all the King's knights, sat dozing pleasantly after an excellent dinner of roast venison. Half sleeping, half waking he was considering what a happy state of affairs existed now that the King had returned from the Holy Land and was bringing law and order back to his dominions. Already England was at peace and Richard had restored much of that land which Philip Augustus, King of France—stealing an advantage because Richard was far away —had taken from him in Normandy.

William Marshal, known in the days of his youth as the finest knight of the age, renowned for his integrity and as a man who was not afraid to offend the King even though it could mean risking his life—and therefore cherished by wise kings such as Richard and his father before him—was now in his mid-fifties but still strong and with the weight of experience to lean on, appeared to have gained rather than lost from the passing of the years.

He had deplored the King's absence from the country, for, while he accepted the fact that Richard had made a vow to bring Jerusalem back to Christendom, he had believed that a king's first duty was to his own kingdom; he had been against the excessive taxation which had had to be imposed in order to raise money for the crusade, but he had been indefatigable in getting together the funds required for the King's ransom when it had been discovered that Richard was in his enemy's hands in the castle of Dürenstein.

Now, his brother John's attempt to take the crown from him during his absence had been foiled and Richard was restored to his people. As William saw it, the prospects were fair—or as fair as they ever could be, considering the vulnerability of the dukedom of Normandy situated as it was on the very borders of French territory.

His wife Isabella came into the room and looked at him with affection. She was a good wife and he had married her when Richard had come to the throne. She had brought him not only fine sons but riches, for her father had been Richard de Clare Earl of Pembroke and Striguel and, although the King had not yet confirmed William in the 'full peace and name of earl', the earldom was in his possession, and that ceremony would be performed in due course. Before his marriage he had been known as the 'landless knight' and had had little to recommend him but his noble birth and unrivalled skills. Henry II had recognized these and put him in charge of his eldest son Prince Henry (after he had been misguided enough to crown him so that the boy had had the title of King while his father still lived—one of the gravest mistakes that usually wise monarch had ever made, for the boy, as was to be expected, became arrogant, immediately flaunting his title and flouting his father, finally making war against him and, with his brothers, bringing him in sorrow to the grave).

Smiling at Isabella William said: 'I was back in the past, thinking of the time when Richard came to the throne.'

She looked at him gravely. 'You thought then, William, that your hopes of rising in the world were ended for ever.'

He nodded. 'And that death and imprisonment would be my lot.'

He lapsed into silence, thinking of that time when Richard was his enemy because he was making war on his father Henry II, whose staunch henchman he, William, was at that time, and how he had come face to face with a defenceless Richard and could have killed him. He had had no wish to do that, but he had satisfied himself by calling him traitor and killing his horse from under him. And soon afterwards Henry had died and Richard was the King.

He mused: 'I shall never forget it, Isabella.'

'I know. You have told me many times how you waited for him to order you to a dungeon and how instead he told you that he could trust one who had served his father well to serve him.'

'I was determined he should never regret that decision,' said William.

'Nor has he. He could never have had a more faithful knight and full well he knows it.'

'He has been good to us, Isabella. He is generous to his friends. Open, honest, forthright ... a man after my own heart. I knew he meant our family well when he commanded me to carry the gold sceptre at his coronation and my brother John the spurs, and how right I was!'

'And he allowed us to marry.'

'The most important benefit of all,' he answered.

'Well you have served him well ever since. I wonder when we shall be hearing of the birth of an heir.'

'He has not long returned to Berengaria. But he knows his duty and that the dissatisfaction his subjects feel will end when he gives the country an heir. He is young and vigorous still.'

'But they have been married so long.'

'But parted.'

'It seems to have been a strange marriage.'

'It was certain to be. The King loves battle better than women.'

'It seems unnatural that a man cannot want sons.'

He smiled at her fondly. She was proud of hers. He did not want to say that Richard preferred the company of his own sex to that of women and it was only his meeting with a hermit in a forest, when he was hunting and temporarily alone, who had so harangued him about the life he led and prophesied disaster, that had made him consider reforming his ways; and when shortly afterwards he had been laid low with a fever which threatened to end his life he had decided to return to Berengaria and do his duty by his country.

It was late, thought William. But better late than never. Richard was a man of immense strength and apart from the fever which periodically attacked him he was very healthy. If he could produce a son or two and live until they had reached maturity, that would be good for England.

'I doubt not,' he answered his wife, 'that when his son is born he will be as delighted with him as any father would be ... and more so, considering the importance to the realm. I trust that soon he will be sending me news that the queen is expecting.'

'Poor Berengaria. Hers has not been a very happy life I fear.'

'Such is the fate of queens, my dear.'

She sighed. 'I dare swear one should be grateful that one was not born royal.'

It was pleasant to have her so satisfied with her lot. She never referred to the riches and title she had brought him for she considered herself the most fortunate of women and he hoped she would long continue to do so.

As they sat talking together there was a sudden clatter of horse's hoofs in the courtyard. William stood up hastily.

'Who can it be?' he wondered.

Isabella was at the window.

'It looks like a messenger.' She turned to him, her eyes shining with excitement. 'I wonder if it is ... It seems so odd. We were but talking of it a few minutes ago.'

'Come,' said William, 'we will go and see.'

They hurried down to the courtyard but one look at the face of the messenger was enough to tell William that the news he brought was not good.

He had dismounted and a groom had taken his horse. William cried: 'What news?'

'Ill news, my lord.'

'Tell me. Let me know the worst.'

'The King has been wounded ... mortally some say.'

'It is not possible. In what action?'

'At Chaluz against Odamar of Limoges and Achard of Chaluz.'

'This makes no sense to me.'

'My lord, you were unaware that treasure was found on the land of Achard of Chaluz. News reached the King that gold figures had been discovered by a ploughman and claiming that as the suzerain this belonged by right to him he went forth to demand the treasure be given up. Achard declared that what had been found was nothing but a pot of old coins but the King did not believe him and attacked the castle. During the attack an arrow went into the King's shoulder.'

'This is impossible,' cried William. 'A foolish quarrel over a pot of coins.'

' 'Tis so, my lord. The King sent for me. He is mortally ill and in great anguish. He has tried to pull the arrow from his shoulder but in doing so has broken it and it remains imbedded in his flesh and is mortifying. He has sent me to you commanding that you go at once to Chinon and there take charge of the royal treasure.'

'He will recover,' said William. 'He *must* recover.'

The messenger shook his head. 'I saw his face, my lord. There was death there.'

'Come in and refresh yourself,' said William. 'You will be weary from your journey. I must to Chinon with all speed.'

Isabella came out and seeing her husband's face asked what ill news he had received.

William told her. She was bewildered. 'What will this mean?' she asked.

'He has faced death many times. Always he has recovered. We must hope.'

While William Marshal was preparing to leave for Chinon yet another messenger came to Vaudreuil. This one brought the news that Richard Coeur de Lion had died of the wound he had received from an arrow shot by Bertrand de Gourdon, a nobleman of Quercy who bore a grudge against him and who since had declared that he was ready to suffer the greatest torments if need be, for he would die happy having seen Richard on his death bed.

So the King was dead. What was to follow?

*   *   *

Arriving at Chinon, and assuring himself that the royal treasure was well guarded, William asked Hubert Walter, the Archbishop of Canterbury, who was by good fortune in Normandy at the time, to come to him at once. Realizing the gravity of the situation Hubert lost no time in complying with this request.

William embraced the Archbishop and took him to a private chamber where they could talk together without being overheard.

'What think you of the news?' asked William.

The Archbishop shook his head gravely.

'It could be disastrous.'

'Everything hangs on the next few months.'

'If he had but lived with his wife; if he had produced sons...'

'Any son they had had would as yet be a minor.'

'That would not have disturbed me. He could have been tutored and there would have been a king.'

'There is a king now,' said William.

'Who? John or Arthur?'

'It must be John,' insisted William.

'Nay, my friend, the true heir to the throne is Prince Arthur.'

'In the direct line of succession may be, but I for one could never support Arthur's claim.'

'You mean you will give your allegiance to John!'

'I deplore that it is necessary, but I see no other way.'

'My good friend, Arthur is the son of Geoffrey and Geoffrey was older than John. Therefore according to the law of succession Arthur is the true heir.'

'The selection of kings does not necessarily depend on direct succession. Suitability must be considered and Arthur is a child.'

'But John is dissolute and unfit for the crown.'

'The English would never accept Arthur.'

'They would accept the fact that he is the true heir to the throne because that is what he is.'

'Nay, Archbishop. Henry II named John as his heir—even to come before Richard.'

'That was wrong. Richard was the elder brother and more fitted to reign. The people would never have accepted John while Richard lived.'

'That I agree with and Richard had no intention of standing aside for his younger brother. Henry realized this in his last moments, when John's true nature was revealed, and would have approved of what was done. But now Richard is dead and the natural heir is John.'

'You are wrong, Marshal. Arthur is the true heir.'

'A boy who has never been to England, who speaks no English, brought up in foreign courts! The English will never accept him. Moreover, John would be determined to take the crown, and there would be continual strife. Many would be behind John. They are prepared for him to follow his brother. He has lived in England. He is English. They will not take a foreigner and little more than a child at that. Arthur I have heard is haughty and proud and has no love for the English. Prince John is the one who is nearest to his father and his brother Richard. John should follow him.'

'Marshal, is this really your wish?'

'It is, my lord, for it seems but good sense to me. A son has a closer claim to his father's inheritance than his grandson can have. It is right that John should take the crown.'

'There will be conflict over this. Arthur will have his supporters and John will have his.'

'I consider it right and in the interests of the country that John should be offered the crown,' said the Marshal stubbornly.

The Archbishop inclined his head. 'So shall it be. But know this, Marshal, and remember what I say, for the day will come when you will question your decision. I promise you that nothing you ever did have you so much cause to repent of as you will have of this.'

'If you are right,' answered William judiciously, 'and it may be that you will be proved right, still I know this should be and that I am but following the will of my masters—King Henry II and Richard the Lion-Hearted—in proclaiming Prince John King of England.'

'So be it,' said the Archbishop but he continued to shake his head sorrowfully.

In spite of his firm assurances that he had done the right thing, William Marshal was very uneasy; after all, if there was such sturdy disagreement between two men who wished the crown and the country the greatest good fortune—which it would assuredly need—how was it possible to expect the people to be of one mind?

Of one thing all could be certain. With two such claimants to the throne there would be trouble.

Oh, why had Richard to die at such a time—and all for a few coins in a pot!

*   *   *

Joanna, the King's sister, was on her way to Normandy. She had determined to make the journey before her pregnancy prevented her. She and her husband, Raymond of Toulouse, needed help and she believed that Richard could and would come to their aid; he had been a kindly and generous brother to her, except on one occasion when he had planned to marry her to the Saracen Malek Adel in order to further his treaty with Saladin, but she had always believed that he had never

been very serious about that. Indeed when she had in-
dignantly refused he had made no effort to coerce her and the
event had not interfered with the devotion between them.

Richard had been a hero to her when as a young girl she
had travelled out to Sicily to be married to the king of that
island and Richard had conducted her across Aquitaine.
Later she had joined him in Sicily when the island had been
seized by Tancred; she had become companion duenna to his
wife Berengaria before her marriage to Richard and afterwards had been Berengaria's constant companion until she
herself had married Raymond of Toulouse.

She had often thought of Berengaria with pity, and wondered how she was faring. She knew a great deal about the
married life of the Queen of England for she had been with
her during the first years of her marriage to Richard. He had
never been actively unkind to her; he had merely behaved as
though she did not exist. Perhaps it would have been more
comforting to have lived a stormy life with him; dislike
would have been easier to bear than indifference. How
embarrassing it had been—for both she and Berengaria knew
that he was constantly seeking excuses to avoid her.

Joanna would have liked to explain to Berengaria: It is
not you in person who does not please him. It is the fact that
you are a woman. He does not like our sex. It is extraordinary
that one who is so strong, so vital, with every characteristic of
manliness so firm in him, should lack this one. People talked
as much as they dared of his one-time passionate friendship
with the King of France, of his close ties with favoured
knights, of the devotion of boys such as Blondel de Nesle, the
minstrel who had travelled across Europe in search of him
when he was incarcerated in the fortress of Dürenstein, and
had discovered his whereabouts by singing a song which they
had composed together and none had sung but them. In the
beginning though, poor Berengaria had known nothing of
this.

And when Joanna had married Raymond she had said
farewell to her companion of several years and had gone to
her new life. Raymond had not disappointed her and they
had a beautiful son—Raymond like his father—now two years
old, and she had found contentment in her married life. Her
husband's court was one where beauty was appreciated; he
loved music; and poets and troubadours were encouraged; in

the great halls of his castles songs would be composed and judged; religious views were aired and there was great freedom of thought throughout his domain. Alas, this had been noticed and reported to Rome and since it seemed to the leaders of the Catholic church that some of the doctrines freely discussed were subversive and could harm that powerful body, it was made known to rival barons that if they attacked Raymond, Rome would be behind them.

This knowledge had stunned both Raymond and Joanna; there had merely been one or two skirmishes at first but now the hostility was growing more marked and it was because of this that Joanna had decided that she would approach Richard and ask his advice for she had no doubt that he would come to their aid.

She and Raymond had decided that she was the one to put the case before him; he would listen to her; moreover, he had always been a man to respect family ties. She remembered well his indignation when he had arrived in Sicily to find her Tancred's prisoner and it was not only the thought of her rich dowry which Tancred had confiscated which made him delay his journey to the Holy Land to right her wrongs.

As she travelled towards Normandy she was contemplating the pleasure of her reunion with Berengaria who, she had heard, was now with Richard. That was good news. Perhaps by this time Berengaria was in the same happy condition as she herself; she hoped so. How Berengaria would love a child! And Richard must realize that it was necessary to establish the succession.

Her mission was not of the happiest and she was deeply concerned for Raymond, but there should be compensations at the end of her journey.

Ahead of her lay the Château Gaillard, and she was filled with pride as she contemplated it ... this magnificent castle which Richard had declared should be the finest in France— and it was. The great fortress glittered in the sun as though flaunting its defiance to the King of France and any who might come against it. Its mighty rectangular bastions, its seventeen towers, its curtain walls, its casements cut in the rock, proclaimed the might of the man who would always be remembered as the Lion Heart, her brother Richard who had never failed her and she knew never would as long as he lived.

Alas her comfort was to be shattered. Richard was not at his castle. He had left for Chaluz for he had heard rumours of great treasure which had been found there on the land of one of his vassals.

She set out for Chaluz unaware of the tragedy which awaited her there.

The battle was over. The castle of Chaluz had fallen to Richard but, though Richard had won his pot of coins, he had lost his life in doing so.

Everyone seemed stunned by the news. There had been about Richard an aura of invincibility. Often, being a victim of a virulent fever—which had pursued him all his life—he had now and then come near to death but always he had risen from his sick bed as strong as he had been before the attack. This time, however, death had caught up with him through an arrow shot by a certain Bertrand de Gourdon.

At least she could be reunited with Berengaria. They embraced warmly and Berengaria took her to her private chamber that they might share their grief in secret.

'He was too young to die,' was all Joanna could say.

Berengaria wept silently. 'Such a waste of life,' she said. 'Mine too, for mine is ended now.'

'You were together at the end,' said Joanna soothingly.

'In a way. He never wanted to be with me. It was just that he felt he must do his duty.'

'Berengaria, are you with child?'

She shook her head.

'More is the pity,' said Joanna.

They mingled their tears and found comfort in each other's company. Each was wondering what the future could hold for her. Berengaria—a queen without a husband—(in truth she often thought she had never really had one) with no child who would give her a reason for living. It would be a return to the old pattern, existing uneasily—no doubt on the bounty of relations. Perhaps she could go to her sister Blanche who was married to the Count of Champagne. In whatever direction she looked the future was fraught with uneasiness. While Richard lived she had always hoped that life would be different, that some spark of affection might be kindled. If they could have had children—say two sons and a daughter—then he would not have felt the need to get more and there might have been a certain peace between them. It was the physical relationship which had repelled him; and because he was a king and it was expected of him to provide an heir it had hung like a shadow between them—something which must be done and being distasteful to him it must be to her.

Joanna's thoughts were sombre. She was thinking of Richard's death caused by this trivial arrow at this unnecessary siege when he had come through a hundred battles with the fierce Saracens in the Holy War. It was an ironic twist of fate that he who was so noble and had earned the title of the Lion-Hearted, should have ended his life in such a petty cause. Moreover, now that he was dead who would help her and Raymond against their enemies?

Berengaria in due course talked of the last days of Richard's life, of the terrible agony which beset him and how he had forgiven the man who had killed him.

'That was noble of him,' said Joanna. 'And what I would expect of him. Bertrand de Gourdon will bless him to the end of his days.'

Berengaria answered: 'His days are over. Richard forgave him but others did not. You remember Mercadier?'

'Wasn't he the general who led Richard's mercenaries? Yes, I do remember that Richard thought highly of him and that they were constantly together.'

'He was beside himself with grief and rage when Richard died. So much so that he defied the King's orders and commanded that Gourdon be put to death in the most cruel way he could think of.'

'But Richard had pardoned him!'

' 'Twas so and what was done will not be laid at his door. Bertrand de Gourdon's eyes were put out before he was flayed alive.'

'Oh my God,' cried Joanna. 'Is there no end to this violence?' She put her hands to the protuberance of her body and felt the movement of her child there. 'It seems an evil omen. I wonder what will become of this child and of us all.'

Berengaria hurried over to her and put her arms about her. 'Be thankful, Joanna,' she said, 'that you have borne one son and carry the fruit of your husband's continued love for you.'

Then Joanna was ashamed and reproached herself for her

selfishness. Berengaria's was the tragedy. There was no child to remind her of her husband's love; there was indeed none of which to be reminded.

*　　　　*　　　　*

Queen Eleanor was in Chaluz; she too had come with all speed when she heard of her beloved son's condition. His death was the greatest blow which fate could have dealt her. She was seventy-seven years of age; he was but forty-two. Ever since his birth and those days when he had been her champion in the nursery in her battles against his father, he had been at the centre of her life. She had loved him as she could love no other; valiantly she had fought to hold his kingdom together when he was absent on his crusades; and now that he was home and seemed set fair to reign for many years and she had at last retired to the seclusion of the Abbey of Fontevraud, she was called forth to be with him during his last hours on earth.

Her grief was such that as she told her daughter Joanna— whom she loved only second to Richard—and her daughter-in-law Berengaria for whom she had always had a fondness, her only comfort was that she herself could not have long to live, for a world which did not contain her beloved son Richard had little in joy to offer her.

So the women who had loved him mourned together and found a little comfort in talking of him—of his greatness, of his valour, of his love of poetry and music, his talent for composing them.

'There was never one such as he was,' said Eleanor. 'Nor will there ever be.'

She would see that his wishes were carried out. 'He told me,' she said, 'that he wished his heart—that great lion heart—to be buried in his beloved and faithful city of Rouen, the home of his ancestors the dukes of Normandy for so many years. And his body is to be buried at Fontevraud at the feet of his father. He repented at the end of his life of the strife between them. God knows it was not of his making. Henry was to blame for the conflict between him and his sons. He was a man who could never let go anything once it had fallen into his hands, and he lost sight of the fact that his sons were men.'

She smiled, looking right back to the turbulent years when

she and Henry Plantagenet had been first passionate lovers and then equally passionate enemies.

Yes, Richard's wishes should be carried out. She would serve him in death as she always had in life.

She would go back to Fontevraud and spend the rest of her life there and she would make some show of repenting for her sins, which secretly she could not regret for she knew that if by some miracle she could regain her youth and vitality she would commit them all over again and she was too much of a realist, and her mind was still too active and lively, for her to be able to deceive herself that it would have been otherwise.

Now she took stock of her daughter, who was so obviously pregnant.

'Take care of yourself, my dear child,' she said. 'It is tragic that Richard cannot help Raymond. Your husband must be strong against his enemies for you will get little help from John.' She frowned. 'John will be the King now. It could not be my grandson. Arthur is too young. He is all Breton and the English would never accept him.'

'Mother,' said Joanna, 'do you not think that there will be those who will attempt to put Arthur on the throne?'

'There are always those who are ready to find a cause for conflict,' she said. 'In England though, John will be safe. It is here that he must take great care. Philip is always ready to seize a pretext for attack. It will always be so, for the kings of France are the natural enemies of the dukes of Normandy. Oh God,' she went on, 'I fear for John. I fear for Normandy and England ... This is a tragic blow not only to us, my daughters, but for the kingdom.'

Then with characteristic energy she made plans for them. Joanna must go back to her husband without the help she had come to ask from Richard; as for Berengaria she might stay with Joanna for a while and then perhaps join her sister until she could make plans for her future. Her brother Sancho the Strong would no doubt welcome her at his court; and although Eleanor did not say so, in her thoughts came the notion that perhaps a husband would in due course be found for Berengaria. She was still of an age to bear children. Oh yes, it might well be she would yet make a marriage that was more truly one than that with the late King of England.

But now there was nothing to do but mourn.

They took him to Fontevraud that his wishes should be

carried out. His heart had been taken from his body and it was said that it astounded all who beheld it because of its size. He was indeed the Lion-Hearted. They dressed him in the robes he had worn when he had been crowned in England; and so they laid him in his tomb. The women who had loved him wept for him, and Hugh of Lincoln, with whom he had had many a difference during his lifetime and who had often reproached him for the life he led, performed the last rites of the Church over his body, and while he prayed for his soul he wept for the passing of one who for all his sins had been a great king.

John and Arthur

AN uneasy atmosphere had prevailed in the Court of Brittany since the arrival of that unexpected visitor, Prince John, Count of Mortain, brother of Richard the First of England—a man whose reputation was such as to lead the people to believe the legend that the Devil's blood had at one time infected the House of Anjou and that the Prince of Darkness had come to Earth again in the person of Prince John.

John had been guilty of almost every known sin during the thirty-two years he had lived to plague those around him, so it would seem that he had plenty of time left to him to commit more; and he showed every intention of living up to those expectations.

He was under medium height—a small man in a family of tall brothers. Richard was a giant in comparison and John had always been very much aware of the advantage that gave him. Lest any should be under the impresson that a lack of inches implied weakness he was determined that all about him should be aware of his importance, so he surrounded himself with companions who applauded all his actions, knowing that if they did not they would be out of favour which could result in disastrous consequences for them; he dressed in a flamboyant manner—his clothes must be of the most costly material and he liked to adorn himself with fine jewels; he strutted through the castles he visited as though he owned them and was the overlord of all; he was greedy and extravagant, his temper was as violent as that of his father had been, yet Henry II had always endeavoured to be just, even when his rage was in possession of him; John had no concern with justice. The only thing that mattered to him was his own pleasure; and one of his greatest delights was to see people cringe before him while he taunted them with the power he held over them. Because he was aware that his brother Richard had power over him, he was determined to remind everyone else he had power over them.

He hated Richard because he was jealous of him and bitterly he coveted what was his. Richard was known as the Lion-Heart and secretly John knew that he himself was John the Coward. Richard was the greatest general of his age; John was not interested in war except when it was victorious. Then he would enjoy pillaging the towns, setting fire to the buildings and raping the women. But it did not always turn out like that; and as one of his greatest pleasures was to sport with women he reckoned he could do that without having to face the preliminaries of war which might not always bring the results he sought.

He was comparatively pleased with his lot. He was the youngest son of a great King; and he often laughed to think how he had deluded his father. Almost to the end Henry had believed that his beloved youngest was the only one who loved him. Loved him! As if John ever loved anyone but John. He believed it was folly to do so. How could one get what one wanted if one was ever swayed by emotions towards others which could be self-detrimental? It had given him a great deal of pleasure to realize how he had pulled the wool over his father's eyes. Henry Plantagenet was supposed to be a wise king, and yet his youngest son had deceived him completely, and while Henry was talking of leaving his kingdom to the only son who loved him, John was making preparations to desert him and join Richard, which at that time was the profitable thing to do.

But his father had discovered just before his death what a perfidious son he had. Some said it hastened his death. So much the better, thought John. He was finished, that old man. But there had remained Richard.

How he had rejoiced when his brother had gone off to the Holy Land. He didn't often resort to prayer but he had then—urging God to send a poisoned arrow through his brother's heart. It did not seem an unreasonable request since Richard was constantly in the midst of fierce and bloodthirsty Saracens. How like Richard to escape!

John congratulated himself that he had come very near to taking the kingdom. That would have served Richard right. If a man was a king he should be in his kingdom not gallivanting over the world trying to win glory by conquering Jerusalem. Which, John thought with great satisfaction, he had failed to do; and moreover, found himself the prisoner of his enemies. A curse on those who rescued him and particularly on young Blondel who had gone out singing all over Europe until he found him and making such a pretty story of it that the people regarded their errant king as a hero of romance.

Well, that was in the past and there was the future to think of.

Richard, curse him, was back; strong and healthy and only just turned forty—ten years older than John, but what was ten years? They all said he looked like a god and that he was invincible. The King of France, who had, while Richard was in the hands of his enemies, been prepared to work against him to such an extent that he would have put John on the throne, as soon as Richard returned had cried off. It seemed that everyone was afraid of Richard. He was said to have some mystical quality. He was the great hero—*Coeur de Lion.* Yet he had no heir and was chary of getting one.

John laughed aloud at the thought. There had been their father lusting after every woman he saw and being a king not inclined to deny himself the pleasure of their company which in the circumstances they would find it very difficult to refuse; and he John was of a similar nature. His father had a romantic streak; he liked to get a woman to his bed with fair words and promises and he was said to have an unrivalled gift for this; with John it was different. He dispensed with such preliminaries. He liked a woman to show fear; it made the experience so much more exciting for him. Well, there they were, his father and himself—and he had no reason to believe that his brothers, since dead, were any different and he was sure they had enjoyed this pastime as well as that of hunting the deer or the boar. But Richard was different—Richard the strong man, the Lion Heart—he had no fancy for women but chose his beloved friends from his own sex.

John could never think of that without giving way to gusty

laughter. It was his weakness—just as the tertian fever was; and it seemed comic to John because both weaknesses were so alien to the image which Richard had always presented to the world.

It was a most convenient state of affairs, for Richard, being what he was, seemed unlikely to get himself an heir and while Richard was disinclined to do this and Berengaria remained unfruitful, the crown of England was well within John's grasp.

That was what he wanted. He longed to possess it. He could work himself into a violent passion just thinking of it. His father had promised it to him—that was when he was fighting against Richard. Yes, Henry II had actually named him as his heir. But Richard was there to claim the throne and their mother was behind him. Richard had always been the favourite with her; yet she had been a good mother to him so he couldn't complain too much—not that he would dare. He had always been afraid of her and it wouldn't have been so easy to deceive her as it had been his father. People had their peculiar ways. Take his mother for instance—a strong woman, a realist if ever there was one and a born ruler even though she was a woman; yet she had a weakness which was her love for her children. She knew that he, John, had worked against Richard, had done everything in his power to snatch the crown while Richard was away—and she was determined to hold that crown for Richard and had shown her intentions clearly—yet when Richard had come home and might have been expected to kill John, or at least shut him away in a prison—which, from their point of view they should have known would have been a wise thing to do—they had pardoned him. He suspected that his mother had pleaded for him with Richard, and the result—forgiveness and brotherly affection at least outwardly between them.

Richard had been slighting of course, saying that John had been led astray and making it clear that he did not fear him because he didn't believe him capable of conquest. Insulting—but it served John's purpose at the time.

What he hoped for now was for Richard to die before having planted the fateful seed in Berengaria. A good strong attack of that fever—and there would be Richard, heir-less departed for ever; and all John would have to do was stretch out his hands and take the crown. But there was one other consideration and it was for this reason that John had come to Brittany.

Arthur! How he hated that boy. What airs the young fellow gave himself. He was haughty in the extreme and Frenchified too for the boy had spent a good many years at the court of France.

It was very unfortunate that Arthur's father Geoffrey had been the elder brother. If only their births had been reversed—and he was Arthur's father! John smiled wryly, lustfully contemplating Arthur's mother, Constance. No longer young—she was mounting up to forty—she was still a comely woman who had had her adventures. Geoffrey had married her to get control of her estates of Brittany, and they already had a daughter, Eleanor, when he died from injuries received in a tournament, to which sport he was much addicted. He had left Constance with child which, alas, was born male and healthy and provided the reason for John's uneasiness.

Arthur! The very name irritated him. His grandfather Henry had wished the boy to be named after him, but Constance backed by the Bretons, was obstinate and they had chosen Arthur because of the associations of that name. He had pretensions to the throne of England, therefore let him be named after the legendary British king.

John disliked the boy's name as much as he did everything about Arthur.

The arrogant little devil, he thought. He should be taught a lesson. He would like to put his hands round that boyish throat and strangle the life out of the creature. Nothing would give him more exquisite pleasure; as it was he had to play the avuncular role, listening to the boy's bright conversation and exchanging smiles with his doting mother. It amused him in a way to play this game. Deceit always stimulated him; he had a natural gift for it. So he was enjoying his stay at this Court and this pleasure was increased because he knew he was regarded with suspicion and that many people would be relieved when he had gone.

He had no intention of going yet. There was too much fun to be had here. He had brought with him a few of his friends who were daring enough to join in his adventures. When they went out riding he would contrive with them to help him elude the party and ride on with Arthur. When he had the boy to himself he would dally in the woods and he always enjoyed returning late to the castle and watching the relief on Constance's face when she beheld her son, because he knew what agonies of fear she had undergone when she thought he was alone in the woods with his wicked uncle.

What should he do to amuse himself on this sunny April day? He might call his friends together and they could ride out into the woods—force their way into some cottages and look for girls, and on finding them drag them shrieking into the woods. A fine game, but one they had played so often that it could pall; moreover, they had to remember that they were in Brittany and the arrogant Constance and her friends would not hesitate to complain to the King of France or perhaps Richard, and at this time John had to play a subdued role, for Richard had not so long ago forgiven him for his rebellion on condition that he mended his ways.

Besides, his thoughts were too serious to be diverted by such commonplace pleasures as the rape of village girls. From a window he saw Constance going into the gardens and she was alone. He hurried down to her.

He watched her for a few seconds before she was aware of him—in his mind stripping her of her garments and assessing her possibilities as a bedfellow. She would not be a mild woman—not like his poor Hadwisa. He was heartily sick of that one and he was going to get rid of her. He had determined on that. Why not? Her lands were safe in his keeping and he had made no secret of the fact that that was all his marriage was about. She had no children—he had decided that he would avoid that complication so that when the moment came to cast her off there would be no question of the issue of the so-called marriage. He laughed to consider how the Church had been against it and how with Richard's connivance he had flouted the Church. The Gloucester inheritance had been worth a certain inconvenience for the addition of that to his possessions had made him one of the richest men in England. But there was a blood-bond between them. They were related through his great grandfather Henry I who was Hadwisa's great grandfather too—in her case her royal blood came down through the bar sinister, but blood was blood all the same and that old fool the Archbishop of Canterbury had ranted about consanguinity. He had not cared; being rather glad, for he saw from the first that

Hadwisa would not interest him except through her possessions.

So he had no need to worry about Hadwisa. When the moment arrived she would be discarded like some old garment one gave to a servant when one had no further use for it.

An idea had been forming in his mind for some time. What if he married Constance? Then if Arthur were his stepson as well as his nephew the boy would be completely in his power. Of one thing he was certain if the opportunity should arise and Richard die without heirs he was not going to be cheated by Arthur.

Constance turned, startled when he came up behind her—rather silently for the pleasure of seeing her momentarily off her guard. She was indeed a good-looking woman and being rather tall she gave the impression of looking down on him. He would soon stop her giving that impression if he married her.

'How beautiful you are, Constance,' he said. 'I always said my brother Geoffrey was the most fortunate of us all in his marriage.'

'You are very kind,' she said coolly. Her eyes were wary; she was like a tigress who suspects some attack on her cubs. Not without reason too.

'Ah,' he went on, 'it is good for families to be together. Not always possible with those of our rank, but rest assured, Constance, that I intend to seek every opportunity of being with my delightful sister-in-law. It does me good to see my niece and my nephew. I say, what a charmer Eleanor is becoming. And Arthur! How proud you must be of the boy.'

'I am well content with my children,' she answered.

'And may I say what good work you have done with Arthur.'

'You may indeed say it, but whether I can claim the credit is another matter. You know he has spent much time at the Court of the King of France.'

'And a thorough little Frenchman that old scoundrel has tried to make of him.'

'I have reason to be grateful to the King of France,' she answered shortly. 'I can't agree that he is old or a scoundrel.'

'You are a stickler for accuracy, my dear sister-in-law. Philip is certainly not so aged but wily you must admit.'

'As becomes such a ruler,' she answered.

'My brother, the King of England, has reason to distrust him.'

Her lips curled. 'One hears that there was once such a great friendship between them that men marvelled.'

John came closer to her leering slightly. 'Ah, that friendship. Our brother—yours in law, mine in blood—is a man of many parts.'

'It would seem so.'

'He has not been over good to you, my dear Constance.'

'One learns to be wary.'

'You and I have a great deal in common,' said John.

'Is that so?'

'Indeed yes—both having been married ... after a fashion ... and not married one might say.'

She raised her eyebrows and studied him coolly.

He went on. 'You know I went through a form of ceremony with Hadwisa of Gloucester. It was what my brother wished. He had just taken the throne and he thought her lands would be a way of providing for his young brother without making demands on his purse.'

'Had you no wish for the match?'

'You should see Hadwisa.'

'I gather you are not pleased with your wife.'

'Shall I say that she is as different from you as one woman could be from another.'

'That would tell me little.'

'Except that you being so attractive, she would necessarily be the opposite.'

She shrugged her shoulders impatiently.

He went on: 'It was sad for you, dear Constance, when Geoffrey died so unexpectedly. Who would have believed it possible when he was playing in a joust?'

'Those jousts were too realistic. They were more like actual battles than a game.'

''Twas so and Geoffrey loved them. And he left you with Eleanor but a baby, and Arthur on the way.'

'My children have always been a great comfort to me.'

'And an anxiety. Admit it.'

'When great inheritances are entailed that is inevitable.'

''Tis sad for women. More so than for men. I know how you suffered through Ranulf de Blundevill.'

He saw the expression flit across her face—one of hatred and revulsion; and he titillated his senses to think of this fine woman forced to marry a man she hated. He wondered what had taken place between them and thought of himself with Hadwisa in the first days of their marriage when he had struck terror into his poor shrinking bride and had thus obtained the only pleasure he ever had from her.

How different from Hadwisa was Constance. On the death of Geoffrey she had been forced into the marriage by her father-in-law Henry, the King at that time; but she had no intention of submitting to such indignity as Ranulf would have forced on her. She had run away from him and returned to Brittany where the people rallied round her and showed their intention to protect her from a man she hated; as for the King of England he was at that time too busily engaged elsewhere to enforce his will.

She was a strong woman, Constance. She had ruled Arthur's Duchy for four years with great strength of purpose and during that time she had endeared the Bretons to her to such an extent that they were ready to defend her and their heir from all invaders.

'I've always admired you, Constance,' said John. 'I was so pleased when I heard you had escaped from that beast Ranulf. But you do not regard him as a husband do you? That is how it is with me. You see we are in like case.'

'I doubt Hadwisa ever caused you the anxiety the Earl of Chester caused me.'

'I have the advantage of being a man, dear sister. You are a woman and women need men—good men—to look after them.'

'Some of us are not so ill-equipped that we cannot look after ourselves.'

'And you are one of those rare women. Ah, Constance, how I rejoice that we are good friends. Do you?'

'In a world fraught with dangers it is always good to have friends.'

She hoped that she did not betray the fear which had come to her. What was John implying? Why had he come here? Could it really be that Richard was considering making a match between them?

Horrifying thought. This monster—for she knew he was that—wasted his time exchanging fair words with her. There

was not one of her advisers who had not been on the alert
from the moment he had arrived at her Court. She had
ordered that Arthur was to be watched and that if it were
possible he was never to be left alone with his uncle. If anything happened to Arthur while John was near, John would
immediately be suspected and that would not help him. But
how could she be sure how foolish John would be? He was
not noted for his wisdom.

It was certainly not inconceivable that Richard and his
advisers might have some idea of a marriage between her and
John since there was a question as to who—John or Arthur—
was the rightful heir to the throne. Such a marriage could
mean that John might rule until Arthur was of age or on
John's becoming a kind of regent.

Never, she thought. I would not trust my son in his hands
... not for a moment.

That she was married to Ranulf de Blundevill, Earl of
Chester, and John to Hadwisa of Gloucester would be no
impediment. Those marriages could be set aside without a
great deal of trouble. Marry John! He would be a thousand
times worse than Ranulf. Besides, there was Guy. Her expression softened as she thought of her lover. He might see her
from one of the castle windows and if he did he would come
to rescue her from her odious brother-in-law. They had talked
of the Prince only last night and Guy had said he was in Brittany for no good and that they must take double care of
Arthur.

She turned away from John, murmuring that she must
leave him now, but when she walked towards the castle he
was beside her. She went quickly to her apartments and there
she asked one of her trusted women to bring Guy de Thouars
to her. When he came and they were alone she embraced
him.

'Oh Guy,' she said, 'I'm afraid ... afraid for Arthur.'

'Arthur is well cared for, my love, while we are here.'

'There is something in John's mind. I can see it. He came
to me in the gardens. He has some plot brewing.'

'We must be careful of him, and we are. We knew that
from the start.'

'I see him watching Arthur.'

'Oh yes, he does not forget that Arthur has a greater claim
to the throne of England than he has.'

'That's what terrifies me.' She leaned her head against him and he rested his lips on her hair. 'This is peace,' she murmured. 'Peace for just a few minutes.'

'Nay, my love, longer than that. Arthur is well protected. His faithful squire sleeps across his door.'

' 'Tis necessary while John is here.'

'I wish he would go away.'

'Then he would be somewhere else plotting against Arthur.'

'At least he would not be so near him.'

'Nay. 'Tis better he were where we can keep an eye on him. We will continue watchful. Never for one moment will we allow Arthur to be alone with him.'

'Yet in the forest...'

'He is always followed. I have seen to that. John but seeks to plague us. He would not allow harm to come to Arthur when it was known that they had been together. The people of Brittany would kill him before he had time to escape and Richard would not forgive him. He knows full well that that would be the end of his hopes.'

'Life is so cruel,' said Constance vehemently. She was thinking of her brief life with Geoffrey—perhaps it had not been idyllic but Geoffrey had been young and handsome and had a certain charm and it had resulted in her two children Eleanor and Arthur; it was after his death the nightmare had begun. Ranulf! She shuddered at the thought. What right had the King of England to give her to a man she loathed because it suited him to do so? That had been no marriage. She had fought desperately against its consummation and had quickly escaped from Ranulf, and the people of Brittany had rallied round her and she had had four years when she had governed the dukedom, and cared for Arthur, bringing him up in the way she wished him to go. Alas, Ranulf had after that time captured her and kept her a prisoner in his castle of St. Jean Beveron but not before, with the help of good friends, she had been able to send Arthur out of harm's way to the court of the King of France.

It was the good people of Brittany who had helped to release her from her prison and fearing that the King of France might use Arthur to gain his own advantage, she had him brought back to her and thus they were together again; but never for a moment must Constance forget how important her son was to the affairs of Europe. There was the King of France on one hand and the King of England on the other, both seeking to use him against each other; but the real enemy was John—the uncle in whose way he could possibly stand, for in the minds of some people Arthur was a step ahead of him in the succession to the throne.

'I almost wish Arthur were not his father's heir,' said Constance. 'There are times when I wish we could go away together ... you, I and my children, and forget Arthur's inheritance.'

'Do you really wish that, Constance?' Guy asked wistfully.

And she could not answer truthfully because Arthur was her son and her love mingled with her ambitions for him. Arthur could be King of England and she could not forget that.

'If Arthur were safe on the throne of England, in command of possessions here, if he were a few years older...'

'While Richard lives the boy is safe. No harm will come to him. Come, my love, forget your troubles. The boy is safe. None could be more carefully guarded.'

'All the same,' said Constance, 'we will be wary of John.'

*   *   *

When John left Constance he went into the schoolroom where Arthur sat with his tutor. The boy's fair head was bent over his books and John was amused to see how alert the tutor had become since his entry.

'Ah, nephew,' said John breezily. 'I find you at your study. That is good. A boy can never learn too much. Is that not so, my good man?'

The tutor had risen. He bowed to John and replied that learning was an admirable asset to all.

'Then we are of one mind.' He nodded. 'I wish to be alone with my nephew,' he added.

The man had no recourse but to leave; but he would not go far, John thought with a smirk of amusement. His orders would have been: Keep near and send word that Prince John is alone with the young Duke; and someone would be at hand to make sure no harm came to Arthur. He would do his best to lead them a merry dance.

'Such a beautiful day,' said John. 'Not one to be poring over books.'

'Lessons must be learned,' said Arthur.

'What a model pupil you are! I never was. I preferred the hunt and the good fresh air to poring over books.'

'I can well believe that,' replied Arthur. Insolent young dog, thought John with a sudden uprush of temper. Be careful, he advised himself. It's necessary to play the good uncle here.

Arthur went on: 'My mother thinks that I must spend much time in study and so did the King of France.'

'I'll warrant you and young Louis had good sport together.'

'We hunted, we fenced and studied the art of chivalry...'

'All that a prince should know, I'll warrant—and more also. Come, we will go and ride together, eh ... just the two of us.' He said that very loudly for the sake of the listening tutor. Now there would be panic.

Like most young people Arthur loved to feel a horse beneath him; he had inherited the Plantagenet love of the chase from his father; and although he did not like his uncle—and being young and a little arrogant and well aware of his importance, he made little effort to hide the fact—he could not resist the suggestion that they should ride.

'Come. Let us go.'

Arthur stood up. He was going to be tall and good looking, resembling his late uncle Henry, who was the best looking of all the sons of Henry II. His sojourn at the Court of France had had its effect on him; his manners were courtly and he wore his clothes with grace. The haughtiness was there though; there was no doubt that Arthur was well aware of his importance.

They rode out side by side, their followers around them.

Constance, with Guy beside her, watched them from a castle window.

Guy said: 'Don't be afraid. There are trusted men with them.'

'You know what he does. He contrives to get him away. Why?'

'Because he finds great joy in torturing you.'

'He's a monster.'

'I have heard that said of him.'

'I would to God he would go away.'

'He cannot stay here for ever. But when he goes let us not slacken our care. It may well be that Arthur is safer while he is here, for if aught happened to Arthur then he would be immediately blamed.'

'I wish he would break his neck.'

'I doubt you are not the only one who prays for that happy event. Nay, my love, do not fret. Arthur is with his friends and they will watch over him. This is for John a light diversion. One of his greatest delights is to frighten people and that is what he hopes to do now.'

'A thousand curses on him.'

'Amen,' said Guy.

*   *   *

How pleasant it was in the forest. The boy's face was alight with his love of the chase. John noted the clearness of his eyes and the freshness of his skin. He was too healthy to please his uncle.

A boy ... nothing more. Twelve years old and to stand so much in his way! The people of England would never accept him, but over here they would. Normandy, Anjou ... oh yes, they would be ready enough. And the King of France would doubtless like to see a minor on the throne of England and if he threw in his lot with Arthur...

When he thought of that his temper started to rise and he must keep it in check to a certain extent. Moreover, it hadn't happened yet. Richard still lived.

They gave chase to a fine buck. Hunting was exciting; he loved the way in which the frightened animal fled; he liked the killing not to be accomplished too quickly. That took the fun out of hunting.

There was no chance on this occasion to get Arthur alone; no sooner had he eluded one than another rider seemed to appear. Madame Constance had given her orders. 'Never leave Arthur out of sight when he is with his uncle John.'

He laughed aloud. He guessed Constance was now in a fever of anxiety and so would she remain until they returned to the castle. They would dally just to keep her in suspense.

The buck was slain; the bearer would take it to the castle.

Arthur had shouted. 'We go back now. I have had enough.'

You have had enough, my little nephew, thought John. What of your uncle?

John said: ''Tis such a pleasant day. Who knows there

may be another buck finer than the one we have captured lurking near.'

'Nay,' said Arthur. 'My mother cares not for me to be away too long.'

'Oh, but on this occasion she knows you are in the care of good Uncle John.'

Arthur was too young to dissemble. He opened his blue eyes very wide and began: 'Oh but...' He stopped.

'Yes, nephew?' said John coaxingly.

''Tis nothing,' replied Arthur. 'I have had enough of the chase though. I wish to see my mother's delight when she sees the buck.'

'We will not go yet,' said John. 'Such a fine young fellow has no wish to be governed by women.'

John spurred his horse and started to ride away certain that Arthur after such a gibe would follow. Arthur shouted after him: 'This is not women. It is my mother.' And galloped off in another direction.

'Curse him,' muttered John. 'The young coxcomb. I'd like to whip him till the blood flowed.'

But there was nothing he could do. His own followers, knowing well from past experience that Arthur's departure would mean that the Angevin temper was on the rise, were aware how wise it was not to be too near their master. A cut of the whip could leave a life-long scar as a reminder of an ill-chosen word or action.

John rode off, his men a little distance from him, muttering curses against Arthur, the boy, the chit, who might easily stand between him and his ambitions.

It was dusk when he returned to the castle. He was in an ill mood. The groom hurried to attend to him and as he came from the stables he saw a man standing in the shadows. He paused. The man appeared to be a beggar and one of the contradictory characteristics of the violent Plantagenet Prince was that he was noted for his goodness to beggars. He rarely passed one without giving a coin which was strange for, although he spent lavishly on himself, he was known to be parsimonious with others. But a coin or so to a beggar was little compared with the gratitude it produced and he enjoyed distributing largesse to these people and earning their thanks. It was a cheap way of winning approval and one he rarely resisted.

So even now, in his evil mood, he paused to find a coin for the beggar.

'My lord,' said the man, 'I am no beggar. I come in this guise with great news for you.'

'News!' whispered John. 'What news?'

'The King of England is dead.'

'*No.*'

'' 'Tis so, my lord.'

John seized the man's arm. 'How could it be?'

'It was at Chaluz. It was said that treasure had been found and Richard wanted it.'

'He would,' said John. 'Go on, man.'

'In the siege an arrow pierced his shoulder. It could not be withdrawn and festered. He is dead. Long live King John.'

'You'll be rewarded,' said John.

'May God preserve you, my lord. I have come in stealth that you might know what has happened. Soon the news will be abroad ... here ... in this castle ... everywhere.'

'And what would happen to me here?' asked John. 'Because if they knew at this moment they would be for putting Arthur on the throne.'

'I thought my lord you would wish to leave in all haste for Chinon.'

'For Chinon and the royal treasure,' cried John.

In the castle Arthur was telling his mother of the fine buck they had brought in, and the smell of roasting meat was in the air. But when the company assembled in the great hall it was discovered that Prince John and his followers were not present.

'Can they have gone at last?' cried Constance, her voice joyful.

'It would seem so,' said Guy, 'but I wonder for what reason.'

They were to discover that the next day.

Richard dead. Then Arthur must be Duke of Normandy, Count of Anjou and King of England.

But by that time John had reached Chinon and possessed himself of the royal treasure.

John is Crowned

WHAT a thrill it was to ride into Chinon. At last that for which he had longed and prayed was ready to fall into his hands. Richard dead! The man who shot the arrow ought to be rewarded; he could not have pleased his new King more. He laughed aloud. What would be the reactions of the lords knights and barons if he said, 'Bring that man before me.' They would bring the man, wretched and fearful, and he would play with him for a while so that he believed dire torture awaited him and then he would offer him lands and title. 'You have served me well. Go in peace.'

Of course it could not be like that. Just at first he would have to follow the conventions a little. But by God's ears, he thought, when I am King with the crown safely on my head, then I shall do as I wish and men will like it or suffer for not liking.

What a glorious future! Blessed man who shot the arrow, you are my good and faithful servant. Old Lion Heart is no more. The terror of the Saracens, the great crusader, who deserted his own country to win glory in the Holy Land, is just a corpse now ... dead and gone and all his glory with him. And the way is clear for John.

Arthur—Bah! what had he to fear from Arthur?

Never had the castle of Chinon looked so beautiful as it did on that April morning. Never had John felt so pleased with life.

Now would come the first test. What if the custodian of the

treasure refused to hand it to him? But there was no question
of how he should act. He would run the fellow through and
take it by force.

Into the castle he rode. There was no resistance. He
thrilled with delight. They recognized him as Duke and
King.

The treasure was his.

There was a message from his mother who had already
given orders that the treasure was to be handed to him. She
was at Fontevraud where the funeral was taking place. John,
now Duke of Normandy, Count of Anjou and King of England was to come to Fontevraud to pay his last respects to his
brother.

John hesitated. None should give orders to him. Then he
saw the folly of resisting. His mother knew the procedure and
she was on his side, a fact which should make him exult. Any
resistance Arthur and the Bretons might put up would be
quickly overcome. His mother carried great influence and he
must be humble for a while. That was the part to play and he
always enjoyed playing those parts which deceived people. To
play the sorrowing brother now, a little weighed down by the
realization of his heavy responsibilities, was a part he could
do well and find a great enjoyment in playing it.

Being in possession of the Angevin treasure, he prepared to
ride to Fontevraud. But first, on his mother's advice, he sent
for Bishop Hugh of Lincoln, the most respected of English
Bishops, whose presence, as Eleanor said, would impress the
people.

John realized this and was amused to think of himself in
the company of such a man, for in the past he had been guilty
of great levity towards such, and Hugh had a most saintly
reputation.

However, for the time being he must curb his high spirits
and show a serious mien to the people.

Hugh arrived and gave him his blessing. John noted with
some asperity that the Bishop was not inclined to treat him
with great respect even though he acknowledged him as
King. These churchmen seemed to look on everyone else as
their children. He would not endure his preaching for long
and the fellow would have to take care how he treated his
new sovereign. Richard had not allowed them to bully him
although he had taken notice of the old hermit in the woods

who had upbraided him for the life he led. Ah, but not until he was laid low and on the point of death!

As everyone knows, thought John laughing, death beds are the place for repentance; before reaching them one should make sure of committing enough sins to make the grovelling for mercy worthwhile.

'God's blessing on you, my lord,' said Hugh embracing him.

John thanked him and suggested that they return to England with all speed.

He was longing for the ceremony in Westminster Abbey and he wouldn't feel completely happy until the crown was on his head. A king was not considered to be a king until after that all important ceremony had been performed. And with Arthur in the shadows it couldn't be done too quickly for him.

Hugh began by refusing to go to England. That was impossible for him at this time. What he would do would be to accompany the King to Fontevraud for it was well that John should visit his brother's grave.

Here we go, thought John. The Church dictating to the Crown already. Very well, my old prelate. Just for a while ... until I am firmly in the saddle—and then you'll have to get out of my way before I trample you underfoot.

It was not long before they reached Fontevraud there to pay homage to the graves of Henry II and Richard.

John knelt by the grave of his father and thought of those last days of the old man's life when he had deserted him because it was to his advantage to be with Richard at that time. He couldn't help feeling a little uneasy in such a solemn place; he could clearly remember his father's eyes as they had followed him and he had called him the only one of his sons whom he could trust. John had laughed inwardly at the time, and congratulated himself on his fine play-acting telling himself what a clever fellow he was. But here in the solemn atmosphere of the abbey he felt a twinge of something which might have been conscience but was more likely to be fear of what reprisals the dead might take. Then there was Richard, freshly laid in his tomb—Richard, for whose death he had prayed a hundred times and more. Could it be that the dead did not leave this earth when they died, that they stayed to haunt those who had wronged them? Morbid thoughts. It was that old ghoul of a bishop standing over him so disapprovingly, determined to maintain the war between Church and State.

It was all fancy. Those two were dead ... finished ... no more earthly glory for them; and their departure meant that John had what he had always longed for.

He rose from his knees, and going towards the choir door, knocked. From behind a grille a nun appeared. The Abbess was away she said, and the rule was that none must be admitted in her absence.

Thank heaven for that, thought John. He was weary of these pious pilgrimages. He wanted to have done with them and get to England. Oh the glory of his coronation! He remembered Richard's which was not really so long ago and how envious he had felt that Richard was the one who would wear the crown and carry the orb and sceptre. My turn now, he thought exultantly. He was thankful to the old Abbess for being away.

He turned to Hugh and said: 'Tell them that I promise benefactions to their house. I pledge this in my name. Perhaps in return they will pray for me.'

Hugh looked at him sceptically. He did not trust the new piety in one of whom he was well aware rumour had not lied. 'I could promise nothing in your name until I was sure that the promises would be met. You know full well how I detest falsehood, and promise given and not fulfilled is that.'

'I swear,' cried John, 'that what I promise shall come to pass.'

'Then I will give the sisters your message, but if you should break your word, forget not that you are offending God.'

John bowed his head in assumed piety.

As they left the church the Bishop began a lecture on the need to govern well. The new King would have to bring a seriousness to his task; God had entrusted him with a great mission. It was to his advantage to carry it out to the best of his ability.

'I shall maintain the crown,' boasted John. He brought out an ornament on a gold chain from under his jacket and showed it to the Bishop.

'You see this amulet. It was given to one of my ancestors and passed down to me. My father gave it to me. That was when he wished that I should follow him on the throne. The legend is that while this stone is in the possession of our family we shall never lose our dominions.'

'You would do well, my lord,' answered the Bishop tersely, 'to trust in the Chief Corner Stone.'

John turned away with a grimace.

They stood for a moment in the porch on the walls of which had been sculptured a scene of the last judgment. God sat on his throne and on one side were depicted the torments which awaited the sinners and on the other side the angels on their way to heavenly bliss.

'I beg of you, my lord,' said the Bishop, 'take good heed of this. See what awaits those who offend against the laws of God.'

'Look not at them, good Bishop,' retorted John. 'See rather those on the other side. The angels are taking them to Heaven. That is the path I have decided is for me.'

The Bishop regarded him uneasily. This virtue had descended too suddenly to be plausible.

*   *   *

They travelled on to Beaufort where Queen Eleanor with the sorrowing widow Berengaria and John's sister Joanna were waiting to receive him.

His mother embraced him warmly.

'This is a sad day for us all,' she said. 'Your brother, our great King, struck down in his prime by this madman's arrow.'

'Alas, alas,' replied John. 'He who survived the Holy Land and cruel incarceration in an enemy castle to come to this!'

He was studying Berengaria intently. What if after all she were pregnant. The thought was too horrible for contemplation. She would have to be disposed of before she brought another rival on to the scene. It was bad enough for Arthur to be there.

He turned to Joanna, clearly pregnant.

'My dearest sister. This is a sad occasion. I trust it has done no harm to the child you carry.'

Joanna turned away to hide her tears. 'He was so wonderful,' she said.

'We share our grief,' murmured John, forcing his voice to tremble. 'And my dear sister-in-law ... how sad for you.'

He took Berengaria's hands and looked into her face. Don't dare to be pregnant! he was thinking. No, you are not. Richard never wanted you to be. He had no wish for a son.

'Come to my private apartments,' said his mother. He had to admire her. She had retired to seclusion they had thought, but events like this would always bring her out to fight for the family; he thanked his good fortune that she had decided that he was to inherit the throne. What if she had let her choice rest on Arthur? No, with her, a son came before a grandson.

When they were alone together he could see at once that she was uneasy. She was bitterly mourning for Richard. 'This has been such a sad blow to me,' she said. 'I had never thought it possible that he would go and leave me here. I used to worry about him when he was in the Holy Land and during that terrible time when we did not know where he was. But when he came back—as strong and as brave as ever, I never thought he could go before I did and leave me lonely.'

Fighting his resentment John took her hand and kissed it.

'You still have one son, Mother,' he reminded her.

'You, John ... the youngest of them all. And you have become the King.'

'It is a great responsibility.'

'I'm glad you realize it.' She looked at him shrewdly. 'It will not be easy. You know that. You will have more conflict to face than Richard ever did.'

'Yes,' he said, his mouth tightening. 'There is Arthur.'

'William Marshal believes that you come before Arthur.'

'William Marshal!' The joy showed briefly in John's face. There was one of the most influential men in England, a man renowned for his integrity. Others would follow him.

'I have sent him to England to prepare the people for your reception there and to urge them to accept you as the rightful King.'

'You have always been the best of mothers.'

'Marshal, with Hubert Walter, will convince the people that you are the true King.'

'The Church must be involved, I dare say.'

'Hubert is Archbishop of Canterbury. He will perform the coronation. His approval is essential.'

'And you think he will give it?'

'If he wavers, Marshal will persuade him. John, you will have to curb your levity.'

'All that is past. I recognize the responsibilities I have for my crown.'

'Then that is well. You must always be just. Think of your father. Oh, he had his faults but taking everything into account he was a good and worthy ruler. The people accepted him because he was just. Try to follow his example.'

'I shall not follow Richard's example by leaving my country in the hands of men like Longchamp while I go off in search of glory.'

'Richard had a mission. He had vowed to go on a crusade. He saw that as his first duty.'

John clasped his hands and raised his eyes piously to the ceiling. 'Mine shall be to my country.'

Eleanor looked at him sharply. 'John,' she said, 'this is the most important time of your life.'

'I know it well.'

'You will have to walk with the utmost care.'

'I know that also.'

'Philip will have to be watched. It may well be that he will try to put Arthur in your place.'

'Think you that I shall allow it?'

'We must see that it does not happen.'

He was silent for a while. Then he said, 'Poor Berengaria. She looks fatigued.'

'She has suffered much. His death was a great shock to her.'

'I was wondering ... is it possible ... If it were so it would create an issue ...'

Eleanor looked at him sharply. 'You are afraid that she might be with Richard's child.'

'It is a possibility.'

Eleanor shook her head.

'It is not so.'

'But possible ...'

'Think you that this has not occurred to me. I have spoken with her. It is not possible.'

John was deeply relieved.

'Then there is nothing to fear,' he said, 'but ... Arthur.'

*　　*　　*

Bishop Hugh was growing increasingly apprehensive. He

was of the opinion that Arthur would have been the better choice. True he was Breton and had been brought up for some of his formative years at the Court of France, but he was yet a boy who could be moulded. It might be that John as son of the late Henry the Second was closer to the late King Richard than Arthur—and yet John was an uneasy choice.

To consider his past record must make all churchmen shudder. Setting his exploits in Ireland, and his treachery to his father on one side, there was still the life he led. The last King's departure from the orthodox in sexual relations was deplorable, but it had not affected his rule; he had never had favourites who had influenced him.

Hugh was surprised that Queen Eleanor, who was a very wise woman, and William Marshal who undoubtedly had the good of England at heart, could have let their choice rest on John. The line of succession was not so rigid that it could not be changed for expediency. A king's son was his natural successor but if that son should show himself to be unworthy it was quite acceptable to select the next candidate. It was a moot point whether Henry the Second's youngest son or the son of an older son was the heir to the throne. If Richard himself had had a son how different it would have been. What alarmed Hugh was that the Archbishop of Canterbury believed Arthur to have been the better choice and had been overruled by William Marshal.

Of course William Marshal was a man with a strong sense of duty and he was in close service with King Henry II. It could be that he remembered that it was his old master's desire that John should be King and this was why he supported the claim of the younger son rather than that of the grandson.

In any case, it appeared that John was to be the next King and they must try to make the best of it.

He went to John's apartments in the Castle Beaufort and there found him with one or two of his companions—young men whose tastes were similar to his own.

The Bishop asked if he could speak to John alone. The young men regarded him rather insolently and John hesitated; he would have liked to tell the old prelate to go, but his common sense warned him that until that coronation ceremony he had better be a little careful.

He waved his hand and the young men sauntered out.

'What is it?' asked John somewhat testily.

'Tomorrow is Easter Day,' said the Bishop. 'You will of course wish to take communion.'

'Not I,' cried John. ' 'Tis not to my taste.'

The Bishop was horrified, and John laughed at him. 'My good Bishop, I have not communicated since I was able to make up my own mind on such matters and I have no intention of doing so now.'

'You are now a king...' The Bishop paused and added ominously: 'Or hoping to become one. It is necessary for the people to see that you are worthy of the crown.'

'What has communion to do with kingship?'

'I think you know. If you are to govern well you will need the guidance of God.'

'I have no qualms that I shall know how to govern.'

'Others might have.'

John narrowed his eyes. The insolence of priests! Was he the King or wasn't he? The answer to that was of course, No, not yet.

Not yet. That was what he must remember. He must get that ceremony performed.

He said: 'I know I have lived a sinful life. I intend to reform now this great burden has been placed upon my shoulders, but if after all these years I communicate—and there are many who know that for years I have abstained— they will think my repentance over sudden. Let me come gradually back to the good life. If I attend the High Mass that will do for a start. It will show people that I am making a beginning.'

The Bishop said: 'God will know exactly what is in your heart.'

'Assuredly,' answered John with his eyes downcast.

There was no point in further persuasion, the Bishop told himself. Time would show what attitudes John would take and the people would accept or reject him accordingly.

When the Bishop had gone John recalled his friends. He gave them an account of what had happened mimicking the Bishop.

'He thinks he is going to govern me. We are going to have some fun with Master Bishop, my friends.'

They applauded wildly; it would have been unwise not to do so.

They were with him at the High Mass. John liked them to be there because he felt over-bold when it was necessary to amuse them with his daring.

There was one point which shocked Hugh profoundly, when during the offertory John approached jingling some gold coins in his hand and did not put these into the dish which was there to receive them but stood for a while looking down at them.

Hugh said sharply. 'Why do you stand there staring at the coins?'

John looked at him slyly. 'I was thinking that a little while ago I would never have put them into your hands. They would be in my pocket. I suppose now I must give them to you.'

Hugh was scarlet with indignation.

'Put them in the basin and go,' he said shortly.

John hesitated for a moment and then did as he was bid, putting the coins in one by one as though with the greatest reluctance.

The Bishop was angry and deeply disturbed that a future monarch could behave so in God's Holy house! It did not augur well for the future, and he was indignant as he went to his pulpit and prepared to deliver his sermon. John was seated immediately below and with him were a few of his dissolute friends.

Was it possible, wondered Hugh, to make this young man understand that unless he behaved like a king he could never be a successful one? He would do his duty and try to sew a few ideas which might bear fruit.

He had prepared a sermon which he would preach before John and he had meant its bearing to be on the duty of rulers to their people. He enlarged on the subject, stressing the disaster that could come through careless and wanton behaviour. A king must be high-minded and must put the good of his country before his own pleasures. He could not stress this enough.

He was aware of the murmurings and nudgings that were going on in that pew but ignored them and the more they persisted the more he had to say about the duties of a king to his subjects.

'A king must never forget that he serves his people under God...'

There was a giggle from John's pew and, when one of the young men quietly slipped out, Hugh was astonished to find that he was making his way round to the back of the pulpit.

'My lord Bishop,' said the young man in an audible whisper, 'the King says will you bring your sermon to an immediate end. He is weary of it and wants his dinner.'

Hugh, colour heightened, continued to preach while the young man went back to his seat.

Oh God, thought Hugh, what will become of us!

The service over, Hugh left the church. He would take his leave tomorrow. There was no point in staying with the King. He would go back to England and consult with the Archbishop of Canterbury and tell them that he had indeed been right when he had suggested Arthur would be a more suitable king.

The next day the Bishop of Lincoln said farewell to John.

John, his friends still round him, cried: 'This is a sad leave taking, Bishop. I shall always remember your sermon to me on my accession.'

The young men tittered and John could scarcely contain his laughter.

'Then,' said the Bishop with dignity, 'perhaps it has not been in vain.'

The Bishop with his entourage rode off and John entered the castle there to enjoy the venison which was being prepared for him. Over the table he talked with his friends of the good sport they would have. They should see what it was like to be the faithful friends of a king.

But while they feasted, messengers came to the castle. It was clear by their looks that they brought ill news. They were taken immediately to John who fell into a rage when he heard it.

Philip was on the march; he was backing Arthur and the Bretons, and Constance, with her son Arthur and her lover Guy Thouars, was leading an army against him. Moreover, no one had put up any resistance. Cities had surrendered; custodians of castles had declared themselves in favour of Arthur; and with the backing of the King of France the situation was perilous. Evreux was in Philip's hands and he was already in Maine. Moreover, barons in such key places as Touraine and Anjou were swearing fealty to Arthur.

'What can I do?' cried John. 'What forces have I here?'

He must get to Normandy. He rose from the table, gave orders to make ready and in a short time was riding for Le Mans, as yet not in his enemy's hands.

He was surprised by his lack of welcome. The people did not want him. His reputation was well known to them. There was a young boy whose father came before John in direct succession and he was the one whom they wanted. Moreover, the King of France was backing Arthur. They did not want John.

It was an uneasy night John passed in Le Mans and as soon as dawn broke he was ready to get out of the place because he knew how dangerous it would be to stay. Philip was not far off, and the people were hostile. To become Philip's captive before he had been crowned a king would be disastrous.

Arthur, he had heard, had done homage to the King of France for Anjou, Maine and Touraine. The impudence! These were his dominions. Normandy was safe. Normandy had been the proud possession of his ancestors since the days of Rollo.

Its people would be true to him.

He must go with all speed to Rouen.

*   *   *

How different it was in Rouen. The people there wanted him. As he rode into the town they came to cheer him. These were his faithful subjects. Here in this city the brave heart of Richard was buried. Close by was the great Château Gaillard—Richard's Saucy Castle. This was the territory of the great dukes who for many years had reigned there in defiance of the Franks. Every King of France wanted to take Normandy from the Normans and every Norman Duke swore they never should. This was the land of William Longsword, Richard the Fearless and William the Mighty Conqueror. The people of Normandy would never support those who were upheld by the French.

The Archbishop of Rouen, Walter—he had the same name as the Archbishop of Canterbury—came at once to welcome John.

'My lord,' he said, 'it is necessary that you be proclaimed Duke of Normandy without delay. The people are with you. The last thing they will tolerate is the rule of a Breton, particularly when he is, as many believe, the tool of the King of France. Here you are indeed welcome and it is the universal wish that the ceremony take place without delay.'

John was quite ready to go through the ceremony at the earliest possible moment. The fact that Constance and her friends, including the King of France, were on the march had sobered him. He told the Archbishop with a seriousness rare to him that he placed himself in his hands, at which the Archbishop blessed him and announced that the ceremony would take place on Low Sunday which was the 25th of April—nineteen days after Richard's death.

John in the cathedral, the coronet decorated with golden roses placed on his head, swore on the Gospels and relics of the saints, that he would uphold the rights of the Church, that his laws would be just and he would suppress evil.

The Archbishop then attached the sword of justice to his girdle and took up the lance which had always been used by the Normans instead of the sceptre as in the Church of England.

It was while the lance was being handed to him that John heard his friends giggling close by and he could not resist turning to wink at them and assure them that he was still the same merry and irreligious companion who had shared their sport and that he was merely indulging in this solemn ceremony because just at the moment he must go along with the old people; and because his head was turned, the lance which the Archbishop was at that moment putting into his hands, slipped and fell to the floor.

There was a horrified gasp from all who beheld this and a soft murmur spread through the Cathedral.

At this solemn moment the lance, the symbol of Norman power which had been handed down and grasped firmly by every duke of Normandy had fallen from the grasp of this one.

It was an omen, and what could it be but an evil one with the King of France in arms against them and some believing that Arthur of Brittany had a greater claim to the ducal crown?

John refused to be depressed by the incident. He would laugh about it later with his cronies.

After the ceremony there was good news. The indefatigable Eleanor had left her seclusion once more and placed herself at the head of Richard's mercenaries led by the brilliant

commander Mercadier—he who had inflicted such terrible
punishment on Richard's slayer—and she was driving the
French and Bretons back from the territory they had gained.
Meanwhile, the people of Normandy were rallying to John
and he was soon ready to march on Le Mans.

He took it with ease and was exultant, remembering their
cool reception of him such a short while before. He was going
to show them what it meant to incur the wrath of King John.
He was no Richard who only on rare occasions let the
Angevin temper take over. John was going to show people
right from the beginning what they must fear if they went
against him.

He burned the houses. Every one of them must be de-
molished, he cried, and the castle was razed to the ground
while the leading citizens were brought before him.

'You were very inhospitable to me but a short time ago,' he
said. 'You were very haughty, thinking you had the King of
France with you. Where is he now? Tell me that? He has
deserted you. He left you to my mercy. Now you shall
discover how merciful I shall be.'

His eyes narrowed. 'Put them in chains,' he growled. 'Put
them in the darkest dungeons. We'll leave them there.
There they can brood on what it means to set themselves
against King John.'

The men were taken away. They had heard stories of his
cruelty. Now they would experience it.

Flushed with success John cried: 'What we have done with
Le Mans we will do to those others who have given them-
selves freely to the cause of the King of France and little
Arthur.'

But his advisers reminded him that the conquest of Le
Mans had not been difficult because the King of France had
already left, and if he were going to march on Anjou he
needed a bigger army. Meanwhile, he should go to England
and there let the ceremony of coronation be performed so
that he could show the world that he was in truth the King of
England.

John needed little persuasion. War in itself did not appeal to
him. It was the conquest he liked. He had enjoyed ravaging Le
Mans and working himself up into a rage over the people's
perfidy to him while he enjoyed to the full making them pay
for their decision to support the wrong side.

But to go to war again, a war which could drag on end-lessly, for Philip was a wily adversary and Constance he knew would find many to rally to Arthur's cause, did not appeal.

He agreed to leave the conquest of Anjou for the future.

He would sail for England and his coronation.

*　　*　　*

The day after he arrived in London John was crowned. That was on the 26th of May. The Abbey had been hung with coloured cloth. Sixteen prelates, ten earls and a host of barons graced the ceremony with their presence; as was the custom at a coronation the Archbishop of Canterbury presided. The Bishop of York protested that the ceremony should not take place until the Archbishop of York was able to be present; but as he was not on the spot it was decided to offend him if need be by continuing without him.

The Archbishop addressed the gathering in an unexpected fashion which appeared to be a justification of the selection of John and exclusion of Arthur.

'The crown is not the property of any one person,' he announced. 'It is the gift of the nation which chooses who shall wear it. This is by custom usually a member of the reigning family, and a prince who is most worthy of wearing it. Prince John is the brother of our dead King Richard—the only surviving brother and if he will swear the oaths which this high office demands, this country will accept him as its king.'

John gave assurance that he was ready to swear any oaths which would put the crown on his head.

'Will you swear to uphold the peace of this land,' asked the Archbishop, 'to govern with mercy and justice, to renounce evil customs and be guided by the laws of that great King known as Edward the Confessor, these laws having proved beneficial to the nation?'

'I swear,' said John.

The Archbishop warned John against attempting to evade his responsibilities and reminded him of the sacred nature of his oath.

So John was crowned King of England but he refused to receive Holy Communion after the ceremony of crowning which was a custom of the coronation and was looked upon as sealing the oaths a king had just taken.

There was much feasting after they had left the Abbey and John and all the guests had to do justice to the twenty-one oxen which had been roasted for the occasion.

The next day he received the homage of the barons.

He was now truly King of England and Duke of Normandy.

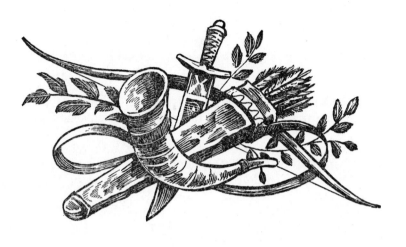

The Girl in the Forest

SURROUNDED by serious men, somewhat overawed by the
ceremonies of centuries, remembering stories he had heard of
his great ancestors William the Conqueror, Henry the Lion
of Justice and even the virtues of his own father Henry II,
John was temporarily ready to be guided.

His first task was to receive William Marshal to let him
know of his appreciation of what he had done and to express
the hope that William would serve him in the same selfless
manner as he had served his brother and father.

William assured him of his loyalty and John could not help
being impressed in the presence of such a man. He confirmed
his title of Earl of Pembroke which had come to him through
his wife and showed himself ready to listen to William's
advice.

William was pleased that England had accepted him; and
that Normandy too was with him. They would regain Anjou,
he promised John. When a new king came to the throne there
were always those who thought they had a greater claim. The
main trouble would come from the Continent, but all the
kings since the Conqueror had been faced with that difficulty.

It was from the North of England, however, that the first
threat came.

William, King of Scotland, known as William the Lion,
had sent messages to the effect that if John wished him to

maintain the loyalty he had given to Richard he, William, would need to be compensated by the return of Northumberland and Cumberland to the Scottish Crown. Faced with the antagonism of Philip and armies under Constance and Arthur, John had replied placatingly to William saying that if he would wait until he returned to England he would be happy to settle all his claims.

Now that he was back William wanted the territories he had claimed and sent another messenger to say that if they were not given up immediately he would perforce be obliged to take them.

William Marshal was inclined to think that the King of Scotland was bluffing and had no intention of engaging in a major war, but it was important that this did not take place, for clearly John's first task was to win back Anjou and the property which Philip had taken from him.

'Offer to negotiate with him,' advised William. 'Send him a soft placatory note and while your army is preparing for the Continent you might meet him somewhere. The Archbishop of York could conduct him over the border and you might travel to the Midlands and see him there. You must not give way. Parley with him. Make terms. Your father was an adept at such diplomacy.'

John was irritated by the Marshal's frequent references to his father, but he had to accept them none the less. He mustn't forget that William had been instrumental in getting him the crown and there had been opposition to it. He dare not offend William Marshal ... not until he was more secure of course.

John wrote to the King of Scotland as William Marshal dictated and a meeting was arranged at Northampton. When he reached that town there was no sign of William but a peremptory demand awaited him to the effect that if the territories were not restored immediately the large army which was on the Scottish borders would invade England.

John was in a quandary. How could he take on a war in the North when he had so much to regain on the Continent? This was not what he had thought of as kingship. Wars ... wars ... continual wars. What fun was there in that? He had always thought his father liked wars—though, when he came to think of it, Henry II was more of a diplomatist than a soldier. He had once said that he won more honours by negotiating and getting the better of his enemy at a conference than he ever had through fighting.

That was how John wanted it to be.

He had a stroke of real luck which was so unusual that it might be suspected of being contrived.

William of Scotland, ready to invade England, had visited one of the shrines of a Scottish saint; and while he knelt there a voice was heard warning him against invading England which would bring sorrow and disaster to Scotland.

This had the desired effect. He disbanded his army and decided to shelve the matter of the Northern Provinces. It couldn't have been more opportune from John's point of view, and he was able to forget trouble on the northern border and sail for the Continent.

*   *   *

Joanna, with Berengaria, had reached Rouen where they planned to stay for a while as Joanna's pregnancy was nearing its end. Those were sad days. Both Queens were overcome by grief at Richard's death and they would sit together talking of his virtues. Berengaria would forget the long years of neglect and remember only that brief period after his repentance when they had been together. Joanna liked to talk of the days when he had taken her across Aquitaine on her way to Sicily. She recalled clearly how the sun had glinted on his armour and how nobly he had sat his horse.

'It seemed inevitable that he should die young,' said Joanna. 'One could not imagine Richard's ever growing old.'

Berengaria said: 'Perhaps in time I should have had a child. I envy you, Joanna, in your happy state.'

'To love is not always a happy state,' Joanna comforted her. 'There are continuous anxieties. In Toulouse we have a beautiful estate, fertile lands, faithful servants and good friends. But there are those who persecute us because we do not think as they do, and because we fear that Rome is at the heart of these persecutions we are afraid. It is for that reason I am here.'

'I know, Joanna. But you have your husband who loves you, dear little Raymond and the new child who will soon be with us.'

'And Richard is dead. My beloved brother ... I never

believed that he would not come back when so many thought
he was dead. What a day of rejoicing it was when Blondel
returned to tell us that he had found him! Ever since he took
me to Sicily I had told myself Richard is here. Richard will
protect me. You see he came to Sicily and I knew that as soon
as he arrived I should cease to be Tancred's prisoner and it
came to pass. My beloved brother and champion! He would
have saved us from those who now persecute us ... and he is
gone, so what will become of us?'

'You have your husband. He will protect you.'

'He is but the Count of Toulouse. Richard was ruler of
England and his dominions here. Sometimes the weight of
this tragedy descends on me and I feel life is more than I can
bear.'

'That is no way for a mother to talk,' said Berengaria in
mild reproof.

'You are right, my dear friend and sister. What should I do
without you?'

'We shall always be together. I will stay with you Joanna,
as long as you want me.'

'You know I should always want you but it may be that a
husband will be found for you.'

Berengaria shook her head. 'I have done with marriage,'
she said.

Joanna was on the point of saying that because one marriage had been a failure it did not mean that a second would
be, but that seemed to cast censure on Richard, so she was
silent. He had scarcely been as good a husband to Berengaria
as he had been a good brother to her.

That night Joanna's pains started. They went on all
through the next day when it became clear that all was not
going well.

The doctors were grave when Berengaria questioned them
anxiously. Queen Joanna had suffered a great shock on the
death of her brother and this had had an adverse affect on her
health. She should have rested in Toulouse instead of travelling to Chaluz to see Richard.

The next morning the child was born, a poor sickly infant
who was clearly not destined to live more than a few days. He
was hastily baptized before he died.

Joanna lingered for a while but it was soon apparent that it
could not be for long.

Berengaria was with her during the day and night, for Joanna found great comfort from her presence.

She said: 'I am dying, Berengaria. Nay, do not deny it. I know it well. I can see the angel of death beckoning to me. There might be a few days left to me, but no more. I must repent of my sins and prepare myself to make my peace with heaven.'

'You have led a good life,' comforted Berengaria. 'You need have no fears.'

But Joanna talked of her mother in the peace of Fontevraud and said it was her wish that before she died she should be veiled as a nun of Fontevraud.

She had one more request. She wanted to be buried in the Abbey of Fontevraud beside her beloved brother Richard whom she had survived such a short while. They would lie together, she said, at the feet of her father.

So she received the veil the day before she died and then her body was taken to Fontevraud where Queen Eleanor received it and carried out her daughter's wish.

Berengaria, who went to the funeral, was stricken with grief. The companion of so many years when they were in the Holy Land together and she gradually understood the nature of the man she had married, was gone for ever. The future looked bleak before her. She could go to her brother's court or that of her sister. Neither promised her any great joy.

As for Eleanor she was stricken and for the first time looked her great age.

She was not bitter as Berengaria expected she might be; she was merely resigned. 'I have lost the two I loved best,' she said, 'and that in the space of a few months. My life is over. What is there left for me now but to wait for death.'

She would go into complete seclusion. She would remain at Fontevraud with the remains of her husband, and her beloved son and daughter.

'My work is done,' she said, 'and there is nothing for me now but to wait for death.'

*   *   *

John, meanwhile, had arrived in Normandy at the head of a formidable army, and in one or two skirmishes with the French army was victorious, which led to a meeting being arranged between himself and Philip. The French King

wanted the Vexin for himself and Anjou, Maine, Poitou and
Touraine for Arthur, but with an army behind him John was
in a position to snap his fingers at such demands; the result
was war. John's good fortune was that William des Roches,
who was leading the Breton army for Constance, Arthur and
Guy Thouars, could not agree with Philip and there was
dissension between them. So greatly did they fear the King of
France and his intentions towards Arthur that in a moment
of panic they decided to place him temporarily under the
protection of John.

John was delighted. He was in Le Mans at the time and he
welcomed William des Roches with open arms.

'Ah, my good lord,' he said, 'it pleases me that there are
some wise men in the world. This conflict with my own
nephew breaks my heart. I have never ill wished the boy. I
would his mother could be made to understand this.'

'I am doing my best to make her do so. The King of France
is quite perfidious. I never trusted him.'

'Nor I,' said John. 'Where is Arthur?'

'Not far from here. I will bring him to you, my lord, if you
will promise to guard him until such time as he is safe from
the King of France.'

'Bring him to me with all speed. I will guard him with my
life.'

John was inwardly exulting. The folly of others was always
exciting. They were actually going to put Arthur under his
protection! And Constance would be with him. That was
highly amusing. He had to be grateful to William des Roches
for quarrelling so fiercely with the King of France that he saw
Philip was the very essence of villainy beside whom his other
enemies seemed like saints.

From the castle tower John saw the party riding towards
the castle—young Arthur between his mother and Guy de
Thouars. He was Constance's paramour of course. That was
obvious. John's eyes narrowed as he thought of the sport he
could have with those two if the opportunity arose, but his
main concern must be with Arthur of course because Arthur
was the great threat to his security and he was the very heart
of conflict between them.

Rubbing his hands he went to greet them.

'My dear, dear Constance,' he cried. 'It does me good to
behold you. And Arthur! How you have grown, nephew!

You are indeed a man. And here is the Viscount de Thouars, your *very* good friend. I thank you, my lord, for taking such good care of my sister-in-law and my beloved nephew.'

She was wary, that woman. It had been against her judgment that they were here, he was sure. She would never trust him. But how frightened she must be of the King of France to have allowed Arthur to be brought to him!

Arthur was too young to hide his resentment. He knew John had been crowned King of England and the arrogant young creature thought that honour should have been his. It was maddening to think that quite a number of people agreed with him. A dangerous boy, this one.

That was why he was going to be very welcoming to him.

Constance said: 'We wish to shelter here for a short time. Our stay will not be long but if you would give us hospitality for a while we shall be grateful.'

'I want no gratitude for that which can only give me great pleasure. Come into the castle. A feast is being prepared. I want you to know how happy I am to see you. I have always deplored that there should be conflict between us. Now we can talk as friends of any difficulties which may have arisen between us.'

Constance exchanged glances with Guy. Any differences! Only the usurpation of a throne! How could she have allowed William des Roches to persuade her to bring Arthur here? She only had to be in John's company for a few moments for all her suspicions to be aroused. Surely Philip of France would have been the better choice even though there was disagreement between him and William des Roches. She had greatly feared that Philip would imprison Arthur. But what if John did the same? She knew then that she feared the King of England more than she did the King of France.

She was given a magnificent bedchamber and Arthur had the adjoining one. When they were alone together Arthur said: 'My uncle seems very kind.'

She smiled wryly. 'It is when he is most kind that I trust him least.'

There was a scratching at the door. Constance went to it and opened it cautiously. She fell back with relief. 'Guy!'

Guy lifted his finger to his lips. 'Depend upon it,' he whispered, 'there will be those to watch us. I like this not. We should never have allowed William des Roches to bring us here.'

'But we are here now,' said Constance, 'and must needs make the best of it.'

Guy shook his head. 'I have heard whispers,' he said. 'John will never let Arthur leave here. At first he will soothe us with soft words but his intention is to make Arthur his prisoner.'

'That must never be,' cried Constance.

'So think I. God knows what would happen to Arthur if he fell into that monster's hands.'

Constance clung to his arm.

'Oh Guy, what shall we do?'

'We are not spending a night in this castle. I have given orders to men I can trust. Tonight when the castle is quiet we shall steal out to the stables and horses will be ready. We shall not stop riding until dawn.'

She leaned against him her eyes half closed. 'Oh Guy, how thankful I am that you are with us.'

*   *   *

All through the night they rode towards Brittany where they could feel safe for a while. With dawn they came to rest at the residence of a knight whom they could trust.

Before they continued their journey Constance talked seriously to Guy about the dangerous position which Arthur was in. 'It is strange,' she said, 'that as soon as I see John I sense that which is evil in him, although when I am not with him I can be led to believe that he is not as bad as I really know him to be.'

'Never forget,' said Guy, 'that he fears Arthur will take what he wants, and which many believe by right is Arthur's. Arthur will never be safe while John lives.'

'It terrifies me. I would to God someone would kill him as they did his brother.'

'It may happen, but until it does let us be on our guard.'

'I know not what I would do without you, Guy.'

'You know that you will never have to do without me. Constance. Let us marry.'

'And the Earl of Chester?'

'That was no marriage. You could surely get a dispensation. Marriage which was never consummated is no marriage at all.'

'Guy, there is a priest here. He shall marry us. Then I shall know that we shall never be parted.'

'It is what I hope for,' he said.

And so immediately after their flight from Le Mans, Guy and Constance went through a ceremony of marriage.

When John heard that Arthur had escaped he fell into such a fury that none dared approach for the rest of the day. He threw himself on to the floor and rolled among the rushes, cramming handfuls of them into his mouth, grinding his teeth in his rage and then shouting to everyone what he would do to Arthur and his mother if ever they fell into his hands again.

*   *   *

Queen Eleanor was feeling her age, which was not surprising considering what it was. Few had lived as long as she had. In two years she would be eighty years old. There had been a time when she had thought she was to be immortal; but since Richard's death she had lost that driving will and determination to live and some force had gone from her. It had surprised her that she had considered for a while settling down in Fontevraud and leading a semi-pious life of seclusion. How she would have laughed at herself a few years ago; now it seemed a quite desirable way of passing the time left to her.

But it was not be be so. Experience had made her wise and she was naturally astute. She had immediately seen what a precarious position John was in, largely due to the existence of Arthur. None could be more aware of John's weaknesses than herself, but he was her son and in her opinion he came before her grandson. She would therefore do everything she could to maintain him on the throne.

Her duty had seemed clear to her. The peaceful life at Fontevraud must be ended and she must go to Aquitaine in order to hold it for John. If she did not, she was well aware that it would fall to Philip.

That she should ever be reluctant to go to the beloved country of her birth amazed her; it was only because the days of holding court were over and she knew she would be nostalgic for her youth—and even for the days when she had left that desirable state some way behind—and young men had composed their songs of praise to her beauty with words and music which throbbed with desire for the lady of Aquitaine. But who could honestly sing such songs to a woman close on eighty!

Some might try but she would laugh them to scorn if they did and they would soon desist.

The fact was that she must return, swear fealty to Philip as a vassal to France for Aquitaine and take up the reins once more—to hold them until such a time as they could safely be passed over to John. Then she would go back to Fontevrault to that life of quiet and seclusion which had suddenly become attractive to her.

She was often anxious wondering how John would be able to stand up to the wily subtle King of France over whom Richard had held some spell, and wondering too how Philip felt about Richard's death. As in every aspect of their relationship there must be contrasting emotions. While Richard lived there was no chance of Philip's regaining those territories he so earnestly desired; but now John had stepped into Richard's shoes? There were times when it was better not to look too far ahead especially when it was likely that one would not be alive to see the catastrophe. But such was her nature that while she lived she would do everything to avoid it.

Messengers arrived at the castle, forerunners of a royal cavalcade at the head of which was her son John. She immediately gave orders for the preparation of a banquet, and went up to a turret to watch for the arrival. It was not long before she saw them approaching and she went down to greet them.

She embraced John warmly and together they went into the castle that she might hear what news it was that had brought him.

'I met the King of France at Les Andelys,' he told her, 'and there is a truce between us. It is this that I wish to discuss with you.'

'How did you find Philip? More amenable than usual I'll warrant,' she said, a glint in her eyes and an excitement gripping her to feel herself once more at the centre of affairs. A life of seclusion for her! How would she endure it!

She was amused by Philip's predicament. What a complex

creature he was; and the fact that he was the son of her first husband had always made her interested in him. She would have enjoyed having him for a son; and she often wondered how a poor monk like Louis had managed to beget him. Philip was clever; in fact she wondered whether there was any man alive to compare with him in mental agility. He was ambitious but preferred to make his conquests through diplomacy and clever juggling than through fighting, which was the best way in the end if the desired result could be achieved. That had been her second husband's virtue. Henry II had had a reputation as a great general and yet if he could avoid battle he did so. This she had always seen as the secret of his successes in his early days. Philip resembled him in that way. Richard—straightforward, seeing but one side to every question—had believed that war was the decisive weapon. It often was, and when conducted by the greatest soldier in the world, invariably successful, but it was the wily ones like Henry II and Philip who often achieved their ends at least cost.

It was strange that Philip, who had once so passionately loved Richard, should now be in love with a woman. But in love he must be to allow a relationship to affect him politically.

His first wife Isabella of Hainault had died some years before, leaving him a son, Louis. Three years after her death he had married Ingeburga, a princess of Denmark. As soon as the ceremony had taken place he took a violent dislike to her and refused to live with her. As was the custom in such cases with kings he at once trumped up a case of consanguinity which would render the marriage null and this was immediately confirmed by a French court which did not wish to displease the King.

It was not always easy though to rid oneself of a royal princess, for her family rallied to her and popes who were often amenable when one side was important and the other less so, liked to be a little more careful when dealing with royalty on either side. Thus Pope Celestine quashed the decision of the French court and forbade Philip to marry again. Two princesses refused the honour of becoming Queen of France fearing that they might not please Philip and their fate be like that of Ingeburga; but then he met Agnes of Meran and her beauty and grace charmed him to such an extent that he was determined, in spite of the Pope, to marry her. This he did. Celestine might have bowed to a *fait accompli* but his successor Innocent III was of sterner morals and, moreover, determined to exercise his power. He wrote to Philip to tell him that his conduct had brought upon him the wrath of God and the thunder of the Church and if Philip continued to live with Agnes he would impose the Interdict on him which meant that there would be no religious ceremonies and festivals in France.

Philip was furious and declared that he would do without the Pope. He had recently been fighting in the Holy Land, he said, and he noticed that the Saracens such as the great Saladin seemed to get along very well without the blessing of Rome.

This was the state of affairs at the French Court and Eleanor knew that although Philip might show bravado outwardly, he would inwardly suffer a few qualms—if not exactly on religious grounds; he would know that to go into battle without the Church on his side would have its effect on his followers.

So now Eleanor was smiling slyly, realizing that Philip would be far more ready to come to a conference with John with the Interdict threatening him than he would otherwise.

'Philip was ready to be reasonable,' John told her.

'I'll warrant he was. He has his affair with the Pope to occupy him at this time.'

'We talked,' said John, 'and we have come to agreement. He has accepted me as the heir of all that Richard held in France.'

'Then we should rejoice,' said Eleanor. 'But doubtless you have had to make concessions.'

'I have had to give up the Vexin.'

'A pity, but naturally he would want something.'

'And I have agreed to pay him 20,000 marks.'

Eleanor grimaced, but a cunning look had come into John's eyes. Agreeing to pay was not actually paying and he had little intention of keeping that side of the bargain. Philip might well be prepared for that, for he would have long ago summed up the man with whom he was dealing.

'And,' went on John, 'here is something that will please you: my niece, your granddaughter Blanche, is to be betrothed to young Louis.'

Eleanor smiled and nodded. 'So our little Blanche will be the future Queen of France.'

'I knew that would please you. But the best is to come. Philip recognizes that I am Arthur's overlord.'

'Ah,' said the Queen. 'Then you have indeed done well.'

'There are some who think I have given away too much and they are nicknaming me John Softsword. By God's teeth if I were to catch those who mocked me in that way I'd flay them alive.'

'Words are of no great importance, and in getting Philip to agree that Arthur must do homage to you you have done very well. Blanche should be brought from Castile before Philip has the chance to change his mind.'

'I'll send for her.'

'Nay,' said the Queen. 'That's not good enough. I shall go to Castille and bring her myself.'

'*You* ... you are capable of the journey?'

'The day I am not capable of doing what I know must be done to hold the throne for my son, I shall be ready to be laid in my tomb. That day is not yet. I shall prepare for the journey at once.' Her eyes shone with pleasure. 'I shall be happy indeed to see your sister Eleanor. It is so rarely that I see my children and then briefly.'

'The journey will be arduous.'

'My son, my life has been made up of arduous journeys.'

Eleanor was as good as her word. She made immediate preparations to leave for Castile and soon she was on her way.

*　　*　　*

John was pleased with himself. He knew that people had compared him with his brother Richard and whispered that he lacked his skill to rule. They should see. Hadn't he already made a treaty with the King of France? Hadn't he got an admission from him that he was Arthur's overlord?

Now was the time for enjoyment and what better than the chase.

He gathered together his intimate friends—young men daring like himself, who applauded everything he did and made him feel that he was indeed the King. It was good to ride out in new forests and, after Eleanor had left, he spent days in hunting on his way north to Normandy. Like his

ancestors, he loved the chase and to be in at the kill and to see
a panting animal at bay gave him a pleasure so intense that it
could only be rivalled by seeing human beings in a similar
state of terror.

He was riding ahead with a party in the forests between La
Marche and the Angoumois when he countered a party
coming in the opposite direction. At their head was a very
young girl. She could not have been more than thirteen years
old but as he looked at her something happened to John
which had never happened before. That she was the most
beautiful girl he had ever seen occurred to him immediately
as it must to everyone else; but she had more than beauty.
She was dainty, imperious, mischievous ... all in the most
beguiling manner and he had an intense desire to seize her
and carry her off.

He called a halt and the riders came up to him.

'Tell me,' he cried, 'where do you come from and who are
you?'

The young man who was riding beside the fascinating
young girl replied: 'I am Hugh de Lusignan, son of the
Count of La Marche and I might well ask what you are doing
in my father's territory?'

'My good fellow,' said John, angry lights leaping into his
eyes, 'I tell you this: you may be the son of the Count of La
Marche and call this land yours. I am the Duke of Aquitaine
under whom you hold this land. It would be well for you to
remember it.'

The young man leaped from his horse and bowed low to
John whose good temper was restored.

'Come, come,' he said, ' 'twas a mistake easy made. Who is
this lady whom you escort?'

'She is my betrothed, my lord. Isabella, daughter of the
Count of Angoulême, who is being brought up in my brother's
household.'

'Charming,' said John. 'Charming, charming. The son of
the Count of La Marche, you say. Well, a merry day to
you.'

With that he nodded and rode on. His friends were
astonished. They had seen the familiar look in his eyes as he
had surveyed the girl and had expected him to take some
action. It would not have surprised them if they had beaten
off her protectors and abducted her.

He was thoughtful—unusually so, and it was clear that he was thinking of the young girl.

When one of them spoke to him, he did not answer. Instead he murmured: 'The Count of La Marche. How many years think you before that marriage takes place?'

'The girl is very young, my lord. 'Twould have to be two years at least.'

'If it ever does take place,' said John with a smile.

He couldn't get her out of his mind. He dreamed of her. It was ridiculous, for she was only a child. She had looked at him in an odd way, too. There was nothing childish about that. Perhaps she was overawed, for she would know he was not only her father's suzerain but King of England.

Why couldn't he stop thinking of her. He could see her face clearly—that thick curling hair about the oval contours and the expression in those wonderful eyes that was half innocence, half knowledge. What an intriguing girl.

His instinct was to carry her off and seduce her without delay. Rape if necessary. Would it have been necessary?

But the daughter of the Count of Angoulême, the betrothed of the son of the Count of La Marche, could not be treated like a peasant. The Lusignans were a powerful family. They could raise the whole of Aquitaine against him, because the people didn't want *him*, and he knew it. They accepted his mother joyfully because she was one of them. Hadn't she been brought up there as the heiress of Aquitaine? But they had hated her husband and her sons. Richard had had to fight incessantly to hold that rebellious land. Much as he deplored the fact that he had not seized the girl John knew very well that he had been wise not to.

He kept thinking about her. No woman could satisfy him now. Always he would see the lovely haunting face of the fairy-like child in the forest.

*   *   *

He could not forget Isabella of Angoulême and it occurred to him that if he had not already a wife he might have made a match with Isabella. There was some grounds for it. After all, the Count of Angoulême would surely be pleased to see his daughter Queen of England; and such an alliance would no doubt change the antagonism of Aquitaine towards him. Of course Isabella was already affianced to one of the Lusignans and the Lusignans were a great fighting family. They wouldn't be pleased, but one cannot please everybody all the time.

The more he thought of Isabella the more he was determined to marry her, for he realized that he could not abduct her and carry her away and keep her with him while she pleased him as though she were a girl with no important family; and he would never really enjoy sexual encounters with other women until he had satisfied his desire for this one.

There was only one way of getting Isabella and that was through marriage.

True he had been married for the last ten years, since just before Richard's coronation he had taken Hadwisa of Gloucester as his bride in order to possess himself of her rich lands. That he had done to his satisfaction and they had made him a wealthy man. It was long since he had seen Hadwisa; she loathed him and that had been the only attraction he had found in her, and he had had a certain amount of pleasure in inflicting his attentions on her only for that reason. Had she wanted him he would never have gone to her. But as she grew older and knew him better she steeled herself against her revulsion and that did not please him. She, however, achieved her wish, for he had rarely seen her during the last five years.

But a king must consider his successors. He did not want to be like Richard and leave no one to follow him. He wanted a son and delicious little Isabella should provide him—once he had rid himself of Hadwisa.

How? He could have her poisoned. No, better not. It would look suspicious if he married Isabella immediately afterwards and he wanted no delay in his marriage. After all he and Hadwisa were cousins and she had been very worried about the connection and tried to prevent the consummation of their marriage in the beginning.

The simplest way was a divorce. Or perhaps even that was not necessary. He would bring up the old charge of consanguinity. That should not be difficult because after all there was a strong relationship between them through Henry I who was the great grandfather of them both—although Hadwisa came down through the illegitimate line—for his grandmother, Matilda, and Hadwisa's grandfather, Robert of Gloucester, had been half-brother and sister. It was a strong blood tie and therefore it should be comparatively easy to dissolve the marriage.

None of his ministers would dare deny him a divorce. The Pope might be awkward though as he was being over the marriage of Philip of France. But if Hadwisa agreed it should not be difficult. Then he would be free ... free for Isabella ...

As soon as he returned to England he rode to Marlborough Castle where Hadwisa lived.

She came down to the courtyard to greet him in the customary manner and to offer him the stirrup cup which he always made her drink first in case she had it in mind to poison him. Not that he really feared that. Hadwisa had no spirit; but one could never be sure with the quiet ones.

'Ah, Hadwisa,' he cried. 'I trust I see you well.'

She drank from the cup without his pressing her to do so and handed it to him. He drank it and threw it from him. It clattered on to the cobbles as he leaped from his horse.

'Come, Hadwisa. I have much to say to you.'

He slipped his arm through hers and was amused to feel her tremble. Did she think he had come to stay and spend the night with her? She was more repulsive than ever now that he compared her with Isabella. But he could still enjoy letting her fear what might be in store for her.

It might be amusing to torment her just once more. No, better not. What if he got her with child? He didn't want that complication now. One of his excuses for ridding himself of her was going to be that she was barren and it was a king's duty to get sons.

All the same he led the way to her bedchamber and waited a while for her to try to calm herself, to pretend that she was not fearful of what ordeal lay before her.

But he was too impatient for Isabella to enjoy plaguing Hadwisa. His one great desire now was to be rid of her.

He sat sprawling in a chair, his legs stretched out before him and regarded the tips of his boots. 'Well, Hadwisa, it was not much was it, this marriage of ours? You know why, do you not? We should never have married in the first place. The blood tie was too strong. Our lusty great grandfather should have remained faithful to his wife and then, my dear Hadwisa, you would never have been born.'

She bowed her head. She did not want him to see the hopeful lights which she knew must be shining from her eyes.

'When I married you,' he went on, 'I was but the brother of a king. It seemed possible that Richard would have sons whom the people would say came before a younger brother. So I was allowed to marry you who, though of some royal blood, had come by it in a dubious manner.'

'I was rich,' she reminded him sharply.

'There you have a point,' he said. 'Our great grandfather was generous to his bastards.'

'It may have been that, like his grandson, he found they served him well, even more loyally perhaps than his legitimate sons.'

She had some spirit after all.

'Well,' he said, 'perforce they must. They would fare ill if they did not. A legitimate son has rights which a bastard would have to toady for.'

'I cannot believe that my grandfather ever did that. By what I hear of him he was a most noble gentleman and the King was well aware of it.'

John made an impatient gesture. 'I have not come here to talk of the merits of bastards,' he said. 'Hadwisa, you have come to great honour. Some might say you are a queen.'

'Is not the wife of the King a queen?'

'If he decides that she is. You remember you were never at Court. You were never beside me when I travelled. You were not crowned with me at my coronation. It is the custom for a queen to be crowned with her husband. Does this give you some idea of what is in my mind?'

He could see her heart beating wildly under her bodice. With hope, he believed. Oh yes, she wanted to be rid of him. She loathed him. She might easily have tried to poison him if she had had the courage. She had hated those occasions when he had turned his attentions on her even more than he realized. He would love to torment her now but he was too impatient to be rid of her.

'The fact is, Hadwisa,' he said, 'that you have not given me a child. I have been married to you for ten years and although I admit you have not had so many opportunities, there have yet been some. I am a king. I must have an heir. So since you cannot give it to me there is only one alternative left to me. I must try elsewhere.'

'You want to declare our marriage no marriage,' she said calmly.

'Failing that, there could be a divorce.'

'There would be no difficulty,' she said eagerly. 'The Archbishop of Canterbury was much against our marriage.'

'Oh yes, old Baldwin. He ranted, did he not? The blood tie is there, Hadwisa.'

'Then you should marry again and perhaps this time you will get heirs.'

She was thinking: I pity your bride. But her relief must necessarily be stronger than her pity.

'This is what I have come to tell you. I believe there will be no difficulty in releasing me from this marriage. I have already set matters in motion. I have chosen three bishops from Normandy and three from Aquitaine. I have no doubt what their verdict will be. The Pope will not interfere unless you raise a voice against it.'

She said almost breathlessly, 'You may rely on me. I shall raise no voice against it. I shall be happy with the conclusion you have come to.'

'Then all is well,' he said.

He stood up and looked about the room. He had had a little sport here, but not much. He had quickly tired of her terror.

'Good-bye, Hadwisa,' he said.

'Good-bye John,' she replied in a subdued voice and never had she been so happy to say good-bye to anyone before.

He rode from the castle in high good humour.

Isabella, Isabella, he was thinking. I shall soon have you.

*   *   *

It must not be too obvious. He must wait for the verdict of the bishops. He had enjoyed explaining to them in a sanctimonious manner. 'I have given this matter great thought. Hadwisa of Gloucester has been a good wife to me and I hesitate to put her from me. If I did not think it was the will of God...'

They had looked at him a little suspiciously then and he knew he had gone too far so he had continued: 'I must confess that it is the succession which is uppermost in my mind. I need a son. The country needs an heir. I want to do my duty to my people.'

They considered a while but not for long. It was good that the King should end his unfruitful marriage. It was true that when a king had a son it was the best thing possible for that son to follow his father to the throne. If there was no direct heir there was invariably conflict. It had happened so recently with John and Arthur.

The Bishops decided—all six of them—that it would be good for John's subjects if he married a wife who could give him an heir.

John was a free man and the Pope, after all the fuss there had been when he had married Hadwisa and the fact that they had been forbidden by the Church to live together, could not but agree. The only point which could have made him hesitate was if Hadwisa herself had raised an objection.

John was content. There was no fear of that.

He now amused himself by pretending to look round for a bride. He did not want anyone to know that he had found her already. He was going to discover when the time was ripe what a good thing it would be for him to marry Isabella of Angoulême.

In the meantime he discussed the possibility of his remarriage with William Marshal.

'Richard did well by marrying Berengaria of Navarre,' he said. 'Navarre has been a good friend to our house. I would wish to preserve that friendship.'

William Marshal agreed that it was wise to do so.

'But Navarre is threatened by Castile and Aragon because they are allies of the King of France. Now I have thought what a good policy it would be to use Portugal as an ally, which could be achieved.'

'I see,' said William Marshal, 'you are thinking of the Portuguese King's daughter. She is marriageable. It is an excellent idea. We should send envoys at once to Portugal.'

'Let it be done without delay,' said John.

So it was; and when he was alone he laughed heartily to consider the excitement in the Portuguese Court at the prospect of alliance with the King of England who owned large dominions on the Continent.

'No, my Princess of Portugal,' he whispered. 'I am not for you, and you are not for me. There is only one who will do for me. Isabella.'

Isabella

IT was some years before John had seen her in the forest that Isabella had become betrothed to Hugh de Lusignan. She would never forget the day when her parents had sent for her and explained that a husband had been found for her and his family wanted her to go to them that she might be educated in the manner expected of a Lusignan and grow to love her husband before she became his wife.

At that time Isabella had known very little of the world outside the Angoumois over which her parents ruled. In some measure she ruled them. That she was beautiful in no ordinary way had quickly become obvious to her. She heard it whispered; she saw it in people's eyes when they looked at her; in fact she was always a little shocked if people failed to react to her beauty which they did only on rare occasions. Perhaps some old Bishop would look upon her just as though she were an ordinary child. Poor old thing, she would think, I suppose he's half blind.

She never lost a chance of looking at her reflection. It delighted her even when she was very young. Those beautiful long eyes with the thick black lashes; eyes that were of a blue so deep that it was almost violet; her thick dark hair was a cloud about the perfect oval of her face. She had been born a beauty and would remain one to the end of her days.

It was natural that there should be a certain imperiousness about her. Her mother used to say to her: 'Never forget that you are descended from the Kings of France and the French Court is the most elegant and most intellectual in the world.'

Naturally her mother would think so because she was the daughter of Peter de Courtenay who was a young son of King Louis VI of France. Isabella knew that her mother considered herself of higher social standing than her father. He, however, being Count of Angoulême, was a man of influence and because she was their only child she was of great importance to them.

When she was very young Isabella learned that they had hoped for a son; she was very glad that they were unable to get one because she knew that if they had she would have been of less importance to them, and one thing Isabella hated was not to be the centre of attraction.

She believed that at the Court of Angoulême she was the most important figure even though she was only a little girl. Her mother watched over her with the greatest care; her father gave instructions to her attendants and governesses that she was never to be left alone. That was a nuisance but because it meant they were so anxious for her she accepted it and would have been put out to see it slackened.

She worked hard in the schoolroom because she had a natural aptitude for learning and she liked everyone to know how clever she was. She wanted to be first in everything. There was no doubt that she was the most beautiful child any of them had ever seen; but she wanted also to be the cleverest. True she had to work a little harder to achieve that but she was purposeful and made a point of getting what she wanted.

There was a great deal of talk about Richard Coeur de Lion who was Duke of Aquitaine of which the Angoumois was a part. She learned that Richard was a great fighter. He had left his country to go to the Holy Land in an effort to restore Jerusalem to the Christians and the world seemed to think he was some sort of hero saint. Not so her father. He hated Richard.

Isabella used to listen to the talk between her father and mother, for she was allowed to go into their bedchamber in the morning and sit on the bed while they gloated on their beautiful child. This appealed to her greatly; she lapped up their admiration but at the same time she liked to keep her

ears open for interesting gossip and they were not entirely
discreet before her, thinking her too young to understand.
But although she was young she could always store up these
comments and brood over them later and ask naïve questions
which very often gave her the answer she needed.

Isabella liked to know what was going on.

According to her father Richard was an arrogant overlord,
and a king who left his kingdom to go to another land to
fight—even in a holy cause—was not a good one and a bad
king was not a good duke. Therefore, Aquitaine was ill-
governed and the Count of Angoulême was not going to
swear allegiance to such a man. He preferred to do so to the
King of France.

Of course the Countess was in agreement with her husband. She was always ready to lean towards what was French,
which was natural enough since that was the country of her
birth.

There was always a great deal of talk about the Lusignans,
an important family who lived in Poitou which bordered
on the Angoumois. At one time this family had been bitter
enemies of the dukes of Normandy but they were great
crusaders and in the Holy Land, they had come into contact
with Richard Coeur de Lion. In a common interest, the
enmity had disappeared and during the Holy War Guy de
Lusignan and Richard Coeur de Lion had become such close
friends that Richard had supported Guy's claim to the crown
of Jerusalem—when it should be regained—against the King
of France who had supported Conrad de Montferrat. Guy
and Richard had fought side by side, and as a result their
friendship had strengthened and this had extended to the
whole family. Thus the Lusignans of Angoulême were supporting a different side from their close neighbour in the
perennial quarrel between the Kings of France and England.
There was another reason for rivalry and disagreement between them. Both families coveted the rich territory known
as La Marche which lay to the east of the Angoumois.

Richard had been secretly pleased that the desire to possess
La Marche kept those two powerful families suspicious of
each other and therefore turned their thoughts from planning forays into neighbouring Anjou.

When Richard had died, Hugh de Lusignan, the eldest son
of the House, had with great temerity managed to capture

Queen Eleanor while she was out riding one day and with even greater daring had declared to her his intention of keeping her prisoner until she gave him La Marche.

With Richard dead and all her tact and skill needed to put John on the throne Eleanor had given way and had bought her freedom for the surrender of La Marche.

The Count of Angoulême was angry that Hugh de Lusignan had that which he had coveted; he had to be placated and the Lusignans had had the clever notion that the best way of settling their differences was by a marriage contract.

Hugh was in his twenties—a young man of pride and strength, worthy to be the head of his house. The Count of Angoulême had a daughter. She was not yet twelve years old it was true, but her lack of years could soon be remedied. With every passing week she grew nearer to maturity and it was only a matter of waiting a year or so before she would be ready for matrimony.

Isabella knew there was something afoot. Members of the Lusignan family rode over and at their head was Hugh. Isabella watching from a window saw him arrive and when he looked up, she smiled at him. He stood there legs apart watching her for a few seconds and she was excited because she knew that he was thinking—as almost everyone else did—how pretty she was.

Her mother came to her room and dismissed the servants.

'I have something to say to you, Isabella,' she said. 'Now listen carefully. Some very important gentlemen are visiting us. You will meet them and I want you to be very charming to them.'

'Why?' asked Isabella.

'There is a very special reason.'

'What reason?'

'You will know all in good time.'

'But if I am to be especially nice to them I want to know now.'

'You are too young to understand.'

Too young! This was absurd. She was not too young for anything. She knew a great deal. She listened; she asked questions; she trapped people into admissions. She knew about the maids who went out into the shrubbery when it was dusk to meet the men servants. She had hidden herself and been at first greatly astonished by their activities and although she had seen them repeated many times she always liked to watch. This excited her more than anything she knew. So she was certainly not too young to know why she had to be particularly attractive to the Lusignans.

'Is it something to do with my betrothal?' she asked slyly.

Her mother stared in astonishment. 'How could you know?'

'Because you said I was too young to understand. When one is considered too young it is usually something to do with men and women together.'

The child was astonishing, thought her mother.

'What do you know of such things?' she demanded.

'Not as much as I should like to, I fear.'

'It is nothing to be fearful about. Such knowledge will come in due course. When you have a husband you will know what is good for you to know.'

'Am I to have a husband then? Who is it? Hugh de Lusignan?'

The Countess hesitated. Then she said: 'Yes. You have guessed aright.'

Isabella clasped her hands together and said: 'I like him.'

'Then that is well.'

'He is a beautiful man,' cried Isabella. 'He looked up at the window when he was entering the castle and smiled at me. I think he liked me.'

'Of course he liked you. Did you expect him not to?'

'Of course not,' said Isabella.

'Now you will be dressed in a gown I shall choose for you and I shall take you down to the hall and present you to Hugh.'

'Will he take me away with him now?' she asked.

'Certainly not, my dear child. He will meet you and if he likes what he sees there will be a betrothal.'

'And if I do not like what I see?'

'You have already said you like him.'

'But if I had not?'

'Girls in your position must marry where their family wishes them to.'

'So you wish me to marry Hugh?'

'It will be good for our families if you do.'

'Is that why Hugh wants it?'

'He will only want it if you are charming to him and he thinks you beautiful.'

'I will be charming and he will think me beautiful because everybody does.'

'This betrothal will please your father. It is very important that there is friendship between our families.'

'So I shall be a wife now.'

She was thinking of the servants in the shrubbery and she thought: I shall know now. Her observations had taught her that it was not only servants who behaved in such a manner. Her turn would come and something told her that she was going to find the exercise highly diverting and every bit as enjoyable as they clearly did. She couldn't wait to indulge in such pleasures.

'My dear child, it will not be for a year or two yet.'

'Not for a year or two! Why should I wait?'

'Because you are but a child.'

'Bess the kitchen girl is but a few months older than I ...'

'What are you saying? Bess. Kitchen girl! My dear Isabella, you are not giving me your serious attention.'

But she was of course and she was very disappointed that she must wait for her marriage.

Now she set about the task of charming Hugh. He was tall and looked very strong. He was wonderful. He was very handsome and was, her mother had told her, a great soldier. He thought she was beautiful; she saw that at once by the way in which he kept looking at her. He laid his hands on her shoulders and she smiled up at him.

He said, 'Your daughter is indeed a beauty, Count. Would to God she were but three years older.'

She wanted to shout: I am as wise as others who are three years older. I am not a child ... except in years. I know about marriage and I don't want to wait for it. Forget I am not yet twelve years old.

But even she dared not say that, with her father and mother looking on.

Her mother said she could go to her own chamber. She pouted a little and said could she not stay.

'Your father and our guest have business to discuss,' she was told.

She tried to linger but her mother had taken her by the arm and was leading her gently away leaving the two men while her father and her husband-to-be talked together of the union between Lusignan and Angoulême, the dowry, when the wedding would take place and what was to happen in the meantime.

* * *

Her mother came to her chamber and sat on her bed. Isabella, rosy from sleep, raised herself. How lovely she was! thought the Countess. It was small wonder that Hugh had found her irresistible and deplored the fact that she was so young.

'You are to leave us, my child,' said the Countess sadly.

'I am going to be married?' cried Isabella.

'In due course. But first you are to leave your home and go to that of your future husband.'

'When, Mother?'

'Within a few days.' The Countess shook her head sadly. 'It is always thus with daughters. They must leave the family with whom they have spent their childhood and go to that which will be theirs for the rest of their lives. You won't forget us, Isabella?'

'Forget you, Mother! How could I? And my dear father too. Oh no, I shall never forget you.'

She threw her arms about her mother's neck but even then she was thinking of the strong body of Hugh de Lusignan and wondering what his embraces would be like.

'You must not fret, my darling.'

Fret. She was all eagerness to go.

'I shall see you and my father often, shall I not, Mother? We shall be near neighbours.'

'We must make sure that comes to pass.'

'We will, we will. I shall insist.'

Her mother smiled fondly. 'It will be as your husband wishes,' she reminded her.

Oh no, thought Isabella. It shall be as I wish.

She smiled complacently. She had no doubt that she would get her way with Hugh as she had with her parents.

'Now we must busy ourselves with preparations for your departure. It is inconvenient that there is so little time.'

She was not inconvenienced at all. She was excited. She wondered how long she would have to wait before they considered her old enough to marry.

In a few weeks she left her father's castle and was escorted by her parents and some of the men-at-arms to the castle situated in the heart of Lusignan country between Poitiers and Niort.

The stone walls of the castle glittered in the sunshine and although she had seen other castles there was a special quality about this one because it was going to be her home. Within those walls she would become the bride of Hugh de Lusignan who was also known as Hugh le Brun. He was rich, he was clever and he was strong. She was delighted with her bridegroom and as she rode towards the castle with her parents she was determined to prove to him that although she was not yet twelve years old she was ready for marriage; she might be innocent but she was not ignorant. She might be a virgin but she was anxious to cast off that not very exciting state; and because she was already aware that the arts of seduction would be second nature to her, she was going to set herself the task of making Hugh the Brown forget that she was only a child, and she had every hope of success.

The family of Angoulême were given a very warm welcome in the ancestral home of the Lusignans and those present marvelled at this since they had always been natural enemies—always fighting for possession of La Marche, always trying to take a little territory from each other, seeking it seemed reasons for quarrels. And now because of this beautiful child's betrothal to the son of the clan all was peace.

It was certainly a time for great rejoicing.

Isabella was given a bevy of attendants only a little older than herself; and Hugh declared to her parents that in this household she would be treated with all honour. He would be absent for long periods, but his brother Ralph would take his place in the household, and Ralph swore to the family that he would make it his personal duty to see that no harm came to his brother's betrothed whose beauty and charm had already won all their hearts.

Isabella's family, though sad to part with their daughter, rode away without misgivings knowing that the Lusignans were to be trusted on such a point of honour.

They comforted each other as they rode back to Angoulême.

'It has to happen,' said Count Aymer. 'All parents must face it.'

'If there had been others it would have been easier to endure,' replied his wife Alice.

'Alas, that we had but one child.'

'It makes her a considerable heiress though,' said Isabella's mother, 'and if we only had one at least the one we had must be the loveliest girl in the world.'

'You speak with a mother's fondness which may obscure her vision slightly.'

'Nay, I heard said by one of the Lusignans to another—not meant for my ears: "When did you see a more perfect creature? Thus must Helen of Troy appeared to those about her."'

Aymer laughed. 'I hope our Isabella will not cause as much trouble as that woman did.'

'Hugh delights in her already. I feel sure he will wish to hurry the marriage.'

'He must needs wait. She cannot marry at twelve years.'

'She is not as immature as some twelve-year-olds.'

'No, my lady, I will not have her forced into the marriage bed before she is ready for it.'

'You are right. There must be a few years wait yet. But perhaps when she is fourteen.'

'We shall see.'

And so they rode back to Angoulême. But the castle there had lost something with the departure of Isabella.

*   *   *

Isabella set out to charm her new family and succeeded admirably. Hugh was already in love with her and chafed against delay. This delighted her, but she did not want him to know this. She chose a hundred little ways of keeping close to him, of clinging to him, calling attention to her helplessness which she knew he found so appealing; she carefully chose ribbons for her hair which would be most becoming to her unusual colouring and enhanced her beauty in every way. Not that anything so obvious needed to have attention called to it. She exulted in her beautiful face, her perfect little body which irritated her a little because it seemed to her so slow in reaching maturity.

She would prance naked before the young girls who were in attendance on her and demand to know if she was not a little more grown up than she had been the day before. She compared herself with them and demanded to know if they had lovers. Those who had, found favour with her; she would give them ribbons with which to adorn their hair before she sent them off for a tryst; and payment for these favours meant that she wanted a detailed description of everything that had taken place.

She was their adored little mistress; she was unlike any other they had served.

'What a wife you will make my lord Hugh, my lady,' they declared.

'Yes, yes,' she cried impatiently. 'But it is all waiting and I am ready now.'

She was obsessed by the subject. She told the girls that Hugh would be so mad for her that he would insist on the marriage taking place without delay.

They laughed and said that would not be difficult. He was half way to that state already and they swore it was only because he feared to offend her parents that he did not insist on the wedding.

Each day she contrived to be with Hugh; her eyes would light up at the sight of him and she would throw herself into his arms which was not very decorous, but he seemed to forget that. She would clasp him tightly about the neck and press her face against his.

'Is it not wonderful, Hugh, that you and I will one day be married?'

'I never wanted anything so much,' he told her earnestly.

'Do you wish I were not so young?'

'I think you are perfect as you are.'

'But wouldn't I be more perfect if I were of an age to marry?'

'One cannot improve on perfection,' he reminded her.

She believed that her very youth was part of her attraction to him. In one way he didn't want her to grow up. He wanted to keep her as she was—pure, he thought, unsullied by the world which meant she had not yet coupled with a man. That he desired her, she had no doubt; and yet he wanted her to stay as she was.

How contradictory! Perhaps she had something yet to learn of the ways of men.

*   *   *

This was the state of affairs at the time of the encounter in the forest. She could not forget the man who had looked at her so intently. That he thought she was beautiful was obvious, but that was a common enough reaction. There had been something more than that. No one had had quite that effect on her before. She knew instinctively that had she been alone at the time, perhaps the daughter of a woodcutter or a forester he would not have hesitated for one moment. He would have seized her on the spot. She was aware of an over-whelming sensuality in this man which Hugh lacked; it was a quality—or perhaps one should say a vice—which she under-stood perfectly because she now knew that she possessed it herself. She had wished—though fleetingly—during those first moments in the forest that she had been a humble cot-tage girl.

That man had desired her in a way Hugh never had and the experiences she would have had with him would be different from any she could share with Hugh.

He was not handsome as Hugh was. Hugh was tall, square-shouldered with a strong jaw and keen eyes; he was a fighter. This man was different. He was not very tall; she calculated that he could not be more than five feet five inches. There were many men who were no taller but she was comparing him with Hugh. He lacked the nobility which she had admired in Hugh; his mouth was sensual; his eyes a little wild; he was dark and swarthy—no, not handsome by any means. But he was a king—King of England, Duke of Normandy, Count of Anjou ... he was a very important man, far more so than Hugh who had had to leap from his horse and show that he was in the presence of one who was far above him.

King of England! And how he had looked at her! Hugh had never looked like that, even in those moments when she embraced him and thrust herself against him outwardly art-less, inwardly artful, he had never looked quite like that.

She had sat there on her horse, her blue hood—the colour of speedwell flowers and so good for bringing out the blue of her eyes, falling from her hair, her cape flowing about her—a lovely picture she knew.

How he had looked at her! As no one ever had before.

Then he had ridden away. Hugh had been silent and she could not lure him from his mood with all her wiles.

'Tell me about that man,' she demanded.

'He is John of England,' answered Hugh.

'And Duke of Normandy and Count of Anjou.'

'He has many titles.'

'He is not exactly well favoured.'

'He has an evil reputation.'

'How so?'

'He has done that which would be beyond your under-standing.'

'You mean ... with women?'

'And others.'

'He has been cruel in war?'

'He is to be feared,' answered Hugh. 'A man would think twice before he offended him.'

They were silent as they rode back to the castle. All interest in the hunt had left them both.

Isabella dreamed that she met John alone in the forest; in her dreams she saw his face coming closer and closer—hungry, demanding, lascivious.

She awoke in fear and wished that she had gone on dream-ing.

I shall never see him again, she thought, and did not know whether she was glad or sorry.

She thought of Hugh, so handsome, so strong. He would be a good kind husband and she would have no difficulty in having her way with him. She smiled to herself to realize how she would rule him.

Why could he not see that it was time they married?

She told her women of the encounter with King John. They whispered of him. Such stories they had heard of him! When he was young he had gone to Ireland. He had had to leave though; he spent his time jeering at the natives and raping their women.

She listened avidly.

'Had I been alone in the forest when I met him...' she began.

They shrieked in horror and silenced her.

'You would never be allowed out alone, my lady; and even King John would have to respect your rank.'

She was silent imagining it.

The girls marvelled at the obtuseness of those about her and in particular Count Hugh.

Didn't they see it was time the Lady Isabella was married? True she was young, but girls such as she was needed to be married young.

The King's Infatuation

An embassy had arrived from Portugal. John received it with outward eagerness. He was greatly amused to note how excited its members were at the prospect of a union between the two countries.

And rightly so. The daughter of the King of Portugal to be Queen of England, or so they thought! How mistaken they were going to be! And the expense of entertaining them and that of sending a return party to Portugal was well worth the satisfaction he got from the affair. It was good too that he should be so sought after; it showed that he was feared, and to be feared was to be respected.

The King of England was free to marry; such news would send a quiver of excitement among ambitious men with marriageable daughters. How envious they would be of the King of Portugal ... for a while.

'My lord,' he cried, 'what pleasure it gives me to receive you here. I believe the King's daughter will be an admirable wife to me. I long for the day when I shall receive her here so let us arrange these matters without delay. I will send an embassy to Portugal that negotiations may go ahead with all speed.'

The embassy prepared to return to Portugal accompanied by those members of John's entourage who would complete the settlements so that in a short time the marriage could take place.

In the meantime John sent for William Marshal that he might speak with him on matters in Aquitaine which were causing him some dismay.

Queen Eleanor had recently returned from Spain where she had travelled to collect her granddaughter Blanche. The journey to Spain had been arduous but she had found great pleasure in being reunited with her namesake, her daughter Eleanor Queen of Castile. They had been delighted to relinquish young Blanche to her care for the child's marriage with the heir of the King of France would indeed be a glorious one.

Blanche was a pretty child and an obedient one; she would make a good wife, thought Eleanor, and she believed Philip would be pleased with her. But how she had felt the rigours of the journey! The rheumatic pains in her limbs had increased and crippled her and she felt angry with the passing years which had taken her youth with them. During that journey she often thought of the one she had experienced with Louis, her first husband, when she had been young and desirable and very desirous. Long ago days! So much had happened since then. She would not want to go back and live it all again; but she wanted to cast off the stiffness of her limbs and she wanted to rid herself of this perpetual tiredness.

It was a difficult journey. She relied so much on Mercadier who was in charge of her escort; she had always liked the man because he had so admired Richard and during the journey they talked continually of her best-loved son; she would sing Richard's songs to him and accompany them on her lute. Mercadier had as many memories of Richard and had stories to tell her of him which she had never heard before.

She said to him: 'Oh, my good friend, you do not know how you have relieved this journey of much of its tedium. When you talk to me of Richard I feel young again. I can see him so clearly as a child in my nursery. He always defended me—no matter who came against me, and I remember an occasion when he ran to the King, his father, his fists clenched and pummelled him because he thought he had treated me unfairly. That was the sort of son he was to me then and always.'

Mercadier would tell her of some exploit in battle and they would be sad together.

And then one day—it was the week which began with Easter, when they were resting in Bordeaux—Mercadier had gone out into the streets but he did not return.

She felt sick, old and tired when they brought the news to her. He was a swaggering man, a typical mercenary to whom soldiering was his livelihood and the meaning of life. He had become involved in a brawl with a knight who served another mercenary captain. They had drunk together, boasted together and quarrelled together; and that was the end of Mercadier. In the heat of the quarrel his opponent drew his sword an instant before Mercadier did. He was bleeding to death on the cobbles of an inn yard.

'My old friends are dying all round me,' cried Eleanor. 'It is so sad to grow old.'

She had no heart for the journey. She would see her granddaughter married and return to Fontevraud and there live out the rest of her days which could not be many and she was not displeased by the thought.

John had met her at Bordeaux where Philip and Louis had joined them and the two young people had been married. It was a touching ceremony. Blanche was so pretty and showed every sign of becoming a beautiful woman and Louis was a boy of noble bearing.

The married pair returned to the Court of France with Philip and there was amity between the Kings of France and England.

'There is nothing,' said Eleanor, 'that cements friendship between countries as much as a royal marriage. I am too old for these jaunts now. I shall go back to the Abbey to rest a while.'

'Do so,' said John, 'and I'll swear that in a short time you will be as vigorous as ever.'

She smiled sceptically and they took their leave of each other.

He was thinking of Eleanor's departure for Fontevraud now and decided that it could be a reason for his taking a journey through Aquitaine, there to confirm the allegiance the vassals of that area owed him and to bring to their notice that he had his eyes on them.

'I suspect the Lusignans are not as loyal as I would wish

them to be,' he told William Marshal.

'They have La Marche now; they should be content,' replied William.

'Content! When are such as they ever content? Moreover, they have some sort of truce with the Count of Angoulême. By God's teeth they could join forces and attack Anjou together.'

'I doubt not that our armies would soon subdue them if they started such tricks.'

'Perhaps. If we caught them in time. But 'tis better to prevent these uprisings and this can be done by letting them know that we are watchful of them. It is time I did a tour of the neighbourhood and received fresh oaths of allegiance from men such as the Counts of La Marche and Angoulême.'

William Marshal agreed that it never came amiss for the suzerain to visit his vassals and now that there was a truce with Philip since the marriage between young Louis and Blanche, this seemed a good time to do it.

'The embassy will be arriving in Portugal very soon,' the Marshal reminded him. 'You might wish to keep yourself in readiness for that and perhaps after your marriage visit these states.'

'I feel,' said John, 'that this is a matter of some necessity and a king must put his duty before his pleasure.'

When John became most sanctimonious the Marshal grew a little uneasy. But he could not think of a reason why John should wish to travel through Aquitaine apart from his duty to keep the barons there in good order.

John went on: 'To tell the truth it is this truce between Angoulême and La Marche which makes me a little uneasy. I hope this friendship of theirs is not of long duration. I'd rather have them sparring together than joining up.'

'It could be a firm friendship,' said William Marshal, 'for Angoulême's daughter is betrothed to Hugh the Brown.'

' 'Tis so, I have heard. She is a child is she not? Something may happen before the marriage takes place.'

'She is not far off marriageable age and is already being brought up with the Lusignans.'

John shook his head and murmured: 'One never knows. Sometimes these marriages don't take place. In any case, I shall go among them and they can take their oaths of allegiance. It will remind them that I have my eyes on them.'

'And when you return I doubt not that we shall be arranging your wedding.'

'I doubt it not either,' replied John, a smile curving his lips.

*   *   *

Isabella saw the messengers arriving at the castle and she wondered what news they brought. She ran down to the courtyard accompanied by two of her attendants. They stood back and watched the grooms take the horses while the messengers were brought into the hall.

Hugh was there.

Isabella ran to him and caught his hand. He pressed hers with affection and eager as he was to hear the news, he had time to smile down at her.

The messenger said: 'My lord of La Marche, the King of England is on his way. He will be here before the day is out. He wishes to assure himself of your allegiance and will want you to swear your oaths afresh.'

'He is coming solely to me?' asked Hugh in amazement.

'Nay, my lord. He is visiting every castle in this neighbourhood. To save him time he wishes you to send a message to the Count of Angoulême. He would have him swear his oath here in your castle that he need not make the journey to him.'

'It shall be done,' said Hugh.

Isabella uncurled her hand from his. She turned and ran out of the hall and went to the bedchamber which adjoined that shared by her attendants.

They came running in to tell her the news she already knew.

'My lady, my lady, King John is coming here.'

She did not want to talk to them, which was strange. She wanted to be alone.

He was coming here. She would see him again—the man whom she had encountered in the forest and whom she had never forgotten. They would see each other again. What would he be like then? Would he look at her as he had in the forest? Why was he coming here? To make Hugh swear his oath. A notion came to her that there might be another reason. Could he be coming to see her?

No, even she could not believe that. Beautiful as she was, he was a king and he must make his vassals swear allegiance now and then. There was a perfectly good reason for his coming. He would remember her, she was sure, but it could well be that he had forgotten the meeting in the forest.

Whatever it was she could scarcely wait to see him.

She ran to the top of the castle to see if she could see a party approaching. How would he come? Royally of course, with pennants flying. He would ride at the head of his men; he would come into the country and Hugh would have to be waiting there. Poor Hugh, he was of little account compared with this man. She had liked to see the manner in which Hugh was lord of his castle and how her father had talked of him as though he were of great importance. She had thrilled at the thought of the power Hugh wielded over so many people. And with her he was soft and yielding and she would have her way with him; what she wanted she would wheedle out of him. She knew and exulted in the knowledge. And now had come this man—this King of England before whom Hugh must bow the knee. He was the all-powerful one—the over-lord.

It was exciting; it was thrilling. Which ribbon should she wear in her hair? He would be there this night. There would be feasting in the great hall. Perhaps she would play the lute for him and sing a song—it would be a song of love and long-ing which Hugh said fondly she sang as though she knew all about it.

In the castle they said: 'The Lady Isabella looks more beautiful than ever. She is so excited at the prospect of seeing her parents again.'

*   *   *

It was as she had thought. He came most royally. The heralds announced his arrival and the sound of their trum-pets sent shivers of excitement through her. She had decided against ribbons for her hair and shook it loose about her shoulders; she wore a blue velvet gown caught in at her tiny waist with a golden girdle.

She was in the hall when he entered. She would have known he was the King by his garments alone. He wore the usual loosely fitting gown buckled at the neck, with sleeves wide at the top caught in at the wrists, but the cloth of this garment was of the finest material she had ever seen. It was silk decorated with gold. He wore a cloak of royal purple which like his blue silk gown was decorated with gold tracing. The belt which caught in his gown at the waist glittered with magnificent jewels and these he wore on his fingers, at his throat and at his wrists. She had never seen a man shine so and she was enchanted by those beautiful gems.

Hugh was bowing to him, but she saw the King's eyes wandering round the hall until they came to rest on her.

She hastily curtsied, lowering her eyes, and when she lifted them she saw that they were upon her and the look in them was the same as that which he had bestowed on her in the forest. The notion came to her then that he had come here not so much to accept Hugh's homage and that of her parents but to see her.

She heard him saying: 'Who is yonder little girl?'

Hugh answered: 'She is Isabella, daughter of the Count of Angoulême, my betrothed, who is being brought up in this castle.'

'Present her to me,' said the King.

She came forward; her eyes alight with excitement, her cheeks faintly flushed.

Hugh's hand was on her shoulder, pressing down, implying that she should kneel.

She did so and then she felt the King's hands on her raising her up.

'Why,' he said, 'it is such a pretty child. You are a most fortunate man, Hugh.'

And his eyes were burning into her saying something which she could not fully understand and yet to which she could respond.

Hugh pushed her gently aside and led the King to the apartment which had been prepared for him. Isabella went to her room, her attendants twittering round her.

'What think you of the King?' they whispered.

'His reputation does not lie.'

'I shivered when he looked at me.'

'I did not see him look at you,' said Isabella sharply.

'He did, my lady, before he found you. Then he had eyes for no one but you.'

She laughed. 'Is he really as wicked as they say, think you?'

'More so,' was the answer.

'Come prepare me for the banquet. It will be such as we
have never had before. It is not often that we entertain a king
here.' She could scarcely wait to see him again.

In the banqueting hall he sat beside Hugh. He was
pleased, he said, that Hugh was now in possession of La
Marche. 'Oh you stole a march on us, my good Hugh,' said
the King waggishly. 'How dare you imprison my mother and
then force her to give up La Marche?'

'It seemed the only way of getting a decision, my lord.
And I promise you it is better for your territories to live in
peace than to wage perpetual war one on another.'

'And you will see that there is peace here, my lord Count.
You have done well to make a truce with Angoulême. And
where are the Count and Countess? Did they not hear that I
wished them to present themselves?'

'They will arrive tomorrow, my lord. 'Tis the soonest they
could get here. They sent word that they would leave at once
on receiving your orders.'

'Then that is well. I may rest here and enjoy your hospitality for a few days instead of making the tedious journey to
Angoulême. Ah, I see there your little bride-to-be. She is
charming. I will have her sit on my other side and that will
show everyone in what high esteem I hold you.'

He beckoned to her and she came to stand before him,
bowing in a most delightful way. He had been right. He had
never seen a girl like that before. Twelve years old. What
would she be like when she was eighteen? He knew instinctively that there was one who could give pleasure such as
he had never known before.

'Come, my little one,' he said, 'sit beside me.'

He took her hand, his hot fingers pressing it firmly. He
drew her towards him and held her there for a moment. 'You
must not be overawed by one who wishes you as much good as
I do. Come, be seated.'

His hands touched her as she sat.

The venison was carved. As the highest ranking nobleman
present Hugh stood behind the King's chair and served him.
This ceremony was one which appealed to the King for there
were moments during it when Hugh must actually kneel
before him. It was good for the little one to see the man they
had chosen for her husband kneel to one who was so much
greater. John knew that power was one of the most potent

ingredients of sexual attraction with some females. Many an otherwise virtuous woman had surrendered to him because he was the King's son, King's brother and later the King. Rank could be a powerful aphrodisiac. He picked out dainties from his platter and fed them to the lovely child beside him. Now and then he would look at Hugh. 'You see, my lord, how I am determined to honour you.'

The meal over, the minstrels played. Isabella had been brought up to love music and taught to sing and play, and when John was asked if he would care to hear her sing for him he replied that this would give him great delight.

So she sang for him a song of love and longing. By God's ears, he thought, I would never want to leave my bed were she put in it.

Twelve years. What a delectable age! And never known a man yet. He would be the first. He must be. He would be ready to give a great deal for that one.

He wished that she were the daughter of some poor knight whom he was visiting so that he might say: 'Your daughter pleases me. She shall share my bed this night.

This was different. What if he abducted her? He would have the whole of Aquitaine rising against him. Angoulême would unite with the Lusignans and all hell would be let loose. Have her he must, and he would, but he would have to be more subtle.

The song had finished.

'I trust it pleased you, my lord,' she said.

'I have rarely been so pleased,' he answered her.

'Tis true, he thought. And she is excited. What passion is in that exquisite little body, just begging to be awakened. My task, good Hugh, not yours. This child shall be my bedmate ... and soon, for I shall go mad if there is too much waiting. I want her now while she is twelve years old, untouched and yet eager to be. What a combination of pleasure awaits me.

Her parents would be here the following day. He would have a proposition to make with them.

Others sang. They bored him. He watched Isabella. Every now and then their eyes met; he would smile at her and there would be her answering response.

How irksome the waiting was.

He retired for the night and she went to her bedchamber. She scarcely slept. She was thinking of him all the night.

The next day she walked in the gardens of the castle with her attendants. She looked up and saw him at a window watching her. She shivered afresh even though it was warm and sunny.

When she went up the stone staircase to her apartment he was waiting there, close to the door. No one else was in sight.

'Isabella,' he whispered.

'My lord!'

He held out his hand and she put hers into it. Then she was seized and held against him. As his hands caressed her body she began to tremble.

'You excite me,' he said, 'as I never was excited before. Do I excite you?'

'Yes, my lord,' she answered.

He kissed her then again and again. She was gasping but making no attempt to protest or escape.

'You are warm-hearted,' he said. 'I sense it. You long to experience the sweets of life.'

'Oh yes, my lord,' she murmured.

'As yet no man has known you.' Then he laughed and whispered: ' 'Twill not be for long. There's joy in store for you.'

'My lord, I hear someone on the stair.'

'Do you then?' he answered. 'So part we must ... and you are for me, forget it not.'

'I am betrothed to Hugh,' she answered.

'Remember this. It is the custom of kings to have their way, sweetheart. And this King is more determined to have his than most.'

He released her then and she ran to her room. She looked at the patches on her skin where he had kissed her.

She knew that something very exciting was about to happen.

*   *   *

Her parents arrived the next day. How delighted they were to see her!

Her mother wished to know if she were happy in the Lusignan household.

'Very happy, Mother,' she said. 'Everyone is kind to me.'

'And you are behaving as we would wish, daughter?'

'I think so, Mother.'

Her father embraced her.

'The Lusignans are delighted with you,' he told her. 'Hugh told me so. You are a good child.'

'Yes, Father. The King of England is here.'

'It is for that reason that we owe this visit.'

'Yes, Hugh told me.'

'Have you been allowed to see the King?'

'Yes. I sat beside him at supper. Then I sang to him. He was most gracious.'

'That is well. I hope you were not too forward.'

'The King did not seem to think so.'

Her parents looked at her apartment and spoke to the young girls who attended her. The Countess wanted to assure herself that they were suitable to wait on her daughter.

Then they went down to the hall where several other heads of noble families were assembled that they might do homage to the King their suzerain.

When the ceremony was completed John said he would like to walk in the gardens and he invited the Count and Countess of Angoulême to walk with him.

He said that he was delighted by the friendship between their house and that of the Lusignans. 'It is always good,' he commented, 'to see these family feuds ended.'

'It was an excellent idea to unite the families through the betrothal of Hugh the Brown and our daughter,' agreed the Count.

'Ah, your daughter. She is enchanting.'

The Countess smiled. 'She has been admired for her beauty ever since she was more or less a baby.'

'She's a little enchantress. I tell you this; she has cast a spell over me.'

The parents smiled fondly but John's next words quickly dispersed their smiles.

'So much so,' said John, 'that I want her for myself and I shall not rest until she is mine.'

The Count and Countess appeared to have been struck dumb for they could not find the words to express their shock and amazement.

John said: 'You are overcome by the honour I would do you. Your daughter is the most enchanting child I ever saw. She is ready for marriage. I never saw one so ripe and ready for the plucking. My dear Count and Countess, you will bless the day I sent for you to come to the Lusignan stronghold. For there I saw your daughter and the moment I clapped eyes on her—which was at a previous meeting in the forest—I was in love with her. I want her and I will have her and you will give her to me with the utmost joy.'

It was the Count who spoke first. It seemed to him that the King had gone mad. He had heard stories of his terrible rages, how he struck people or anything that was in his way, animate or inanimate, how he threw himself about and would do himself a damage if there was no one else on whom he could inflict his fury. This must be a prelude to madness.

But he now appeared to be calm enough. 'Yes,' he said, 'I want Isabella. So much do I want her that I am prepared to face anything and anyone to get her. She is to be the Queen of England. What think you of that, my lord Count?'

''Tis a great honour, my lord, but she is betrothed to Hugh the Brown.'

'Hugh the Brown! The petty Count of Lusignan! I am offering your daughter a crown. Duchess of Normandy, Countess of Anjou, Queen of England. You are no fool, Count.'

'It is honour beyond our dreams,' said the Countess.

'My lady, you know a good prospect when you see it. I am so enamoured of your daughter that I will risk anything to get her, for no sooner did I see her than I knew I must have her.'

'She is but a child, my lord, as yet.'

'She is no ordinary child. There is a woman in that adorable immature body. My woman.'

'Isabella has always been much admired. We know that she is possessed of exceptional beauty. You honour us greatly, but her betrothal...'

'Bah! It shall be as nothing. You will take her away with you this day ... back to Angoulême. I will come with you and there I will marry her without delay.'

'The Lusignans would never permit her to go.'

'Do you have to ask their permission as to what you do for your own daughter?'

'In the circumstances we should have to. My lord, your admiration for her has been noted and we are in the heart of Lusignan country. It seems certain that they would never permit us to take her today.'

John was silent for a while.

Then he said: 'I have it. We will go from here this day leaving Isabella here. Then in a week you will ask the Lusignans if they will permit your daughter to visit you for a few days. You have been with her and you miss her very much. They cannot object to parents wishing to have a visit from their daughter.'

'And then, my lord?'

'I shall come to Angoulême and there I will marry Isabella. As you know I am free to do so. Then instead of being the Countess of La Marche, your daughter will be the Queen of England. Come, good Count and Countess, you will find it far more profitable to ally yourself with the House of Anjou and royal Plantagenet than with the Lusignans. Your daughter would never forgive you if you attempt to spoil her chances.'

'It is my daughter of whom I think,' said the Countess. 'She is a child. She has grown accustomed to Hugh de Lusignan, and she is reconciled to the fact that she is to marry him.'

'You'll find your daughter is happy with the change.' He laughed aloud. 'I can promise you that.'

Then they went into the castle together and the Count and Countess of Angoulême told their host that they must leave. There were matters claiming their attention in Angoulême.

They said farewell to their daughter and left.

*   *   *

The next day the King left the castle and rode off in the opposite direction.

He had taken a brief farewell of Isabella. She had stood before him in the hall and suddenly he had lifted her from her feet and kissed her mouth. He had whispered: 'Soon we shall meet again.'

Then he put her down and in an aside to those standing by he said that he found children enchanting. As though, she thought momentarily angry, she were but a child to be petted. But she remembered his words and the brief embrace they had had on the previous day and she knew that he was acting for those watchers.

He rode away and she was with the crowd who stood at the castle gates watching; then she had gone up to a turret to see the last of the cavalcade.

The castle seemed very dull when the guests had departed. Had he really meant it when he had said they would soon meet again?

Everyone in the castle seemed to be talking about him. She went down to the kitchens to listen to the talk there. Servants knew so much.

She heard how he had been called John Lackland by his father when he was born because there were so many elder brothers to share out the King's possessions. He had been to Ireland where he had shocked the natives with his wild behaviour. He had several illegitimate children. His weakness was women and he could never have enough of them. Had they noticed his clothes? All those jewels! His father had never cared for fine clothes; he had the hands of a lackey for he refused to wear gloves; and he ate standing up so that none would have known he was a king. John was different. He was always dressed in fine clothes and jewels. He always wanted everyone to have no doubt from the moment they saw him that he was the King.

The visit was the most exciting the household had ever known. King Richard had been very friendly with the family because of the crusades; now it was good to think that King John was on such excellent terms with them.

But listening to talk of him was poor consolation for his presence.

And what would happen now? He would go away and forget her. Would he? The way he had looked at her and held her surely had meant something? But then he liked all women.

The days passed. Nothing very amusing happened.

Shortly after the King's departure Hugh had to go away to settle some revolt on the borders of his territory. He said farewell to Isabella and kissed her tenderly.

'Soon,' he told her, 'we shall marry. I begin to think that in spite of your tender years we might go through the ceremony. As for the consummation...'

He did not finish and she did not seek to remind him as she had on other occasions that she was not so young as they all presumed her to be.

'My brother Ralph will take over my position in the castle. He says his first duty will be to protect you.'

She watched Hugh ride away rather sadly for in spite of the

impression John had made on her she was still deeply attracted by Hugh. In fact it had occurred to her to wish that Hugh were the King. What a fine King he would have made!

A few days after Hugh's departure came a message from the Count and Countess of Angoulême. They missed their daughter and they wondered if Hugh would allow her to pay them a short visit.

Hugh being away Ralph could see no reason why he should not grant Isabella's parents what they asked.

Within a few days, surrounded by a considerable entourage, Isabella was riding to Angoulême.

*   *   *

Isabella welcomed the change. It would be pleasant to be home for a short while. She was feeling a little depressed, for her attendants had talked constantly of John since his visit and she had heard a great deal about his many mistresses.

Could it have been that he had behaved with her as he did to all attractive females? Was it really true that she being so young and inexperienced of the world had believed there was something special in his treatment of her?

She was soon to discover the truth. As they came close to Angoulême she saw a party of riders in the distance and recognized the King at the head of them. Excitement possessed her as he galloped up to her.

He brought his horse close to hers and looked at her.

'I feared I had imagined so much beauty,' he said. 'But nay, you are even lovelier than in my dreams.'

'My lord, I am glad to give you pleasure...'

'There has never been such pleasure as we two shall know together,' he told her. 'God's eyes, I would we were alone now. I would the priest had mumbled his words over us. But soon it shall be so. You and I will ride on to your father's castle and as we ride I will tell you of the future I am planning for you.'

He had turned his horse and kept it close to hers. He waved his hand for the rest of the two parties to fall behind. Then he and Isabella rode on close together some way ahead of the rest.

'I cannot take my eyes from you,' he said. 'Ever since the day in the forest you have shared my bed ... but only in my thoughts. I am going to make that a reality. I shall wake in the morning and find you there. My little Queen.'

'What does my father say?' she asked.

'What can he say? What can he do but thank God for his good fortune and go down on his knees and bless the day King John saw the loveliest maiden in the world before she was thrown away on a count not worthy of her?'

'Hugh is a very fine man,' she said and was surprised that she felt a certain resentment to hear him maligned.

'Forget him, sweetheart. You are no countess. You are to be a queen. I am going to marry you. Yes, sweetheart. It's to be marriage for us. Your parents are beside themselves with joy for this great good fortune which has come to them through you. I had a wife who was no wife to me. I hated her as much as I shall love you. It makes me laugh to speak of her with you beside me. She was as different from you as one woman could be from another. She gave me no children. I gave her little chance to. It will be different with us. But I'd not have you bear children too soon. You are too young for it. I'd not have that perfect little body spoilt. Nay, we'll keep it as it is, shall we ... for a year or two? And then we'll start our sons. Why do you not speak, Isabella?'

'I had no idea that this would happen.'

'Did you not know when I held you against me ... and talked to you? Could you not guess how urgently I needed you?'

'I did not know...'

'My innocent sweetheart, you are but a child. Never mind. I'll teach you to be a woman. There'll be a warm welcome for you at Angoulême and then the priest shall wed us and I'll carry you to my bed.'

At the castle her parents were waiting for her. They looked very solemn but she saw at once that they were reconciled to the change of bridegroom.

When she was in her chamber they came to her and dismissed all her attendants.

'You realize, Isabella,' said her father, 'what a great honour this is for you, for the family and for Angoulême?'

'I am to be a queen,' she said.

'Queen ... duchess ... countess ... yours will be one of the highest positions in the world.'

'You are pleased with me, Father?'

'There is not a father in the land who would not be pleased to see his daughter made a queen.

'There is one who will not be pleased to see me a queen,' she reminded them. 'What of Hugh?'

'He must perforce accept what is inevitable.'

'We have been betrothed, Father.'

'Thank God the marriage was delayed.'

'You thought I was too young for Hugh. Am I not too young for the King?'

'The King thinks not. He likes your youth.'

Her mother looked anxious. 'There are matters which you must try to understand.'

'Your mother must talk to you,' said the Count.

She laughed at them. 'I know of what you would speak. I have looked about me and I know well what happens between men and women. I know what the King wants of me.'

'You are old for your years, my child,' said the Countess, 'and perhaps that is well.'

Isabella could not stop thinking of Hugh—so tall and kind. She had tried to lure him into forgetting her youth but he would not be lured. There was something honourable and noble about Hugh; it made her a little sad to think of how angry he would be when he had heard that her parents had taken her away from him to give her to King John.

'You are to prepare to leave for Bordeaux at once,' said her mother. 'You are to be married there by the Archbishop. The King will have no delay, he is so eager for the ceremony.'

'Should not Hugh be told?'

'My dear child, certainly not! The great point is to get the marriage over before anyone can try to stop it. The King will be very angry if we do not all meet his wishes. Therefore you must prepare without delay.'

It was exciting to have a wedding. She thought of herself wearing a crown. It would be most becoming. Within a few days they were riding to Bordeaux and there the Archbishop married them.

There was feasting in the castle that night but at an early hour John left the feast with his bride.

'I am hungry for only one feast,' he told the company.

She was very young—a child really, but the sensuality was

there as he had known it would be. He was rarely mistaken in women.

Young as she was she could give passion for passion. He blessed the fate which had sent him into the forest that day. His hopes of her had been high and they had not been one whit disappointed.

During the days of the honeymoon which were spent mainly in the bedchamber, for he would not rise until dinner time, he became even more infatuated with his child bride.

The Crowned Queen of England

WHEN the King of Portugal heard that even while the embassy from England had been on its way to arrange the marriage of his daughter, John had married Isabella of Angoulême, he was furious. This was an insult. There had been no warning. They were preparing to receive the embassy with all honour when the news had come. At first it had seemed incredible; but when it became obvious that it was indeed true the King decided that there was nothing to be done but send the embassy back with all speed. He would not lose his dignity by complaining of this insult to himself and his daughter but he would not forget.

Hugh de Lusignan was stunned when he returned and found that Isabella had been taken away. Ralph explained to him that he had received a request from her parents which did not seem an unreasonable one. Surely it was natural for parents to wish to see their child from time to time.

Hugh had to admit that had he been at the castle he would have acceded to the request.

'Did you not know that that lecher was there waiting for her?' he demanded.

'How could I know this?' cried Ralph. 'Had he not been here and sent for the Count of Angoulême to come here to save himself the journey to Angoulême?'

'We have been deceived by both the King and the Count of Angoulême,' cried Hugh in anguish. 'Was not Isabella solemnly betrothed to me?'

'There can be no gainsaying that.'

'Then this cannot be.'

'Alas, brother, it is.'

'And he has married her already! But she is only a child.'

'Methinks that she was older than her years.'

'Oh God in Heaven! To think of her with that lecher!'

'Brother, you must put her from your mind.'

'What can you know of this? She is so exquisite. I had treated her with tenderness and care ... I had put off the marriage solely because of her youth. I did not want her to be frightened. I loved her dearly, Ralph. I had planned our future together ... and now to come back like this and find her gone ... and gone to him. You know his reputation. How think you he will be with her?'

'You must put her from your mind, I tell you,' repeated Ralph. 'She is lost to you. She will be going to England soon to be crowned Queen.'

'She was *snatched* from me!' cried Hugh.

'You must face the fact, brother, that she may have gone with the utmost willingness.'

'How could that have been?'

'There is a certain glitter about a crown. I'll tell you this, Hugh, there was a wantonness about her. You were bemused by her. God knows she is an exquisite creature. I never saw a girl or woman to compare with her. It may well be that you will have reason to rejoice that it has turned out as it has.'

'You talk of what you do not understand,' said Hugh shortly. 'Isabella was betrothed to me. I love Isabella. I shall never love another woman as long as I live, and that's the plain truth.'

Ralph shook his head. 'Would to God it had been any but myself who let her go.'

'Nay, Ralph, anyone would have thought it well to let her go to her family. We have been thoroughly deceived. But I shall not let it pass. I shall tell you this, Ralph, I am going to be revenged on John.'

'What can you do?'

'I shall kill him,' declared Hugh.

'Nay, do not act hastily. Do not speak without caution. Who knows what may be carried to him.'

'I hope my words *will* be carried to him. I loathe him. I despise him for a cheat, a liar and a lecher. He should never have been given the crown. That should have been Arthur's. And by God I swear I shall never forget this foul deed. He shall die for it and I shall send someone without delay to him to take him my challenge for mortal combat.'

'You think he will agree to meet you?'

'He must ... in all honour he must.'

Ralph shook his head. 'You cannot talk of honour to one who has none and knows not the meaning of the word.'

'I have made up my mind,' said Hugh. 'I shall challenge him to mortal combat.'

*   *   *

His servants did not dare disturb John in his bedchamber, and it was dinner time each day before he emerged from it and then with great reluctance.

He was living in a world of sensuality where nothing was of the least importance to him but Isabella.

He had found that he was not mistaken in her. She was sexually insatiable even as he was and on this ground they were completely in tune. He had recognized this quality in her; it was at the very essence of her tremendous attraction. She was indeed the most beautiful creature he had ever seen; her immature child's body was just beginning to blossom into womanhood and could be compared with the most perfect piece of sculpture except that it was living. He delighted in her. To guide her, to teach her in erotic arts was the greatest joy; and she scarcely needed tuition. Such was her sensuality that she reacted instinctively. For some time she had been trying to force open the floodgates of her voluptuous desires. She had tried with Hugh whose honourable instincts had restrained him; John had no such scruples and for a while she was glad of this.

So they returned early and rose late. The marriage bed was more important than anything during those first weeks.

John said during those days of his honeymoon: 'I now possess everything that I could desire. The crowns of England and Normandy ... and my most cherished possession of all: Isabella.'

One day when he emerged from the bedroom to take dinner which was awaiting his arrival at the table and which was served after midday, he was told that messengers had arrived from Hugh de Lusignan.

'Hugh de Lusignan?' he cried. 'What does that fellow want with me?' He grimaced. 'Can it be that it has something to do with the Queen? I'll send for him when I am ready to see him.'

He went back to Isabella who had risen languorously from the bed and was wrapped in a gown of blue lined with fur, her beautiful hair in disorder about her shoulders.

'There's a fellow to see me,' he said. 'He comes from Hugh de Lusignan. What insolence to send him.'

'What does he want?' asked Isabella.

'That we have to find out.' He lifted her face to his and looked into her eyes. Then he slipped the robe from her shoulders and marvelled at her beauty. She studied him through veiled eyes and she was thinking of Hugh who was so tall and handsome, and she was angry with him because he had resisted all the indications she had given him. She wondered briefly what would have happened if he had not.

She was a queen though and it delighted her to be a queen.

John pulled the robe up over her shoulders. He took her hand and pulled her to her feet.

'I'll not look at you now, my love, or it will be no dinner for us. I see that. You are more attractive than a thousand dinners.'

He went to the door and called: 'Bring the Lusignan's messenger to me now.'

Then he turned to her and drawing her to the bed sat with her upon it. He held her hand pressed against his thigh as the messenger entered.

'So you come to disturb me when I am engaged with the Queen,' he said. 'What is your message?'

'I come from Hugh de Lusignan, who challenges you, my lord, to mortal combat.'

Isabella said involuntarily: 'Oh no.'

John pressed her hand. 'Your master is insolent, my man, and you brave to bring such a message to me. I like not such messages and I like not the people who bring them. Has it struck you that I might decide to make you so that you could carry no further messages?'

Isabella saw the sweat which appeared on the man's brow. She remembered him as one of Hugh's esquires in the castle.

She said: ''Tis no fault of his that he brings such a message.'

John smiled. Everything about her delighted him; even her interference. She didn't want the man punished. Therefore he should not be.

'Nay,' said John, 'the Queen is right. The insolence comes from your master. You but obey your orders. Go and tell him that if he is so eager for death I will appoint a champion to fight with him.'

The man, delighted to get away, bowed his head and John waved a hand to dismiss him.

When he had gone John turned to Isabella. 'Insolent fellow!' he said. 'He would invite me to mortal combat. Does he think that I would demean myself by fighting with him? Nay, he shall have his fight. There'll be plenty who will be glad to do me the honour.' He pulled the robe from her shoulder and buried his face against her flesh. 'Think you he will report to his master that he saw us thus? 'Tis what I trust he will do.' John began to laugh loudly. 'Master Hugh will mayhap be more eager than ever for mortal combat when he realizes all that he has missed in life.'

There was no responsive laughter from Isabella. She was thinking of Hugh—whose good looks had been such a delight to her—lying cold and still with blood on his clothes. But that would not happen. She felt that in combat it would not be Hugh who was the vanquished.

But she had lost temporarily her appetite both for dinner and sexual excitement.

*   *   *

When Hugh received the message he was filled with fury.

'The coward!' he cried. 'Of course he is afraid of combat. He knows full well what the result of that will be. Does he think I'll be satisfied with some mercenary captain whom he will pay to take his place? Did you see the King?' he asked the messenger.

'Yes, my lord.'

'And the Queen?'

'Yes, sir.'

'Together?'

The messenger nodded.

'How looked the Queen?'

The messenger looked puzzled.

'Contented with her lot?' suggested Hugh.

'Yes, my lord.'

Such a child, he thought, and he wondered what would become of her.

He went to his brother and told him that the King had refused to meet him in person.

'Did you expect him to?' asked Ralph.

'No. I always knew he was a coward.'

'Such men always are. The best thing, brother, is to forget this insult. Find yourself a bride—a good and beautiful woman who will give you sons. There are many who would be happy to mate with the Lusignans.'

Hugh shook his head. 'No, brother,' he said. 'At least not yet. There is one thing I am pledged to do and that is to take my revenge on John of England.'

'How so?'

'You ask that? You, a Lusignan, who understand the state of this country. The King of France has entered into a truce with him but it is an uneasy one. The Duke of Brittany—and he has many to support him—believes himself to be the true heir to all that John has seized. Rarely was a crown so precariously poised on any head. I am going to do all in my power to dislodge it. I swear this to you, Ralph, that ere long Normandy will not belong to its present Duke but to the King of France whose vassal I shall be. Richard was a friend to our family. John is an enemy. I shall not rest until I have taken my revenge on this voluptuary who has robbed me of my bride.'

'Bold words, brother.'

'And meant, Ralph, meant from the bottom of my heart. You will see.'

*   *   *

Even John had to realize that it was time he was on the move. Moreover, Isabella was ecstatic at the prospect of being crowned Queen of England. She was thrilled at the thought of crossing the sea because she had never yet seen the sea. Her excitement about her new life added zest to John's days. He began to see things afresh through the eyes of a young girl and he found the experience exhilarating.

Thus they set out on their journey.

They called first at the Abbey of Fontevraud where the Queen Mother received them.

She was enchanted by Isabella. She saw in her son's young bride something of what she had been so many years ago. A freshness, a youthful outlook on life and that overpowering sensuality which was at the very root of the secret of her power to move John so deeply.

The young girl made Eleanor feel her age more acutely. The journey to Castile had been too much for her and she had been glad to get back to Fontevraud where she could daily visit the graves of her husband, her son Richard and her daughter Joanna.

'My life is over,' she told Isabella. 'Sometimes one can live too long. Perhaps the fates would have been kinder to me if they had taken me when Richard died.'

There were some pleasures left to her, though. Thinking over the past was one; and sometimes she could throw herself back so clearly that everything became as vivid as though it were happening at that moment.

'Live fully, child,' she said, 'that is the secret of it. I used my time ... every minute of it; and now I can look back and remember. There were years when I was imprisoned and even then I made the most of every hour.'

She thought a great deal about John and was uneasy doing so. She knew him well and she felt that it had been the greatest tragedy that Richard had died when he did. How ironical it was that, just as he had come home from the Holy Land and had been released from his incarceration at Dürenstein, that wicked man had shot an arrow at him that had killed him, so that there was only John.

She knew what John had done. He had taken Isabella from Hugh de Lusignan by a trick, for they would never have let Isabella go if they had known she was going to the King. Did John think that that would be forgotten? There would be retribution, she knew. Was John, uxorious, living in a state of euphoria, thinking only of bed and Isabella, unable to realize what a storm his actions might well have aroused, or was he simply ignoring this? The Lusignans would be against him. He might have gained the Count of Angoulême as an ally but that was not much of a gain to be set beside the enmity of the Lusignans. What of the King of Portugal nursing his wounded dignity? And there were Arthur and his mother with her new husband Guy de Thouars just waiting for a chance to rise. And more important than all, Philip of

France. What was *he* thinking at this moment? Laughing no doubt to think how recklessly John was gambling with a kingdom.

But I am too old to concern myself, thought Eleanor. My day is done. And what could I do in any case? I could warn John. As if he would listen! He hears nothing but the laughter of that child of his; he sees nothing but her inviting person and he cannot see the jeopardy in which he has placed himself while he is bemused by dreams of new ways of making love.

She could warn the girl perhaps. Voluptuous she certainly was, and knowledgeable with a knowledge such as her kind were born with. Eleanor knew, for she had been like that herself. But what did Isabella know of the world outside the boudoir?

'The King is deeply enamoured of you now, but it may well be that he will not always be so,' Eleanor warned her.

Isabella looked startled. She could not believe that anyone would fail to be in love with her.

'Men like change, my dear,' said the Queen.

'You mean John will no longer love me?'

'I did not say that. He will always see in you the beauty that you have; it is a beauty which is always there. Age cannot destroy it. You have that sort of beauty, Isabella. I will dispense with false modesty and tell you that I have it. When I married John's father he was enamoured of me. It was an unsuitable match in many ways. The reverse of you and John, I was his senior by some twelve years. That did not stop us. We were lovers ... even as you are now. But scarcely had the first year of our marriage passed when another woman was carrying his child.'

Isabella drew back in horror.

''Twas so. I did not discover it until he brought her child into my nurseries. I never forgave him, and that set up a canker in our hearts ... both of us. Our love turned to hate. Now had I been wiser I might have said to myself: It is the way of men. He must go forth to his battles and we were parted, and so he took his women. Had I realized that his dallying with the light women he met on his journeys did not alter what he felt for me, we would not have been such bitter enemies. Perhaps then our children would not have learned to hate him and fight against him. I think a great deal about this now I am old. I go down to his grave and talk to him as though he were there. I go over our life together and say to myself: Ah had I done this ... or that ... we might have gone in different directions. We might have been friends instead of enemies, for there was always something between us. Often we called it hate but with people such as we are, love is near to hate. Ah, I see I tire you. You are asking yourself what this old woman is talking about. Why, you say, does she tell me this? Have I not a husband who adores me, who thinks me the most perfect being in the world? Has he not said he possesses all he could desire? Yes, so it was with Henry and with me in the beginning. My child, what shall you do if John betrays you with other women?'

She thought a while then her beautiful eyes narrowed. Then she said very deliberately: 'I shall betray him with other men.'

Eleanor said gently: 'I trust it may never come to pass.'

*　　*　　*

How excited Isabella was to see the sea! She wanted to run into it and catch it with her hands.

She stood gazing at it in wonder. John watched her indulgently.

'Such a lot I have to show you, my love,' he said.

They went on board their ship and he found it hard to draw her away from the deck so enthralled was she. She was excited beyond words when she beheld the white cliffs of her new kingdom.

'You shall be crowned ere long,' John told her. 'The most beautiful Queen England has ever known.'

He was excited to be in England which always seemed more home to him than any other land. England had accepted him when some of those who lived in his overseas dominions had been prepared to take Arthur. It was because England would never have accepted Arthur that men such as William Marshal had come down in his favour. So he owed a lot to England; and now he was going to honour that land by giving it the most beautiful woman in the world to be its Queen.

He called together a council at Westminster and there, glowing with pride, he presented Isabella to them. They could not but be moved by such charm and beauty and the unfortunate affair of the Portuguese embassy seemed to have been forgotten, as was the manner of his snatching Isabella from the man to whom she was betrothed. After all, the troubles of Hugh de Lusignan were scarcely something for the English to worry about.

There would be a coronation for the Queen and the people loved a coronation. They had wondered why the King's previous wife had not been crowned with him. There had been rumours then that he was thinking of casting her off. They might have been sorry for her, but here was a new bride and there would be rejoicing in the streets, dancing, bonfires and perhaps free wine. Therefore, it was a matter for rejoicing; and when the people saw the exquisite child who was to be their new Queen they were enchanted by her. The cheers for Isabella resounded through the city.

Hubert Walter, Archbishop of Canterbury, came to Westminster to perform the ceremony. The King had given orders that the Abbey was to be strewn with fresh herbs and rushes on the great day and a certain Clarence Fitz William received thirty-three shillings for doing this. There was one chorister whose voice was considered the most beautiful heard for many a year. He was known as Ambrose and the King ordered that he should be given twenty-five shillings to sing *Christus vicit*.

John wanted his people to know that this coronation was as important to him as his own had been. He wanted the whole country to welcome Isabella, to see her in all her youth and beauty and to applaud their King for possessing himself of such a prize.

They were willing and so Isabella, amid great rejoicing, was crowned Queen of England.

No one could doubt John's joy in his Queen and his determination to honour her.

*   *   *

They were happy—John and Isabella. She continued to delight him; he was sure he would never tire of her, nor look at another woman only to compare her with Isabella to her great disadvantage. Isabella was supreme; with her child's body and the deep sensual appetites of an experienced woman, and he thought little of anything but the times when they could be alone together. As for Isabella everything that happened was so new to her; and apart from her sensuality she was an inexperienced child of twelve. Novelty delighted her and she had plenty of that; to be the centre of an admiring circle was not new to her but it never failed to delight her; and to find that English strangers were as surely delighted with her as the people of Angoulême was a delicious discovery. Sometimes she thought of poor Hugh the Brown and she wondered if he were very sad. She hoped so for she could not bear him to forget her. Sometimes she thought of what it would have been like if she had married him. How different he would have been from John. Hugh was very handsome and he had never understood what she was really like as John had from the moment they met. Something within her still hankered after Hugh, but life was too exciting for brooding. She loved her golden crown and the homage of the people. The coronation had delighted her. She could have endured a great deal to win the title of Isabella the Queen, so she enjoyed travelling through the country with John which they did immediately after her coronation.

She loved fine garments—so did John; she could not hope to wear such splendid jewel-encrusted clothes as those which belonged to him but he gave her rich presents. For travelling in the winter he ordered for her a *pelisson* with five bars of fur across it to keep out the wind. After her coronation five ells of green cloth and another five ells of brown were sent to her so that she might command her seamstress to make it into a gown for her. The King gave her jewels too and how she enjoyed appearing with him at the head of a table while all others looked on with amazement at her sparkling gems and beauty.

She could regret nothing while life promised such excitement.

Their journey through the country was leisurely, for they stayed in the castles of the nobility and there John would receive the homage of his barons which would be extended to Isabella.

By Christmas they reached Guildford and the feast of Christmas was celebrated with much feasting and merriment. Games were played in which the Queen took the central part and for once John was prepared to stand aside and let the limelight fall on someone else. They danced, they sang, they feasted and they drank; and the King would not leave his bed until dinner time.

Up to the north of England they travelled through Yorkshire to Newcastle and Cumberland right up to the borders of Scotland. By March they had reached the Pennines and greatly daring they battled their way through this range of wolf-infested mountains. Life was full of adventure for the young Queen who until she had met John had never been very far from Angoulême—the only journey she had made being that to the castle of those whom she had then believed would be her new family.

It was Easter time when they reached Canterbury. Here they were greeted by Hubert Walter the Archbishop, and during Mass in the Cathedral he placed the crowns on their heads in accordance with an old custom so that it was like being crowned again.

After this ceremony they went to the Archbishop's palace where a banquet had been prepared for them. John was delighted.

'It is rare,' he told Isabella, 'that a King of England is on such fair terms with his Archbishop.'

They would return to Westminster he told her and there they would hold Court and she would learn more of what it meant to be Queen of England.

She was delighted with the country—although the winter had been more rigorous than that to which she was accustomed but she was young, her blood was warm and she had her *pelisson* with the five bars of fur to protect her from the fierce winds.

Alas, their pleasurable meanderings through England were coming to an end.

The Easter festivities were no sooner over when a messenger arrived from Eleanor. It seemed that it was impossible for her to retire from life, for she could not resist watching closely what was happening in her son's dominions. She had been more aware than he was of the trouble he was stirring up when he more or less abducted the betrothed of Hugh de Lusignan.

Now she had disquietening news for him. If he were wise he would prepare to leave England immediately. In short, what had happened was that after John's marriage the Lusignans had naturally been infuriated with the Count of Angoulême whom they considered had deceived them cruelly by being a party to his daughter's marriage with the King after they had pledged her to marry Hugh, and that feud, healed by the betrothal, burst out again. John must remember that Hugh's brother Ralph was Seneschal of the castle of Eu in Normandy so that the trouble could spread into the Duchy.

The Lusignans, filled with hatred towards John, had declared they had thrown off their allegiance to him and had approached the King of France asking him to accept them as his vassals. Philip, like a wily spider, sitting in his web watching for unwary prey, was congratulating himself on the turn events had taken.

'There is only one thing to be done,' wrote Eleanor. 'Gather together an army and come at once.'

John was a little petulant at the prospect of having his pleasure spoilt, but his mother was insistent and in his heart he had known something of this nature would happen soon.

While he was digesting his mother's news another messenger arrived.

This one came from the Count of Angoulême who had the same story to tell.

The Lusignans were on the march, vowing vengeance. Moreover, Arthur's stepfather Guy of Thouars, was proving himself a clever strategist. In Arthur's name he was amassing an army. There was trouble then not only from the powerful Lusignans and the King of France but from Arthur.

Arthur must not be victorious.

John made up his mind. He must prepare to leave England. He would need a big army so he sent envoys throughout the country commanding his barons to come with all speed to Portsmouth with their followers, for he planned to cross to the Continent without delay.

*　　*　　*

There followed the first clap of thunder from a storm which was to grow big.

Many of the barons had been consulting together and were recalling the good old days before the reign of Henry II when they had indeed been rulers of their estates. None of them could remember that time but the stories had been handed down through their grandparents and parents. In the days of Stephen a baron was a baron. He was the king of his own lands and held jurisdiction over those who passed through them. They forgot that during that time it was not safe for travellers to go on to the road and that many of those who did were captured by cruel and avaricious barons and either held to ransom or robbed and tortured for the sport of other baron guests. This was a situation which to all decent men was intolerable and the rule of Henry II had wiped it out, much to the relief of almost every inhabitant of the country apart from those unscrupulous men who had profited from this barbarism.

Henry II's stern but just laws had made the country safe again and that King was such that none would have dared to go against him; but when Richard had come to the throne and had enforced taxation in order to pay for his crusade the people had grown restive. But the knowledge that he was engaged in the Holy War made them little inclined to revolt against such taxes because they superstitiously feared they would offend Heaven by doing so and would consequently suffer more harm than if they gave up their money. So they paid up; and when Richard was taken prisoner and came back a hero they were proud of him. All who saw him declared that even towards the end of his life he had the appearance of a god.

And then he had died and there was John. In the first place John lacked those impressive good looks, that kingly bearing and world-wide reputation. John's image was tarnished before he came to the throne. They had all heard of his exploits in Ireland and when, as Count of Mortain, brother of the King, he had ridden through their village they had hidden their daughters. It was well known that when Richard was away he had plotted against him without much foresight and wisdom and consequently been forced to humble himself and crave pardon when his brother returned. They knew that that pardon had been given and Richard had been heard to say that his young brother had been led astray and in any case he was not to be feared because he would never be able to make a conquest and if by good fortune a kingdom fell into his hands he would not be able to hold it against a foe.

That clearly indicated Richard's contempt for John. It may well have been why, the barons now reasoned, he had at one time named Arthur as his heir.

And now, there was trouble on the Continent. The barons

cared little for the Continent. They were English now, for though many of them had Norman ancestors, Normandy now seemed far away; it was their estates in England which they cared about and they had no desire to pay with their money and perhaps with their lives to help the King hold territories on the Continent while their affairs in England were neglected.

Some of the more bold of them now called together all those who had received a summons from the King and they met at Leicester where they decided they would make a stand against the King's orders.

They would not accompany him in his proposed war unless in return he did something for them. They wanted the old privileges which their baron ancestors had enjoyed returned to them.

John was in Portsmouth awaiting their arrival when he received the message. Immediately he flew into a rage. Isabella was with him and this was the first time she had seen one of his rages. He had been so delighted with his marriage, so absorbed by Isabella that nothing irked him at all; he had been content to put aside anything that was unpleasant and give himself up entirely to enjoying his marriage.

But this was too much. They had dared defy him as they would never have defied Richard or his father! They refused to come, unless he complied with their conditions.

'I'll see them in hell first,' he screamed and threw himself on to the floor.

Isabella watched him, round-eyed, as he rolled back and forth clutching the rushes, tearing at them with his teeth and spitting them forth as he kicked out madly.

'John,' she cried. 'Please ... please to not do that. You will do yourself an injury.'

For once he did not hear her. He lay kicking violently at anything which came within range and when, frightened, she ran out of the room, he did not even notice her going.

When his fury had abated a little he sent for the messenger. The man came pale and trembling, for the news that the King was in one of his raging tantrums had reached him.

'Go to these rogues,' shouted the King, 'and tell them that if they are not in Portsmouth within the week I will seize their castles and lands, and what shall be done to them I leave them to guess.'

The messenger made off with all speed, his one desire being to put as great a distance between himself and John as possible.

'Now,' cried the King, 'which is the nearest castle of these rebel barons?'

He discovered it belonged to a certain William of Albini.

'They shall see that I mean what I say,' he declared. 'We will take this Castle, raze it to the ground and hang all those who stand in our way as a lesson to the others.'

John was on the march, Isabella temporarily forgotten. His mouth was set in a firm line; his eyes were slightly bloodshot; there was a strength of purpose in him which all those about him recognized and they wondered whether they had mis-judged John.

That was victory, for before they had reached the target castle, William of Albini sent out a body of men with his son offering him to John as a hostage until he, William of Albini, could gather together his forces and present himself to the King at Portsmouth.

John laughed aloud. He had won the day. This, he thought, is the end of these barons' petty revolt. This will show them who is their master.

All believed he was right, for the barons were now arriving at Portsmouth with their men and the money he had com-manded them to bring.

Being John he must have his sly joke with them.

He collected the money they had brought which was to keep them and their soldiers during a long stay on the Continent. His eyes glistened as it was counted.

Then he said: 'You have disappointed me, gentlemen. You show me that your hearts are not in this fight. You live smug and content on your lands here ... lands which but for my noble ancestor known as William the Conqueror would never have been yours. You forget the land of your fathers which has been in my family's possession since Great Rollo came and took it from the French. It is in peril, gentlemen, and you would rather stay behind and live in ease and comfort. The curses of the Conqueror on you! Stay behind. Do you think I want chicken-hearted men serving with me! Go back to your lands. I will take but your money. It will buy me soldiers whose profession it is to fight and will serve me better than you.'

With that he dismissed them.

He laughed aloud in high good spirits. He felt strong, invincible; and in such a mood he crossed the Channel.

*   *   *

Philip was considering the new turn of affairs. Never for one moment had he diverged from his ultimate goal which was to bring back Normandy to France and not only Normandy. Every acre of land which was in the possession of John, Philip was determined to bring to the crown of France. Politically nothing could have pleased him better than the accession of John, though he would always think of Richard with sadness in his heart. He would never forget their friendship, for nothing had been quite so important to him in his life as that; but now Richard was gone he could devote himself to his great task which he had always made clear was to make France as great as it had been under Charlemagne.

John was a weakling. Oh, he could strut and swagger but at heart he was not a bold man. He was a bully and bullies were cowards; he was vain in the extreme; he was no strategist. All Philip's hopes lay in John. So he would forget his regrets for Richard and rejoice that fate had given him John to deal with.

He did not at this time want to indulge in another war. Wars were rarely decisive and with a man like John it should not be impossible to get the desired result without a great deal of unnecessary bloodshed and destruction.

Timing was all important and at this particular moment it was better to go along with John and not let his true intentions be known.

Of course it was clear that this foolish act of John's in abducting Hugh Lusignan's bride was one which should be exploited to the full. The Lusignans, feeling themselves to have been shamefully injured, were yearning to take revenge. That was good. But not just at this time. He would keep the wound open and festering; but he was not yet ready to go to war against John. That time would come. Then he would go to the aid of Arthur and his supporters; Arthur should swear fealty to him; he would offer him his little daughter Marie as a bride. True she was not yet six years old and Arthur had been affianced by Richard to the daughter of Tancred of Sicily; that was of no account. Then he, Philip, would have his hands on Normandy and John's possessions on the Continent and, who knew, perhaps he could in due course stretch out to the crown of England. After all William the Conqueror had done just that when he had been only a Duke of Normandy.

But not yet. As the true strategist he was, Philip had always known when to wait and when to act. Some might say he had been overcautious, but wise men knew that he was invariably right.

Therefore, when John reached Rouen he was met by placatory messengers from Philip who informed him that the King of France had urged the Lusignans to end their rebellion until he and the King of England had met and come to some agreement.

Puffed up with pride after his recent triumphant skirmish with the barons, John mistakenly believed that Philip was afraid of him and agreed to meet the French King at Les Andelys.

When the meeting took place Philip was gracious and invited John and his beautiful bride to Paris.

*   *   *

How Isabella revelled in the luxury of the Court of France. Philip was very courteous and determined to make them accept his friendship.

'You must have the best of all lodgings,' said Philip. 'Yes, I will hear of nothing else. My brother John and his beautiful bride shall have my royal palace and I with my Court will move to one of my other residences.'

This delighted John. He was eager to show Isabella off to his rival who professed himself enchanted by her charms. The Queen of France—of whom Philip was deeply enamoured since he was braving the wrath of the Pope for keeping her—seemed to John a poor creature in comparison with Isabella though without that bright star she was fair enough.

Isabella, basking in the admiration of the French, seeing new sights every day, leading a life of complete excitement, ceased to think of Hugh the Brown, only to remember now and then how dull life would have been had she married him.

She loved Paris with its grand buildings, its river, its people who were not unlike those of her native Angoulême. There were banquets in the palace almost every day; and she danced and sang to the applause of all concerned.

The King of France flattered her and complimented John on acquiring such a beautiful bride. John preened himself and laughingly told how he had duped the Lusignans and having seen her in the forest had determined to marry her.

' 'Tis clear,' said the King of France, 'that you have not been disappointed.'

'I never knew a woman capable of such skills,' John told him. 'Young as she is ... and a virgin when I married her ... yet she is as well versed in the art as an experienced whore— but with a fresh innocence if you understand.'

'We all understand,' replied the King of France, 'that it must need exceptional skill to keep you abed till midday.'

John laughed aloud.

'So they are talking of that, are they?'

'It reached my ears,' said Philip.

'Why not? I know of no better way to spend the time.'

Philip nodded and he thought: How long will you hold your possessions, John? I'll prophesy not many years. Then you will learn, brother, that a king must have other ways of spending his time than in his bed.

Philip was delighted. He could see his goal nearer every day.

At the table he talked to John of serious matters. Isabella was there and John was conscious of little else, holding her hand one moment, stroking the soft fair flesh ... flashing messages to her with his eyes to which she responded in a languorous manner.

Good, thought the King of France. I'll have it all my way. He'll not care as long as he can go to bed with his wife.

' 'Tis a mistake,' he said, 'to go into battle against the Lusignans. Unnecessary wars should be avoided.'

John nodded sleepily. He said: 'They have risen against me.'

'With reason,' said Philip. 'You could hardly expect them to remain passive when such a prize was snatched from them.'

John laughed. 'Such a prize would be wasted on Hugh the Brown.'

'That may well be,' said Philip. 'Why should you not submit the Lusignans to trial? They have stirred up rebellion. They have opened up their quarrel with Angoulême. Ralph has made trouble in Normandy. Bring them to trial for forgetting their oaths of allegiance to you and causing trouble which could have resulted in war.'

John hated to be told what he was to do. He was capable of ruling without Philip's help and he'd have him know it. But to go to war was not what he wanted. It would mean Isabella wouldn't be able to accompany him. That was unthinkable.

So he would agree with Philip; and when he had the Lusignans on trial he would see that they were found guilty of treason and he would sentence them to prove their innocence by fighting in a duel with opponents who should be chosen for them. This was a perfectly legal method of settling disputes. It was believed that if a man was innocent, God was on his side. If he were guilty then he would be defeated because God would be on his opponent's side. John kept a company of expert duellists who had never been defeated and if he wanted to rid himself of an enemy he contrived to sentence him to one of these duels knowing that it was invariably a good way of getting rid of him, for however skilled he was with a sword it seemed hardly likely that he could do better than a man who had spent all his time practising the art in the King's cause.

The duel sentence was preserved for men of high rank. There were other less aristocratic methods of carrying out the same principle—such as plunging the accused's hand in a pail of boiling water to retrieve some object which had been placed at the bottom of the pail. If the damaged hand later festered the man was considered guilty. There was another punishment in which a naked man whose hands and feet were tied together was thrown into a river or any water that was handy. To float in such circumstances meant that he was supported by the devil and he was immediately rescued and put to the death; to sink meant that he was receiving no such aid and he was rescued. If in time all well and good; if not, well, he died anyway. These punishments had been in existence since the old pagan days but no one had at this time seen fit to change them.

Thus, when John agreed with the King of France to bring Hugh the Brown to court where he himself would stand with him that their cause might be judged, he had no intention of appearing himself; and had decided that he would sentence Hugh and certain members of his family to meet duellists who should be chosen for them.

The Triumph of Mirebeau

THE Duchess Constance lay in her bed feeling exhausted. She had given birth to a daughter, the Princess Alice, and had, since the child had been born, felt her strength slowly ebbing away.

She was listless, idly wondering what the future held, and with her was the certainty that she would not be there to see it. The child lay in its cradle, a healthy little girl; the third of her children. What would become of that little one? There would not be the storm about her inheritance as there was about that of Arthur—yes, and even Eleanor, for Eleanor was the granddaughter of Henry II and as such in certain circumstances could be an heir to England, Normandy and Anjou.

She stirred uneasily and her daughter, who had been seated in the window, came at once to the bed.

'Is there anything you need, Mother?' she asked.

'Nay, Daughter. But sit and talk to me a while.'

'Should you not reserve your strength?'

'For what, my child ... death?'

'Do not talk so, Mother. You are going to be well. It was just a difficult birth and it has exhausted you.'

'I always believed that one should face the truth however unpleasant. I hope you will do that, Eleanor.'

'I shall try to, Mother.'

'I lie here and wonder how it will end. I have terrible fears for Arthur. Sometimes my mind is plunged in melancholy. I cannot say exactly why but it is like some terrible foreboding.'

'It is because you are weak, Mother, that you feel thus.'

'No, 'tis not that. It is as though I can peer into the future and see horror there.'

'If it eases you to talk of your fear, Mother, do so.'

'How can I talk of that which I do not understand? I see it there and you and Arthur are at the centre of it. It is my punishment for my ambition perhaps. I was so delighted when I married your father because he was the son of a king and I hoped one day that Arthur would take his place.'

'It may be that he will.'

She shook her head.

'Mother, what has come over you? You always believed that one day he would have what was his by right.'

'Yes, I believed it and I worked for it. Your stepfather Guy has worked for it. Listen to him, Eleanor, when I'm gone.'

'You are not going,' said Eleanor firmly.

Constance smiled. 'I would you and Arthur were a little older. I wish I could have lived another five years. That was all I would ask.'

'You are young yet and newly married. What do you think your husband would say if he heard you talk like this?'

'He will grieve for me sorely, Eleanor. He truly loves me.'

'Of course; as I do and Arthur.'

'I know. And it is because I love you all so dearly that it grieves me so much to leave you. Eleanor, listen to Guy. Take care of your brother. Oh, I know he is a duke and thinks himself a man. But I greatly fear John.'

'Yes, Mother, I know. So do we all.'

'John is a monster. He has his follies but do not underestimate them, my child. Even now he is with the King of France. What do you think they are plotting?'

'Philip is our friend, Mother, not John's.'

'You should not put your trust in kings, Daughter. Philip is our friend today and John's tomorrow. Philip's desire is to get for himself what John now owns and is by right Arthur's. That is Philip's part in all this.'

'He has been good to Arthur.'

'Only to serve his own purpose. I would like to see Arthur

stand alone, with mighty armies behind him. I would like to see him and Guy ride together to victory.'

'It will come.'

'Eleanor, watch over your brother. Do not let him be too trusting, particularly of his Uncle John.'

Eleanor swore that she would do her best to carry out her mother's wish but she insisted that Constance would soon be rising from her bed and doing all that she had done before. She was merely suffering from the depression which often follows a birth.

So it seemed for a week or so and then one day her condition changed for the worse. She sent for Arthur, Eleanor and Guy.

She said: 'This is indeed the end. My loved ones, take care of each other.'

They knelt by her bed, Arthur who was but thirteen years old, Eleanor who was not much older, and Guy who had loved her for years and had so recently married her.

Thus died Arthur's mother, and that day the young Duke lost his best friend and adviser.

*   *   *

John was at Chinon with Isabella. He was amused to think how anxious the Lusignans would be to have him so close. He laughed to Isabella about it as they lay in bed together.

'I'll warrant they will keep a close watch on the tower. Imagine it, sweetheart, they won't know from one day to the next when I shall be bearing down on them with an avenging force. Hugh will be trembling in his shoes.'

Isabella frowned. 'It is not his custom to tremble,' she said.

'Oh, you would defend him then?'

'I would speak the truth,' she answered a little defiantly.

'You are but a child,' he said. 'What do you know of these matters?'

'I know Hugh better than you do. You forget I lived in his castle for a while.'

'Do not remind me of it,' he said, 'or I might fall into a rage. You have seen my rage ... once. Before I had you I was always in and out of them.'

'Then I have brought you some good for I confess when you lie on the floor and kick you look ... mad.'

She had knelt up on the bed her hair falling about her

shoulders. He lay back feasting his eyes on her.

He caught her wrist.

'Are you trying to anger me, little Isabella?'

'I must speak the truth,' she answered.

'Virtuous little wife,' he said. 'I too will speak truth and tell you that I like not to hear you defending Hugh.'

'I do not defend him. I say that he is no coward. Ask anyone. They will tell you the same. He fears no man—not you nor the King of France, and if you say he is trembling in his shoes I will say that I do not believe he is.'

He pulled her down beside him. 'If you were not so pretty I might be angry with you.'

'Why should I worry about that when I am pretty enough to divert your anger? And I will tell you this, that if I were not, I would still say what I thought.'

'She has spirit, this Queen of England.'

'Would you wish her otherwise?' she asked him, stooping over him and putting her soft cheek against his.

He caught her in a fierce embrace. 'I would not have her other than she is,' he said.

'So I thought I,' she answered.

But later he remembered that she had spoken too warmly in Hugh's favour and he felt displeased.

*   *   *

There was to be a visitor to Chinon. It was Queen Berengaria. She had heard that the King was resting there a while and would come to visit him and his Queen.

'Poor Berengaria!' said John to Isabella. 'She had a sad time with Richard. He was a strange man. He didn't care for women. *You* wouldn't have liked that, my Isabella, would you?'

'Perhaps he would have been different had I been his queen.'

'Ho. The vanity! Nay, Richard chose his loves from minstrel boys. You know the story of Blondel. I used to wish I'd cut out his tongue before he went singing round the castles of Europe.'

'You were not fond of your brother?'

'Fond of Richard, who took the throne from me when my father had promised it to me!'

'And Richard promised it to Arthur at one time. Poor John, you were hard done by.'

'Ah, but I came into my own did I not?'

'You did.'

'And secured the greatest prize in the world ... snatched it right from under the nose of that Hugh of whom you speak so highly. Why so? What happened that you should grow warm in praise of him? By God if he ever laid his hands on you I'll have him flayed alive.'

She laughed up at him provocatively. 'Forget not that I was betrothed to him.'

'And did he take advantage of that? You were a virgin when you came to me, I'll swear.'

'Ah yes,' she said, 'I was a virgin but a somewhat regretful one.'

'You mean ... you tried to seduce him and he would have none of it?'

'He is a man such as you could not understand, John.'

'And you did?'

'Yes,' she said, 'I did. He thought me too young and would never touch me.'

'Different from me, eh?'

'As different as it is possible to be.'

'And now I have him, Isabella. He is going to be brought to Court and there he will be sentenced to fight a duel, and I shall make sure he is not the victor.'

'Are you afraid of him?'

'Afraid of a petty count! What mean you?'

'That I might like him better than I like you.'

She had gone too far. She had seen the red lights in his eyes.

She ran her lips over his face and murmured: 'Could you be as foolish as that? Poor Hugh, if he could but hear you now.'

She knew how to rouse him and she did.

There was a slight change in their relationship. She was no longer the child who marvelled at everything that was happening to her; she was taking a great deal of the pomp and luxury, the sexual excitement for granted. She had a will of her own and had never been faced with serious opposition.

She knew though that John was capable of the utmost cruelty. At the moment he wanted nothing but her; yet when he had talked of Hugh and had believed for a moment that she was more interested in her one-time suitor than he wished her to be, there had been such vicious cruelty momentarily unveiled in his expressive face that she had felt a tremor of alarm.

It was pleasant to welcome Berengaria.

'Poor Berengaria!' Isabella called her. What a sad life she had had! John joked about her relationship with Richard, when Berengaria had always been watching and hoping, and Richard ignoring her.

She was sad too but she was clearly impressed by Isabella's startling beauty.

They talked together in Isabella's apartment and Berengaria said how pleased she was to see John so happily married.

'It is wonderful,' said Berengaria wistfully, 'to know such happiness as you must. It is so obvious that the King is deeply enamoured of you. You are so young. Is it possible that you are not yet fourteen years of age?'

' 'Tis true,' replied Isabella. 'But I believe I am in advance of my years.'

'You would need to be—so young and yet a wife. I was much older than you when I married.'

Isabella wondered what she herself would be like when she was Berengaria's age.

It was pleasant to bask in her admiration. At the same time there was something depressing about Richard's Queen. She was so clearly an unhappy woman and she was too given to talking of the past. She kept bringing John's sister Joanna into the conversation, and Joanna was dead—had died in childbirth. Apparently she and Berengaria had been great friends.

To talk of women dying in childbirth was not a pleasant topic for a young wife, although John had said that he did not want children yet because they would spoil her body and he liked it as it was.

Berengaria explained to John what a desperate position she was in. She had settled in Le Mans which was part of her dowry but she owned lands in England and she hoped that John would compensate her for these.

John was affable: as always he was very ready to promise because he never considered it necessary to honour his promises.

'My dear sister,' he said, 'you may rest assured that I will do everything within my power to help you. Now let us see what I can do. You shall have Bayeux and there are two castles in Anjou which shall be yours. It is only right that they should be. Richard would have wished it,' he added piously.

Berengaria wept a little. 'I wish Richard could hear you now,' she said. 'I don't think he thought you would be so good to me.'

'I am accustomed to being maligned,' replied John. 'Of course I was wild in my youth. What man worth his salt is not? But with responsibilities one changes. I have decided to give you a thousand marks a year.'

She kissed his hand and told him Heaven would reward him.

'For,' she said, 'but for you, I should be little more than a pauper and have no alternative but to throw myself on to the mercy of my family. I had considered going to live with Blanche my sister, but much as I love her I should hate to accept her bounty.'

'You may trust me to see that you are well provided for,' said John.

When she left Chinon Berengaria took an affectionate farewell of John and his young Queen.

'What will become of her, I wonder,' said Isabella as they watched her ride away.

'She will go and live with her sister Blanche of Champagne,' said John with a smile, who had no intention of giving her what he had promised. Why should he, he reasoned. Let her sister provide for her.

'Richard was never a husband to her,' said Isabella. 'She must have been very miserable.'

John gripped her arms, putting his face close to hers. 'What would you have done, my desiring and desirable one, had you been married to Richard?'

'Find lovers,' she answered promptly.

He laughed, but he remembered that later.'

*   *   *

When the day arrived for John to meet the Lusignans in a court set up by the King of France and presided over by him, John failed to put in an appearance.

This was exactly what Philip was hoping for. He had taken

advantage of the truce between them and was prepared now to go into action. By not appearing John had given Philip the excuse he needed to go against him. As a vassal of Philip for Normandy he had insulted the King by flouting his wishes.

John, said Philip, must be taught a lesson.

He sent to Brittany asking that Arthur come to him as he would knight him and accept his fealty as Count of Anjou, Duke of Brittany and all the land with the exception of Normandy which was now in the hands of John.

Guy de Thouars realizing that this meant Philip was now prepared to help Arthur against John, most joyfully travelled with his young stepson to *rendezvous* with Philip.

This was the signal for John's enemies to rise; and the Lusignans caught up with Arthur at Tours and there pledged to support him in his efforts to take from John not only his Continental possessions but the crown of England as well.

*   *   *

In the Abbey of Fontevraud the aged Eleanor was resting after the strenuous journey to Castile. She could congratulate herself that although it had impaired her health still further yet it had been a success and her granddaughter was indeed married to the son of the King of France. She had never lost sight of the fact that it was in that direction that real danger lay.

John was more or less firmly established on the throne of England; if he could keep a strong hand on his Continental possessions he would get through that dangerous period which followed accession to the throne. He was married to a beautiful young wife and if they had sons the people would be pleased to see the succession assured. The threat came from Arthur of course; but now that Constance was dead he must have lost a certain amount of support. Eleanor could not mourn Constance—a woman whom she had always disliked. Perhaps Constance was too forceful, too much like herself. Looking back it was easy to understand that she wanted her son to have what she had considered his rights and there were many men who would have agreed with Constance. After all, her son was the son of an elder brother. Constance had made an error of judgment when she had refused to allow Arthur to be brought up in England.

Had she? Would Arthur have been alive if she had?

She had always prided herself on never blinking facts. What was she doing now? Was she being like Henry, refusing to see what was obvious? She had given her allegiance to John because he was her son and meant more to her than her grandson did—moreover, at the back of her mind was her dislike of Constance. I would never allow that woman to rule, she had promised herself; and as Arthur was a minor, very much under the influence of his mother, it seemed a likely conclusion that if ever he became King, Constance would indeed be the power behind the throne.

Well, she had given her support to John and so had William Marshal: and with two such adherents he had won the crown. It was now his responsibility to keep it; and she had earned a rest.

It was strange that her idea of pleasure now should be to lie late abed, to listen to the bells, to join in the life of the Abbey, attending prayers, giving herself to meditation, retiring early, reading, resting, sleeping. It was what one came to at eighty.

Not that she had become pious. She had always been too honest with herself for that. She could say, Yes, I have led a sinful life and it would have been better for others and myself, too, if I had practised virtue. 'But God,' she said, 'You made me as I am. You should not complain. Had You wanted me different, You should not have sent me into the world equipped as I was.'

Trying to find some virtue in herself she could say with honesty that she had loved her children, and had unswervingly worked for their good. Even though Richard had been her favourite, she had never failed any of the others. And to think that she had outlived so many of them, so that of five beloved sons there was only John left!

John, King of England, was safely married and deeply enamoured of a young wife; soon they would be giving her a grandson. She could rest in peace.

But it was not to be. This was due to herself, she would be the first to admit. Although she wished to live quietly she must know what was happening and she sent out some of her servants whose duty it was to discover what people were saying, or if there was revolt anywhere, and come back and report to her.

It was in this way that she learned that the Lusignans were

rising. She had expected that of course. They were a proud
family and not of a nature meekly to accept a wrong done to
them. That they would make trouble with the Count of
Angoulême was certain, but that was a small matter which
should be comparatively easy to settle. There was more than
that.

The French King had honoured Arthur, which meant that
he was inviting him to take up arms against John. Philip was
on the march; he had already harried the borders of Normandy and one or two castles had fallen to his forces. The
Lusignans were joining forces with Arthur and Guy de
Thouars, and a mighty uprising against John was coming
into being.

More news came. Philip was advancing into Normandy
within ten miles of Rouen.

How could Eleanor remain at Fontevraud when such
disaster was threatening her son? Clear-headed, with the
judgment born of long experience, she knew that there was
work for her to do. She must hold Aquitaine for John otherwise the Lusignans with Arthur would take it.

The days of peace were over. It mattered not that she was
old, her joints stiff, and that her body cried out for rest. She
would not have been Eleanor if she had not prepared herself
for a journey, and that day set out for Poitiers.

There she proposed to fortify the castle and hold it against
intruders.

She forgot that she was old. The fighting spirit was as
strong as ever and in her heart she was glad to be at the
centre of events again.

*   *   *

Arthur with his stepfather, Guy de Thouars, and with a
formidable army behind him had reached the town of Tours,
where he rested for a night at the castle. Since his mother had
died he had become more self-reliant. Now he must make his
own decisions without his mother to remind him that he was
after all only a boy. People around him had become more
respectful; they came to him whereas once they had gone to his
mother and he was realizing how important he was and
relishing his position.

Being so young he was inclined to give himself an aura of
authority to remind people of his importance lest they should

forget it. Even Guy's attitude towards him had changed since his mother's death. His was a great inheritance out of which he had been cheated by his wicked uncle.

'But we are going to win back that which has been stolen,' declared Arthur.

'Rest assured,' cried Guy, 'that is our intent. I have promised your mother to serve you with my life and that I will do.'

His sister Eleanor, still grieving for her mother's death, joined them and asked if there was any news.

'My dear sister,' said Arthur, 'you should not be with us. This is no place for women.'

'Nonsense, Arthur,' replied Eleanor, 'I want to be with you and Guy and so shall I be.'

'We could forbid you,' Arthur reminded her; and she smiled and told him that although he might be the Duke of Normandy, Count of Anjou and King of England as well as the Duke of Brittany, he was still her young brother.

Arthur frowned, displeased. Everybody must understand that he had put his childhood behind him. *Everybody,* he emphasized.

Eleanor slipped her arm through his. 'What airs you give yourself these days, brother!' she said.

'Arthur is growing more aware of his position every day,' said Guy. 'From here we shall be going to Poitiers,' he went on, 'Eleanor, Arthur is right. You should not be with the army.'

'Where should I go?' asked Eleanor. 'To Brittany? There to wonder what is happening to you all? I couldn't bear it. Now that Mother is gone I want to be with you and Arthur.'

'We shall send you away if there are any signs of fighting,' Arthur told her. 'I'll not have my sister in danger.'

Guy smiled at her. Let the boy have his way, he implied. It is right for him to feel his position for he will be a ruler one day and must prepare himself for it.

While they were speaking messengers came with news that Queen Eleanor had left Fontevraud and was on her way to Poitiers.

'She must not be allowed to get there,' cried Arthur, 'for if she does the whole of Aquitaine will rise up to help her. She may be my grandmother but she is no friend of mine.'

'It is difficult to be a friend of a grandson if it means being an enemy of a son,' Eleanor reminded him. 'What a pity that there have to be these rifts in families!'

'It is no use getting sentimental,' Arthur told her sharply. He turned to Guy. 'What are we going to do about my grandmother?'

'As you say we have to prevent her reaching Poitiers and that means we must lose no time in going in pursuit of her.'

'Then why are we wasting time?' asked Arthur imperiously.

*   *   *

It was a hard journey. With a very few supports, all she could muster at such a short notice, Queen Eleanor had ridden with as much speed as was possible from Fontevraud. She was exhausted at the end of the day and when news was brought to her that Arthur was in pursuit on one hand and the Lusignans were coming up from the South to join Arthur she said that they must take refuge immediately and if possible defend themselves.

The castle of Mirebeau was near at hand. 'We will make our way there,' said Eleanor, 'and let my son John be told that I am being pursued. I am sure that then he will come to my rescue without delay.'

She was received into the castle by loyal friends, and realizing the danger they made ready for a siege. Eleanor was not greatly perturbed.

'I'm too old for panic,' she said. 'If they kill me I shall die, which I expected to do soon in any case though in my own bed. And if they take me prisoner, well, it will be a short imprisonment. But I know my son will come with all speed when he knows what a predicament I am in.'

She went into the keep and watched from a window. It was not very long before she saw the approaching army led by her grandson.

She knew the castle could not hold out long because it was ill-defended and unprepared for a siege and in a very short time Arthur's men had broken through to the inner courtyard.

She picked out her grandson. How young he is, she thought. Just a boy! He couldn't be much more than fifteen. It's too young to have to take decisions, to have to fight for a crown, she thought.

A noble-looking boy though—one of whom a grandmother could be proud. A little imperious perhaps. That was natural, for too much responsibility had been thrust on him at too early an age and he made a good pretence of being able to carry it.

Geoffrey's son! How like his father he was! And an orphan now. Poor Arthur, what would be his fate? she wondered.

He was the enemy of course. At any moment now, his men would break into the keep and confront her. She hoped they would let her talk to Arthur and she would try to explain to him how she bore no animosity towards him; she was merely following a principle because she felt her son John had a greater right to the throne.

Arthur looked up and saw her at the window. His formidable grandmother of whom he had heard so much! He wondered what he would say to her when they broke down the last door and he confronted her.

He felt very uncertain. He would ask Guy to take her prisoner perhaps. It would come better from him; and they would shut her up where she could no longer work for John and cause the people of Aquitaine to rise up in support of her.

He called a halt to the fighting. Hugh de Lusignan and Guy asked him what his orders were now that they were on the point of attaining their object.

'We have captured the Queen Mother,' he said. 'But if we break down the door of the keep what shall we do with her?'

'We could ride on,' said Hugh, 'to one of my castles and hold her there, for we should keep her prison a secret.'

'This we shall do tomorrow,' said Arthur. 'The men are tired now. Let us stay here for the night and leave at dawn.'

Both men agreed that it seemed a good idea and the soldiers were delighted with the decision. They could help themselves to food from the kitchens and wine from the cellars. They had ridden far and fought hard and the object was achieved, the Queen Mother being their prisoner. They were entitled to enjoy a few hours respite before going on duty again.

So the night passed.

Eleanor in the keep waited, at first expecting that she would be confronted by her grandson or Hugh or Guy, and told to make ready for the journey to wherever they were going to take her.

Can it be, she thought, that I shall once again be a prisoner? It was ironical when she considered it. First her husband and now her grandson. She would have liked to have had a word with Arthur. Perhaps that would be granted her.

She could not sleep, which in the circumstances was to be expected. In any case she reminded herself the old did not need a great deal of sleep.

Where was John? she wondered. Had he received her cry for help? Would he come with all speed or would he be unable to tear himself away from Isabella? If she were with him the answer would be no.

It would be interesting to see. Life was always full of interest or so it had seemed to her; that was the secret of her ability to enjoy being alive while she was philosophical enough to be prepared for death.

Arthur lay awake but only for a short while. This was a victory. To have captured such an important person as his grandmother would show the world that because he was merely a boy he was a general too. He would plan and use his armies to advantage. He had to show them that he knew how to act, because people dismissed him slightingly as a boy. And one day soon he would come into his kingdom and his wicked uncle would be defeated for ever. He had such good friends— his prospective father-in-law Philip of France; Guy, his step-father, whom his mother had loved and who had promised to serve him faithfully; and Hugh de Lusignan who had his own special grudge against John.

Arthur slept peacefully.

*   *   *

Hugh de Lusignan was thinking of Isabella. She was never very far from his thoughts. He would go over and over again in his mind that terrible day when he had heard of her marriage to John. He had been stunned, unable to believe there could be such perfidy. And Isabella who must have been willing was only a child really and her father would have pushed her into it. She could not be blamed. He thought of her charming ways, the show of affection, the artless manner in which she had clung to him. He had re-strained himself against her beguiling ways, reminding himself of her youth, and then that lecher had taken her and, child that she was, had married her. *He* had had no respect for her youth. The sly innuendoes had reached him. He knew that they lay abed half the day.

Isabella! He would never forget her—her youth and her charm and the promise that was in her; he would never forget either that John had deceived him and taken her from him.

He would always love Isabella but he would never blame her. And he would always hate John.

They were up with the dawn.

'There must be no delay,' said Hugh. 'I would we had left last night.'

'As soon as breakfast is over we will leave,' promised Arthur.

The servants came in with pigeon pie which would make an excellent breakfast.

'Let us eat quickly and be gone,' said Hugh.

'When I have finished,' Arthur answered, 'I will go to my grandmother and tell her to prepare to leave and that she is to be our prisoner.'

But he did not do so, for while he was still at the table there was a shout from without. An army was making its way to the Château Mirebeau.

*   *   *

When John heard that his mother, who was on the road to Poitiers in order to hold Aquitaine for him was being pursued by Arthur and Hugh de Lusignan, he acted with a speed which was unusual with him.

He saw at once the importance of this. If Eleanor were captured he could lose Aquitaine and what heart that would put into his enemies! Philip penetrating into Normandy with Arthur and Hugh in the South would put him into a very uneasy position.

He had to rescue his mother at all costs.

All through the night he rode with his army and just before dawn they arrived at Mirebeau. Great was his delight when he discovered that the enemy was still there.

They stormed the castle. It was an easy victory, for John's forces greatly outnumbered those of Arthur and Hugh. Exultantly Arthur and his sister Eleanor and Hugh among others were taken prisoner and John himself went up to the top of the keep to escort his mother to safety.

The old Queen's eyes were shining with delight. John at last was behaving like a son of hers. She was proud of him.

*   *   *

This was John's greatest victory. William Marshal who had ridden with him lost much of the uneasiness he had experienced since he had been adamant in supporting John's claim to the throne.

John was proving himself to be a king after all. There could not be a better turn to events. Two of the most important leaders of the revolt against him were in his hands.

'We must lose no time in letting Philip know that Arthur is your prisoner,' he said.

'Philip shall be informed at once.'

'And Ralph de Lusignan must know that his brother Hugh is in your hands.'

John licked his lips with pleasure at the thought.

'This day's work has saved us many a battle I doubt not,' said the Marshal.

John was proud. It was the sort of battle he enjoyed—quick and decisive and bringing glory at the end.

He embraced his mother, who congratulated him on the speed with which he had acted. Her praise delighted him, he replied. And if she were proud of him he was doubly so of her. For she had sought to save his duchy for him and he knew that she was tired and longed to rest.

'Depend upon it if I were needed I would rise from my death bed,' she answered.

She took her farewell of him; that which she had set out to do no longer needed to be done. Aquitaine was safe, for Arthur and Hugh were no longer in a position to threaten it.

'That will soon be common knowledge,' said John.

Eleanor went back to Fontevraud there to rest, for now the ordeal was over she realized how it had exhausted her.

When she had gone John prepared to return to Normandy.

He was in high spirits. There were two prisoners over whom he wanted to gloat—one was his nephew Arthur and the other Hugh de Lusignan.

First he sent for Arthur. He prepared himself very carefully for the interview and put on a red satin mantle decorated with rich gems; he wore a girdle set with pearls and diamonds and the baldrick which held up his sword glittered with emeralds. He was a dazzling sight.

He sat sprawled in a chair. He did not care to stand for he was very conscious of his lack of inches and always felt better on such occasions when he was seated.

Arthur, who was brought in by two guards, made a show of indifference but was not able to hide his nervousness altogether.

John surveyed him maliciously.

'Ha, my young nephew who would be King. How fares it, Arthur?'

'It has gone ill with me,' said Arthur, 'but it will not always be so.'

John raised his eyebrows and leisurely took off his gloves, one adorned with a massive ruby, the other with a sapphire. He flung them nonchalantly on to a stool.

'You set your hopes a little high, nephew.'

'I think not.'

'Well, you will doubtless be able to brood on the matter in your prison.'

'So you will send me to prison?'

'Where do you think I should send you? To Westminster Abbey to be crowned King?'

'I did not think that.'

'There you showed some sense. Why could you not be a good boy content with your very pleasant Duchy of Brittany?'

'Because I have a right to other possessions.'

'You mean mine? Have a care, boy. I might not like such talk.'

'Then why do you bring me here if not to speak to me?'

'I expect you to show humility, to fall to your knees, to admit your fault and beg for clemency.'

'That I shall never do.'

'Nay if I had that tongue out you would never be able to.'

That made the boy grow pale. No doubt he had heard tales of this uncle's methods.

John enjoyed his fear. He narrowed his eyes. 'Take care, boy,' he said. 'I like not those who would take what is mine. You will be my prisoner, at my mercy. Know you this: that whatever I order my servants to do they will do—they dare do aught else.'

'I would rather you killed me than...' began the boy and his voice was shrill with terror.

'There are many ways of punishing your arrogance, nephew, and I could do them all. I could put out those haughty eyes, tear out that tongue.' His eyes slid over the boy's slender figure. 'You are scarce a man and I could do that to you which would mean that you would never know manhood. What say you to that?'

Where was the haughty would-be-King now? It was a frightened child who stood before him.

'I ... I ...'

'Come speak up, boy. What say you to these suggestions? Come speak. I like answers when I ask questions and my temper is not of the most mild. You may have heard this.'

'I would say,' said Arthur, 'that you would not do these things even if it were your power to.'

'It is in my power to. You should know that.'

'But ... you would be reviled. The whole world would rise against an uncle who did such to his nephew who was but fifteen years old.'

'Do I care for the world's opinion? Nay, nephew, I do what I will. But I spoke but to frighten you and to impress on you that I need obedience. If you do as you are told, it may be that no harm will come to you. Take him away,' he said to the guards. 'And, Arthur, think of what I have said. Ask yourself what it would be like to be without that of which a word from me could rob you.'

Arthur was led away.

He'll not sleep easily tonight, thought John laughing.

And now for Hugh.

He was a good-looking man. He stood there showing no fear so that it was hard to believe that he felt any. Isabella had said that he was never afraid. Could it be that she had a fancy for him?

John was glad he was seated. He would look very small beside Hugh de Lusignan. He stroked his red mantle; the touch of gems was reassuring. Hugh might look noble but he, John, looked royal.

'So you are my prisoner,' he said.

Hugh bowed.

'You should have made off last night. An error of judgment.'

' 'Twas indeed so,' agreed Hugh.

'And now you are my prisoner. You who have caused trouble in my realm and done everything you can to bring about revolt.'

Hugh was silent.

'You know what we do with traitors.'

'I am no traitor, my lord.'

'No traitor when you stir strife in my realm?'

'I was under no obligation to serve you and made no secret of my quarrel.'

'You were commanded to meet a duellist in combat and refused.'

'I would not have refused to meet you, my lord. It was only one of your hirelings whom I would not face.'

'You have too great an opinion of yourselves, you Lusignans.'

'I beg your pardon, my lord, but we are a great family.'

'Do not speak of greatness in my presence. We are enemies, Hugh the Brown.'

' 'Tis so, my lord.'

'And you are my prisoner.'

'Taken in honourable battle.'

'When you were in the act of taking possession of my royal mother!'

'Who was taking part in war and therefore it was fair enough.'

'Bah! Do not parley with me.'

'As you wish, my lord.'

John sat back and narrowed his eyes. He wondered what he would do to Hugh. He could think of several forms of torture; but he knew that whatever was inflicted this man would preserve that outward calm, that indifference.

There was no fun with people like that. He couldn't have the fun with him that he had had with little Arthur.

But he would humiliate him. That was the best way. Take some of the pride out of him.

He had an idea.

'Take the prisoner away,' he said.

They took him and John sat alone for a little while his brows drawn together in a frown. He was thinking of Isabella and wondering how deep her feeling had gone for Hugh. Could she really have had some affection for him? He was a handsome fellow and Isabella was of course what he would call ripe. Hugh had not seen this; if he had ... who knew what would have happened. Hugh was a fool, better at war than love, no doubt, and he had become a prisoner even in that.

He had no real reason to be jealous of Hugh. But he would humiliate him all the same.

He stood up and shouted. His servants came running.

'There is no reason why we should stay here,' he cried. 'We shall prepare to leave at once for Normandy.'

*   *   *

He was so amused. He had thought of a brilliant idea. He had sent his servants forth to find farm carts—those in which cattle or hay had been carried and in these, securely fettered, he put his prisoners. He laughed aloud to see them—haughty young Arthur, the would-be-King, riding there like a cow to market. Hugh the Brown, would-be-husband of Isabella, like a proud bull going in to be inspected and bid for.

There were others of course but those were the two who gave him most pleasure.

Young Arthur was overcome with shame.

This, thought John unctuously, will be good for him. He was too haughty by far.

It was wonderful to ride thus, the conqueror. People had said that he would never be the king his father or brother were. They sniggered at his lying abed late with his wife. Any of them would have lain abed if they could have done so with Isabella. They had said he would lose his dominions, for the King of France was too wily for him, and ere long Arthur would be on the throne.

And how wrong he had proved them to be!

Philip would be very uneasy, overcome with shame to know that his protégé was in his enemy's hands. And Hugh de Lusignan, too. This would show the upstart barons what happened when they opposed the King.

Oh yes, he was very content with himself riding through Normandy to Caen. He was going to show his prisoners to Isabella. That would be amusing. She should sit with him while they were trundled past. It would be quite a spectacle and how the prisoners would writhe with shame. Mental torture was often more rewarding than the physical kind, he was beginning to realize.

Arthur would not like to be seen in a farm cart chained like an animal.

And bold brave Hugh? What will Isabella think of you then?

*   *   *

Isabella was at Caen waiting to receive him. He hurried her off to the bedchamber immediately.

She laughed at him. It was the longest period they had been apart.

Later he boasted of his victory. 'Speed is what is necessary, Isabella. If I had delayed it would have been victory for them. They would have taken my mother prisoner. Imagine that. The impudence of them!'

'But you were there and stopped them.'

'Aye, and took them prisoner. I have some fine prisoners to show you.'

She pouted slightly. 'I do not greatly care for prisoners.'

'I want you to see these. There is young Arthur himself.'

'He's only a child.'

'Ha, hark who is talking! He's older than you are!'

'I shouldn't like to be your prisoner.'

'Nay,' said John sentimentally. 'I am yours.'

''Tis a pretty thought,' she said.

'And now I wish to show them to you.'

'But I said I did not want to see them.'

'But you will to please me.'

'I thought *you* always wanted to please *me*.'

'I do when your pleasure is mine.'

They laughed together; but he had implied that he was going to insist on her viewing the prisoners.

She didn't want to. She hated unpleasant things and the sight of men in chains gave her no pleasure—particularly if they were handsome men. She was beginning to be a little wary of John. She had seen the redness tinge his eyes and it gave her a qualm or two. She would never forget how he had rolled on the floor and stuffed the rushes into his mouth.

If she were to have her way it would have to be subtly; and she must never appear to go against him.

So she found herself sitting in the courtyard beside him while the farm carts rolled by.

Poor little Arthur, he looked so sad and frightened too. He was such a boy. She knew he was a little older than she was but not much; and she shuddered to think of herself fettered in a farm cart, John's prisoner.

And there was another. She started at the sight of him. Hugh! He stood up in the cart, his head high as though he were quite unaware of where he was. Her heart leaped at the sight of him and a great emotion swept over her. Oh not Hugh! she thought, and was afraid that she had spoken aloud as she knew John was aware of her every movement, and was watching the expression on her face.

Hugh had turned his head and was looking straight at her. What was that she saw in his eyes? She tried to answer him. Oh Hugh, Hugh, I am sorry. It was not of my doing really. They forced me to it.

I wanted to be Queen, she thought. Yes I did. I liked the ceremony and the clothes, the jewels, the people cheering and saying I was beautiful. I like my nights with John—but he frightens me sometimes. Oh Hugh, if it hadn't happened like this...

The cart had passed; she did not look after it but stared at the next one.

'What thought you of your one-time betrothed?' asked John.

She hesitated. She could not bring herself to speak flippantly.

She said: 'I thought he bore himself like a brave man.'

John was silent. He thought: If she had cared for him she would never have dared speak of him like that.

Nay, she is content enough. Are her responses not enough to tell me that?

He gave orders that Arthur was to be sent under strict guard to Falaise; there he was to be held in the utmost security. If he was allowed to escape, he commented, he would not envy those who had been in charge of him. His sister Eleanor should go to Bristol. She was only a girl and he did not fear her. Let her be treated with courtesy.

Others he sent to Corfe Castle in Dorset.

'I have not yet decided where I shall send Hugh the Brown,' he told Isabella. 'But it shall be a strong prison for

that one. Such a bold brave man might well attempt escape.'
She did not answer.

Then he said: 'I have it. It shall be here in Caen. We have some fine dungeons here—damp and cold. You can think of him when you and I are revelling together—but no, your thoughts must all be for me. I'll not have it otherwise.' Playfully he put his hands about her throat. 'You'd not disappoint me, sweetheart.'

'How could I do so?' she asked.

'By pitying poor Hugh the Brown.'

'What good would that do him?' she answered.

'None, my love. None at all.'

They stayed on at Caen through the autumn and John declared they would pass Christmas there.

This they did. There was much jollity, feasting, singing, dancing; and the King and the Queen, it was noticed and remarked on, did not leave their beds until dinner time.

'Put Out His Eyes'

RIDING in the midst of John's guards Arthur was quiet and sullen. He missed his mother; he wondered what was happening to Guy; if only his sister Eleanor were with him there would have been some comfort, but here he was alone with strangers, enemy strangers.

He kept going over the events which had led to this humiliating capture. If only they had taken his grandmother and left Mirebeau with her, victory would have been theirs. How could they have been so stupid as to delay? He had to admit it had been his wish and he had been so eager to have his way. He knew that the soldiers had wanted to stay and he had heard it said that when men were fighting they must not be driven too hard all the time. And after a battle must be given some sort of reward. It had been so wonderful taking Mirebeau with his grandmother looking on at the battle and, as he had believed, wishing she had given her support to her grandson Arthur instead of worthless John.

And then suddenly it had all changed. They were the losers and he had had to ride in that dreadful farm cart—a degradation he would never forget.

Before him lay the castle of Falaise—renowned because it was in this town that his great ancestor William the Conqueror had been born. Was that why John had sent him here, that he might be held a prisoner in the old home of that great ancestor?

William de Braose and his wife Matilda, who were waiting to receive him, came out to the courtyard and William held Arthur's stirrup while he alighted.

'I trust the journey was comfortable, my lord,' he said in a soothing and respectful voice which was reassuring to Arthur.

'I could scarcely be comforted in the circumstances,' replied Arthur.

'My wife and I will do all we can for you, my lord, while you are here.'

Matilda de Braose came forward then and curtsied to Arthur. She was a tall woman with strong features and a deep resonant voice.

She said she had had his apartments made ready for him, and had herself made sure that he should lack nothing for his comfort.

It was a better reception than he had hoped for after his treatment from his uncle.

He was taken into the castle and William de Braose led the way up a spiral staircase. Arthur followed and Matilda brought up the rear.

There was his bedchamber. The bars across the narrow window were the only indication that it was a prison.

William de Braose glanced at them apologetically. 'Alas, my lord, we have to hold you under restraint and the King's orders are that there must be guards outside your door and one must sleep in your room. It is with regret that I must carry out these orders for I know how irksome this can be.'

'We want you to understand,' said Matilda, 'that it is our desire to make your stay in Falaise as comfortable as is possible. If there is anything you need, pray ask for it, and if it is within our power to give it to you, that shall be done.'

Arthur thanked them, adding: 'I had not expected such a gracious greeting. 'Tis different from what I have had hitherto from my uncle.'

'There are those of us who regret the need for this, my lord,' said William, 'but it has come about and we must perforce obey orders.'

'I shall remember your kindness to me,' Arthur promised them.

Making sure of his comfort they left him. He threw himself

down on the pallet and wondered what the future held.

He dreamed that he had escaped from Falaise and that he was marching at the head of his armies. His mother was with him and Eleanor was there too and they were saying: 'I knew you would not remain a prisoner long. You will soon be free from prison, Arthur.'

Then he woke up and felt a little better. Of course he would not stay here long. The people of Brittany would never allow it. They were so loyal to their little Duke. It was not in real battle that he had been beaten; it had just happened by ill luck. Had he left Mirebeau the night before, Europe would have been talking of his victory and he would be half way to regaining all that was his by right. He supposed even the Conqueror had had uneasy periods like this one.

No, he must not despair. He was in the hands of good people who were not going to take advantage of his position. He liked William de Braose and his wife.

*　　　*　　　*

William and Matilda were discussing the prisoner.

'He's but a child,' said Matilda.

'Nevertheless, John is afraid of him, and you know what John is like when he is afraid. He is capable of anything.'

'You don't think he'll give you instructions to murder the child?'

'I wouldn't, Matilda, if he did. But between the two of us I would whisper that he is capable of giving such a command.'

'The whole world would revile him.'

'John doesn't consider consequences when certain moods take possession of him.'

'I would Richard had lived.'

'Aye, there you speak for both of us.'

William was thoughtful. He was one of the most ambitious men of the day. His ancestors had been minor barons who had founded the family in the town of Braose in Normandy and had come over with the Conqueror and acquired lands in Sussex, Devon and Wales. He had proved himself a magnificent soldier on the Welsh border where he had earned Richard's approbation and the two had become friends. William had been with Richard on the Continent when the latter had met his death at Chaluz.

William de Braose was a man who was determined to advance; his ambition was to be the foremost of the barons of England. He had considered carefully on Richard's death which side he would be on and had chosen John, not because he liked John—he did not admire him as he had Richard— but because he believed that John had the stronger forces behind him; and when William Marshal had placed himself with John that was the signal for men such as William de Braose to do likewise. He agreed with the Marshal that Arthur would have little chance in England. John had been by far the safer bet; and to have gone against him and failed would have been the end to all his dreams of riches. Matilda had been with him. A strong forceful woman, she was just the wife he needed.

John trusted him, for he had proved himself a good knight to Richard; and it was for this reason that he had put Arthur in his charge at Falaise.

It was an honour and yet William de Braose hoped that it would not continue too long. He did not want to spend his life as a jailer. He had other plans. But at this stage the fact that he had been appointed for the task showed John's confidence in him, and he was gratified at that. With a man like John one could descend from favour to disgrace in a day. He must make sure that that did not happen to him.

At the same time, just in case John should be defeated he would treat Arthur with especial deference so that should the time come when Arthur was in a position to bestow honours he should not think too badly of William de Braose.

Thus it was that Arthur's stay in Falaise was pleasant enough and his guards were the only outward sign that he was a prisoner.

William would play chess with him and Matilda mothered him in a rather domineering way which sometimes, when he felt young and lonely, he did not dislike.

*   *   *

While John was at Caen William des Roches presented himself.

John received him indifferently as though he did not care whether he saw him or not but William des Roches was a man who was well aware of his importance, even if John were not.

John was still puffed up with pride over his success at Mirebeau. He was going to bask in that glory for as long as he could. It was success, William conceded, but it was not one which affected John's entire life and made his Continental possessions safe for ever. It was merely a successful skirmish. John, however, appeared to have sunk back into a life of voluptuousness on the strength of this one mild success.

Like William de Braose, William des Roches was an ambitious man. Both of them realized the importance of being on the winning side, but if the victor was not inclined to honour William des Roches then he would look about him for other means of using his talent.

William des Roches had been the leader of Arthur's army when it had joined forces with Philip of France; but it was not long before des Roches was quarrelling with Philip, for Philip had destroyed one of the castles which had belonged to Arthur because rebels against him had sheltered there.

William des Roches had protested to Philip that the property of his young lord should not be wantonly destroyed, to which Philip had sharply retorted that what was and what was not to be destroyed was a matter for him to decide.

Clearly, des Roches had thought Philip was no ally for him.

In the heat of his temper he had gone to John and said that he would persuade Arthur and Constance to come to terms with him and give up their claim; but he would do this on one condition: that he, William des Roches, was to decide their actions.

John, rejoicing in the rift between William des Roches and Philip had delightedly agreed, and peace was concluded between Arthur and John—an uneasy one it was true, for Constance had been highly suspicious of John's intentions towards her son.

William des Roches had then worked closely with John. When he had heard that the young Duke was at Mirebeau it was William des Roches who had been one of those foremost in leading the attack.

'If we capture Arthur,' he had told John, 'you will, my lord, remember your promises that I should have a say in the young Duke's future.'

John had promised.

And now he had sent Arthur off to Falaise where his jailer would be William de Braose.

William des Roches was incensed when he presented himself to John, though he did his best to hide his mood.

'My lord,' he said, 'it is good news, Arthur is your prisoner.'

John laughed. 'You should have seen the boy's face when I threatened to castrate him. He believed it, you know. 'Twould be amusing to take from him the opportunity of savouring that of which at this time he is ignorant, I believe. His mother kept him under close restraint, and I doubt he had any opportunity to try his talents.'

'The young Duke is well I trust,' said William.

'The would-be-King has become a frightened little boy.'

'Poor child,' said William. 'I have come for your permission to take over the care of him.'

John raised his eyebrows. 'He is well cared for. You need have no qualms in that respect.'

'I am glad of it. I understand he is at Falaise with de Braose.'

'A good man, de Braose,' said John, 'and one I would always trust. He was a good friend to my brother and has been to me. He likes to profit from his service, but what matters that if his profit is mine also.'

'I am prepared to ride to Falaise without delay.'

'There'll be no need, my dear fellow.'

'Sir, I consider there is every need. You have forgotten our pact. I made the peace between you and Arthur; I have fought for you and you'll remember my reward was to be that I was to have the charge of Arthur.'

'Reward!' cried John. 'Men do not generally ask about their rewards when serving me.'

'They think of them none the less, I dare swear,' said des Roches boldly.

Warning lights were shining in John's eyes. William des Roches was aware of them, but important enough he believed to ignore them.

'They are too courteous ... or perhaps too fearful ... to mention them,' said John meaningfully.

'Then perhaps I should be the same,' said des Roches.

'You were always a clever fellow, William. You ever knew which side to jump before it was too late.'

'Thank you, my lord, for that compliment.'

'You are welcome to it,' John nodded to imply he was tired of the subject and William des Roches took the opportunity to retire.

'Be careful,' warned John as William left. 'Mind which way you jump.'

He had misjudged des Roches who was in a position to do a great deal of harm and he was determined to do it.

That day he deserted John and without delay formed a league of the lords of Brittany, marched into action and took certain castles, thus cutting off John's means of communication to the South.

The rot had set in. The success of Mirebeau was seen to be trivial. With the French King ready to seize any opportunity, with the Lusignans raring to avenge the insult on the head of their house in addition to the abduction of Isabella, and with all those who hated John—and they were numerous—waiting for the moment to come when they could successfully rise against him, John's hold on his Continental territories was growing weaker every day.

He could not see it, for he was still revelling in his marriage which after a brief separation seemed like a new beginning to him.

His supporters began to be anxious. It was as though Isabella's beauty and allurements had been bestowed on her by the devil who was determined on John's destruction, for when he rose from his bed—late in the day—he would be languid after the night's performance and disinclined for anything but to wait for the night to come again.

*   *   *

Isabella thought often of Hugh in his dungeons and wondered whether he ever thought of her. It was not her fault; she did hope he understood that. She had had no say in the matter. Her parents and the King had decided for her.

She shivered with horror when rumours reached her of what had happened to the prisoners of Corfe Castle. They were all dead, for food supplies had been cut off from them and they were left to starve to death in the dungeons.

People were whispering that this was not the way to treat honourable prisoners who had merely followed a leader and been loyal to him.

They had revolted and tried to escape and it was then that John had given the cruel order: 'Let them starve. That will teach them to rise against me.'

She would lie in their bed and think of the terrible things that were happening all around them and how powerful John was and how terrible in anger. He was never angry with her although there had been occasions when he was on the verge of it. She used to wonder what would happen if she ever took a lover. She had to admit that she would have liked to. Such was her nature that she could never see a handsome man without picturing him as a lover. Sometimes she would see one of them looking at her and some sort of understanding would flash between them. It would be so easy—a moment's temptation and they might succumb to it. And what if John discovered?

What would he do? In her wilder moments she sometimes thought she was so eager to know that she would run the risk to find out. That would be folly she realized on those occasions when she saw his temper.

She wondered about him. The same thoughts must occur to him.

He was getting anxious now because there was whispering among his knights. William des Roches had not only deserted him but was raising forces against him. So powerful was the man that the complacent mood following Mirebeau had to change, even for John. He had to see what was happening, for he knew that at any moment Philip could be expected to take advantage of the situation.

John was at last persuaded that he must leave Isabella for a few days and see what was happening in his dominions. He reluctantly agreed to do this and sent Isabella to Chinon.

His enemies, who had laughed at his obsession with his wife which exceeded that for his country, decided this was too good an opportunity to miss. What if they captured Isabella? What could they demand from John for her release?

Thus when Isabella was coming into Chinon she heard that a party of rebel barons were waiting to take her prisoner. The news was carried to John at the same time. He was frantic. She must be brought to him at once; never again would he allow her to go from his side.

He was advised against going to her rescue, for it seemed that it might well have been a trap to capture him. Instead, a strong band of his mercenaries rode with all speed to Chinon and on the road encountered Isabella in flight.

They brought her back to John.

He wept with relief when he saw her, picking her up in his arms and carrying her to their bedchamber.

She laughed at his fears.

'What if they had taken me?' she said. 'What would you have done then?'

'I would not have rested until I had brought you back where you belong.'

'What of your country, John? They say that is in danger of being taken from you.'

'They say!' he cried. 'None would dare! In any case I'd soon have it back.'

'You are losing much.'

'I'll get it back.'

'When?'

'In my own good time.'

'When will that be?'

'When you don't distract me from all else.'

'Do you think that will ever come about?'

'It could,' he admitted. 'But not yet.'

'You are unsure of me,' she said.

'I deny that. You want me as much as I want you. I am as important to you are you are to me.'

'Yes, 'tis true but you show you don't feel that.'

'How so?'

'Well, your attitude towards Hugh the Brown for one thing.'

'I do not understand.'

'He is in chains is he not?'

'Yes, where he deserves to be.'

'You keep him prisoner as you keep Arthur prisoner. You have reason to fear Arthur. What reason have you to fear Hugh?'

'*Fear* Hugh!'

'Well, you keep him in chains. Do you do it because once he dared to love me?'

'I do it because he is an enemy.'

'People say that you are afraid of him—that he might try to take me from you.'

'Who says this? I'll cut out their tongues.'

''Tis whispered here and there. There could be too many tongues involved. Would you want a tongueless household? You could stop this foolish talk by freeing him.'

'Free Hugh de Lusignan?'

'Why not? It would show your contempt for him.'

He was thoughtful. 'Petty lord,' he said. 'He wouldn't dare stand against me. He did not like riding in that cart, Isabella. That wounded him more than a hundred lashes would have done.'

'I doubt that not for a moment. If you released him he would see the humiliation at once. He would say "John despises me. If he did not he would never let me go."'

John laughed. 'That's a woman's reasoning.'

''Tis a true one.'

'Why do you care what becomes of him?' he asked suspiciously.

'I don't. I care only that people should not say you fear him.'

She yawned.

'I am weary of that man,' she said, and kissed him.

He responded as ever but he was still thinking of Hugh.

What if he released him? People would say 'he bears no rancour'. But why should he bear rancour? It was Hugh's place to bear that. What if he sent Hugh back to Lusignan? It would be tantamount to saying that what such a petty baron did was of little concern to him.

*   *   *

William Marshal asked for an audience. John received him with warmth. He must always remember that it was the Marshal who made the way to the throne of England easy for him.

William said: 'Is it indeed true, my lord, that you have made certain propositions to the Lusignans?'

'Aye,' said John, ''tis true.'

He was put out by the incredulous wonder in the Marshal's eyes and quickly made excuses for his act.

'There is trouble in the South,' he said. 'I have too many enemies there. I need friends. If the Lusignans would work for me, the entire aspect would be changed.'

'They are your worst enemies, my lord.'

'Enemies can be turned into friends, Marshal. You know that well.'

'Then they are scarcely worth the effort.'

'The Lusignans were once the friends of my House. My brother and they had a great deal in common.'

'My lord, your marriage makes it impossible for the Lusignans ever to be true friends of your House.'

'I think not. That is why I am freeing Hugh the Brown and the others who are my prisoners. I am demanding certain privileges in exchange for my clemency. With them holding the South for me they will stop enemy penetration. I shall demand pledges from them—a castle or two ... some lands. They can hold La Marche for me and my position will be much happier.'

'My lord, I beg of you consider what you are doing.'

'I have considered.'

'These men will be in one of the most important strategic positions in your dominions.'

'Exactly so.'

'And you believe that they will work for you?'

'I shall extract pledges from them. It will show everyone that I fear them not. In a way it is an act of contempt towards Hugh the Brown.'

'I fear he will not consider it so.'

'You are too set in your ways, Marshal.'

'I fear you will regret this, my lord.'

'I'll warrant I'll make you eat those words.'

'I hope to God you do. Nothing would make me happier.'

'You shall, Marshal. You shall.'

'You are firmly fixed in this decision, my lord?'

'I am.'

William the Marshal turned sorrowfully away. Was it true that John's mind was weakening? And were those voluptuous nights sapping his strength—mental as well as physical? Many were saying they did and it would seem they might be right.

The Marshal was of course proved right. No sooner was Hugh de Lusignan free and returned to his estates than he began to break his pledges and store up trouble for John.

'Pledges given to such a man mean nothing,' he declared. 'He is evil and if it is necessary to dissemble to outwit him then so must it be. I shall not rest until John of England goes back to the title he was born with—John Lackland. For only when we have rid ourselves of him will this land be a happy one.'

John fell into a rage. He could see he had been a fool. He began to shout of what he would do to Hugh de Lusignan if he ever fell into his hands again. Obscenities poured from his lips and his eyes seemed as if they would bolt out of his head.

He had been a fool, he knew. He had listened to Isabella's soft words. Why had she been so interested in Hugh? But it might have worked. If Hugh had been a man whom he could have trusted he could have held the South for him.

As it was he was a traitor and with his stirring up trouble in the South and Philip beginning to emerge with a big army behind him John was getting worried.

He thought of Arthur in the castle of Falaise. What if they rescued him and put him in John's place? That was what they were after.

He ought to have thought more about Arthur. Now William des Roches was working against him and the Lusignans were on the warpath, the situation was growing more and more uneasy.

But Arthur was the great menace.

*　　*　　*

Something would have to be done about Arthur. To think that that silly young boy could cause him so much concern! At least there was something in John's favour: Arthur was his prisoner. If he were of less importance how easy it would be to get him out of the way, but if he were to disappear there would be such an outcry that the whole of Europe would rise up in its indignation. The fact that Arthur was little more than a child would be played on; one could imagine wily Philip making the most of that factor. All the same he must take some action.

Preoccupation with the subject of Arthur got between him and his pleasures; he would think of the boy during the night even, imagining someone rescuing him from Falaise and spiriting him away, getting him to Brittany or the Court of France, and with so many enemies ready to go into action all about him, this made uneasy pondering.

He sought about in his mind for someone whom he could trust and his thoughts alighted on Hubert de Burgh. Hubert was a nephew of the Lord of Connaught who had been a steward to Henry II and found favour with him for good service. Thus Hubert had been noticed by Richard I and when John came to the throne and was pretending to think of marriage with the daughter of the King of Portugal. Hubert was a member of the embassy which was sent to that country.

John's behaviour with regard to that embassy had been to say the least cynical, for while his envoys were actually in Portugal he had married Isabella, which could have meant that the outraged King was so angry that he could have vented his wrath on John's servants. Such behaviour was not unknown and the members of the embassy were well aware of it. The King of Portugal, however, incensed as he naturally was by such an insult, was too civilized to lay the blame just out of spite where it did not belong and the embassy was allowed to return to England in safety.

Hubert de Burgh had shown no resentment of this behaviour, John had noticed, which was strange as Hubert was not a meek man. He was one who cared for the welfare of his country and believed it was his duty to save his king but if he disagreed on a point he would not hesitate to show his disapproval. John's father Henry II and his brother Richard I had cherished such men and in his heart John knew that they were right to do so. The Marshal was such another. He had disapproved of giving Hugh de Lusignan his freedom and he had been right. John saw that now, but only in a measure. It did show the world that he bore him no rancour and that meant that he felt himself to be secure in Isabella's regard. The fact that he had paraded Hugh before her in chains had set people wondering if he harboured some jealousy of such a handsome man. At least, he consoled himself, in freeing Hugh he had stopped that rumour. Marshal would say it was folly to allow his personal feelings to affect the holding of his dominions. But Marshal had never—poor man—known the spell of a woman like Isabella.

But he must stop thinking of Isabella and concentrate on State matters. Where was he? Hubert de Burgh! Yes, he was the man. Hubert would do what he thought right for the good of his king and his country.

He sent for Hubert de Burgh, and he made sure that they were absolutely alone and that there was no possibility of anyone's hearing the conversation between them.

'Hubert, my good man, it pleases me to see you.'

'And I to see you, my lord. I trust you are in good health.'

'As you see,' said John. 'I have sent for you because I am disturbed and you are going to serve me now as you have served me and my brother in the past. I know you are a man whom I can trust.'

'Thank you, my lord.'

'You must carry out my orders and know that by doing so you will serve me and your country well.'

'That is my constant aim,' said Hubert sincerely.

'You know full well that the situation here is not a happy one.'

'No, but...' Hubert paused. He could hardly say to the King: It has always been difficult to maintain a hold on the Continental dominions but if the King were to bestir himself, if he were with his soldiers instead of lying in bed all night and half the day with his wife, it could be different.

'There is one whose presence is a constant menace to our safety here,' went on John. 'He's a rallying point for my enemies. The King of France used him most shamefully. I refer to the Duke of Brittany.'

'Indeed yes, my lord. There are these rival factions. But he is your prisoner now and Sir William de Braose and his wife are, I am sure, your trusted servants and will guard the Duke with the utmost care.'

'I know. I know. But I need your help, Hubert. I want you to go to Falaise and take over the guardianship of Arthur.'

'You are displeased with William de Braose?'

'No, no. But I believe it is your turn to serve me there.'

Hubert was puzzled. He could not understand why he should be a so much better jailer than the Braoses.

John said slowly: 'I want Arthur out of my way.'

Hubert looked startled and John went on quickly: 'Nay, I do not wish you to kill the boy. That would be folly.'

'It would also be murder, my lord.'

John frowned. So he was going to have scruples. He had a pious look in his eyes now. John said: 'You have killed at some time have you not?'

'In battle,' said Hubert. 'That was different. I would not commit cold-blooded murder.'

'That is something I would never allow,' said John with

mild piety. He had learned not to act so outrageously as he once had, for now, with the reputation he had, people were immediately suspicious. Now he had to show himself as a man with faults but who was not really bad at heart. 'Why, my good Hubert, you and I would have no rest at nights if we cold-bloodedly murdered a boy—and my own nephew at that.'

Hubert looked a little easier. 'If, my lord, you wish me to go down and take over the guardianship from Sir William de Braose I will do so at once.'

'That's what I wish. Then we have settled this point. Hubert, it grieves me, these battles which go on. You may have thought I have been remiss. Ah, ·do not deny it.' (Hubert had made no attempt to because he most emphatically did believe this.) 'I cannot bear to think of men done to death merely because they happen to serve a certain lord who wants a certain castle ... I think of their wives, their children ... They haunt me, Hubert.'

Hubert was silently thinking: And what of the prisoners in Corfe Castle? Do they haunt you?

'And so,' went on John, 'I wish to end these wars. I want to live in peace with my people. I want my dominions to prosper. You are a good man, Hubert. Am I right in thinking that you want this too?'

'I do, my lord, as any man of good sense must.'

'Then we are of like mind. But this happy state of affairs cannot be while Arthur could escape at any moment and if he did ... think of the enemies who would rally round him. War ... wars ... It would go on for years.'

Hubert nodded sadly.

'If Arthur were no more...' John saw Hubert's lips set firmly in a stubborn line. He wouldn't kill the boy. He would be afraid to, and in a way he was right for what an outcry there would be. It would be almost like the death of Thomas à Becket all over again. John inwardly smirked to picture himself doing the penance his father had done. Not likely, thought John. I'd see them all in hell first. But he went on: 'Arthur exists and while he exists this danger will be there. My plan is to minimize the danger, and in this you will help me. You will because you want peace and prosperity for my people even as I do.'

'I will do anything to bring this about, my lord.'

'My thanks, Hubert. You have given me your word and I know you to be a man of honour who will not go back on it. So ... you will go to Falaise. You will guard Arthur and in due course you will render him powerless to take the throne from me and so restore peace to our troubled lands.'

'How so, my lord?'

'By putting out his eyes and castrating him. No one would want a blind king, and one who could not produce heirs would not be welcome. Therefore we shall reduce Arthur to ... nothing...'

Hubert had grown pale.

John said: 'That's all, Hubert. You may go now. Go to Falaise, take over the guardianship and ... not immediately ... but in due course ... in five or six weeks shall we say you will send me a message. The deed is done. Then you will have served your country well.'

'My lord, I...'

'You will not go unrewarded ... either way.' John laughed. 'You know me well. You can trust me to reward you ... for your services.'

Hubert was like a man in a daze.

He stumbled out of the King's presence.

*　　*　　*

Hubert de Burgh was riding to Falaise.

What can I do? he asked himself. Five or six weeks. Thank God not yet! There is time to think, to see for myself what can be done.

The sly look in his eyes when he talked of reward! He meant if you do not work for me you are working against me. What a monster it was they had put on the throne.

It is true that if Arthur were not there the throne would be safer for John. All those who rose against him used Arthur as a pretext. If Arthur did not exist there would be peace. Thousands of lives would be saved all for the cost of one.

But Arthur was to live. Hubert thought of a poor sightless boy groping his way about a cell; and he was the one to give the orders that this should be done.

How can I? he asked himself as he rode along. And then: How can I not?

In due course he reached the castle.

He was greeted by Sir William de Braose and his forth-right lady.

'Why has the King decided to change Arthur's jailer?' asked Matilda.

'I know not,' replied Hubert for he was wondering why if such an order had been given to him, it should not have been to William de Braose. He wondered what Sir William's re-actions would have been but he dared not ask. He dared not mention the matter. Not that he wanted to. It sickened him so much that he wanted to thrust it out of his thoughts.

'But you are glad to be relieved of the duty?' asked Hubert.

'I like not to be jailer to a royal boy,' said Sir William.

'He's a child at heart,' said Matilda quite fondly. 'I'm beginning to feel he is like one of my own. He needs affection, that boy. I think he could be happy if no one had ever talked to him about a throne and let him play and learn to be a knight like someone of simpler birth.'

'I can see you have been kind to him.'

'Who knows,' said Sir William, 'when the tables might be turned.'

But it was not only this thought, Hubert knew, which had made them care for the boy. There was a tenderness in most people for the young.

He was taken to the rooms in which Arthur was confined, and Sir William presented him.

'This is Hubert de Burgh who is coming to take our place.'

The boy received Hubert with a touch of hauteur. Poor child, thought Hubert, you little know what fate is in store for you. For all his dignity young Arthur was summing up his new jailer and Hubert's heart smote him, for behind the regal manner cowered a frightened boy. How shall I do it? he kept asking himself. How can I do that to such a child...? Could I do it to the veriest villain? Perhaps. But to a boy. God help me.

Two days later the Braoses left.

*   *   *

Hubert felt that if he got to know his captive he might be able to warn him in some way; he might be able to discover something of his nature. He would sit with him and talk and he often found himself staring at those fine blue eyes and imagining what that face would look like without them.

Between Arthur and Hubert there began to grow a friend-ship which Arthur had not felt for the Braoses. Matilda had been too managing, Sir William too aloof. It was not so with Hubert. There was a sadness about him which matched Arthur's own and Hubert's voice was often very gentle, though sometimes it would be harsh as though he were angry with Arthur simply because he existed; then he would seem to repent and be almost womanish in his attitude. Arthur found this intriguing and for the first time since his captivity he forgot his misfortune.

Hubert noticed that he was laughing more readily; that often for hours he would forget he was a captive. Once he said: 'How glad I am you came, Hubert.'

'Why so?' said Hubert, suddenly in one of his gruff moods. 'Was not Sir William de Braose a good castellan?'

'You are more than a good castellan, Hubert. You are a friend. Do you know, Hubert, that's what I haven't had before. A friend. It is hard for someone in my position to have a true friend. One can never be sure that they might not want something. But what can you want from me? Here I am your prisoner ... and since you came, Hubert, there have been times when I have been glad to be here.'

Oh God, help me, prayed Hubert. I can never do it.

'Why there are tears in your eyes, Hubert. I would never have thought that of you.'

' 'Tis a kind of rheum which affects me.'

Arthur laughed aloud and seized him suddenly in a great hug.

'You lie, Hubert de Burgh. You are a man of emotion, and you are glad ... yes you are glad ... that you and I have had this chance to become friends. Confess it.'

'Well, perhaps I am, but...'

Arthur laughed. 'Say no more. Come, I'll beat you at the chess board. I have to have my revenge, you know, for the last time.'

Together they bent over the chess board.

How clear his eyes are, thought Hubert, and he remem-bered horribly mutilated men who had offended their kings or their overlords in some way.

It is necessary for the peace of the country, he said to himself.

'No, no,' he said aloud. 'I will never do it.'

'You are right,' cried Arthur. 'The next move I have you.'
He had lifted clear limpid eyes to Hubert.

When he looks at me like that I know I never will, thought
Hubert de Burgh.

*   *   *

They talked together. Arthur told him of his childhood,
how he had been scurried from one place to another.

'I soon became aware that I was important and I seemed to
be in perpetual danger. I used to think it would have been
better not to be so important.'

'It is always better not to be too important,' agreed
Hubert.

'There are always people trying to take what is yours. What
do you think of my uncle John?'

'Only that he is the King.'

'Which many say he should not be. But you are his man,
Hubert, I know that, so I would not attempt to trick you into
treachery against him. What do you think of him as a man?'

'I know him only as a king.'

'They say he has a wicked temper. I must confess when I
was with him he frightened me a little. I wouldn't admit that
to anyone but you. I have heard terrible stories of him,
Hubert.'

'In his temper he can act impulsively,' said Hubert, 'even
against himself.'

'Perhaps one day he will do himself an injury,' said Arthur
hopefully. 'I hope he never comes here. Do you think he
will?'

'I know not.'

'I wish I could see my sister. I wonder what he has done
with her? Do you think she is a prisoner as I am?'

'I have heard that she is in Bristol Castle in England and
that she is being treated very well there.'

'I am glad of that. Of course he would not fear her unless I
were dead. Oh Hubert, that has just occurred to me. If I died
then by right she would be the next heir to the throne. What
would that mean?'

'You are young, my lord, to speak of death.'

'Yet I am in such a position that it could occur to me at any
time.'

'Not with me here to guard you.'

'That's a comforting thought, Hubert. I tell myself that sometimes. I lie awake and in the night with the darkness all around me, fears come. Sometimes I think, What if men come creeping into my prison to kill me on King John's commands? That could be, for he does not like me to be alive. I am a threat to him. So many people would rather see me in his place. Then I think: It's all right. Hubert is here and he will protect me.'

Hubert nodded. 'Yes,' he said, 'I will protect you.'

'So then I go to sleep and in the morning I just laugh at my night fears. It's in the night that I like to remember that you are not far off. But I do think a great deal of Eleanor. She is older than I am, you know, and when we were little she used to look after me. I liked being with her then. I wish they had put us together. It would have been pleasant if we could have both been here in Falaise with you, Hubert. You would like Eleanor. She is serene—more so than I, I think, but that is doubtless because she is older. She was never jealous because more was made of me ... being a boy. My mother was always stressing how important *I* was. But it does bother me a little that she is the second in the line of succession. If it was fair, of course, she would really come before John.'

'The direct succession is not considered so important,' Hubert pointed out. 'Although the people like a King's son to follow him, if that son is not worthy then they would rather have the next in line. And as your sister is a girl I don't think there would be any thoughts of putting her on the throne.'

'No, I suppose not. I am the true heir and my sons will be next. I'd love to have sons. I wonder what my sons will be like?'

Hubert closed his eyes. I shall never do it, he thought. Each day it becomes more difficult.

'What ails you, Hubert? Are you tired today?'

'Nay. I am not tired.'

'You are in one of your sad moods. Cheer up. I like to see you gay, Hubert.'

And so it went on; and each day they seemed to grow a little closer to each other.

*   *   *

It was hardly likely that the Bretons would remain passive while their Duke was a prisoner. It was soon known that he was in the castle of Falaise and reports came to the castle that parties of Bretons were riding into Normandy the object of each being to have the honour of rescuing their Duke.

Arthur was excited, for Hubert could not resist telling him the news. They stood at a window together looking out on the road.

Arthur said: 'Why, Hubert, I think you are hoping they will come and take the castle.'

'How can you say such a thing?'

'I know you well. I know your moods. I can almost *feel* your excitement. What would happen if they came here?'

'There would be a siege.'

'And you would be on one side I on the other—you holding them out, I longing for them to break in. Oh, Hubert, what a pity! You and I should be together ... on the same side. I hope we shall be one day. When I gain what is mine by right, you will be my chief adviser perhaps. We shall always be together. You will be my best friend and I shall always remember these days because, Hubert, since you came everything is different.'

Hubert did not trust himself to speak. He pretended to be scanning the horizon.

But no Bretons reached the castle. This was one occasion when John really did arouse himself and he went into action to make sure that they were turned out of Normandy.

He sent a message to the castle, and when Hubert heard that the King's emissary had come and would speak with him alone his heart sank because he guessed what the orders would be.

He received him in his bedchamber and shut the door so that none could hear.

'What news?' he asked.

'The King's orders are for your ears alone. The Duke of Brittany is to be fettered.'

'Fettered! He is safe enough here. I have guards. I watch over him myself.'

'The King's orders. There is another. The King says that you are to do your duty as commanded by him. He expects news without delay.'

Hubert bowed his head.
As he feared the time had come.

*   *   *

'Must I wear these fetters, Hubert?'
'It is the King's orders that you should.'
'But I didn't before.'
'No, but since then, as you know, your supporters have been trying to reach you.'
'So the King is afraid of them?'
'It would seem so.'
'To be fettered so! It is humiliating for a prince.'
'For all men,' replied Hubert. 'They have their feelings just like princes.'
'But the higher a man is in rank the deeper the humiliation.'
'I'll tell you what,' said Hubert. 'When you and I are together we will undo the fetters.'
'You don't like to see me chained any more than I like it myself, Hubert.'
'Of course I don't.'
'Because at heart, Hubert, you care for my welfare, do you not? I believe you hoped my friends would come and take me away.'
There was a lump in Hubert's throat.
'You did. You did,' cried Arthur. 'Confess it.'
'For your sake, yes.'
'Oh dear, dear Hubert. And let me tell you this. I thought: If they take me what of Hubert? John will be so angry. What will he do to Hubert? For he will blame him. I couldn't bear that Hubert. He is such a wicked man. He does terrible things to those who anger him. I would take you with me, Hubert. Yes, I would. I had thought it all out. I was going to tell them. Bind Hubert de Burgh. Make him my prisoner. That was what I was going to do. I would have changed our positions ... and then we could have stayed friends.'
'But it did not come to pass,' said Hubert.
And to himself he said: Oh God, I wish it had.

*   *   *

There was another messenger at Falaise. He too came from

the King. He wished to know if Hubert de Burgh had a message for the King.

'The time has not yet come,' said Hubert.

'I was told to say that the King expects to have news soon. He grows impatient with delay.'

'He shall have news soon,' said Hubert, and he stood at a turret window watching the messenger ride away.

He knew now that the moment had come. All he had to do was give the order and merely stand by and see it carried out.

He shut himself in his bedchamber. He knelt and cried out to God to show him a way out of this terrible situation in which he found himself. But there was no way. He tried to persuade himself. John was right up to a point. There could not be peace while Arthur lived—but if he were a poor maimed creature no one, not even the Bretons, could wish to see him on the throne.

Better for the boy to die, a thousand times better.

There was no way of course. That was clear. He had no recourse but to carry out the King's orders.

He sent for two attendants, loutish men who would perform any deed for money. He knew that they had been used before for brutal tasks and found a certain pleasure in performing them.

They would do their work and do it quickly which was best.

He spoke to them and told them what the King's orders were.

' 'Tis so, my lord,' cried one. 'And not surprised am I. I've been waiting for it.'

'When the deed is done,' said Hubert, 'you two will go from here. You will not mention a word of what has happened. You know the punishment for such as you who think fit to chatter.'

'We'll be silent as the grave, my lord. When should the work be done?'

'Soon,' said Hubert firmly. 'Let us have done with it.'

'We'll do it with the irons, my lord.'

Hubert was shivering.

'Go to,' he said turning away. 'Be ready and wait upon my call.'

He went to his room; he knelt and prayed for strength.

'I would I had died before I were called upon to do this,'

he whispered. Then he rose and went into that room which was now a prison cell and which he feared would shortly be the scene of the greatest tragedy of his life. It would haunt him for ever more, and make him wish he had never been born to play a part in it.

'Hubert 'tis you then. Welcome. Come, take off my fetters. Is it to be chess? Why, what ails you?'

'My boy, I feel unwell today.'

'You are ill? What is it? Tell me. Something terrible has happened. They are going to take you away. I shall never see you any more.'

Hubert sat down and covered his face with his hands.

'It's true,' cried Arthur. 'I shan't allow it, Hubert. Let's run away from here, together. We'll escape to Brittany. High honours shall be yours. We won't worry about the crown and John and all that. We'll just be friends as we have been here.'

Hubert did not answer.

'Hubert, Hubert look at me.'

He pulled Hubert's hands from his face and stared at him aghast.

'I never saw such sorrow in a face,' said Arthur.

Hubert put him from him and stood up. He clapped his hands and the two men came in with the brazier and the irons.

'What means this?' cried Arthur shrilly.

Hubert did not answer. The tears had started to fall down his cheeks.

'Oh God have mercy on me. Oh God help me. Hubert, they are going to burn out my eyes.'

One of the men said: 'Ready, my lord?'

'Not yet,' said Hubert quickly. 'One moment yet.'

Arthur had fallen to the floor; he clutched at Hubert's legs. 'Hubert, my friend Hubert,' he cried. 'You can't let them do this to me. You are my *friend*.'

'Arthur...'

'Yes, Hubert, yes?'

'These are the King's orders. I am his man. I must obey.'

'Not this, Hubert. You could never do this. If you did you would kill yourself because you couldn't bear it. You'd jump from the tower and take me with you ... because neither of us could bear to live ... like that.'

'Mayhap you are right. I could not endure it ... but do it I must.'

'You cannot ... Hubert. You cannot.'

'The irons are hot, my lord,' said one of the men. 'Shall we bind him now? 'Tis hard to do when they struggle.'

Hubert put up a hand to silence them. He knelt beside Arthur on the floor. Arthur took his hand and lifted his face.

'Look at my eyes, Hubert. Do not flinch. Look at them and remember that we love each other. You cannot let them do this. I would never let them do it to you. I promise you that. If they tried to I would kill them rather. Not my eyes, Hubert ... anything but my eyes. Have you ever thought what it would be like never to see the sky again and the grass and the walls of a castle, the flint glistening in the sun? Have you thought what it would be like never to look into the face of a friend, to see him smile, to see his eyes light up at the sight of you? You couldn't rob me of that, Hubert, could you?'

'I must,' cried Hubert. 'I must.'

'You *could* not. I know you well. You will not, Hubert.'

How long the silence seemed to go on. Then Hubert stood up. His voice rang out clear and strong. 'Take away those things. We shall not be using them.'

The men trained to obey without question immediately started to remove the brazier.

They had gone and the silence went on and then suddenly Arthur and his jailer were sobbing in each other's arms.

*　　　*　　　*

'We must think now how best to act,' said Hubert.

'Oh you are indeed my friend,' cried Arthur.

'We are in danger; you must know that well. Thank God I was the one given this foul task. I was sad once because it was given to me but if it had been given to another...'

Arthur shivered. 'None but you would have been brave enough to defy John,' said Arthur proudly.

'Let us not forget that we have defied him. He must not know.'

Arthur clung to Hubert's arms. 'I do fear him, Hubert. I boasted and said I didn't. But I do. I do. I believe Satan is kinder than he is and all the devils in hell less cruel.'

'You may well be right. I shall have to tell him the deed is done, for he will be sending soon to know that it is.'

'What if he comes to look at me? He will. I know he will. He will not be able to resist taunting me.'

'I had thought of that. I must say that you died while it was being done. We must find a hiding place for you, where you can live in peace until the time shall come when you can be free.'

'Where, Hubert, where?'

''Twere safer in this castle for a while. If I can remain here ... it's custodian ... and why should I not? ... we can keep our secret.'

'We will do it, Hubert.'

'And I will say that you are dead and buried.'

'Where should I be buried?'

'I must think of that. But in the meantime I must bribe those ruffians.'

'Can you trust them?'

'By paying them well and threatening them with what I will have done to them if they betray us. They are safe enough, for no one will know that they were here. It is a good plan and I think it will work. I have good friends in a Cistercian Abbey not far from here. They will help me in this and I shall tell the King that I had you buried quietly there.'

'We can do it, Hubert,' cried Arthur excitedly.

'We must do it,' replied Hubert.

*   *   *

In one of the lower rooms of the castle to which only Hubert had the key, Arthur spent his days. Hubert visited him frequently and only a few of his trusted friends knew that the boy still lived.

A coffin said to contain the body of the young Duke of Brittany had been taken from the castle to the Cistercian Abbey and there buried in a secret place.

Hubert decided that he could not trust an account of what had happened to the messenger and would see the King himself.

John received him with alacrity.

'What news,' he cried. 'Is the deed done then?'

''Tis done, my lord.'

'So now he is without his eyes and the outward sign of manhood.'

'My lord during the operation the boy has died.'

John caught his breath. 'How was this? The men were clumsy.'

'The boy struggled. It often happens like this ... He did not survive.'

John nodded. 'Fate has taken a hand then,' he said. 'What of his body?'

'Buried, my lord, in a secret grave.'

'So be it,' said John.

'My lord, I suggest it would be better if I returned to Falaise and lived there quietly for a while until the noise which this will inevitably make blows over.'

John nodded. 'Go back to Falaise. It would be well to keep Arthur's death a secret for a while.'

'I will do so, my lord, with all speed.'

So far, so good. How long can I hope to keep the truth secret? he wondered. And then what will become of me? Oddly enough he didn't care. He was in a state of exultation which he had not known since the day John had ordered him to put out Arthur's eyes.

The Body in the Seine

THE news that Arthur was dead was spreading through Brittany and the Bretons were forming an army to come against John whom they suspected of murdering their Duke.

Arthur had been John's prisoner; he had been in the charge of John's men; and now it was being said that he was dead and they wanted to know how he had died.

In the castle of Falaise Hubert heard the news and in the secret chamber where Arthur now lived he told him about it. The excitement of the adventure was wearing off and Arthur was having to face the difficulties of living in cramped quarters. He could only emerge from his room by night when he might go out on to the parapet, ever watchful that he might be seen. Hubert could not visit him as frequently as he would have wished for he feared to attract attention by doing so. The days were therefore long for Arthur and the nights were terrifying, for he often dreamed that he was bound fast while cruel men came to him with hot irons in their hands.

He longed for the coming of Hubert and knowing this Hubert could not resist taking certain risks, and he came more often than he knew he should.

He told him that the people of Brittany were incensed and that they were determined to avenge him.

'I knew they would,' cried Arthur. 'They will march against John—and what joy there will be when they know that I am alive and unmaimed. I shall never forget what I owe to you, Hubert.'

'Let us pray,' replied Hubert, 'that one day you will be at peace with your own people.'

'I shall never forget what my uncle would have done to me. He is a wicked man, Hubert. That he takes my crown I understand, for many ambitious men would have done that, but to give orders to put out my eyes—that I shall never forget. He is bound for hell surely, Hubert, and may it be that the gates of that place soon open to receive him.'

'Let us think,' said Hubert, 'of your future rather than his. If the Bretons are successful the King of France will no doubt join them. Then it may well be that you will be free.'

'Freedom. I dream of it when I am not dreaming of ... other things. It seems to me the most beautiful thing on earth ... better than a crown ... not better than one's eyes though. Everything I would barter for them, even freedom. Now I see things differently, Hubert. I notice the birds and the trees. The sky was beautiful at dawn and as I watched the sun rise I said: But for Hubert I would not have seen that. It has all become precious to me, Hubert. I see things which I wouldn't have noticed before.'

'Do not speak of it,' said Hubert. 'You unman me.'

'I love you unmanned, Hubert, for methinks that unmanned you are a better man than you could ever be cold and strong and in command of your emotions.'

Thus they talked and each time when Hubert locked him in his room and carefully put the keys on the belt which never left him he thought: But how long can this last?

When he was alone he salved his conscience because he was a loyal man at heart and he had disobeyed his king. He would never have thought of disobeying Richard but John was not Richard. He had assured himself that the Bretons, believing Arthur to be dead and themselves without a leader, would have no heart for the fight. He had promised himself that they would reason: Arthur is dead and therefore the cause for conflict is removed. Without Arthur, John's claim to the throne is the right one.

As if they would. They wanted revenge for murder. So they were on the march. The King of France expressed himself outraged by the death of the Duke of Brittany—so timely for some—and wanted to know how he had died. Here was an excuse for marching against John. Philip was rousing John's enemies against him. He had usurped the Crown of England

and the coronet of Normandy, said Philip, but these were the crimes of an ambitious man; whereas the murder of a man's own nephew—little more than a child—was the work of a barbarous criminal.

John shrugged aside the threats. He was following his practice of spending half the day in bed. There were more exciting ways of passing the time than fighting wars, he said.

There were times though when his rages got the better of him and then he cursed Arthur. Why did the boy have to die? he demanded. What a weakling he must have been. Even in such a moment when he was out of control he did not mention the operation which he had ordered should be carried out and under which he presumed the boy had died.

If Arthur was alive, he said, there would not be all this trouble.

Hubert realizing this, decided that he could salve his conscience by telling the King that Arthur was alive and well. If this could be known, if he could be seen, the trouble would cease. He knew that he could not keep Arthur's existence a secret for ever and this was a good way of letting it out.

He left Falaise and went to see the King, who was at that time residing in Château Gaillard, the great fortress not far from Rouen. No doubt it gave him comfort to be there at such a time, for this château built by Richard Coeur de Lion had been his darling; it was said to be the most formidable fortress in Europe. John would be safe there no matter who came against him.

Hubert was received immediately by John, who remembered that the last time they had met Hubert had had instructions to put out Arthur's eyes.

He shouted at him: 'Clumsy creatures. What have they done? Cannot they perform a simple operation ... without bringing this about?'

'My lord, I have news for you,' said Hubert. 'I would have you know that anything I have done has been in my service to you. Your orders were not carried out in the castle of Falaise. Arthur still lives.'

John opened his eyes wide and a sly smile played over his face. ''Tis true then. Now I can show him to my enemies ... Oh but...'

John was thinking of what Arthur would be looking like ... two horrible inflamed sockets where his eyes had been.

His poor castrated body sent back to Brittany. This would be worse than death.

'My lord,' said Hubert, 'I knew that you would need to produce Arthur and that if you could not there would be trouble, so thinking of your needs I did not have his eyes put out nor his body tampered with in any way. He is your prisoner still ... and as he was when you took him.'

There was a moment of hesitation. Hubert did not know what his fate would be. The King might order that he be dragged away and that done to him which he had ordered for Arthur. Such action would seem to John a just and to him amusing reward. But John had been frightened of the armies rising against him and the thought of being able to produce an Arthur who had suffered no harm was just what he needed.

He said: 'You've done well, Hubert. Let it be known that the boy is safe and well. Where is he?'

'At Falaise Castle still,' said Hubert. 'But living quietly.'

'In hiding?' John laughed. 'You crafty old fox, Hubert.'

Hubert allowed himself to smile. 'And trust I shall always be so in your service, my lord.'

John was still laughing. 'Go back to Falaise. Produce the boy. Let all see that he is alive and well. Ride out into the town with him, making sure he is well guarded. I want the whole world to know what calumnies the Bretons and that old rogue Philip have uttered against me.'

Hubert lost no time in returning to Falaise.

*   *   *

Arthur was delighted. He rode out in the streets of Falaise with Hubert beside him, laughing and talking gaily with his friend.

'Do not fear that I will try to escape,' he said. 'I would not go without you. I shall wait for the day when you and I, Hubert, escape to Brittany together.'

Hubert did not think that could ever be but he did not tell Arthur; he was so pleased to see the boy enjoying his freedom, pointing out the beauties of nature which he had scarcely noticed before, occasionally putting his hands to his eyes when Hubert knew he was offering a silent prayer for their preservation.

*   *   *

John and Isabella, lying in bed during the mornings in Château Gaillard, talked idly of trivial matters though sometimes John mentioned State affairs.

Much as he was still enamoured of her, he had not been faithful to her. On the occasions when they had not been together—which were not many—he had found opportunities for sporting with other women. He had reminded himself that as King he had a right to do as he pleased and if Isabella objected she should be told this. But when he was with her he preferred these peccadilloes should be kept a secret from her and he warned his followers that any who tattled of them might find himself without a tongue to repeat the offence.

She knew of course what he had planned to do to Arthur and she had deplored it. Arthur was a pleasant-looking youth and she did not care to think of handsome men being maimed in any way. She enjoyed life and she liked to think of others doing the same. She was good-hearted as long as being so did not curb her pleasures. She disliked that viciousness which she was discovering more and more in John and she often thought of the different life she might have had with Hugh de Lusignan.

Now as they lay in bed John mentioned Arthur and how Hubert had disobeyed his orders.

'And rightly so,' said Isabella.

'I am not sure of that. True I am glad he did not carry them out but when I give orders I expect them to be obeyed.'

'And are mightily glad when they are not—since they are the wrong orders.'

He twirled a piece of her hair round his finger.

'I don't know that I shouldn't show him that I won't be flouted.'

'He did what he did for your sake. He thought it was right, and so it proved.'

'You seem to be much concerned about his fate.'

'I like thanks to be given where they are due.'

'And you do not forget that he is a handsome man and young Arthur is a pretty boy, eh?'

'I cannot see that that is at issue.'

'Can you not? I can. You have a fondness for attractive men.'

'Is that not obvious since I have married the King?'

He wound a strand of her hair round her throat.

'Do not have too much fondness for others,' he said.

'Why should I when I have one?'

'Some like variety.'

'As you do?' she asked.

He was wary. What had she discovered? Nothing, he was sure. They would all be too much afraid to tell her. And if she did know she would be angry and not hesitate to show it. He did not want that. She was still the best, still the only one he really wanted. It was strange that after so long she could still excite him. He reckoned that they would have to have children soon. That was a measure of how his feelings were changed towards her. In the beginning he had not wanted her body changed; he had wanted to keep that virginal look which so excited him. But nature was changing her. She was as beautiful as ever—most would say more so. But she was no longer the child she had been in the first year.

'I found the perfect mistress and that she is my wife gives me complete satisfaction.'

'That is well then,' she said.

'Well? Just well?'

'It means that I do not have to vent my rage upon you.'

'You think I would fear that?'

'You would, John.'

'Nay,' he said, suddenly angry. 'I'd have you know that I am King and do what I will.'

'It might well be that I would let you know that I am Queen,' she answered.

'What mean you by that?'

'That what the King may do so may the Queen.'

' 'Tis not so. By God, if you were unfaithful to me I'd make you regret it.'

'As I would if you were to me.'

'How could you do that?'

'There are a hundred ways which it is not beyond a woman's wits to discover. But let us not fret about what is not.'

He was relieved. She did not know.

He started to talk about Arthur and it suddenly occurred to him that it would be a good idea if he went to Falaise to see the boy.

*   *   *

When a messenger arrived at Falaise Castle to inform Hubert that the King was on the way he was filled with apprehension. He went at once to Arthur and told him.

Arthur turned pale. 'Why should he come here, Hubert?'

'We shall soon know,' replied Hubert. 'In the meantime we must prepare for him.'

'I hate him,' said Arthur fiercely.

'Keep control of your feelings.'

'I'll try, Hubert. But it is not easy when you hate someone as I hate him. When I think of what he would have done to me...'

'Do not think of it.'

'I can't help it, Hubert. I think of it constantly.'

'He will not harm you ... yet,' said Hubert. 'He may well be coming in peace. It may well be that he will want you to ride out with him to show the people that you are alive and well.'

'I will never ride in amity with him.'

'I beg of you take care,' said Hubert.

But by the time John arrived at the castle Arthur had worked himself up into a frenzy of apprehension and hatred. How could he help it towards someone who had wanted to rob him of his precious eyes and had actually commanded it to be done?

I will hate him for ever, thought Arthur.

The King came to the castle and strode in arrogantly. There was something about Falaise which threatened to subdue him. He supposed it was because it was in Falaise that his great ancestor the Conqueror was born. In these cold stone-walled rooms the young William had played at the skirts of his low-born mother. All his life William the Conqueror had been held up as an example. Even his father had talked of him with awe. Consequently John had never liked Falaise. He seemed to sense the old man's disapproval and he imagined what he would say if he could see the state of Normandy today and be aware of how John lay in bed half the morning with his seductive wife. Great William had never understood such emotions. He would have been very impatient with them.

But what was he doing, thinking so of one who was long dead? He was alive and he was the King of England and Duke of Normandy and so he intended to remain and if he were not the great soldier his ancestor was, it might be that he was more subtle.

He had come to see Arthur and to talk to him. He would try to make the boy see reason. That was the object of his visit.

Hubert de Burgh received him. A good servant, although he did take the law into his own hands. He would give him a reprimand for that, but Hubert would say he did it to serve him and he would have to accept that, because it certainly had. If Arthur had really been dead, all hell would have been let loose over Europe. If he had been blinded and castrated what howls of rage there would have been. No, it was not good policy to have ordered those things to be done—though it would have served the ambitious boy right had it happened to him.

'Well Hubert,' he said, 'I have called and will stay here for a night before being on my way. And while I'm here I must see this boy, this nephew of mine who is causing me so much trouble and see if I can talk him into good sense.'

'He is coming now to greet you,' said Hubert.

And there was Arthur. He stood still for a moment looking at his uncle. Oh God, prayed Hubert, do not show your hatred so clearly, Arthur.

John saw it for he laughed aloud and went forward with outstretched hands.

'Nay, nephew, do not kneel.'

Arthur raised well-marked eyebrows, for he had had no intention of kneeling to one whose rank he considered but for usurpation did not equal his own. For in his opinion he Arthur was King and Duke whereas John, if he lost the crown which he had usurped, would be a mere Count.

'I have to see you, nephew,' went on John. 'There is much we have to say to each other. But we will talk later. After we have eaten, for I smell venison and I am hungry. Good Hubert, being aware of my coming, I see has prepared for me.'

Hubert said he would have them hurry in the kitchens so that the King did not have to wait long for his meal.

He himself conducted John to the best of the bedchambers and Arthur was left in the hall looking after his uncle with undisguised hatred.

In the bedchamber the King turned to smile at Hubert.

'Methinks my nephew gives himself certain airs,' he said.

'He is but young, my lord, and has much to learn.'

'Let us hope that he has the good sense to learn his lessons,' said John.

He feasted in the hall and complimented Hubert on the venison. He drank freely of the wine and looked about him for the comeliest of the women with whom he would spend the night.

But first he must talk with Arthur for he did not wish to linger in Falaise.

At last he and Arthur were alone together. Arthur's heart was beating wildly. All he could think of was: He gave the order. He commanded them to put out my eyes.

He would remember it always, he knew, whenever he was in the presence of his uncle John. To think this man was his father's brother and he had ordered that that should be done to him! Hatred filled Arthur's heart. Hubert had warned him: Take care. Do not offend him. Think before you speak. But all Arthur could think of was: He ordered that they should put out my eyes and but for Hubert it would have been done.

'Now, nephew,' said John, 'it is time you and I understood each other.'

'I think I understand you well,' replied Arthur coolly.

'Then we shall be able to talk good sense. It is no use your thinking that you have a right to what is mine. You are but a boy. You have to grow up.'

'I *have* grown up, in the last months.'

'You have grown a little older, but I want you to stop this foolish conflict. Thousands of men have died and more will because of your obstinacy unless you withdraw your claim to England, Normandy and all that is mine. Promise me you will. If you did that doubtless we should be very good friends.'

'There is that between us uncle which prevents that.'

'Then by God's ears let us remove it.'

'That is not possible.'

'And why not? Why not?'

'Because what you have is mine and I shall not cease to claim it.'

'You talk like a fool. Haven't you seen what happened to you when you made war on me? You thought to capture your grandmother and look what that brought you to.'

He saw the shiver pass through the boy's body and he smiled grimly.

'You see, my dear nephew, you have much to learn. Give me your word that you will give up your claim to the crown. I will have a treaty drawn up and we will both pledge our solemn word. When that is signed and sealed you shall go back to Brittany. How's that?'

'I could not sign away my birthright.'

John sighed elaborately. He felt too drowsy to lose his temper; he was thinking of the woman who would be waiting for him in his bedchamber if she did not wish to displease him, and he did not think she would. He wanted to be with her and he was impatient with foolish young boys.

'If I had no legitimate son then the crown would go to you,' said John. 'Is that not just?'

' 'Tis most unjust that you should hold that which is mine.'

John yawned. 'Think of what this means, nephew. Remember what happened to you at Mirebeau. You were my prisoner then. You do not want to remain my prisoner all your life, do you?'

'That would not be. My people would never allow it.'

'I see you are in a stubborn mood and I waste my time in trying to make you see reason. I shall leave here tomorrow.' Arthur could not help showing his relief and John smiled. 'I see that fact does not cause you any great sorrow,' he went on. 'But when I go I want you to think very clearly. You have been my prisoner. It has not been a very happy experience for you.'

Arthur cried out: "I know full well what you intended to do to me.'

For a moment John's lazy mood dropped from him. His eyes flashed and he cried: 'Remember it. Think of it when you consider what I have said to you this night. It would be well for you, nephew, if you set aside your claim to what is mine and were content with your dukedom of Brittany. I will leave you now to your thoughts.'

John rose and went to his bedchamber.

He forgot about Arthur but the next day he remembered.

*   *   *

A week after John's visit to Falaise the King's messengers

arrived at the castle. There were orders for Hubert de Burgh.

The King was pleased with his custodianship of the castle and wished him to remain there. He had a fancy though to remove his nephew and shortly after the arrival of this messenger, guards would be coming to the castle to take Arthur to another castle of the King's choosing.

When Hubert read the message he felt sick with grief. So he and Arthur were going to be parted. How much had John guessed? Had he believed that Hubert had spared Arthur's eyes because he felt he would serve his king better by doing so or had it been out of affection for the boy? Arthur did not hide his feelings well. He knew he had shown his hatred and fear of John; he would most certainly have betrayed his affection for Hubert. This John would think was the reason why the boy kept his eyes.

It would amuse John to separate them. He did not see why if Arthur would not do as he wished he should do anything for Arthur.

'What is it?' asked Arthur fearfully. 'Is it orders from John?'

Hubert knew that he could not keep the news from him for long and in any case it was better for him to be prepared.

''Tis ill news indeed. He is going to separate us.'

'No, Hubert, no. I won't hear of it.'

Hubert said: 'It won't be for long.'

'Where am I going. Hubert?'

'I have not been told. But he is sending a guard for you. It could arrive at any time.'

'Oh Hubert, let us get away from here. Let us go to Brittany.'

'We could not do it, Arthur. The King has set guards to watch over you. He knows that I have an affection for you and fears what I might do. We should never be allowed to escape from here. We should be caught, imprisoned and then you can imagine what would happen to us.'

'I would I could kill him,' cried Arthur.

'Hush, do not speak so. The best plan is to go calmly with his guards. I will discover where you are.'

'And we will escape to Brittany,' said Arthur.

'Who knows?' murmured Hubert, for there could be no harm in letting the boy hope.

'I know why he is sending me away,' said Arthur. 'He tried

to make me promise to give up my claims and when I would not and showed him that I hated and despised him he told me to think of it and remember my imprisonment. He was thinking of my eyes, Hubert. I could see that in his.'

'Take care, Arthur.'

'I will.'

'He will not dare to harm you,' said Hubert comfortingly. 'We have seen that. He has learned his lesson. He knows what would happen if he did. So you will be safe ... though his prisoner.'

'I shall watch for you, Hubert. You must come to me.'

'I shall try,' said Hubert.

It was only a few hours later when the guards arrived in Falaise.

From a turret Hubert watched the departure until he could see them no more. Then he turned away and went mournfully to his bedchamber.

My poor unfortunate child, he thought. Would you had been born a shepherd or a swineherd. What will become of you now?

*   *   *

Arthur did not know where they were taking him. He held his head high but he was sick at heart. He had not dared look at Hubert at the parting. It would have been too shameful if he had burst into tears. He knew too that Hubert—that dear good saviour—felt as he did, so Arthur tried to think of his hatred of his uncle and so stifle the emotion which his love for Hubert aroused in him.

They came along by the river—and there was the Château Gaillard, such a castle as he had never seen before. There had never been such a fortress. How formidable it looked in the sunshine.

The man who rode beside him said: 'See, my lord, King Richard's Saucy Castle. None could take it. That was what the King intended.'

They were reminding him of course of the might of King John. I hate him, hate him, he thought. He tried to rob me of my eyes.

And at last they came to a city that from a distance looked like a mighty castle, for it was enclosed in a strong stone wall and there was the river flowing past on its way to the sea.

He knew that he had come to Rouen, the capital city of Normandy, which should, he reminded himself, be his if he had his rights.

He must remember Hubert's words. He must try not to offend them. Never never must he forget what could so easily have happened to him in the castle of Falaise.

He was taken into the castle—the stronghold of Norman kings almost since the days when Rollo first came to Normandy. He was treated with respect. His apartments were not like a prison but there were guards outside his door. Still it was a comfort to have some freedom. He might go to the battlements at the top of the tower and look down on the city, on the housetops and the river and the city wall. If Hubert were here it would be bearable, he thought.

Each day he went to those battlements and looked hopefully to see if riders came this way. He dreamed of plans which could be carried out—of Hubert's coming to him and carrying him off in a sack as he had heard the Seneschal of Richard the Fearless had done in years gone by, long before the birth of William the Conqueror and himself.

Life was only bearable if he passed the days dreaming of escape. Sometimes he thought a party of Bretons would storm the castle. There would be a siege and he would creep out to the besiegers and place himself at their head. What joy that would be when he was reunited with his own people. But he liked best the fancy that it was Hubert who came to rescue him.

But the days passed and neither the Bretons nor Hubert came to Rouen.

*   *   *

A visitor did in due course come to the castle of Rouen.

John could not get out of his mind the memory of that boy in the castle of Falaise and now at Rouen. The manner in which his eyes had flashed, the haughty way in which he held himself, showed that he was well aware of what had been planned for him in the castle of Falaise. He would remember it all his life; it would be spoken of. Doubtless if he were free he would find some means of communicating what had happened to Philip of France. John could well imagine what use Philip would make of such information.

Arthur was a menace—the greatest menace of his life

really. What a pity he hadn't died at birth.

John wondered how many people knew that he had given the order to put out the boy's eyes and castrate him. Hubert knew. Oddly enough he believed he could trust Hubert. There was a nobility about the man which John could recognize; there was loyalty too and Hubert would not work against the crown even though he did not agree with what was being done. Somehow that boy had moved him and that was why he had saved his life. Hubert would not betray his king though ... not unless he thought it was for the good of the country. His father had always said: If you have a good man respect him, even though at times he may speak against you, for if he speaks from honesty and honour he is a man to grapple to you for he is worth all the flatterers in the kingdom. Although John hated to be crossed and that drove him into a frenzy of rage, when he was calmer he realized the truth of this. So he would hold nothing against Hubert de Burgh.

But he was glad he had separated him from Arthur. He must come to some terms with the boy. If he could only delude him into signing some document in which he would renounce all claims to the possessions which were now in John's hands he could with a few strokes of the pen deprive the Bretons of their reason for waging war on him.

He was tired of war. It seemed a king's life must be spent in this futile occupation. The victory of today was the defeat of tomorrow and castles passed from hand to hand as the battle swayed.

There were more interesting ways of spending one's time. It was aggravating to have to leave one's bed in the early hours of the morning to be on the march, to be prepared to storm some castles, to spring to the defence of another. It wearied him. Then there was the possibility of being struck by an arrow. Three Kings of Britain had fallen in that way: Harold at Hastings, Rufus in the forest and Richard at Chaluz—and all three in less than one hundred and fifty years. Why should a man put himself into such danger when he would have a very comfortable life? As John saw it a king should travel through his possessions being respected and honoured where he went; there should be feasting, singing, dancing at the various castles which he visited; there should be women only too eager to share his pleasures. He would of course prefer to have Isabella with him, and they would lie abed until dinner time as they used to. It was not asking a great deal, only what he thought of as a kingly existence. But there were those who stood in his way of enjoying it.

Chief of these was Philip of France: he would never stop trying to make himself lord of all French territory. It was three hundred years since Rollo had taken Normandy, and yet Philip still dreamed of getting it back, and he would go on trying to do so as the French kings had for all that time. There was nothing he could do about Philip; but he could do something about his nephew and if he could prevent his continually harping on his claims, if he could render him powerless, he would have removed one cause of conflict.

He decided that now Arthur was at Rouen and Hubert de Burgh was not there to caution him and advise, he would go and see him. So John set out for Rouen.

It was the 1st of April when he started the journey, travelling through the fertile lands of Normandy. He was thinking of his nephew and made up his mind that he would not leave Rouen until he had extracted from him an oath to give up his claims. He felt irritated by the need to have to come to Rouen without Isabella for he had decided on the spur of the moment not to bring her with him. He did not want anything to distract him from this matter of coming to terms with Arthur, but when he left her he always wondered what she was doing. The fact that he was never faithful to her during their partings made him wonder whether she was faithful to him, and while he shrugged aside his own adventures as natural and to be expected, the thought of hers could send him to the edge of one of his rages so that he would be inclined to let it flow over whoever came near him and offended him in the slightest way.

He needed to keep his mind clear to deal with Arthur so he did not want it to be disturbed by outside influences. Perhaps he should have brought Isabella with him. No, he could not be at all sure what was going to happen at Rouen and it was better to be alone.

He was pleased by his reception at the castle. There was a flurry of excitement at his arrival and serving men and women were scurrying in all directions. Arthur came to greet him sullenly and he spoke to him in a jocular fashion and told him that he had come to talk with him and to be his good uncle.

Arthur was subdued, and they feasted together.

Tomorrow, thought John, I will talk with Arthur.

He knew the castle well. Often he had stayed here. He remembered how he had gone with a party of men down to the stone steps where boats were moored, for the river was close by. They had rowed up that river to Les Andelys over which the Château Gaillard stood guard. He had always been thrilled by that castle and wished that he had built it instead of Richard. It was the castle to outshine all castles. He knew that Philip of France ground his teeth in envy when he saw it; it was like a sentinel standing on guard protecting Rouen, that favourite city of all the Dukes. When Arthur had signed that document in which he would admit he had no claim to John's possessions, John would swear that on his death without heirs everything should go to Arthur. They would sail up the river to Rouen and there they would ride through the town together and all should know of the amity between them. And once he had signed that document proclaiming that Arthur should be his successor if he died without heirs he must have children without delay.

That would be the right thing to do. The first stage of his relationship with Isabella had passed. He had adored her child's body, but she wasn't a child any longer and she must fulfil her duties and give him children. That would keep her out of mischief. So what he must do was get Arthur to sign and then get Isabella with child; and signing that document was the purpose of his coming to Rouen.

It was dusk of the next day when he and Arthur were alone together.

John said: 'Pray be seated, nephew. I have something of great importance to say to you. It is this: You and I must come to terms. I want us to be good friends.'

'Are you going to give up what you have taken from me then?' asked Arthur.

'I said we should come to terms.'

'Pray tell me these terms you have in mind,' said Arthur.

'You are to give up all claim to my possessions. Ah, wait. Do not sulk like a foolish child. If I die without heirs you shall be my successor.'

Arthur shook his head. 'I want what is mine now.'

'You must not act like a spoilt child, Arthur. I have the crown of England and the lands over here are mine too. I have been accepted by the people. What do you think the people of England would say if they were asked to accept you?'

'Doubtless they would say I was their rightful king since my father was your elder brother.'

'You are a foreigner, Arthur. You have never been in England. You don't know the English.'

'I know who is their rightful king.'

'So do they, nephew, and it is John.'

'John usurped the crown. Richard named me as his heir. The King of France proclaims me.'

'And I wear the crown,' taunted John. He was wishing he had it with him so that he could wear it on this occasion. That would have been amusing. 'You can save us and yourself a great deal of trouble if you accept what is. Now I shall have a document drawn up which you will sign and when you have signed it you and I will be good friends.'

'That is something we shall never be.'

'Have you made up your mind to that?'

'Yes, I made up my mind when you sent orders to blind me and rob me of my manhood.'

'What talk is this?'

'''Tis a statement of facts. I know you for the wicked man you are and if you think I shall ever enter into any agreement with you, you are mistaken.'

'I think you will, Arthur.'

'Why should you think that?'

'Because you are going to see what is best for you.'

'And you think it is good for me to sign away my inheritance?'

'There are worse things to lose than your inheritance as you came near to discovering.'

'You are a devil.'

'I am a man who will have his way.'

'And I have no more to say to you.'

Arthur rose and went to the door but before he reached it John had seized him.

'Take your hands from me—liar, coward, lecher ... I hate you. I will work against you until the end of my days.'

'So all my kindness to you is of no avail.'

'Kindness...' Arthur threw back his head and laughed.

A sudden blow sent him reeling. He fell against the wall and for a few moments he looked into a face which was distorted by rage. John's temper had taken possession of him and he made no attempt to curb it.

Another blow sent Arthur staggering to the floor, blood spurting from his mouth. John picked up a stool and hit him with it again and again ... on his head and on his body.

Arthur moaned in agony and then he was silent.

John kicked him, laughing demoniacally.

'What now, my brave cockerel, what now? What say you, eh? What say you, King of England, Duke of Normandy, Count of Anjou ... You should have been content with being Duke of Brittany.'

He was foaming at the mouth; his eyes were staring out of his head; his blood was pounding with excitement as he went on kicking Arthur.

And then he was aware that there was no response from Arthur. He no longer moaned; he merely lay slack and still as if oblivious to the pain which was inflicted on him.

John stopped suddenly, his rage sliding away from him.

He knelt down.

'Arthur,' he shouted. 'Stop shamming. Get up, or by God's teeth I'll kick you to death.'

There was no response.

'Arthur,' cried John shrilly, but the boy lay still.

He's dead, thought John. I have killed Arthur. What now?

*   *   *

He must act quickly. If Arthur were found thus there would be an outcry. They would know who had killed him and it would be used against him. He imagined such knowledge in Philip's hands.

Curse Arthur! He had been a plague to him ever since he had been born.

His rage started to get the better of him and he kicked the boy again.

He must not. He must be calm. He must think clearly. What was he going to do? He must get rid of Arthur's body. How? It would be obvious to any observer what had happened and it would be widely known that he was at Rouen and had been alone with the boy. This should not have happened.

He should have controlled his rage. He should have had Arthur murdered in a traditional royal manner—poison for instance, or neat strangulation, but to have battered the boy to death...

Curse him.

There was blood on the floor. He must have help. There was one of his servants—a strong man who had had his tongue cut out. John used him now and then because of what he thought of as this qualification. He had said to him once: 'You are a fortunate man, for tongueless you can serve your King well.' Had the tongue been removed by him he might have had to be wary for these creatures could harbour thoughts of revenge for years when one would have thought the matter might be forgotten by reasonable men. But this man had no grudge against John and John had craftily decided that because of his usefulness he should be cherished.

Locking the door of the room in which the dead boy lay, John went in search of the silent man. He found him in the stables, for he loved horses and was usually there when not engaged on his duties. John took him back to the chamber of death. There was only need to point to Arthur and the man understood—the loss of his tongue having sharpened what was left to him.

John said: 'He must be removed. Let us throw him in the river.'

The mute nodded and indicated that they would need to weight the body so that it would sink.

'We'll weight it then and take it to the river,' said John. 'Then we'll throw it overboard. There are boats moored down there. How shall we remove him?'

The man went to the window, indicating that he would throw the body out.

'Good man,' said John. 'That is the answer. Wait though ... until it is later. Then the castle will be quiet.'

John left the mute to guard the body behind locked doors while he went down to join the castellan and his wife. He was excited. He was rid of the boy. Arthur would be forgotten in time and that menace was removed.

It was past midnight when Arthur's body was thrown from the window. They tied a stone about his neck and carried him to a boat which they rowed along the river towards the sea. They threw the body overboard and then came back to the castle.

The next morning a jewelled button which was known to belong to Arthur was found on the stones beneath his window. There were some traces of blood there—the mute had removed all those in the room where the murder had taken place.

It was said: 'Arthur has escaped. He must have lowered himself from the window; and he hurt himself in falling, hence the blood.'

It was expected that soon there would be triumphant news from Brittany that their Duke was with them.

But none came.

*   *   *

Two fishermen out in their boat one night were amazed to haul in a heavy load and to their horror they saw what they brought in was the body of a young man with a stone securely tied about his neck.

Uncertain of what to do they rowed for the shore, left the body in their boat and went at once to the lord of the near-by castle. When he heard what they had to tell him he went with them to the boat and examining the features of the dead boy he had a suspicion as to who he was and when he noticed the jewelled buttons on his garments he guessed.

Arthur had been at the Castle of Rouen. There were already rumours in circulation that he had disappeared. There could be no doubt who this was.

'Say nothing of this,' said the lord of the castle, 'on pain of your lives keep silent.'

The frightened fishermen were only too eager to promise to do so.

Everyone knew that to talk of this could cost them their tongues.

Very secretly the body of Arthur was buried in the church of Notre Dame des Prés close by Rouen but there was no indication of the identity of the corpse. None wished it to be known by King John that they had had any hand in the disposal of the body. Their safety lay in secrecy, for who could know what unpredictable turn the King's anger might take.

Thus Arthur was buried but it was hardly likely that he could be so easily forgotten.

'Where is Arthur?' the Bretons were asking the question and the King of France joined his voice to theirs. They wanted to know why King John's nephew had suddenly disappeared.

Death at Fontevraud

DISASTER was threatening from all sides and John was haunted by memories of Arthur. Not that he suffered remorse because of what he had done, but fear was there. If it were ever known that he had murdered Arthur with his own hands he would be discredited throughout the world and there were so many waiting to take advantage of him.

He rejoined Isabella and plunged into such a life of voluptuous pleasure as even he and she had not experienced before. He would stay in bed, refuse to see messengers, always fearful what news they would bring. His generals and his ministers were dismayed. They didn't understand this man who at one time was eager to take everything and at another behaved in the manner best calculated to lose it.

Philip was the first to take advantage of such a situation. Arthur had died on Maundy Thursday; two weeks later Philip had taken Saumur. He was joined by Hugh de Lusignan and the Breton army. The whispers about Arthur's whereabouts were now becoming angry demands.

William the Marshal came to John and begged him to bestir himself.

'Philip is undermining us at all strategic points,' he pointed out.

'I am in no mood to go to war yet,' replied John.

'Philip is in just that mood,' retorted the Marshal grimly.

'Leave be. Leave be,' growled John. 'Send a deputation to Philip and ask if he is prepared to make a truce.'

'My lord, why should he? He has his army on the march. He is joined by allies. Why should he consent to make a truce merely to suit your convenience?'

'Go and ask him,' cried John, and because the Marshal could see the signs of temper rising he could do nothing but take his leave and carry out the King's orders.

As he had known Philip laughed them to scorn. If John could humiliate himself so utterly as to beg for a truce now he must be in a sorry state, and the result of that foolish strategy was to set Philip planning more intensive invasions into John's territory.

Those barons who had no love for John, although they had sworn allegiance to him as their suzerain, wavered in their loyalty. What was the use of a weak King who lay in bed with his wife half the day when the mighty King of France was marching on their castles? Philip captured many; and some surrendered, glad to change their allegiance.

William the Marshal presented himself once more.

'My lord, my lord, I beg of you give consideration to what is happening. The King of France has taken your seneschals. Do you know that there are those who will not surrender to France?'

' 'Tis to be hoped it is so,' said John. 'Have they not sworn allegiance to me?'

'For their loyalty many of them have been tied to their horses' tails and dragged to prison.'

'I am glad they are good and loyal men.'

'They are the prisoners of the King of France, my lord. Does that not move you to action? Philip is making himself master of your lands, your goods. He is taking your inheritance bit by bit.'

John laughed unpleasantly. 'Do not excite yourself so, Marshal,' he said. 'Let the King of France enjoy himself. I shall win back every castle, every acre of land which he has taken from me.'

'When shall you start, my lord?' demanded William Marshal. 'When you have lost the whole of Normandy?'

The Marshal strode out and left the King.

John hesitated a moment before shouting after him: 'Come back, you insolent dog.'

But William Marshal pretended not to hear and John knew that there was a man he had to keep working for him. In that moment he felt a twinge of fear. He was losing his grip, he knew. And here he was in Falaise of all places—the castle most associated with his mighty ancestor. Was William watching from the shades now? Was Arthur with him? What would the Conqueror think of Arthur's murder? One thing, thought John cynically, he would not condemn the murder of Arthur so much as he would the loss of the Norman castles.

He must bestir himself. He thought of the Pope. Philip had not been on good terms with Rome since his defiance over Ingeburga of Denmark whom he had married and put from him. In her place he had taken as his queen the Austrian Princess Agnes of Meran. The Pope had protested and Philip had said some harsh things about Rome, which would not be readily forgotten.

If Innocent would intervene in his favour John might be able to bring about a truce. John therefore complained to the Pope that Philip was making war on him most unjustly and he begged the Pope to help him keep the peace.

This was always a good way of bringing hostilities to at least a temporary halt; for there would be deputations from Rome to be met and discussions to ensue. John thought this would give him an opportunity to remain living as he wished to do without his generals and men such as the Marshal getting excited about Philip's aggression.

Philip, however, was too clever to be duped in this way. Whatever the Pope said he was going on with his war. It was true, as John had predicted, that he had offended the Papal embassy by telling them he had no intention of taking orders from Rome and that his attitude towards a vassal of his—as John, Duke of Normandy was—was his affair.

John saw that prevarication from Rome could avail him nothing because Philip was going to ignore it completely. It was inevitable therefore that he bestir himself.

But he was too late, Philip had already turned his attention to that bulwark of Norman strength, the great château built by Coeur de Lion, the Château Gaillard, which if it fell would open up the way to Rouen and the whole of Normandy for Philip and thus enable him to congratulate himself that he was on the road to fulfilling his great ambition—to make France as great as it had been in the days of Charlemagne.

*   *   *

It has come at last. The French were besieging Château Gaillard, the last bastion of the Dukes of Normandy. How long could it hold out? wondered John. He was in the castle at Rouen, the scene of Arthur's murder. He had no wish to go to that castle but it was all that was left to him.

He knew that his generals and advisers, men such as William Marshal, were disgusted with him. Only loyalty held them to him. How Hugh de Lusignan must be exulting now. How the Bretons must be rejoicing. Did they hope to discover their Duke and set the ducal coronet of Normandy on his brow? John laughed. Arthur would not look well in that.

Château Gaillard, Richard's pride and joy, the castle which had proclaimed the dukes of Normandy masters of the land—about to fall to the French.

They were blaming him, he knew. They were whispering together of how he had lain abed with his wife while his castles were falling one after another to the King of France.

'Let them,' he cried aloud. 'I'll win them all back.'

But he knew in his heart that he couldn't. Sometimes he had fantasies that were like nightmares that all the past dukes of Normandy congregated about his bed: Rollo, William Longsword, Richard the Fearless, the Conqueror himself, the most forbidding of them all; even Rufus, who would have nothing much to boast of, Henry I the lawyer king, Stephen, who was not much either, although he was a great soldier, soft in battle though for different reasons from John; and his own father, Henry II. How angry he would be. And Richard ... well, Richard, what did you care for your lands when you left everything to go off on the Crusades?

It is going fast, he muttered. Normandy is going. Well, I still have Anjou, Poitou and England of course. I am still King of England.

He wished he were in England, away from it all. He would go soon. He would have to when Gaillard fell, and Gaillard was going to fall. How could they hold out against the besiegers much longer?

William Marshal came to him, sick with grief, and sorrow-
ful.

'My lord, this is a sad day for Normandy.'

'Cannot they hold out at Gaillard?'

William Marshal shook his head. 'Philip surrounds the
place. There is no way of breaking through. Everything has
been left too late.'

'Cheer up, Marshal. I have good friends and all that is lost
will be regained.'

'My lord, I think I must tell you, there has long been
discontent among the Norman barons.'

'Treason!' cried John.

'I'd scarcely call it that, my lord. They say that you were
disinclined to protect them. They have seen many captured
by the French and held prisoner, their lands and castles
taken. They say that if you are not prepared to stand by them
then they must perforce seek another master.'

'Philip?' snarled John.

''Tis so, my lord. Philip sends his spies among them. It is
hinted that if they wish to live in peace they should swear
allegiance to him and accept him as their suzerain which he is
by rights ... so says he. For you, the Duke, are his vassal for
Normandy and they being your vassals are in truth his. He is
offering them exemption from conquest if they will come
over to him.'

'They cannot do that, Marshal. They would be traitors to
Normandy if they did.'

'They say Normandy has not cared for them and they will
offer themselves to France.'

'My God,' said John, 'has it come to that then?'

'It has, my lord. The commander of Gaillard has communicated to Philip that if you do not come to his rescue
within the month he will surrender, for he can no longer
hold out.'

'What then?' asked John.

'My lord, we are in no condition to go to their aid, and all
the castles from Bayeux to Anet have pledged Philip that
once he is master of Rouen they will surrender to him.'

'If Gaillard falls ...'

'Then Rouen would be lost and with Rouen Normandy.'

'We will regain everything ... everything,' cried John. He
raised his face, his eyes suddenly alight with excitement. 'I

will go to England. I will talk to my barons there. I will raise a great army. And I will come and take from Philip everything he has taken from me ... aye, and more also.'

William Marshal regarded him sadly.

'So,' went on John, 'I shall leave for England but soon I shall return.'

When William Marshal had gone John went to Isabella and told her that they were going to England without delay.

'I am weary of this place surrounded as I am by traitors. We are going back to England. There we shall have peace.'

'And what will become of Normandy?' she asked.

'Philip will take it for a while ... but only for a while.'

She did not answer and he said suddenly: 'Why do you look like that? You are like everyone else. You think it is my fault.'

Still she did not answer and he shook her. 'Speak,' he cried. 'Speak.'

She looked at him fearlessly. 'Mayhap if you had been more of a soldier...'

'It was your fault. You kept me chained to your bed.'

That made her laugh.

'Where are the chains?' she asked.

'You are a witch. You bewitched me.'

'Nay 'twas your own appetites which chained you.'

'You fed them well.'

'As was my duty.'

They began to laugh and again she thought of Hugh who would have been so different.

'We'll go to England,' said John. 'We'll have a family. That will please them. It's about time you gave me sons.'

'I am ready.'

'Away from this cursed place. I've had enough of it. I long for Westminster.'

'When do we go?'

'I have already sent on the baggage. We'll slip away in the early morning before they arise.'

'Why?' she asked.

'Because they will reproach me. Old Marshal thinks I should stay here and fight. I'll swear he's telling himself that that is what Richard would have done.'

'I shall be glad to be gone,' she said.

'It is well that we are away. When Gaillard goes Rouen will soon follow, depend upon it.'

'And we do not wish to be here when that happens?'

'You speak truth there. So ... very soon we'll be in England.'

The castle retainers woke one morning to find the King and Queen had gone. William Marshal explained that the King had returned to England to arouse the barons there to action and to acquaint them with the need to raise an army to save Normandy.

But no one believed the King would do that; and they thought that since he had taken his Queen with him he did not intend to return soon.

Shortly afterwards Château Gaillard fell to the French, and it was clear that Normandy would soon be lost.

*   *   *

Queen Eleanor in the Abbey of Fontevraud knew that her end was near. She was eighty-two years old—a great age. Few had lived so long. She had lived life to the full and had borne many children. She often thought back over the years and dreamed that she was young again. She could not complain she supposed; it had been an exciting life.

She could not cut herself off from the outside world as the nuns did. She had her family, she reasoned with herself; she cared for them still and she must know what they were doing that she might pray for them.

She still mourned Richard. It was but five years since his death and she had loved him so dearly—best of them all. He had been born to be king—with all the kingly virtues, save one. It was a pity that he had so little love for women and had disappointed her and his people by not begetting a son. Then she thought of poor Berengaria whose life had been so different from her own and she wondered what she was doing. Did she still think of the time when she and Joanna were in the Holy Land? If she did she would be mourning Joanna's death.

Death, thought Eleanor, is constantly with us—and now it is my turn.

One of her messengers came to the Abbey, for she often sent them out on errands since she must know what was happening in the outside world.

She could not believe it. It was not possible. The messenger assured her that it was.

Château Gaillard fallen to the French!

Richard's beloved castle. She remembered when he had built it. How he had called it his darling daughter and he had loved it as he could never have loved a child. It was the perfect castle, the impregnable fortress, the gateway to Rouen. And it had surrendered to the French!

Oh, Richard, she thought, I could almost be glad that you had not lived to see this day.

What other news? The King had gone to England. Rouen was ready to fall and so was the whole of Normandy. In a short time it would all be in Philip's greedy hands.

Oh, my son John, she thought. That it has come to this. It should never have been. Arthur perhaps. But no. He was but a child and the English would not have him. Would they not? How did they like John? And where was Arthur? He had disappeared mysteriously. He had been in Rouen and John had gone to Rouen. Could John tell them where Arthur was?

If he had escaped by jumping out of a window, as some believed, where was he now?

She was old and she was tired. And Normandy was all but in the hands of the French. And what could she do? Richard was not here to comfort her. If you had lived, my Lion Heart, this would never have happened. You would never have let sly Philip triumph. But all that is left is John...

Oh, John my son, what will become of Normandy, of England, with you at the helm?

How times had changed. In the old days she would have ridden to Poitou. She would have declared her intention of holding it for John, of raising an army, of going into battle for Normandy.

But she was too old now and there was nothing to do but turn her face to the wall.

And so in her eighty-third year she died in Fontevraud and they buried her by the side of the husband she had loved and hated; and they made a statue of her which they laid on her tomb. Serenely the stone figure looked on the world—the strong features clearly marked, wearing the gorget, wimple and coverchief over which was the royal diadem. In the hands had been carved a book and there this statue remained to remind the world that Eleanor of Aquitaine had once lived her turbulent life.

And so John lost not only Normandy but his mother.

An Election at Canterbury

HIS mother was dead. At least she could not reproach him, and she would have done, comparing him with Richard much to his disadvantage. A plague on them all! Those Norman barons who had gone over to Philip, those English barons who were criticizing him for losing his family's inheritance!

'I'll get it back,' he boasted to Isabella. 'This is but the fortunes of war.'

He did not want to hear what was happening in Normandy, though he knew that castle after castle was falling to Philip.

'Let them go,' he shouted. 'Knaves. Traitors. By God's feet, when I regain my territories they shall suffer for it.'

He was playing chess when news was brought to him that Rouen had fallen. Rouen! Rollo's Tower, the greatest of all Norman cities in the hands of the French! No duke of Normandy would have believed that could ever be possible.

The messenger came and stood beside him. He did not look; he merely nodded and continued to stare at the pieces on the board. Then very deliberately he moved his bishop.

'They'd better make what terms they can and so preserve their ancient privileges and customs,' he muttered. Then he shouted to the baron with whom he was playing, ' 'Tis your move, man. What are you gaping at?'

His opponent moved with apparent carelessness which was,

in fact, calculated. He knew it would not do for John to lose the game as well as Normandy.

John could not be indifferent to what was happening. People were saying: 'So Normandy is falling. What of Anjou and Poitou? Is he going to lose every acre of his overseas territories?'

He would make a truce with Philip, he decided; but when Philip heard of this he laughed aloud. There would be no truce, he said, until John handed over Arthur; and he added ominously: 'Alive or dead.'

So the spectre of his nephew was rising up to haunt John. It seemed that Philip suspected that Arthur was dead and if not directly murdered by John, on his orders. However, he knew very well that John was unlikely to produce the boy, nor would he confess his guilt; but Philip was determined to make the most of John's discomfiture on the matter. Philip turned his attention to some of the notable barons, such as William Marshal and the Earl of Leicester, who held lands in Normandy. These barons naturally did not want to be dispossessed, nor did they wish to swear allegiance to the King of France. It was a delicate situation, for it could be that Normandy had only temporarily passed into Philip's hands. Philip suggested therefore that they should pay the sum of five hundred marks each for the privilege of holding these lands for a year, and at the end of that time if John had not regained Normandy, they should swear allegiance to Philip and declare themselves vassals of France.

This seemed a fair enough arrangement and the barons agreed to enter into it.

Being the man he was, as soon as he arrived in England William Marshal had acquainted John with what he had done. John received the news mildly enough. 'I understand well,' he said. 'You are loyal to me and this is the only way you can hold your lands. Depend upon it, before the year is up I shall be back in Normandy.'

William Marshal had not been sure of that, but he was greatly relieved at the King's acceptance of what he had done.

A few weeks passed while every messenger from the Continent was awaited with breathless suspense, and suddenly John woke up one morning with a change of mood. All his slothfulness had dropped from him.

He sent for William Marshal. 'The time has come,' he said,

'to go into the attack. Philip will have Aquitaine if we do not act. I shall go up and down the country raising troops and money that I may show the King of France that I am now ready to stand against him.'

'It is late in the day,' said the Marshal.

'What, Marshal, no stomach for the fight?'

'My stomach is ever ready in a good cause.'

'And you think this is not one? Are you so eager to swear fealty to your French master?'

'You know me too well, my lord, to make such an accusation with any seriousness.'

Indeed he did, and he could not do without the Marshal. He knew that well enough too. But there was a growing haughtiness among these barons. It was detectable even in William Marshal's attitude now. They were criticizing him for what happened in Normandy. He wanted to scream at the Marshal but he was obsessed now by the desire to go into the fight and he could not quarrel with men like this one at such a time.

William Marshal was thinking how unpredictable John was. This burst of energy was now as compulsive as his sloth had been. For what could one hope from such a king? Sometimes, thought the Marshal, it would seem good for England if we were conquered by the French. Better to be ruled by clever Philip than this king who at times gave the impression that he was verging on madness.

'So you do not think we should fight for our rights?'

'I think we should have done so earlier, my lord.'

Yes, it was insolence. But be calm, John warned himself.

'There is a time,' said the Marshal, 'when action should be taken and if opportunities are lost it is sometimes unwise to try to make them later.'

'You have your views, Marshal,' said John, 'and I have mine. I shall start travelling the country today to amass my army.'

*　　　*　　　*

The year which Philip had granted to the barons for holding land in Normandy had passed and it was necessary for them to return there and show allegiance to the King of France and to swear 'liege homage on the French side of the water'. Philip was delighted with this arrangement for it meant that several of the leading barons of England could not in honour take up arms against him on the Continent.

How it was possible to serve one master on one side of the water and another on the other was something to which it was difficult to reconcile oneself, but William Marshal had seen that it was the only possible way in which he could keep his possessions in Normandy and as he, among other barons, was feeling his loyalty to John slackening every day, he at last made the decision that it was the only way out of his dilemma.

Meanwhile, John had spent the winter going up and down the country raising money—never a popular activity—and letting it be known that a rift between himself and his barons was making itself felt. He was going to take an army to France; he was going to win back what the French king had taken and he was determined on this. The people must realize that they were in a dangerous predicament. With Philip in Normandy it was possible that he might be contemplating an invasion of England. Were the people going to allow their country to be overrun by the French, for that was the danger.

Such prophecies brought people to his banner and he was not displeased by the result of his work. Conditions were against him, for the hard winter had made food scarce and dear, and the first signs of rebellion among the barons made itself felt. They incensed him by refusing to swear allegiance to him unless he upheld the rights of the kingdom. He ground his teeth in rage but so desperately did he need to build up his army that he had to promise what they asked.

He commandeered supplies, ordering that men join him, and by Easter he had one of the finest armadas the country had ever seen waiting in Portsmouth harbour to set sail. John went to near-by Porchester to make the final arrangements.

News came from the Continent that Philip was not now amassing his army on the Normandy shores. He had evidently decided that a conquest of England was a tricky undertaking; instead he was turning to attack Poitou.

'By God's eyes,' cried John, 'it is time I was there.'

There was now no indefatigable Queen Mother to hurry to the defence of Aquitaine. He was alone, John thought bitterly, for whom could he trust? There were many people who were trying to warn him against this undertaking. 'Traitors,' he cried. 'Traitors all.'

There were two men who were in particular set against the expedition—one was Hubert the Archbishop of Canterbury and the other William Marshal.

Hubert as Archbishop was almost certain to be regarded with suspicion by John. Relations between them had been far from easy particularly since John's return to England, for the Archbishop, like other members of the community, was beginning to realize that John was a tyrant.

Hubert was more than an archbishop; he was a statesman, and many might accuse him of being more the latter than the former; he was an astute man with the good of England at heart and during the years of Richard's absence he had managed to raise money for his king in the manner which he had learned from his uncle Ranulf de Glanville. When it had been necessary to raise the hundred thousand pounds needed for Richard's release from captivity he had worked closely with Queen Eleanor to produce the money and had managed this seemingly superhuman task with great credit to himself; and following the methods of Henry II he had succeeded in performing a task so painful to the people of England in such a manner that they resented it far less than might have been expected.

He had of course quarrelled with John but in a moment of good sense John had realized that a quarrel could profit him very little and he made peace with the Archbishop.

Now at Porchester, Hubert was preaching against taking an army into France. The invasion had been too long delayed, he declared. It could end in failure and if that army were beaten how could England be defended if Philip decided to turn his strength towards it?

John raged and ranted, as eager now to go into battle as a short time ago he had been determined to avoid it.

William Marshal too firmly believed that the expedition would be a failure, but he had another reason for not wishing to go to France.

The barons, growing more and more distrustful of John, had been deluded into thinking that they were going to defend Normandy. Now they had discovered that this was not John's intention. He was going to do battle with Philip for Poitou and Anjou. While the barons were interested in

Normandy where so many of them had property, they were not equally so in the other dominions. They began to murmur among themselves and when they discovered that the Archbishop of Canterbury and William Marshal were reluctant too, they took heart and said they did not wish to go.

William Marshal, with a number of the barons, came to speak of the matter with John.

'I myself could not go to France to fight,' he said.

'I understand you not, Marshal,' cried John.

'My lord, you know that I and others made a pact with Philip. This we did with your approval, you will remember. We paid him that we might hold our lands for a year, promising that if you did not conquer Normandy by that time we would swear allegiance to him. That time has passed, my lord, and the allegiance has been sworn.'

'You ... traitor!' cried John. 'So you have sworn allegiance to my enemy.'

'With your knowledge, my lord.'

John's eyes began to protrude and his lips began to move although he did not immediately speak. They all saw the signs of the notorious temper.

'Arrest that man!' he shouted. 'I will not have traitors beside me.'

There was a silence. The barons remained impassive. There was not one of them who would raise a hand against the Marshal.

John began to scream. He pointed at William Marshal with a shaking finger.

'By God's ears and teeth,' he shouted, 'I tell you that man is a traitor. He has made pacts with the King of France behind my back. He is my man and he cannot fight the King of France because he has made a vow to serve him. This is a man I have allowed to be close to me. I have given him my confidence and he has betrayed me. Arrest him. Take him away. Take him to a dungeon. Let him there await my pleasure ... and my pleasure will not be yours, Marshal, I promise you that.'

His eyes raked the silent company.

'What's this? What's this?' he cried. 'So none of you move. You stand there. I order and you do nothing ... nothing ... *nothing*!' His voice had risen to a scream. Then he suddenly seemed to grow quiet. 'I see,' he said slowly. 'I see clearly. You are all against me. Every one of you. Traitors ... all of you. By God's eyes, this is an ugly matter.'

He turned from them and strode off.

The Marshal was against him. The Archbishop was against him. And there was smouldering resentment among his barons.

'They shall not stop me,' he screamed at Isabella. 'I'll have my way. Rest assured I will. Nothing will stop me ... nothing ... nothing ... nothing.'

And he went on with his preparations.

*   *   *

William Marshal came to him. He looked sad and contrite and for the moment John's heart leaped with hope because he thought he had come to beg his pardon.

Not so the Marshal. John thought: None would think he were my subject. I could take him and imprison him and put out his eyes. Does he forget that?

No you could not, whispered common sense. If you did the whole country would rise against you. This man is beloved of the barons and the people. Do not delude yourself. You need his friendship.

All the same he scowled at the Marshal.

'Well,' he cried, 'why do you come to me? Why do you not go to the lord you have chosen to serve?'

'There is one I serve on these shores,' said William Marshal. 'There is one I would always have wished to serve. I have been forced to swear allegiance to the King of France when in the land he now commands and I am a man who must keep his oath.'

'So you swore away your honour for your lands.'

'I would never swear away my honour, sire. Has it struck you that if—and by God's grace may it be soon—you regain Normandy you will have strongholds there of those who serve you well. I am one of those.'

'Am I expected to believe that?' demanded John scornfully.

'You must believe as you will, my lord. The facts will remain as they are. I come now to beg you to disband your army.'

'Because you do not wish to fight against your friend?'

'If you refer to the King of France I must say I do not wish to. But my reason for braving your wrath and coming to you is to beg you consider. The facts are these: Philip is now in command of vast territories; he can put more men in the field than you can. You know full well the treachery of the Poitevins. Can you trust them? They would be your friends one day and if it was advantageous to them—as it could well be— they would turn to France. And while you were engaged over there with the flower of your army you would leave this land exposed to the invader. Your presence is needed here. The people are disturbed. They liked not the taxation which has had to be imposed to raise this army. The barons are on the edge of revolt. My lord, you can best serve your interests by disbanding your army and staying here, to hold firmly on to what is left to you.'

'You disappoint me, Marshal. I had thought I could rely on you.'

'You can rely on me now as ever. I have done nothing disloyal. I had your consent to pay Philip that I might retain my lands in Normandy and you knew full well the condition that if you did not regain Normandy in one year I must swear fealty to him. This I did as you must have known I must. And because I have taken my oath of allegiance to him I cannot in honour bound accompany you to France ... if you decided to go—which I hope you will not.'

John clenched his fists and swore but he must not let his temper break out. He had seen the looks in the barons' eyes and he wondered what they would do next.

He said: 'I will summon the barons and talk to them.'

The Marshal looked relieved.

*   *   *

John looked round the company. They were all against him ... all! He had his mercenaries; they would follow him. But no, he could not go against his barons and his ministers.

'You advise me not to go,' he cried. 'Tell me then what I must do.'

Some of the barons thought that a small company of knights might be sent to Poitou, there to help those who were loyal to him.

'A company of knights! Is that going to hold Poitou? Is that going to win back Normandy?' He had become maudlin.

He was in tears. He could rely on nobody. Every man's hand was against him.

'Very well,' he shouted. 'I will dismiss my army. But you won't stop my going. I shall go taking with me a few of my *loyal* supporters.'

The barons gave their opinion that he must not leave the country. It was imperative that during this uncertain state of affairs he remain in England.

'Do not attempt to tell me what I shall do and what I shall not,' he screamed at them forgetting that he had asked for their advice. 'You will not come with me.'

He left them and went out to the harbour where his own ship was anchored.

'Prepare,' he cried. 'We sail at once.'

His captain was astonished to hear that only this one ship was going to cross, all the rest being disbanded.

'Nobody will follow me,' cried John. 'Then I will go alone.'

He set sail in his ship while the rest of the fleet was dismantled and the soldiers he had gathered together returned to their homes.

He did not intend to go to France though. As his temper cooled and the land receded, he knew it would be ridiculous if he went to France with just one ship's company.

He gave orders for the captain to put in at Wareham where he alighted, complaining bitterly that he was surrounded by traitors. He had set out for France to regain his heritage and his subjects had deserted him. The disaster abroad was due to them. See, he had been ready to fight. But they were cowards. They had taken oaths to the King of France, forgetting their duty to the King of England in their determination to save their lands. It would always be remembered against them.

He had come to a sorry pass—not for what he had lost but what he had discovered—the treachery of those who should have loved him best!

Philip naturally took advantage of the situation and in a short time had all of Poitou in his possession with the exception of Rochelle, Thouars and Niort.

*   *   *

Hubert Walter, Archbishop of Canterbury, was feeling his years as he left Canterbury for the town of Boxley where he was going to settle a quarrel between the Bishop of Rochester and some of his monks.

He was getting too old for such journeys and he was suffering from a tiresome carbuncle on his neck which was giving him a great deal of pain. On that morning when he had awakened he felt feverish and had wondered whether to postpone the journey, but it was never wise to allow these quarrels to fester. It was far better he always said to find some quick solution. There was trouble enough in the country. He had been very uneasy of late, particularly since he had been with the King in Porchester when the latter had been there assembling his army to take across the Channel. What violent rages John could fall into! Hubert knew the Angevin temper well; John was not the only member of the family who possessed it for it had been present in almost every member of that family. It might well be true that it had been introduced into their blood by the witch woman whom one of the Dukes of Anjou was said to have married. Henry II had had it, so had Richard to some extent but never had anyone possessed it to such a mad degree as John. He seemed to verge on madness when it flared up in him and to be possessed by the Devil himself. It was alarming to contemplate that such a man was at the head of the country.

Often the Archbishop thought of the King and wondered what had happened to young Arthur who had so suddenly and mysteriously disappeared. He had been in Rouen; John had gone to Rouen; and that was significant. The Archbishop prayed that John had not been guilty of some foul deed which could only bring disaster to him and, through him, to England.

They were good friends now, but conflict could arise between them at any moment. All monarchs resented the Church, but John more than most and he was not the sort to attempt to behave with diplomacy.

Often the Archbishop wondered whether it would not have been better to have brought Arthur over to England and trained him to become its king.

All this he was thinking as he jogged along on his horse. The heat was great—or was that his fever? The nagging pain of the carbuncle was growing more insistent; he would be glad to rest for the night. By the time he and his retinue came to the town of Tenham he was quite exhausted and very ready to sink into a bed. He could eat nothing and his servants, he could see, were anxious on his behalf.

'Please let me rest,' he said. 'After a good night I shall be fresh for tomorrow's journey and pray God we shall soon have completed our business and be back in Canterbury.'

But in the morning he was certainly not ready to set out again. The carbuncle was throbbing painfully and the fever had increased. He was a little delirious and he agreed that he must rest here for a few days.

As the day wore on the fever grew worse. Nor had it improved on the next day; and on the third day after his arrival at Tenham he was dead.

It was necessary to inform the King without delay of the death of his Archbishop; and a messenger set out from Tenham as soon as it was known what had happened.

John was at Westminster with his Queen when the messenger arrived. He was taken straight to the King because it was clear that the news was of the utmost importance.

'My lord,' cried the messenger, 'the Archbishop of Canterbury is dead.'

John stood up and a low smile spread itself across his features.

'Is it true then?' he asked.

'My lord, it is. He died of a fever and a carbuncle at Tenham.'

John turned to Isabella with a smile. 'Did you hear that? He is dead. Hubert Walter, Archbishop of Canterbury, is dead. Now for the first time am I truly King of England.'

*   *   *

When news reached Canterbury that the Archbishop was dead the Monks of St. Augustine called a conclave at which they discussed the appointing of a new Archbishop. This was according to a long-standing tradition for the Canterbury monks had the right, which they were very eager to maintain, to elect their Archbishop.

The Abbot pointed out that the death of Hubert was a great tragedy which they must all deplore but it could be an even greater one if an Archbishop were elected who had not the good of the Church at heart. They must therefore come to a decision to select a worthy successor to Hubert and without much delay send to the Pope for his permission that the man of their selection might take the office which was so important to the Church.

They disbanded and arranged to meet again within a week. But before that time John had arrived in Canterbury.

He had come, he said, to pay his last respects to the Archbishop, his dear friend and adviser. He then extolled the virtues of Hubert, inwardly amused as he turned their differences to displays of amity. Such a situation appealed to his sense of humour.

'We must make sure,' he told the Abbot, 'that we appoint a worthy successor to our good Hubert. He would be distraught, looking down from Heaven, if we appointed one who was the wrong man. Of course it is impossible to find one of his worth but we must ensure that he who follows is capable of wearing the mantle so tragically discarded by himself.'

'We have been thinking deeply of the matter,' said the Abbot.

John was alert. So you have, have you? he thought. And you would like to put up your man, somebody who would bow to Rome. I know you churchmen! Nay, my old abbot, the next Archbishop of Canterbury is going to be *my* man as old Hubert never was.

'It is a matter which all those who have the good of the Church ... and the Court ... at heart, must consider deeply. I myself have been thinking and it seems to me that I could not find a better man than John de Grey, Bishop of Norwich, who has been a very good friend to his country.'

The Abbot was dismayed. John de Grey was the King's man. It had been said that Hubert was more a statesman than a churchman but at least he had always had the good of the Church at heart. John de Grey would work entirely for the King and this was clearly why the King had decided on him.

The Abbot did not reply and John went on to extol the virtues of Hubert.

'Alas, alas we shall never see his like,' he said and thought: Thank God for that.

He was present at the ceremonial burying of the Archbishop and lingered for six days in Canterbury making himself agreeable to the monks, never again mentioning that he was determined on the election of John de Grey but nevertheless making up his mind that as soon as he returned to

Westminster he would send envoys to the Pope. The fact that this had to be done infuriated him as it had kings before him. The yoke of Rome was never very comfortable for a royal neck. It was for this reason that uneasiness always existed between Church and State, and therefore imperative for the King that this most important office should be filled by a man who would work for him. John de Grey was that man.

As soon as John had left Canterbury the Abbot called another meeting.

'It is clear,' he said, 'that the King has decided to put forward the Bishop of Norwich. He is the King's man; he will do exactly as ordered and that means that if the King demands the abolition of the Church's privileges, the King's Archbishop will do as ordered. That will not serve the Church well.'

One of the monks reminded the Abbot that it was their privilege to elect an Archbishop and ask the Pope's sanction for his appointment.

'That is exactly what I suggest we do.'

'Against the King's wishes?' asked one.

'That is not a State matter,' replied the Abbot firmly. 'It is for the Church to choose and as it is our privilege to elect the Archbishop, let us do so. We will then send him in person to Rome to solicit Papal approval but not before we have placed him on the Archbishop's chair.'

There were some of the more timid monks who talked of the King's displeasure but the Abbot pointed out that not only must the Church stand against the State when necessary but that they who were the monks of Canterbury, where the martyr St. Thomas à Becket had shown his defiance to the crown, must inspire their countrymen to do their duty and that lay with the Church. They would, secretly by night, elect their Archbishop, go through the ceremony of putting him on the Primate's throne and then send him to Rome. By the time his election was known he would have the Pope's consent and when that was given, the King could do nothing.

The monks saw that unless they were going meekly to accept the King's man, this was how they must act, so they attended the secret conclave and elected their sub-prior Reginald—a pious and scholarly man who had proved his devotion to the Church. They went through the ceremony at the altar and set him on the throne. Then it was agreed that he should set out for Rome without delay and tell the Pope that he had been elected by the monks of Canterbury and that all he needed was the Papal sanction for his office.

'It is imperative,' said the Abbot, 'that none should know what has happened here tonight until you have the Pope's sanction, so I am going to ask you to swear an oath of secrecy.'

Reginald declared that nothing would draw the information from him and he eagerly took an oath swearing absolute secrecy.

Then he set out for Rome.

*   *   *

As soon as John left Canterbury he sent for John de Grey, his Bishop of Norfolk.

The King was in a good mood. With de Grey at the head of the Church in England he could look forward to little interference in that direction and he was congratulating himself on having the very man for the post.

'My dear Bishop,' he said, 'it does me good to see you. I have plans for you. What say you to Canterbury?'

'Canterbury, my lord!'

'Oh, that makes you open your eyes, does it?'

'My lord, I know that Hubert is dead...'

'Interfering old man. His idea was that he would make the State subservient to the Church. He did not say so but the implication was there. Well, now he is no more and we must find another to take his place. Because I know you have been my friend and will continue to be so, I have decided to appoint you Archbishop of Canterbury.'

'My lord!' John de Grey was on his knees kissing John's hand.

'My dear Bishop,' said John. 'I am sure that you will serve me well as you have in the past. You have been a good secretary and friend, and I know that, with you on the Primate's throne, I shall have done with these trying and interfering old men who would presume to tell me my duty.'

'I shall serve you with all my heart and soul,' the Bishop assured him.

'I know it well and now I shall send envoys at once to Rome, though it irks me to, but so must it be. Then, my dear friend, when you are my Archbishop we can work together

for the country's good and keep the Church where it rightly
belongs.'

A good day's work, thought John, when he said farewell to
the Bishop of Norwich.

*   *   *

Pope Innocent III, born Lothario of Segni, was a man of
great intellectual powers. He had been destined to become
Pope ever since the time—some sixteen years before—when
he had become a Cardinal under his uncle Pope Clement III.
Highly educated, he had a lawyer's mind and was deeply
interested in world affairs. He was not content with being the
figurehead to whom the Church throughout the world was
answerable. He considered all kings and rulers to be subject
to the law of the Church and therefore they were under his
control no less than the clergy.

Every Pope was aware of the conflict which it seemed must
inevitably arise between Heads of States and the Church and
he was more determined than most of his predecessors to keep
all subservient to him.

Hubert Walter had been an ideal Archbishop of Canterbury; a strong man who had been a statesman as well as a
churchman; it was such men whom Innocent wished to see at
the head of the Church throughout the world.

He was surprised, therefore, when Reginald arrived in
Rome to ask for his sanction of his appointment as Archbishop of Canterbury. He had never heard of Reginald and as
the man had arrived with some secrecy he realized that there
must be people in England who would not be eager to see
him as Primate. He learned that Reginald had already been
elected by the monks of Canterbury, though neither the King
nor the Bishops had set their seal of approval on this choice.
He would make careful enquiries.

He sent emissaries to Reginald and demanded to see his
credentials. Reginald assured them that he had been elected
by the monks of Canterbury whom ancient tradition allowed
to select their Archbishop. In his appeal to the Pope he
signed himself Archbishop Elect.

The Pope was not greatly impressed and laid the matter
aside, while Reginald was left chafing with impatience in
Rome. There were many who knew why he was there and to
them he talked more freely than was discreet, insisting that

he had been properly elected and had even been throned in the Primate's chair. Every document he signed as Archbishop Elect and very soon the object of his mission was well known throughout Rome.

It was hardly to be expected that no one would consider it worthwhile reporting this state of affairs in England. John was at Westminster when he received a caller who had come from Rome with news which he thought should be laid before the King.

John, who had shelved the matter of the election of the Archbishop because while there was no Archbishop the riches of the See, which were considerable, were at his disposal, was furious.

The monks at Canterbury had dared attempt to outwit him. They had selected their man and sent him to Rome for the Pope's approval. The perfidy of such an act infuriated him.

He shouted for his servants. 'Prepare for a journey. I am leaving for Canterbury without delay.'

When the King travelled—which was frequently—none could be unaware of it. He would be at the head of a cavalcade with the Queen riding beside him and not far behind him would be litters and their bearers in case they should get tired of riding. Following them were their ministers, knights, courtiers, musicians, entertainers and the rest; then would come the wagons filled with bedding and cooking utensils and perhaps some piece of furniture of which the royal pair were particularly fond. Servants of all types came behind the wagons and as the party progressed it would be joined by pedlars, harlots, strolling players, all out to earn something from this stroke of unexpected good fortune in being able to join up with the royal party on the move.

Thus the monks of Canterbury heard that the King was coming their way and when this happened they guessed why, and were thrown into a panic. The Abbot's first act was to send a messenger at once to Rome to repudiate Reginald. He had been indiscreet and had not kept his part of the bargain, and therefore they were justified in disowning him.

Meanwhile, John and his retinue arrived at Canterbury and John paid an immediate visit to the Abbey and demanded that the Abbot and his chief subordinates stand before him. They quailed before his rising temper.

'By God's ears, teeth and feet,' cried John in a voice which echoed through the vaulted chamber, 'I'd know what this means. You traitors, you scoundrels! So you have elected your Archbishop, have you? You scheming curs. You have lied to me. You have accepted John de Grey and all the time you have been hiding the fact that you have elected a man to the Primate's throne.'

' 'Tis not so, 'tis not so,' cried the Abbot trembling. 'Nay, you have been misinformed, my lord.'

John looked a little better humoured. 'How is it then that I hear you have elected your sub-prior Reginald? You have sent him to Rome for the Pope's sanction. He prates that you have already enthroned him. By God's eyes, I'll have you know that I shall soon unthrone him.'

' 'Tis not so. 'Tis not so,' was all the Abbot could say.

John seized him almost playfully by the shoulders and looked into his face. John at such moments was terrifying; the blood tinged the whites of his eyes and the pupils were completely exposed; his teeth were bared and expressions of cruelty and sadism chased each other across his face.

'Nay, 'tis not so, 'tis not so,' he mimicked. 'For I know this, Sir Abbot, you would not be so foolish as to cross me thus. Did I not come here and tell you that *I* had appointed John de Grey?'

'You told us, my lord, that you believed he would be a good Archbishop.'

'And you agreed with me, so it is not conceivable that you could have so deceived me. You would do no such thing. How could you, a godly man, so lie and on such a matter too? All Heaven would rise against you—as would your earthly master, Abbot. By God's limbs, no punishment would be too great for one capable of such perfidy. It pleases me that you are innocent of this: I should not care to be called on to do my duty in your case. It would have to order that tongue to be cut out ... since it was capable of uttering such lies.'

The Abbot by this time, together with the monks, was reduced to such a state of terror that their only desire was to placate the King.

'My lord ... my lord...' he babbled.

'Come, come,' said John. 'Speak up. You are an innocent man and innocent men have nothing to fear from me. What is it you would tell me?'

'That ... that we will elect an Archbishop now while you are with us, my lord, that we may have no fear of offending you.'

'Well spoken,' said John. 'We will elect John de Grey. Then we must perforce send a deputy to Rome for confirmation from the Pope. A fact which irks me, but nevertheless must be. Come, my good friends, we will proceed, for I see we are in complete agreement on this point.'

So before John left Canterbury, his protégé, John de Grey, had been elected Archbishop and it was arranged that a deputation be sent to Rome to inform the Pope of the election and to procure his sanction.

* * *

When Reginald heard that the party had arrived in Rome he was furious. That the deputation came with the King's authority was indeed disconcerting, but he was a man who was determined to have his rights. He had been elected Archbishop, had even gone through the ceremony, and he was not going to be brushed aside if he could help it. He sent further proofs of his election to the Pope who by this time had received the deputation from the King.

Meanwhile, the bishops had learned that there were two candidates for the archbishopric and neither of these men had their support. Those who were in Rome immediately sent their protests to the Pope.

Innocent was irritated. This was all very unorthodox. First the secret election was greatly to be deplored and he was sufficiently well informed on State affairs to realize that John de Grey was the King's man and that he could expect little support for the Church from him. Although, like all popes, he regarded himself as supreme ruler, none but fools would run the risk of alienating powerful kings, even though the Church he believed should hold sway over temporal rulers; he could not, therefore, openly flout John. But he determined that his man should not become Archbishop of Canterbury.

Innocent believed that when a difficulty of such a nature presented itself a great deal was to be gained by delay, but finally he came up with a decision.

The election of Reginald had not been conducted in a proper manner and therefore he could not give his consent to it. Nevertheless, it had been an election and Canterbury had in fact had an archbishop when John de Grey was elected. Therefore, his election was invalid. The Archbishopric of Canterbury was, in fact, vacant.

This seemed to Innocent an excellent opportuniy for putting forward his own man, and he had the very one in mind. This was a certain Stephen Langton. There should be no objection to Langton, the Pope reasoned, for he was reputed to be the most illustrious and learned churchman of the age. Moreover, he was an Englishman, having been born in that country. It was true he had lived there very little, having studied in the University of Paris where he had lived until a year before. There he had lectured on theology and earned himself a reputation as one of the most intellectual men of the day. King Philip, realizing his abilities, had shown him great friendship; moreover, he was a man of high moral standing.

A year or so before Innocent had made up his mind that such a man must be recognized for what he was and he sent for him to come to Rome where he made him Cardinal priest of St. Chrysogonus. He gave lectures on theology in Rome and had become a friend of the Pope who saw in him a man who could do great service to the church.

Innocent had learned that when Stephen Langton was invited to Rome, King John had written to congratulate him as an Englishman, for his promotion. John had said that he himself had been on the point of inviting him to come to the English Court for he believed that such an illustrious Englishman should reside in the country of his birth that he might bring credit to it. But since he was in Rome and close to the Pope doubtless he should not forget that he was an Englishman.

The Pope was amused. So John thought he had an advocate near the Papal Court did he? He would have to understand that Stephen Langton was no man to be bribed or intimidated. He was one who would stand by his principles in any circumstances, and he was a staunch upholder of the Church and would always support it against any temporal rulers.

He therefore called together an assembly of monks and bishops and told them that his choice had fallen on Stephen Langton and they must agree with him that there was no one more suited to the post and he therefore proposed to elect him Archbishop of Canterbury. The See was vacant, rendered so by the death of good Archbishop Hubert. The secret election of Reginald which, because it had been conducted in an unorthodox manner, was void and the election of John de Grey was similarly so because it had taken place before Reginald had been displaced. Neither of these men seemed so eligible and everyone must agree with him that Stephen Langton was eminently so.

The monks were frightened, but the Pope was at hand and the King was far away, and the Pope could be forbidding. In his hands lay the power of excommunication, which all men feared, for to die with that dread sentence on one meant exclusion from heaven, and eternal damnation.

Nevertheless, the monks were uneasy. They would have to return to England in due course and face the King's wrath. On the other hand it was either that or braving the Pope's. As men of the Church they must fear their spiritual leader more than their temporal one.

There was but one exception. Elias of Brantfield abstained from voting. The rest elected Stephen Langton as Archbishop of Canterbury.

The Spectre of Arthur

JOHN had other matters with which to concern himself at this time. If he were not going to lose the whole of his Continental possessions to Philip he must do something about the matter. He consulted with his generals and ministers and it was decided that if a small force could be taken to La Rochelle, which was still loyal to him, it might be possible to start an offensive and regain some of the lands lost to him. Moreover, La Rochelle would not be able to hold out for long if Philip made a determined attack on it. He could hire mercenaries to fight for him. He declared they were often more reliable than his own knights; a mercenary was in the battle for what he could get and if there were plenty of spoils that was good enough for him. Men of principle, such as the Marshal, were not always as useful as they might have been.

It was in June, while the controversy about the election of the archbishop was going on in Rome, that John and his small force set sail for La Rochelle; and to his great joy when he arrived there it was to discover that Aquitaine was prepared to stand with him, for it was clear that Philip was casting covetous eyes on that Duchy which had no desire to be ruled by him.

After securing his position at La Rochelle John went to Niort, another stronghold which had remained faithful to him. He began to score a few successes which although they were far from decisive, had the effect of making the wary Philip reconsider the position and decide that he was not at this time ready for a major offensive.

The result was that he was quite prepared to agree to a

truce which was to last two years. John was delighted. He had
not hoped for such success, and one of the terms of the treaty
was that Isabella—her father having died—should be declared the Countess of Angoulême. This meant that John had
allies which he had not possessed when he had set out on his
expedition; and, moreover, he had two years in which to
prepare to go to war with France and regain all that he had
lost.

He came back to England in high good spirits, laughing
inwardly at all those knights who had criticized him for lying
in bed half the day and neglecting his duties. This would
show them. When he did take action he was successful. He
had promised them that he would win back all he had lost to
Philip and he would.

Almost immediately on his return he received news of
what had happened in Rome.

The Pope had dared to reject his man and elect Stephen
Langton.

The King's fury was such that it threatened to choke him.
He could only splutter in dismay and all those about him
knew that they were in for one of his major rages. They faded
away from him, fearing that he might give vent to his feelings
on any who were close at hand.

He went to Isabella and told her what had happened.
Tears of rage spurted from his eyes and he plucked at the
jewelled buttons on his cloak, pulling them off and throwing
them about the room.

Isabella languorously asked what ailed him.

'What ails me?' he screamed. 'That rogue of Rome has set
up his man for the archbishopric.'

'Which man?'

'One called Stephen Langton. A great scholar, he says. I
want no scholars. I'll put out the fellow's eyes and see how he
attends to his studies then. Very clever he is said to be, well so
am I, I tell you. So am I.'

'We know,' said Isabella, 'and we know also that you are
the King. How dare the Pope put up his man and can he do
that if you are against it? I suppose he can as Pope.'

John was foaming at the mouth. 'No, he can't. I'll not have
it. Stephen Langton can stay in Rome where he belongs, for
if he attempts to come here he'll soon be lying in a dungeon
minus some vital organ, I can tell you.'

'Be calm, John.'

'Calm! When my authority is flouted? Am I King of this realm or am I not?'

'Undoubtedly you are, so behave like it.'

For a moment his rage was turned on her. 'Do not try me too far, Madam. I have been over soft with you because you have good bed manners, but you are not in bed now.'

That made her laugh and he came to her and seized her angrily. She slid her arms about his neck, and pressed her body against his. He immediately felt the familiar surge of desire. It was strange how she could move him still. It astonished him. She was incomparable. It was some quality ... witchcraft they said. If it was, he didn't mind. He liked it. Still he was glad of the women who now and then replaced her. If she knew about them she'd be mad with rage. He held that against her. She was more in his power than he was in hers.

But this was too important a matter to be shrugged aside by pleasures which he could indulge in at his will. Now he was furious with the Pope and he was going to let the whole world know.

He put her from him and shouted: 'If I gave way the whole world would laugh at me. I appoint an archbishop and the Pope says no and sets up his. No king would stomach that—nor should I. Why do you sit there smiling?'

'Because you would set up a man who would work for you and the Pope would set up one who would work for him. The stronger man will win.'

'And you know who that is.'

'You, my King. You of course.'

He was not going to be side-tracked with soft words. He was going to show Rome and England that he was the King who would rule his own country and that included the Church within it. He was not going to have the Pope setting himself up over the King.

He set out at once for Canterbury and again the Abbot and his monks were thrown into a panic when they heard of the King's approach.

He summoned them all to meet him and although his rage was great it was by this time somewhat under control.

He shouted at the assembly. 'By God's teeth, there are traitors here. There are liars and enemies of the King. I forget not that I came here and was told that Reginald had not been elected. Then it seemed he had. And knowing that you had elected Reginald yet you denied it and elected John de Grey. So says the Pope this makes both elections invalid and he would set up his own man. I will not have this man. I ... and I alone, will select my Archbishop. I will have people of my choice, those who work for me and not for themselves or the Pope. You thought to trick me. Do not deny it. I know full well your cowardly ways. In secret you set your choice upon the Primate's throne. A plague on you all. You are no longer monks of mine. Get out! This is no longer your abbey. Go, go ... go! No ... not tomorrow ... nor the next day ... as you are now ... now unless you wish to be cast into dungeons, which you richly deserve. What would be the best punishment for you I wonder—to deprive you of the eyes that looked on that treacherous ceremony or the tongues which applauded it.'

He was amused to see the terror dawn in people's faces at the prospect of these terrible punishments. To threaten them with death could not produce the same concern.

'So shall it be,' he cried. 'If you are not on your way this very day. Where to? you might ask. Go where you will. Go crawling back to the master whom you thought to serve better than you serve me. Go to Reginald and ask him to care for you. You gave him your support ... in defiance of your King ... let him support you now.'

The rage was in control. This was more enjoyable ... to inflict punishment on others rather than himself because when the rages were out of control he came close to injuring himself. How much more fun to strike terror into their hearts.

That day sixty-seven of the monks left Canterbury and made their way to the Continent. John was pleased, for now he was in possession of their lands.

He was in no hurry to settle the dispute—even to install John de Grey—because until there was an Archbishop of Canterbury the riches of that very prosperous See remained in his possession.

*   *   *

John sat down to write to the Pope. He was not going to curb his anger. He wanted Innocent to know that he had no

intention of submitting to his will. He would not accept
Stephen Langton as his Archbishop and he understood well
Innocent's reasons for trying to impose this man upon him.
He wanted to force Papal doctrines on him which as a King
of England he could not accept. It was a matter of amazement
to him that a Pope could have so little regard for the friendship of the King of England as to treat him with such a lack
of respect, as a man whose desires were of so little conse-
quence. John was afraid that he must point out to His
Holiness that he could not—nor would he—accept such
treatment; and if the Pope had so little regard for him, that
was not the case with others. He knew nothing of this man,
Stephen Langton, except that he had been particularly well
received at the Court of King Philip in France—a man who
had shown himself to be no friend to John, indeed he would
find it difficult to name one who was a greater enemy to him.
And this was the man whom the Pope—without the sanction
of the King of England—had chosen to be England's Primate.
This was beyond John's understanding.

Exceedingly irritated to receive such a letter, the Pope
wrote with great dignity reminding the King, in every line,
of his supremacy over temporal rulers.

'The Servant of the Servants of God informs the King of
England that in what he has done there was no cause why he
should tarry for the King's consent, and as he has begun he
will proceed according to canonical ordinances neither to the
right nor to the left . . .'

John scanned the letter with growing impatience.

'We will for no man's pleasure,' went on the Pope, 'defer
the completion of this appointment, neither may we without
stain of honour and danger of conscience.'

John ground his teeth in anger. 'Curse him. Curse him!'
he cried. 'God curse all my enemies . . . and none more than
this one who calls himself the servant of Your servants.'

'. . . Commit yourself therefore to our pleasure which will
be to your praise and glory and imagine not that it would be
to your safety to resist God and the Church in a cause for
which the glorious martyr Thomas has shed his blood.'

Any reference to Thomas à Becket always made John
uneasy. Becket had been the cause of his father's public
humiliation at Canterbury. He must never find himself
forced to do the sort of penance his father had. Curse on all

churchmen who made saints of themselves!

The Pope went on to say that he did not believe John was as ignorant of Stephen Langton's qualities as he implied. True, Stephen had spent little time in England and had been appreciated by the King of France as a man of such outstanding ability must be by all with whom he came into contact. John himself must be aware of his work—if only the revision of the Bible. It was not only in Paris that Langton had enjoyed great fame. The Pope had heard of it in Rome and he knew that John had in England, for had he not mentioned this to Stephen Langton himself when he had congratulated him on being elected Cardinal? John should be gratified that such a man was bringing his great intellectuality to England.

John danced with rage when he read the Pope's reply.

'Does he think we have no men of intellectual stature here? We have our scholars here. Does he think England is populated with the ignorant?'

He sat down and wrote in the heat of his anger once more to the Pope. He would not have Stephen Langton in Canterbury. He had decided on John de Grey and John de Grey it should be. If the Pope did not agree with him, if he withheld his sanction, let him. Why should he be governed by Rome? He was quite prepared to break away if the Pope wished it. Let the Pope do his worst. He was ready for him, but first let him consider how much poorer he would be from all the benefits which he would miss from England, for if John broke with Rome he would not allow his churchmen to journey back and forth taking rich gifts, which he knew they did now. It was not England which would suffer; it was Rome.

This vituperation was received coldly by Rome.

The Pope merely replied that John should give thought to what could happen to him if he continued to offend Holy Church. This was a hint that there could be excommunication for him and an interdict placed on England.

John snapped his fingers and put the matter from his mind. Another event had occurred—a much more pleasant one. In the early part of the year Isabella had discovered that she was pregnant.

* * *

Isabella was delighted. She was nearly twenty years old and

had been John's wife for seven. She had begun to be rather worried about the fact that she had not conceived during that time. It was true that John had not wished her to in the first years of her marriage—and it may well have been that her extreme youth had prevented her from doing so. In those early years neither of them had wanted children and even later the passion between them and the sexual satisfaction which was so necessary to them both was of far greater importance than anything else.

And now she was sure. She was with child.

She had to watch her beautiful body—of which she was very proud—become misshapen. Never mind, it would return to its former beauty when the child was delivered. It would be interesting to have a child, and she hoped for a son.

John was delighted when he knew.

'People have been murmuring,' he said. 'They've been saying we couldn't get children and that it was God's punishment because we were too fond of the preliminary act.' He laughed aloud. 'They were sniggering about us, my love, when we lay abed till dinner time. Remember those days?'

'I remember them well.'

'And no child to show for them! That was strange, they said. They can say that no longer.'

'Do you think it will be a boy?'

'Of a certainty,' said John. 'The first of many.'

'Not too many,' Isabella reminded him. 'Your father had too many and look what happened to some of them ...' She looked at him slyly. 'And their offspring.'

He flushed with sudden anger. He did not like to remember that scene in Rouen castle when he had looked down at the still figure of his rival nephew; nor did he like to think of himself and the mute carrying the body down to the river. Could he trust the mute? What could the man say when he had been so conveniently deprived of his tongue, which was the very reason John had used his services on that occasion.

No matter how careful one was, such news seeped out sometimes. Where is Arthur? was a question which was going to be asked for some time to come and there was one who would be determined to find the true answer: Philip of France.

Isabella should not have reminded him. She had always been over saucy, perhaps because he had been so enamoured of her, but he was less so now. Other women could please him too, although oddly enough he still preferred her. But he would brook no insolence from her.

'People should learn their lessons,' he growled.

She folded her hands together and raised her eyes piously to the ceiling. ''Twould be good for us all to do that,' she observed meekly enough but with sly insinuations.

No matter for now, he thought. She was comely; and he could still say that he was well pleased with his marriage. If she gave him a son, he would be delighted.

Success on the Continent—for not even his worst enemies could say he had not made progress—and an heir at last!

She was only twenty. There were years of childbearing ahead of her.

Yes, he was as delighted as ever with Isabella.

* * *

Isabella was six months pregnant when news came that Innocent had consecrated Stephen Langton as Archbishop of Canterbury.

John laughed sneeringly when he heard and told Isabella that Innocent could have saved himself the trouble, for the election was not going to be recognized in England. He'd not have Langton set foot on his shores, and by God's feet and toes as well, he'd put John de Grey in the Primate's chair.

It was a different matter when the Pope sent instructions to the leading churchmen of England and Wales reminding them of their duty first to the Church; and he named three of them, William Bishop of London, Eustace Bishop of Ely and Mauger Bishop of Worcester—three of the most important— to approach the King and remind him also of his duty.

It was three very apprehensive Bishops who faced John.

He shouted at them: 'Come, my good Bishops, you have come to talk to me. You come straight from your master and I believe you are very bold when you are not in my presence. What ails you now that you tremble?'

'My lord,' said William of London, 'we come on the orders of the Pope.'

'The Pope,' screamed John. 'He is no friend to me, and nor are those who value his friendship more than mine.'

'We would beg of you, my lord,' said Eustace of Ely, 'to listen to His Holiness's commands.'

'It is a King who commands in this country, Bishop,' retorted John.

'In all matters temporal,' Mauger of Worcester reminded him.

'In *all* matters,' snarled John.

'My lord,' said the Bishop of Ely, 'if you would but receive Stephen Langton and give the monks permission to return...'

'You are mad,' cried the King. 'Do you think that I will allow myself to be so treated? You come to threaten me. Is that so?'

'Nay, nay,' cried the Bishops in unison. 'We but come to tell you the wishes of the Pope.'

'That he will lay an interdict on my kingdom. Is that what you would say?'

'I fear, my lord,' said the Bishop of London, 'that if you will not accept Stephen Langton as Archbishop of Canterbury and allow the monks to return there, the Pope will put the country under interdict.'

'As I said, as I said. And let me tell you this,' John narrowed his eyes and his looks were venomous. 'If any priest under my rule should dare to obey the Pope in this matter, I shall take his property from him and send him a beggar to his master the Pope since it will be clear to me that he is no servant of mine and it is meet that he should go to his master.'

'His Holiness will not allow the matter to rest,' began Eustace.

'No, he will send his envoys with dire threats I know that. And I shall let him know who is ruler here. Not him, he must understand, but the King. Tell him this ... you who serve him so well ... that if I catch any of his envoys on my land I shall send them back to their master ... aye, and not in quite the same condition as that in which they came. They'll grope their way back for they'll have no eyes to see with and I'll slit a nose or two for good measure.'

'My lord, I beg of you remember that these messengers would come from His Holiness.'

'Remember it. Remember it. Do you think I should forget? It is for that reason that I shall make them very sorry they ever came this way. As for you, my lord Bishops, I have endured your company too long. It maddens me. It sickens

me. Get out ... while you are still in possession of your organs
for by God's ears, if you are not gone from my sight in the
next few minutes I shall call my guards and you will be
shown what happens to men in this realm who dare defy
me.'

They could see that he meant it, for the temper was
beginning to flow over.

They bowed and hurried out.

John burst into loud laughter as he watched them.

'Farewell, my brave Bishops,' he shouted.

*   *   *

Isabella was lying in at the Castle at Winchester which had
been built by the Conqueror.

It was October and the leaves of the trees were turning
russet, red and bronze. She lay in her bed and waited for her
child to be born, fearful yet expectant, asking, 'Will it be a
boy or a girl?'

Isabella would prefer a boy of course, but it would be
amusing to have a daughter. How she would enjoy dressing a
girl! Would she be beautiful like herself or resemble John
who was scarcely that?

John was getting old now, having lived for forty years.
That mattered little. She was but twenty. It was perhaps well
that she was having a child, for she was no longer as eager for
John's company as she had once been. Sensual in the extreme
she still was—but not for John. During her pregnancy she
had been thinking a great deal of the child and like most
women she had changed a little. But once the child was born
those desires which had been so important to her would
return—but they would not be for John.

But the child was the main concern now. Here she was in
this ancient town of Winchester where it was fitting that heirs
to the throne should be born—Winchester one of the oldest
towns of the country. The Early Britons had called it Caer
Gwent or the White City; then the Romans had come and
named it Venta Belgarum and it was the Saxons who afterwards called it Witanceaster which had become Winchester.

The original castle was said to have been founded by King
Arthur himself and it was in this city that when the people
were weary of the Danish occupation the order had gone out
that all good Saxon women should take a Danish lover and on

a certain night each should, as he lay in bed beside her, cut either her lover's throat or his hamstrings. That had been the order of Ethelred the Unready. She could imagine John's giving such an order.

When her pains started she could think of nothing but the need to come through her ordeal. There were people in plenty about her bed to help her along and the labour was neither very long nor too distressing.

'My lady will give birth easily,' she heard one of them say.

And so it was, for not long after she had been brought to bed her child was born.

It was a moment of the greatest satisfaction when she heard the words: 'A boy. A fine and healthy boy.'

*   *   *

The child was christened Henry after his grandfather Henry II and there was general rejoicing, many expressing the hope that the baby would resemble the King whose name he shared, commenting that they could hardly have expressed such sentiments if he had had his father's name.

His birth had subtly changed the relationship between his parents. Isabella had quickly regained her good looks and her main attraction would always be that inherent sexuality which had been apparent when she was a child and would remain with her until her death, but the pregnancy and the birth had sent John elsewhere and he continued to roam.

Isabella was for a while absorbed by the child and as she realized the satisfaction of motherhood, she decided that there must be more children; little Henry needed a brother or sister and it was always wise for a King to have several children.

After the stormy interview with the Bishops, John guessed the Pope's answer would not be long in coming. He was right. Just before Easter of the following year the interdict was pronounced from Rome and it was to cover England and Wales.

This meant that there was to be no public worship in churches, and sacraments were not permitted to be administered. Services could be preached—but only on Sundays—and not in church for the church doors must be kept closed. They must take place in the graveyards. Women had to be churched in the porch of the church and there were no burial services nor could any person be buried in consecrated ground.

This caused a great deal of distress among the people who feared that this final shame of being buried in a trench might impair their hopes of a heavenly reception.

Aware of the murmurings of the people against him for having incurred this quarrel with the Pope, John's determination to fight the enemy increased.

'The Pope has taken from my people their rights to religious consolation,' he cried. 'Very well, I will show the Pope what I can do to his servants. Any priest who closes his church to the people will forthwith lose his possessions, for I will not allow him to have them when he turns his face against the needs of the people.'

The priests were in a quandary. What should they do? Lose their goods or as they thought their souls? Many of them decided against their goods, much to John's amusement.

'By God's hands,' he declared, 'this interdict makes me grow rich. I am not sure that I should not be grateful to Master Innocent after all.'

The clergy were in trouble whichever way they turned. If they obeyed the Pope they lost their possessions to the King; if they refused to obey the Pope they were excommunicated. Many of them, including the three Bishops who had warned the King, fled the country.

'Let them go,' screamed the King. 'As long as they leave their goods behind them, why should I care? I hope Innocent realizes how he is enriching me.'

He began to cast about for means of gaining more from the situation. He knew very well that some of the rich churchmen kept their secret mistresses and it appealed to John's sense of humour to extract money through them. He sent his men throughout the country to spy out the secret amorous lives of these outwardly moral churchmen. When a mistress was discovered John arranged that she should be kidnapped. He then sent messengers to the churchmen telling them how much would be paid in fines for the return of their mistresses.

This caused the King a great deal of amusement and in spite of the Interdict he was enjoying life.

He had a healthy son who was almost a year old and Isabella had become pregnant again.

Her second son was born at Winchester a little more than a

year after Henry had appeared, so now she had two healthy sons, as though to make up for the unproductive years.

Little Henry was proving to be quite bright and a source of interest and she found that she liked to be with her children. The second boy was named after his uncle, Richard Coeur de Lion, which pleased the people and the two little boys did much to add to the popularity of the King and Queen.

They were not very often in each other's company and Isabella was well aware that he had mistresses. She was not going to accept that without some protest, but as she did not particularly wish for his company she decided against bringing the matter up with him.

She found herself looking round and admiring some of the more handsome young men; they looked at her with fearful longing, no doubt aware of the invitation in her glances and dreaming of the excitements they could share with her, while at the same time they must consider the terrible consequences of being discovered by an irate husband—and such a powerful one.

Danger added to the excitement and Isabella knew that it was in time to become irresistible. She too thought of the consequences. Suppose such an encounter resulted in a child, would it be so important? She had two sons who were undoubtedly John's. John had had a number of bastards, but that was before their marriage. There may have been others later of whom she had not heard, but for the first years of their marriage he had undoubtedly been faithful to her. No man could have been more zealous in his attentions and he had had neither time nor inclination to disport himself elsewhere.

But now there was change. Some wives might have thought it necessary to act with especial care, to placate him, to play the humble wife. But that was not Isabella's nature. Her power was still there as potent as it was when she was thirteen—more so, for now she was so very experienced, and no man could be in her presence without being deeply affected by her; there could have been very few whom she could not move to desire with very little effort. As for the young and the lusty they were ready to risk almost anything for her favours. Anything. Yes they had to consider that. She wondered what punishment John would think up for one of her lovers.

She played with the idea; her looks, her gestures were full of invitation. She wanted a lover who was prepared to take enormous risks for a brief spell with her.

The inevitable must happen. How thrilling it was! The secret meeting, letting him into her bedchamber, wondering all the time if anyone had seen. It was the most exciting adventure she had known for years.

Why had she been content with that ageing man of the violent temper when there were handsome young men who adored her and were ready to risk mutilation for her sake? Mutilation that would be the most terrible John's warped mind could conceive she was sure.

Life had a new spice for Isabella.

*   *   *

John was pleased with his swollen exchequer. The city of London was also pleased because the new bridge which had taken thirty-three years to build had now been completed. It was nine hundred and twenty-six feet long and forty feet wide and supported by twenty unequal arches. It was indeed a worthy sight and a great boon to the people. They were proud of it.

But even the citizens of London were ill at ease and they talked incessantly of the Interdict.

Burial in unconsecrated ground was but just one cause for apprehension. To be denied the comfort the Church could offer was intolerable to a great many people, moreover, they feared the wrath of Heaven on the ungodly of which, if the doors of the Church had been closed upon them, it seemed they must have become. If they had had to go to war, which was very likely, there would not have been a soldier in the army who would not have felt a great sense of uneasiness and have been convinced that God could not be on the side of men who were the victims of the Pope's Interdict.

It was all very well to have defied Rome for a while but it should not continue. He decided therefore that if the monks of Canterbury returned to England he would allow them to do so and that he would be ready to meet Stephen Langton to discuss matters with him.

This was a step in the right direction, said the Pope, and it was arranged for Stephen Langton to come to England in the company of several of the exiled Bishops. The Pope was adamant that if the Interdict was to be lifted John was to obey all the terms laid down by Rome and failing that His Holiness would have no alternative but to excommunicate John.

In due course the three Bishops arrived with Stephen Langton. John met them at the coast and there was an immediate discussion between them.

John said that he would reinstate the monks; he would accept Stephen Langton as Archbishop but he would not receive him or show him favour.

The Bishops replied that unless John conformed to all the Pope's terms he would be excommunicated.

'One clause of the agreement must be fulfilled,' he was told, 'and that is that you must return all the confiscated property to their rightful owners.'

The thought of losing all that he had gained and meekly giving in infuriated John.

'Get you gone,' he cried. 'Tell Innocent to excommunicate me if he wishes. I care nothing for him nor his threats. I shall keep what is mine and chief of my possessions is the right to rule the country of which I am King. Get back to your master before I am tempted to give you your deserts, you traitors.'

The party left without delay and the result was excommunication for the King of England.

*   *   *

As the effect of the excommunication began to be felt the King was mad with rage. It brought home more clearly than anything could have done the power of the Pope. That the land he ruled should be in such fear and trembling of a distant ruler infuriated him more than anything possibly could; and he looked about for victims on whom to vent his wrath.

The Pope's edict decreed that all those who had contact with the King were themselves contaminated. Any who obeyed him were the enemies of Rome and would suffer accordingly. What were men to do?

When Jeffrey, Archdeacon of Norwich, stood up at the Exchequer Table at Westminster and declared that since the King was excommunicated the Church forbade any to act in his name, the King ordered his arrest.

Jeffrey was placed in a dungeon and John himself could not resist visiting him.

'You served the wrong master, Jeffrey of Norwich,' said John. 'You should have thought twice before doing that.'

'My conscience is clear,' answered Jeffrey boldly.

'Let me tell you this, you traitor to your King, you will not long have a conscience to be clear or otherwise.'

'You cannot intimidate me into accepting what a greater Lord than you tells me is sinful.'

'You must be on better terms with Him than you are with me,' said John. 'Let us see how He will look after you in your emergency.'

He then left the cell and ordered that the Archdeacon should be laden with chains. 'I want a cope of lead, a large and heavy one and I order that it be crammed down on our pious Archdeacon's head. Let it crush and suffocate him while he broods on his great virtues and his treachery to his King.'

This was done and men talked of it with awe.

All the bishops and friends of Stephen Langton were to be put into prison and their lands and goods confiscated.

'These churchmen have done very well for themselves,' said John. 'And now they are doing very well for me. This excommunication like the Interdict has its uses.'

But there was in this a certain bravado because the people were turning against him. The barons had always been seeking a reason for revolt and they were very powerful; he feared them even more than he feared the Church.

If they were to turn against him now and ally themselves with the Church, his position might be very difficult. He decided therefore that he demand of the barons that each of them should send one of their sons to the King as a hostage. When the young men were in his power he could be sure of the fidelity of their parents.

While this order was being carried out John was making a progress through the country to assure himself that the people realized his power and that he himself was not deeply concerned over the excommunication.

Passing through the countryside he came upon a crowd of people beating before them a man whose hands were tied behind his back.

The King called: 'What happens here? What is this man guilty of?'

'He is a murderer, my lord. A thief as well,' was the answer. 'He waylaid a man on the road, robbed him and murdered him. He was caught in the act.'

The man trembled. Fearful punishment awaited him. He would doubtless be hanged on a gibbet. It might be his hands would be cut off. But perhaps that was too mild a punishment for murder. He hoped it would be the tree, for to have his eyes put out was worse than death. 'Who was the man the rogue murdered?' asked John.

'A priest, my lord.'

The King burst out laughing. 'Untie his hands,' he said. They obeyed. 'Come here,' ordered the King.

The man stood before him raising fearful eyes to the King's face.

'Go on your way,' said the King. 'You are a free man. You have killed one of my enemies.'

The man bowed low and cried: 'God's blessings on you, my lord King.'

And he ran off as fast as he could.

The crowd fell back in astonishment; there was a murmur of disapproval.

'What's this? What's this?' cried the King. 'If any has anything to say let him speak.'

None dared reply. They knew tongues could be torn out for raising a word against the King.

People talked of the incident. A murderer had gone free, pardoned by the King, because his victim was a priest.

*   *   *

The family of Braose had fallen out of favour with the King since those days when William de Braose had been the custodian of Falaise and had been in charge of Arthur before Hubert de Burgh took over that duty. William, a man of great spirit with a tradition of power behind him, had always defended his rights, and rulers had realized that his was not a family to be neglected. When a Braose had been killed by the Welsh, it was William who had invited a party of Welshmen to his castle as guests, and after they had partaken of his hospitality he, with members of his family, killed them all as a lesson to any who might feel inclined to become their enemies.

He had been in the King's company at Rouen soon after the death of Arthur and he had a very shrewd notion as to what had happened to the young Duke of Brittany. So had his wife Matilda. She was a strong-minded woman; in fact it was said that there was only one person in the world of whom William de Braose was afraid. Although they were aware that there had been gruesome events at Rouen they could not be sure of how the murder had been carried out; and fierce as Matilda was, her maternal instincts were strong and when she and William had been in charge of Arthur in Falaise Castle she had grown quite fond of the boy.

She declared: 'I have disliked and distrusted John ever since Arthur disappeared.'

No matter how earnestly William might warn her to guard her tongue, Matilda would speak when she wished and the thought of that boy's death—perhaps in horrible circumstances—could rouse her to anger.

When a quarrel broke out between her family and the King she was not altogether displeased. She was not a woman to disguise her feelings and secretly—although she knew it was dangerous—she preferred to be on terms of hostility with John rather than those of friendship. At least she could be honest and, forthright woman that she was, that pleased her.

When John had levied taxes on his barons, William had objected and failed to pay and towards the end of the year 1207 John expressed his annoyance that William owed him certain monies and demanded that William surrender his castles of Hay, Brecknock and Radnor as pledges for his debts.

There was another matter which angered John. The Braoses' youngest son Giles was Bishop of Hereford and when John was excommunicated Giles had left England with other Bishops, indicating his objection to accepting John's rule and his desire to be on the side of the Pope.

John's reaction to this was to rage against the whole family. He could not trust them any more. William de Braose had once been a very powerful man, and John was determined to curtail that power; the fact that he had been obliged to give up three of his castles would be a great blow to him and John chuckled to think of how resentful he would be.

'I don't trust these Braoses,' he said. 'I am determined to show them who is the master.'

They should send hostages without delay, for only when he had some members of the family in his charge would he feel he held some power over them. Matilda de Braose guessed that something of this nature could come about. She discussed the matter with her husband and demanded to know what he thought would become of their grandsons if they were put into the King's charge as hostages?

'He will be in duty bound to treat them with honour,' said William.

'When did this King ever feel in *duty* bound?'

'Nevertheless, we shall have no alternative.'

Matilda cried out so that several servants heard: 'I will never allow any son or grandson of mine to go as hostage to the King ... and I have my reasons ... very good ones.'

'You speak with indiscretion,' said her husband in alarm.

'Sometimes it is well for certain matters to be given an airing,' she retorted.

Again he implored her to be discreet, but Matilda was one who would always speak her mind.

In due course the messengers from the King arrived at the castle and asked to have speech with Sir William and his lady. They explained that the King was not pleased with the manner in which they were behaving and he needed two of their grandsons to leave at once in the charge of the messengers. The boys were to come to him where they would be treated as became their rank; and their presence would ensure the good behaviour of the family.

Before her husband could stop her Matilda cried: 'Do you think I would deliver my grandsons to your master! I would never do such a thing. Give up my boys to a man who murdered his own nephew!'

There was a brief silence. The eyes of everyone present were on Matilda. She held her head defiantly and looking at her husband cried: 'It's true. We know it. Others know it too. In time the whole world will know it. And I will not put my grandchildren into the hands of such a murderer.'

Sir William tried to silence her. He laid his hand on her arm and said: 'Pray do not speak thus against the King. If I have offended him I will make good my errors without the surrender of hostages.'

'The King's orders are that you give your grandsons into our hands.'

'Never!' cried Matilda stoutly. 'I will never give them to him. You may go and tell him that.'

The messengers left. Sir William looked after them shaking his head dolefully.

'You should never have spoken so freely,' he said.

'I will not give up my grandchildren to that murderer,' reiterated his wife.

When the messengers returned to the King he demanded to know where the Braose hostages were. The messengers replied that Lady de Braose had refused to give them up. 'So she deliberately disobeyed me,' cried John.

'She said my lord that she would not hand her children to one who had murdered his nephew.'

John turned pale; a horrible sick foreboding touched him.

The ghost of Arthur had returned after all this time to mock him. For a few moments he could find nothing to say. Then the rage swept over him; he spluttered: 'By God's hands and feet. By God's ears and mouth ... they shall pay for this and in particular you, my Lady Matilda.'

He shut himself into his chamber; he threw himself on to the floor. He wanted to bang his head against the wall, but he refrained from doing this. In the shadows he seemed to see a slim boy smiling at him. He thought of those lifeless eyes when they had lifted the body to throw it into the Seine.

Oh yes, Arthur had indeed come back to haunt him.

*   *   *

He was worried now. Matilda de Braose had reawakened the rumour. Now they would be talking of it throughout the country; it would spread to the Continent. Philip would take it up. Philip had never really let it drop, but Philip was far away and people in England had not been particularly interested in the young Duke of Brittany. But now they would be talking. He had lost Normandy; an interdict had been placed on England and Wales; he was excommunicated; and now if this ugly spectre arose they would hold something else against him. It was just what his enemies needed.

A thousand curses on Matilda de Braose. She should suffer for this; and if she were spreading rumours about Arthur it was time she was removed.

Realizing that the messengers would have repeated Matilda's words to John, William guessed what action John

would take and that there was only one way open to him.
John would try to destroy them, so they might as well make
an attempt to hold what was left to them. With his sons he
decided to try to recover those castles which he had pledged
to John until he had settled his debts; but John had suspected
he would try this; he therefore declared that he was a traitor
and that the same name would apply to any who assisted him.

The result was that William found it necessary to retreat to
his Welsh estates, but when it became clear that John was
determined to harry him, he and his family left for Ireland.

One of his daughters had married Walter Lacy, Lord of
Meath, the eldest son of Hugh Lacy one of the conquerors of
Ireland. He had now and then been at odds with John but
was at this time on fairly good terms with him.

In Ireland William felt comparatively safe but he was
apprehensive about the fate of his possessions in England and
Wales. When John knew that he had gone, he demanded his
extradition. The Lacys promised to send him back but day
after day passed and still William and his family remained in
Ireland.

But John could not forget the threats behind Matilda's
words. The family hated him; they were his greatest enemies;
and Matilda had openly accused him of murdering Arthur.
He could not feel at ease until he had rid himself of that loud-
voiced woman. He enjoyed promising himself what he would
do to her when he had her in his power. She must not know
how she had disturbed him; there was nothing she could have
said which would have caused him more uneasiness. Over the
years he had forgotten Arthur; people seemed to have taken
it for granted that he had disappeared and accepted it as a
mystery. Now she had to shout forth her malice. By God's
teeth, if he could but lay hands on her!

And they were in Ireland. It was time the power of the
Lacys was broken there. He had to be watchful, though.
Sometimes he felt that his barons were banding together
against him. No man in his kingdom should have so much
power. Why should these Lacys behave as though they were
kings of Ireland? How dared they shelter a rebel when he
had demanded he be delivered to him?

He would go to Ireland. He would take the power the
Lacys had assumed; he would show the people who was their
rightful ruler; he would establish the supremacy of the crown

over there; and he would bring back the Braoses. He would not rest until he had made that woman his prisoner.

When William de Braose heard that the King had arrived in Ireland he was greatly disturbed.

'God help us,' he said to Matilda, 'if we fall into his hands.'

'We must see that we do not,' she replied firmly.

John, however, had come with a powerful army behind him and the Irish chiefs flocked to Dublin to pay homage to him; he had no difficulty in seizing much of the land which the Lacys had considered theirs; he deposed them and set up his old friend John de Grey in their place. He had failed to make him Archbishop of Canterbury but at least he could show his appreciation of him in some way.

If there was one thing John enjoyed it was easy triumph and he had achieved what he wanted with the utmost ease. He could not stay of course. He must return to England; that was why he sent for John de Grey.

'I do not wish you to stay here,' he said. 'Just long enough to let the people see that this is the end of the Lacys' rule. It cannot be long before the Braoses are in our power and when you have them, I want you to bring them to me in England. I have plans for this arrogant family.'

He could trust John de Grey, who had always been a good friend and now had the added reason for being loyal to John—the promise of the Archbishopric of Canterbury when the controversy with the Pope should be over.

John was a little too optimistic. Matilda was not the woman to submit easily. It was known that she was in residence at Meath Castle and John's men besieged that castle, their purpose being to capture her. She was too wily for them, for she had already left the castle and crossed to Scotland.

Infuriated by this, John seized William and said he personally would conduct him to England.

John realized that he had not finished with the troublesome family so far. When they crossed to England William escaped to one of his strongholds in Wales and there declared open war on the King. John was maddened. It was the woman he wanted. She was the one who was going to spread the scandal all over the world. She was the one who would tell the world that he had murdered Arthur.

*   *   *

It was a rough journey which Matilda and her eldest son William undertook, and it seemed to them both that they had escaped one peril for an even greater one. Clinging to the sides of the boat they had little inclination to think of anything but immediate survival, but when the boat finally did reach the safety of Galloway her first thoughts were of what might have happened to William.

'He has been less fortunate than we have,' she said to her son. 'I shudder to think of what will happen to him in the hands of that tyrant.'

'Father is clever,' said the younger William. 'It may well be that he will think of a way of outwitting the King.'

'John has so much on his side. It won't always be so, William. Rebellion is growing throughout the country. He is disliked everywhere. The barons are ready to rise against him. Your father is one of the first of many. The day will come, you will see, when John will be forced to listen to the will of those he calls his subjects.'

'We will hope so, Mother.'

'It must be so. I only wish that they would band together now and come to rally round your father. What a leader he would make!'

Where could they go now? she wondered. They had reached Scotland but it did not seem a very hospitable land.

A party of fisherfolk who had seen their arrival came out to see who they were and when they realized that they were people of quality, they took them into their homes and gave them food.

One of their party went to tell Duncan of Carrick that they were there and he came to greet them and offer them hospitality of a kind suited to their rank. Gladly they accepted.

Matilda told him who they were and why they had escaped so hurriedly from Ireland; he listened closely, nodding sympathetically but, when they had retired for the night and being exhausted soon fell into a deep sleep, he sent a messenger to England asking what should be done with them.

The answer came back promptly.

Thus it was that while William, having seen that his position in Wales was untenable, had fled to France, Matilda and her eldest son were delivered into John's hands.

*   *   *

They were taking her to Windsor. She knew it well.

What would he do to her there? Imprison her in a dungeon? She held her head high. Whatever he did he would not intimidate her. She was not afraid of him. He was a coward, she told her son William, who rode with her, and it was always a mistake to show fear to cowards.

Windsor, she thought, where the Saxons had built a palace, and which in those days was known as Windlesofra or Windleshora because of the way in which the Thames wound through the countryside! There were some who said its name had come about because travellers had to be ferried over the river with a rope and pole and people had said, 'Wind us over the river'. It was a bleak spot and Matilda thought the real origin of the name might well be 'Wind is Sore' referring to the bleakness of the gales which assaulted the place in winter.

Edward the Confessor used to keep Court here but when William the Conqueror came he had set his mark on the place as he had done throughout England, and there was the Round Tower to proclaim it. It was his son Henry the First who had built a chapel there and made it a residence.

John secretly watched their arrival chortling with glee. Now, my proud lady, he thought, you will be a little less bold, a little less inclined to spread calumnies concerning me.

His mouth tightened. Of one thing he must make sure. She was never to leave this place alive.

He sent for them and when they stood before him he noted that she was as arrogant as ever, although her son William looked a little subdued. He wished that it was her husband he had there. *He* had cleverly made his escape. No matter, it was the woman he wanted most. She was the one who had made trouble and he doubted not led her husband into it.

He dismissed the guards for he did not want anyone to hear any reference to Arthur which he feared she might make. Some women might be a little humble in her desperate position, but one could not be sure of Matilda de Braose.

John looked at her slyly, keeping her standing while he sprawled in his throne-like chair.

'So we meet at last,' he said. 'By God's ears I thought we never should. First you are in Wales, then in Ireland and finally in Scotland. You lead a wandering life, my lady.'

'It was no wish of mine, my lord, that I wandered so much.

I should have preferred to remain in my rightful castle of Hay, or that of Brecknock or Radnor.'

The impertinence of the woman! If he were not afraid of her and what harm she might do him he might have found it in his heart to admire her.

'And now you have come to rest at Windsor. It pleases me to see you here as my guest.'

He savoured the last word. He is a devil, she thought. He will murder us as he murdered Arthur.

'I trust you feel a like pleasure,' he added smiling sardonically; and when she was silent he went on: 'You do not answer me, my lady. I must tell you that when I speak I expect to be answered.'

'I thought you did not want an answer which must be obvious.'

'You are not pleased to be my guest,' he said. 'But you who are usually most eager to speak your mind should say so.'

'And trust I always shall be. I was never one to say one thing and mean another.'

'I know it well, so I believe did that husband of yours. You're a forceful woman, my lady.'

She bowed her head.

'And now you stand before me,' he went on, 'knowing that you have been speaking ill of me. That should give you cause to tremble.'

'I speak nothing but the truth.'

'That is for us to decide.'

'Nay, my lord, it is for the world to do that.'

'You are an insolent woman,' he cried.

She knew that she was looking straight into the face of death but she shrugged her shoulders almost nonchalantly.

'I have said that which has offended you,' she said, 'and I care not because I know it to be the truth. If it is not so, where is Arthur of Brittany?'

'You have not come here to question me. Remember you are my prisoner. You stand there with your son. Your husband has deserted you.'

'Nay,' she said, 'we have been parted through evil circumstances. He is not the man to desert his wife.'

'You contradict me at every turn.'

'I have told you that I shall speak the truth.'

'Very brave, very brave. Save your bravery, my lady. You are going to need it.'

'I know that well. I have spoken outright what has been in people's minds these many years—in fact ever since the night when Arthur disappeared from the castle of Rouen. You cannot keep your sin a secret for ever, my lord.'

John began to shout. 'Guards. Guards. Take this man and woman. Put them in one of the dungeons. I shall decide then what shall be done with them.'

The guards came in. Matilda went out, still holding her head high, and her eyes flashed scorn at the King and although she did not speak, her lips formed the word Murderer.

*   *   *

How could he punish them? When he thought of that woman his rage was almost out of control. He had to be careful though. William de Braose was still free. What could he do if he maimed his wife—put out her eyes or more appropriately cut out her tongue? The spectre of Arthur seemed very real at that moment. Was he never going to forget Arthur? The barons were growing more and more rebellious. Caution, whispered his good sense.

Of one thing he was certain. Matilda de Braose should never leave Windsor.

'Take these two to a dungeon,' he said. 'See that they are fettered. Let them be kept in the same dungeon.'

He smiled to himself. There they could watch each other's misery which would be an added torment.

His wishes were immediately carried out.

*   *   *

Each day he wondered how they fared. How could they be living in that cell from which there was no escape? They had no food and even the valiant Matilda could not live for ever without sustenance.

He thought of her with pleasure every morning when he awoke and sat at table. Succulent flesh, rich pastry—he took great delight in them, more especially because he knew that proud Matilda and her son were starving.

After two weeks he sent his guards down to the dungeon to see what had happened. They were both dead. The son had died first and in her agony the mother had gnawed at his flesh in the very extremities of starvation.

John laughed aloud when he heard.

So died proud Matilda! That would be a lesson to any who thought they could accuse him of his nephew's murder.

But it proved otherwise and after the death of Matilda de Braose the whispering started up as fresh as it had been at the time of Arthur's death.

The Virgin of Dunmow

In the castle of Gloucester, Isabella was delivered of her third child. This time it was a girl and she was christened Joanna. Having borne three children in the space of three years Isabella felt that she could give herself a rest from childbirth. She loved her children but her nature made her more interested in the sexual side of marriage than the maternal.

She was growing more and more disenchanted with John. She could still attract him in a way, although naturally the tremendous appeal she had had for him had slackened a little. He liked to add different flavours to his activities and as he grew older his desires did not diminish.

It was always a daring adventure for a Queen to take lovers because of the possibility of children. Royal children should be those of the King, for illegitimate offspring could cause endless trouble. Isabella was royal enough to be aware of this. But having presented John with three children she felt she had earned a little respite and there were one or two personable men on whom she had cast speculative eyes.

Her inborn fascination for the opposite sex had to be great indeed for them to dare risk the dangers which discovery would mean. As gentlemen of the court they would have experienced from time to time the mad wrath of the King and although he might think it perfectly natural for him to take a mistress wherever he fancied, he would certainly not offer the same liberty to his Queen.

Therefore to one of Isabella's character the thought of

infidelity was irresistible. John was absent a great deal and opportunities offered themselves.

There were one or two men who were ready to take the risk Isabella discovered when she looked about the court for likely partners with whom she could spend her nights. They did not have to be of high birth; their only qualifications were their sexual prowess and their courage.

There were not a great number who had both; but she did find the occasional man who was prepared to risk everything for her favours.

Life was spiced with exciting adventure for Isabella.

*   *   *

John was becoming a little suspicious of Isabella. There was something sly about her. When they met they were as amorous as ever and no matter what women he encountered none of them could really compare with Isabella. He had set spies on his wife where she would least expect to find them but still nothing had come to light about the lovers he suspected her of taking.

Sometimes he would laugh to himself to think of her with them but at others the thought would send him into a mad rage. It would depend a great deal on his mood of the moment, though he knew of course that if he ever had actual proof of her infidelity he would be furious.

Meanwhile, he sought ladies to amuse him. Sometimes they were willing—in fact they almost always were—out of fear of his temper or obsession with the honour of being noticed by the King. But it was the reluctant ones who were beginning to attract him more and more.

When he came to Dunmow Castle to be entertained by one of his leading barons, Robert FitzWalter, the baronial lord of Dunmow and Baynard's Castle, he met Robert's daughter Matilda. That the girl was a virgin was obvious from one glimpse of her, for she was very young and her mother had guarded her well. Moreover, she was the prettiest creature he had seen for a long time and just the sort to soothe those nagging doubts about Isabella's fidelity which beset him from time to time.

Robert FitzWalter was one of the most important of the barons and his possession of Baynard's Castle carried with it the hereditary office of standard bearer to the City of London which meant of course that he was regarded highly by the citizens. He was a great merchant and owned several ships; he was also engaged in the wine trade and because of his importance as a baron the King had granted him several privileges which were useful to him in his business.

And now having seen he had this fair daughter, John was prepared to honour Robert FitzWalter even more.

As they rode together in the hunt in the forest of Dunmow John brought his horse close to that of Robert Fitz-Walter and said: 'By God's eyes, Walter, you have a fair daughter.'

Those words accompanied by the leer on John's face were enough to make any father anxious.

'My lord, Matilda is but a child.'

'A fair one forsooth.'

'Yes, her mother has brought her up very carefully.'

John licked his lips. He had a great fancy at this time for virgins. 'So I see, and it does her credit. Your lady wife will be pleased to hear that the King admires her.'

Robert FitzWalter did not answer, knowing full well that that was the last thing his lady wife wished to hear. Lady FitzWalter was a woman of strong character and stern morals who had brought up her daughter firmly in the light of her own beliefs.

'I will tell her,' said Robert quietly.

'Pray do. I may extend my visit to Dunmow, Robert. I like the place. It pleases me ... as does your daughter.'

When the King talked in such a manner there was only one thing to do. Robert FitzWalter immediately sought out his wife and told her what the King had said.

She turned pale.

'This is terrible. What can we do?'

'I know not.'

'I shall never give my daughter to that lecher.'

'It is impossible.'

'I would prefer to die defending her.'

'Remember what happened to Matilda Braose. Starved to death in a dungeon.'

'This man is a vile tyrant, Robert.'

'I know it well. The barons have known it for years. They will not endure his villainies much longer.'

'But not in time to save Matilda. Our little girl, Robert! I feel ill contemplating it.'

'I know. I know.'

'I'll take her away. We'll leave at once. You must tell him I have taken her on a visit ... you can say it is without your permission. In fact it is better that you do, for he might turn his wrath on you if you do not. Tell him I have taken her away and you knew nothing of it. That I often do it perhaps, that I am a disobedient arrogant wife. Tell him that and that you do not know where we have gone.'

'It's the only way,' said Robert. 'Who knows, if she is out of his sight some other poor girl might take his fancy.'

Lady FitzWalter lost no time. She sent for her daughter and told her to prepare for a journey at once and to be sure not to mention to anyone that she was going.

Thus Lady FitzWalter took her daughter from the Castle of Dunmow.

At supper that night John asked where Robert's wife and daughter were.

'They have gone on a visit.'

'While I am here?' cried John.

'My lord, my wife is a most contentious woman.'

'By God's ears, Robert, it is an insult to me.'

'I trust you will not take it as such, my lord.'

'To leave when the King is here! Why so, man, why so?'

'It seems my wife had arranged this visit and would let nothing—not even your presence—prevent her departure.'

'You have married a scold, Robert FitzWalter.'

'I fear so, my lord.'

'Yet I would not have thought you a meek man.'

'We don different faces, my lord, by our own fireside.'

''Tis true. I have seen the boldest men cowards before their wives.'

'Then here you see yet another.'

John laughed aloud. He was in good spirits it seemed. Robert was delighted. His wife's ruse had worked and John was already looking round at other women.

He did not know that John's men had made him aware of the departure of Lady FitzWalter and her daughter and he had laid plans that they should be intercepted on their way. Lady FitzWalter should be allowed to return to the lord who declared he was in awe of her, but the delectable daughter should be carried to a place of John's choosing where she could await his coming.

*   *   *

The following day John left Dunmow and shortly after his departure Lady FitzWalter returned. She was so distraught that she could hardly tell her husband what had happened. Their daughter had been abducted and she was in great fear as to what was happening to her. They had not ridden far from the castle when they met a party of men riding towards them. The men stopped and asked if they were near Dunmow Castle.

'I told them that they were very close,' said Lady Fitz-Walter, 'and I asked what their business was. The leader of the men bowed and said he knew he had the pleasure of addressing Lady FitzWalter and her fair daughter. That was the sign. It was terrible, Robert ... a nightmare. Two of them seized Matilda's horse and started to drag it away. She cried out but by that time I was surrounded by them, and her horse was galloping away with her with two of these scoundrels. Some of our men gave chase but they were followed by others of the party whose horses were fleeter than theirs. There was a fight and several of them were injured. Oh, Robert, they have taken Matilda.'

'Oh God,' cried Robert, 'it cannot mean...'

They looked at each other in horror.

'How was he ... when he knew we had gone?' asked Matilda fearfully.

'Calm, jocular. He did not seem put out.'

'Could it possibly be...?'

They dared not answer that question.

*   *   *

It was one of his smaller castles, not very far from that of Dunmow. It amused him that it should be so near the home of her parents and they not know it. He expected she would be terrified. What would she be like when she knew who had ordered that she be brought here? They could say what they liked, all women were at heart ready to please the King. It meant something to them to take a royal lover. She might be reluctant at first but not for long.

Her mother would be outraged. Foolish woman! Did

she not know that he was conferring an honour on her daughter?

As he rode to the castle to confront the young girl he was thinking of her mother. What impudence to have removed the girl in that way because she knew that he had designs on her. Had she forgotten what had happened to Matilda of Braose? Did she think that because she was the wife of a powerful and somewhat forceful man she could act against him with impunity? Matilda de Braose had been the wife of a most influential man—though he had fallen low—and Lady FitzWalter should consider her.

By God's ears he would humiliate that woman where it hurt her most. He would show her that her meek little daughter came to him willingly. He would make the girl eager for him. He would flaunt their lust before that prim woman. It was the best way of dealing with her. So as he rode along he made up his mind that he would not force this young Matilda. He would make her come to him of her own free will. Then he would tell her mother this and indeed the prospect of the mother's anguish would give him as much pleasure—if not more—than the deflowering of the daughter.

With this firm resolution he arrived at the castle and went at once to the chamber where they had put the girl. It was in one of the turrets—approached by a stone spiral staircase—a safe refuge for her. She would not be able to escape from this place very easily. That was the last thing she must do. If she did they would secrete her abroad somewhere, find refuge in France most likely. That would not be difficult, for Philip was master across the Channel now and what pleasure he would take in fresh scandal about his old enemy! He would make the most of it, honour the girl, take her to his Court, no doubt find a noble husband for her and hold her up as an example of John's wickedness; he would revive the murder of Arthur. Revive it! He had never let it die!

But he would not think of Arthur now. The years were passing and it was long since the day the boy had died. Who would have thought the scandal could have survived so long? But now he was interested in that tasty morsel, the virgin Matilda.

She stood up as he entered. By God's teeth, he thought, she is a beautiful creature. Her eyes were wide, dilated with terror. She would have heard stories no doubt of the monster he was reputed to be. She clasped her hands together in front of her, as though to guard her body from him, or perhaps to try to hide the fact that they were trembling. Silly, frightened creature! She was so graceful. Like a deer startled by the approach of the huntsmen, poised for flight. But where to, my pretty? Out of the window? Down, down to the ground below, that exquisite body bruised and torn by the rough stone walls as she fell? No, I have other plans for it.

'You must not be afraid, Matilda,' he said, smiling.

To her it was an evil smile although he had meant it to be reassuring.

'You must not be in awe of me because I am your King.'

She continued to gaze at him, speechless with fear.

'You must speak to me when I address you, Matilda. It is not good manners to do otherwise—particularly when you are confronted by your King.'

She swallowed and stammered: 'I ... have nothing to say except to beg you to let me go home.'

'All in good time,' he said. 'But I'll tell you this, Matilda, there will come a day when you will beg me not to send you away. You will ask me not to send you back to the dull home of your father where your mother stands continual guard over you. You will say: I love my King. I wish to serve my King in all ways. I wish to be a joy and comfort to him.'

He put his hands on her shoulders and felt the tremor run through her.

Foolish child! he thought. It was a pity she was so pretty. He would have liked to have shouted: Go home to your mother, you silly little thing. There are women a thousand times more attractive than you are who welcome me.

It was her youth that appealed to him. She was about the age Isabella had been when she had first come to him. How different she had been! This child knew nothing of the passion of men like himself except to distrust and fear it; how different from his gay adventurous Isabella who had longed to experiment with everything that was new.

A great yearning for the days when he had first known Isabella came to him. To be young with Isabella. To start again. Oh, he would have acted just the same. When the Marshal and the barons warned him that he was losing his dominions he would still have stayed in bed with Isabella.

There would never be anyone to replace Isabella. This

foolish shrinking virgin, what had she? She had been nur-
tured by that strict woman whose main desire had been to
protect her. What pleasure could there be in this child—
except the rape of innocence? He had had plenty of that.

He wanted Isabella. He wanted to be young with her
again. What was she doing now? Had she taken lovers? She
was not the sort of woman to live without them. And that
slyness about her ... that acceptance of his infidelities which
had angered her in the first place?

But why was he thinking of Isabella here with this lovely
young girl before him?

It was not that he wanted the child so much as to score over
the mother.

'Now, Matilda,' he said, 'you and I are going to be friends.
I will show you how to get the utmost pleasure out of life.
You would like that would you not, my dear,'

She had closed her eyes and he thought she was going to
faint.

'Please ...' she began. 'Please let me go.'

He put his arms about her and kissed her roughly on the
lips. She gave out a cry of anguish.

The impulse came to rape the girl and get it over, send her
back to her mother and hope he had not got her with child,
for a weak creature it would be with such a mother.

He shook her roughly.

'You silly girl,' he said. 'You are afraid of what you do not
know.'

Her frightened eyes were staring at the door. There was no
one there; she was thinking of escape.

He said softly: 'No use, Matilda, there is no way out.
There is a guard at the door and others on the stairs.'

She showed a spark of spirit then. 'Would they not be
doing you better service guarding your possessions?'

'You are my possession, little Matilda,' he said. 'As all my
subjects are. Subjects, remember! That means they are
subject to my will.'

'My father ...'

'Your father, oh he is a very powerful baron but he and
your mother will learn that there is none more powerful than
the King.'

Her eyes appealed to him to release her. Oddly enough,
beautiful as she was with her large eyes like a doe's, she did

not arouse him. How different from Isabella's long languorous eyes. She was unformed—attractive in a way. How was it Isabella had managed to be voluptuous in her immaturity?

Why did he not take the girl and have done with it? Because he did not want to. He wanted to revenge himself on her mother. That woman's defiance of him could rouse more passion in him than this child's obvious charms.

He would woo her; then he would make the mother aware of her daughter's depravity.

'You should not be afraid, Matilda,' he said. 'I have a fancy for you, 'tis true. But you have been listening to evil tales of me. It is a sad fact that a king is often maligned. There are rumours about him, his deeds are exaggerated. You fear me because you have heard whispers, have you not? Confess it little one.'

She nodded.

'I have to convince you that you have been misled, do I not? I shall have to show you how different I am from the man they led you to believe me to be. Let us talk now of your home and your family. You shall tell me what you best like to do.'

'I best like to be with my mother.'

'Ho, that is baby's talk. We are at our mother's knee when we are children, but as we grow older we realize we cannot spend the rest of our lives there. You will find interests away from your mother and I am going to teach you.'

He took her hand and led her to a bench. He sat there beside her and put his arms about her. He felt her whole body shrink and it made him want to shout at her not to be a fool or he would give her something to be frightened about. But he restrained himself by thinking of the insolence of her mother in snatching her away from him as she had done. Nobody was going to treat him like that. Did she think that because Philip of France had humiliated him, that his subjects could?

Be calm, he admonished himself. You are going to revenge yourself in full on that woman.

He talked to Matilda quietly, of his journeys through England. He was not sure that she was listening and when he rose to go he believed she had ceased to fear him as much as she had when he arrived.

*   *   *

It was a difficult task he had set himself, but having embarked on it he decided to go on. He stayed in the castle to be near her, expecting that in a short time he would have beguiled her into accepting him of her free will as a lover. That was what he wanted. He would say to her mother: Here is your daughter. My willing mistress. Is it not so, my dear Matilda! And she would blush and stammer, for she had been brought up never to tell a lie—and that would be the ultimate triumph.

It had to happen that way. He had determined it should.

There were times when he lost his temper with her.

'Matilda, you like me, don't you?'

Her foolish answer was: 'You are the King.'

'What does that mean?'

'That it would be treason not to.'

'And you know what happens to those who commit treason, my child?'

She hung her head.

Oh she was a foolish creature. He could imagine Isabella in such circumstances. How she would relish such a game as this.

On the day he tried to make love to her, she began to shout for help.

More folly. As if anyone would come to her aid when they knew who her assailant was. If it wasn't for her mother he would let her go.

Fear had changed her a little. It had made her grow up. She might develop feelings, desires. She might realize that there was exciting adventure outside her quiet home. He imagined the marriage which would be planned for her. A powerful nobleman with estates, carefully chosen by the mother; someone who would bring wealth to the darling daughter and be gentle with her. It would do her no harm to be the King's mistress first. She would go to her husband wiser and more able to enjoy her married life.

Every time he visited her she shrank from him. She was never going to come to him willingly. He had to make up his mind whether he should take her by force or give up. Give her back to that woman. Virtue triumphant. Never!

He tried to talk to her reasonably. 'How can I be such an ogre when I am so patient?'

That made a little impression, for she was well aware of what he might have done.

'See how I seek to woo you! I am tender and kind. I have told you how I came to your father's castle and saw you and loved you for your beauty. You are a very beautiful girl, Matilda. I have rarely seen one as lovely as you. But you are unformed, you are a child. Your beauty needs to mature. You need a lover ... a king for a lover.'

But what was the use?

She was adamant.

One day, she stood by the window and said: 'If you come near me I will throw myself out.'

He looked at her in alarm and he knew she meant it.

*　　*　　*

It was no use. She would never give in willingly. Her family would be searching for her. He didn't trust Fitz-Walter. He was too powerful; he was the sort of man who would lead the barons to revolt. All the same he was not going to allow FitzWalter's wife to dictate to him.

And what if they discovered the whereabouts of their daughter? It wouldn't be difficult in the present state of affairs for them to lead the barons to her rescue.

He pictured it with dismay. All those who had been murmuring against him for so long, setting out against him. There could be civil war.

He had had enough of Matilda. She would never give in willingly. He did not want just another rape. He had had enough of that, and it had ceased to appeal as it once had.

What then? Return her to her parents? Never.

But be rid of her he must.

He sent for one of the cooks, a good fellow whom he knew would do a great deal if rewarded for it; and with such a task one was comparatively safe because although he had ordered it, the act had actually been committed by someone else who was as involved as he was.

It was so easy. A hint which was immediately taken.

During the day young Matilda was taken ill. Before the night was out she was dead.

It was later said by those who attended on her that she had become affected after eating an egg.

*　　*　　*

He sent her body back to Dunmow and the young girl was

laid to rest in Little Dunmow Church. Her mother wept bitter tears of anguish and could not stop herself going over and over that moment on the road when her daughter had been snatched from her.

What could I have done? she asked herself. I should have gone with her. I should have died rather than let her go.

But it was no use weeping. Matilda lay in her tomb, poor child, and no tears could bring her back.

'I shall never forget this,' cried Robert FitzWalter. 'I shall be revenged on John. He shall suffer for this. He will wish he had never dared harm my family.'

'What can we do?' cried his wife. 'Nothing will bring Matilda back.'

FitzWalter could do a great deal. His hatred burned so fiercely in him that it became an inspiration.

A Substitute for the Bedchamber

JOHN could not help but be aware that the position of the King of England had deteriorated alarmingly during his reign. The great bogey was Philip Augustus of France, who having taken possession of Normandy and much of John's possessions overseas was in fact now casting his eyes on England itself, and much as William the Conqueror had gazed longingly across the Channel before the invasion, so now looked Philip Augustus of France.

He reasoned that John was no great adversary. How different it would have been to face Richard or his father, Henry II. He felt no such qualms about John. A king who had sported in bed when his kingdom was in jeopardy, who had lost the heritage of his great ancestors, whose country was under Interdict and who himself was excommunicated seemed to have placed himself in a position of which it would be folly for his enemies not to take advantage.

So Philip began to amass an army with the idea that when the time was ripe he would cross the Channel and take the English crown from John.

Even John must be alarmed at this prospect. The loss of Continental possessions meant a respite from perpetual fighting, but the loss of England would be intolerable. He would be no longer a king.

He could not now be idle and spend half the day in bed. He did not wish to. He was travelling about the country most of the time, taking women where he fancied them and enjoying variety.

He made an arrangement with five of the chief trading ports in the country to supply him with ships. These were Dover, Romney, Hythe, Hastings and Sandwich which were known as the Cinque Ports. Later Rye and Winchelsea were added to the original five. He demanded from Dover twenty-one ships, from Romney five, Hythe and Sandwich five each and from Hastings twenty. As with the ships came the men to man them, this was of considerable importance to him. In support for the fleet of ships John was willing to grant certain privileges.

This was a fair enough arrangement and special privileges were granted to the towns, and their merchants were known as barons.

But John was in urgent need of funds and he set about getting these through what he called 'fines'. If a man was accused of some misdemeanour it became possible to buy his way out of his just punishment. 'Bribes' would have been a better way of describing these inequities.

The Jews had always been persecuted and because they had a talent for amassing money, they became one of John's special targets. He gave an order that all Jews were to be imprisoned that they might on the payment of certain sums of money be allowed to go free. Understandably reluctant to part with their worldly goods, many of them refused which so aroused the King's wrath that he ordered them to be tortured. He made it clear that they could preserve themselves from these horrors by the payment of certain sums. From one rich Jew of Bristol the King asked for a payment of ten thousand marks—a great fortune which was all he possessed. When the Jew refused to pay John the money, the King ordered that each day one of his teeth should be pulled out until he had paid the sum. For seven days the Jew held out but by the end of that time he decided that he would part with his fortune rather than endure the brutal extractions.

John was constantly thinking of new ways of getting money. If two people disputed over a piece of land which they did often enough, the one who gave the bigger present to the King would get the land. It was not only money which was passed to the King in this manner; cattle, jewellery, anything of value came his way.

It was often necessary to get the King's consent to marriage if the bride was an heiress, and this proved a valuable source of income to the King. Geoffrey de Mandeville wanted to marry Hadwisa, John's first wife whom he had discarded; she, still a rich woman, was a very good catch and the prospective bridegroom gave the King twenty thousand marks for his permission. Often a little profitable bartering took place and in the case of the widow of one Stephen Falconbridge, Richard de Lee gave the King eighty marks for his permission to marry the lady which John accepted with alacrity. The widow, however, had other plans and offered John one hundred pounds sterling if he would withdraw his permission, which John on the receipt of the money obligingly did. If he heard that a certain widow had no wish to marry he would set about finding a husband for her that she might offer a sum of money to be excused from matrimony. The Countess of Warwick gave him a thousand pounds and ten palfreys that she might be left in peace.

There was no excuse too wild which was not used to extract money. Cities were expected to give bribes that they might conduct their business in a manner suited to them. London itself gave forty marks that it might sell cloth at a certain length; and the Bishop of Norwich who, as a bribe, presented the King with an emerald ring, was fined for delivering it at an inconvenient time when others were present.

Anyone who possessed anything which could benefit the King found himself robbed of it and John took a cynical pleasure in thinking up methods of extraction.

It was not to be expected that the people would meekly endure this state of affairs. The barons were growing restive and more and more people were asking themselves and each other whether they had been unwise in welcoming John as King when they might have had young Arthur; and that raised the question: Where is Arthur? And there was a growing conviction that John knew the answer to that riddle and had in fact taken and played a brutal part in the young Duke's disappearance.

John, while not unaware of the resentment growing up around him, yet maintained an indifference to it. He was the King. They must remember it. Moreover, there was a threat to England from overseas and he needed money to prepare himself to meet it. He refused to allow himself to be perturbed by the resentments which were growing up around him.

His arrogance was becoming intolerable to many and the barons talked together in secret of the state to which he was reducing the country. His bursts of energy were disconcerting, followed as they were by long periods of slothfulness. He was unpredictable; he could be quite amusing and witty at one time but the violent temper could suddenly overtake him so that no one really felt safe for long in his company.

His licentiousness had not decreased with his years, and in his new mood he did not hesitate to demand acquiescence wherever his fancy rested. It might be a serving girl or it could as easily be the wife of one of the high ranking barons—it made no difference to John; if he desired a woman he expected all to remember that he was the King who must not be crossed.

Thus it was when his eyes fell on the wife of Baron de Vesci.

Eustace de Vesci had served Richard well and had followed him on his crusade; after Richard's death he had given his allegiance to John and was becoming more and more horrified to discover how different he was from his brother and father.

Vesci was one of those barons who had been censorious of John's rule in secret; but he was a bold man and did not intend to go on accepting such conduct on the part of the King.

He had a great deal of influence in Scotland because his wife Margaret was the illegitimate daughter of William the Lion and he had often acted as John's ambassador there, where in view of the marriage connection he was well received.

Now this same Margaret had caught John's fancy and Eustace was filled with rage—though he did not show this—that John dared presume that he could make free with other men's wives while their husbands stood meekly by.

But he was well aware of the king's violent temper and at this time all his subjects were at his mercy, a state of affairs that Eustace, in company with other barons, was determined should not continue.

He pretended to treat the matter as a joke, implying that the King could not be serious of such intentions regarding his wife and the daughter of the King of Scotland.

'My lord is gracious in admiring my wife,' said Eustace cautiously.

'She's comely,' replied John. 'She is a woman such as I greatly admire. I have had pleasure from many such. I know a woman's potentialities when I see them. I have had a great deal of practice, baron.'

'I know it well,' was the reply. 'My wife will be leaving this day for a visit to her father.' Eustace was implying that Margaret was not only his wife but the daughter of the King of Scotland.

'She will not leave this night,' said John, 'for this night she and I will bed together.'

Eustace had to restrain himself from giving the King such a blow as would have felled him. But being a quick-thinking man he realized what the result of that would be. Of what use would he be to Margaret, how save her from this lecher if he were confined to a dungeon, and deprived of his hands or perhaps his eyes?

He said slowly: 'Is my lord so set on that?'

'Never was I more set on anything,' replied John. He smiled slyly. He knew Eustace—a man of rather narrow tastes. The sort who would have considered it sinful to amuse himself outside the marriage bed. And Margaret was of like mind. She was afraid of him, he knew. That was one of the reasons for her attraction for him. He doubted she had ever known any man but her husband. He would find her most diverting.

' 'Tis hardly to be expected that a husband would look on such a project with favour,' suggested Eustace.

John conceded this. 'If it were a baron who desired your wife you could object. Just as if he wanted a castle which was yours. You would fight for it with all you possessed, my good Eustace. But if your King decided he wanted a castle which was yours, you would be wise, as you well know, being a wise man, to give it to him. Thus it is with your wife.'

You are a monster, thought Eustace. Do you think I will serve you? From this day forth I will work against you and I will not rest until I have brought about your downfall.

But he did not show his anger. John did understand something of his feelings though and it amused him that this moral man had not the courage to oppose him. He cared for the virtue of his wife but his freedom and his limbs were of more importance to him.

'Why, Eustace,' went on the King, 'I have decided to honour you. After tomorrow you may boast that your wife so pleased the King that he took her to his bed. It may even be that I shall plant a royal seed within her. How would you like that, baron? What if there should be a little prince or princess in your nursery?'

It was difficult for Eustace to restrain himself, but he managed it. To show his disgusted anger was not the way to deal with this situation. John was becoming more gross, even more of a libertine than he had been in his youth; he was capable of any cruel act and the more cynical the better.

Eustace bowed his head and asked leave to retire. He could no longer endure to be in the King's company.

He went to his wife's chamber where she awaited him fearfully. She dismissed her women and when they had gone she ran to him and threw herself into his arms.

He stroked her hair thoughtfully.

'You have been with the King,' she said. 'When will he go?'

'Not until tomorrow.'

She began to shiver.

'I am afraid of him, Eustace,' she said.

'With good reason,' answered her husband grimly. 'He has blatantly asked for you.'

'*Asked* for me!'

'This night he will command you to his bed.'

'I can't do it, Eustace.'

'You know him well. He will force you. This castle is surrounded by his soldiers who would do his bidding. It will not do to refuse him. But listen. An idea has occurred to me. Someone must go to his bed tonight but need it be you?'

'What have you in mind?'

'There are several light women in the castle. There are some I doubt not who would give a great deal for what they think of as the honour of sharing the King's bed. Why should not one of them take your place?'

'You think he would agree?'

'No. But why should he not believe his bedfellow is you when it is someone else?'

'Oh Eustace, how clever you are!'

''Tis not done yet. Let us not be hasty but give much thought to this matter. If we could select the woman, bathe her, dress her hair, perfume her body ... is it possible, think you, that we could deceive him?'

'He has seen very little of me,' said Margaret, 'and I think this mad desire is partly to discountenance you and to prove to my father that even his daughter dare not refuse him. I am sure he could be deceived.'

'He *must* be deceived,' declared Eustace. 'We will select one of the whores, dress her up and send her to him. There is no time to lose. She will need a little tuition. But I intend him to be so intoxicated with wine, so heavy with food that his powers of observation will be numbed; and in the morning early, you must set out on a journey. There must be no delay about that. And you will wait near by until such a time as he shall have left the castle.'

Their very need seemed to endow them with special skills. They found the substitute whom they chose because her hair was very similar to Margaret's. It was washed and perfumed and bound in the same way as hers. The woman was bathed and dressed in a robe of Margaret's and well primed in her part.

It amused her and she was told that if she succeeded she would be well rewarded for the night's work so she was determined to play her part to the very best of her ability.

That night John supped well and drank deeply. Margaret, on his right hand, Eustace on his left, plied him with wine. He was delighted with Margaret and anticipated the night's adventure with excitement. He looked from one to the other with undisguised pleasure.

As the night wore on Margaret whispered that she would go to his bedchamber and there await him. He nodded a little drowsily and turned to smile at Eustace.

'After tonight, my friend,' he said, 'you and I will have shared our experiences. I know the lady will please me as she has pleased you.'

Eustace led him to the door of the bedchamber. There Margaret's substitute awaited him. There was a little moonlight coming through the narrow slit of a window. Not enough to show him his companion's face. He did not doubt for a moment that it was Margaret for she was dressed exactly as the baron's wife had been and her hair was worn in a similar manner.

He kicked the door shut and fell upon her.

Had he been a little more sober he might have been surprised at her response which was hardly what it would have been had the woman been Eustace's wife.

He was amused and exultant. This would show his barons that they must bow to him no matter what he asked.

At dawn, Margaret left the castle and John's night companion slipped out of his bed, her duty done and all that was necessary now was to collect her rewards. It had been a profitable night and some day she would be able to boast that she had slept with the King.

John awoke late in the morning. He remembered the previous night and laughed aloud.

He would not linger at the castle. He must move on.

He was in a good temper as he resumed his journey.

The Prophecy

WITH the passing of each week, John's fortunes seemed more dismal. The barons were grumbling together about him and asking themselves how much longer they were going to endure the rule of a king who believed he could make free with their wives and impose on them the most ridiculous fines which were in fact bribes and impositions.

The members of the Braose family would never forget the fate of Matilda and her son. To put a woman of her age into a dungeon and leave her to starve to death was monstrous, when her only fault had been to refuse the money which was demanded of her family and to defy the King in this matter of sending members of her family as hostages. Very understandable, was the verdict, when one considered the fate of Arthur. And it seemed that everyone now was considering the fate of Arthur. Philip of France was demanding that the young Duke be produced, knowing full well that he never could be. Anything that could be used to discredit John he was going to use.

Eustace de Vesci was arousing the barons against him; not that they needed much rousing. They were only too ready to accuse the King and many of them were meeting to discuss what could be done.

There was one who regretted the course events were taking and who determined to make yet another effort to save the monarchy. This was William Marshall and he came to see John.

The King, who was beginning to realize how friendless he was and that such friendliness could mean he was in acute danger of losing his kingdom, welcomed the Marshal warmly.

'My lord,' said William, 'I come to speak in a straight-forward manner to you which you may not find very much to your liking. Yet speak I must for if something is not done with speed, I see disaster overcoming this country and your kingly house.'

'You may speak as you wish,' said the King.

'Then I will say that it is folly to allow this state of affairs to drift as it is now. The barons are dissatisfied.'

'A plague on the barons!' muttered John.

'You may wish a plague on them, my lord, but forget not that such would infect the entire country, as they are now beginning to infect it with their dissatisfaction.'

'Who are they to show their displeasure?' demanded John. 'Am I their King or am I not?'

'At this time yes,' said the Marshal bluntly, 'but who shall say for how long if matters drift along in the direction they are now set.'

'You are over bold, Marshal, for it would seem you are critical of me.'

'I warned you I was over bold. I ever have been, and if you are not prepared for my boldness it would be well for us both if I retired.'

'Nay,' said John, 'say on.'

'Think how we stand. Interdict! Excommunication! In-ward turmoil, and perhaps most serious of all Philip awaiting his opportunity.'

'By God's ears, I would settle him if he dared set foot on this land.'

'My lord, he has the whole of Normandy. There is little left to you overseas. For the love of your ancestors do not let England pass out of your hands.'

John was afraid. There was one man whom he could trust and that was the Marshal. He had to listen to him. He knew. He had to take his advice, for he knew it would be sound and that Marshal had nothing but the good of England at heart.

'Trouble grew big with the quarrel with Rome,' said Marshall. 'My lord, your first step is to end that quarrel.'

'How so?'

'Accept Stephen Langton.'

'I have sworn not to.'

'It may be so, but my lord, a crown is at stake. If you do not make peace with Rome in a short time a French King will take the crown of England. There are many here who would welcome Philip.'

'Then surely they are traitors.'

'They are men who are at war with the manner in which England is being ruled. There is so much they do not like. Be prepared for treason, my lord, where you least expect it.'

'You, Marshal?'

'I am here to save your kingdom for you, to give you my help and support which is not inconsiderable. Those who murmur against you, love this country. They would serve it well. But they murmur against unfair taxation, the interdict and excommunication and the manner in which you rule. Therefore they believe it would be to the good of the country to take Philip as their King. This would restore Normandy to the crown and with all this and France, Philip would be the most powerful ruler in the world.'

'And you ask me to go humbly to Innocent?'

'I am convinced that now is the time to make peace with Rome.'

'But this will mean breaking my word. I have vowed that never will I have Stephen Langton here.'

'There are times, my lord, when it is wise and most expedient to break one's word. This is one of them.'

'What will people think of me?'

The Marshal's lips curled. 'No worse,' he said bluntly, 'than they do already.'

'And you would urge me to make advances to the Pope, to admit my willingness to have Langton here?'

'I would with all my heart,' said the Marshal, 'for I see clearly that if you do not, you will not long remain King of England.'

Marshal half expected him to fly into a rage. The fact that he did not suggested that he was really frightened of the position in which he found himself.

'I will without delay send an embassy to Innocent,' he said. 'I will even take Langton.'

*   *   *

There was a great deal of excitement in Yorkshire at this

time because an old man who was known as Peter of Pontefract claimed to have had a vision. Peter was a hermit who
lived in a cave at the opening of which people left food for
him; he was said to be a man of unusual powers.

He had prophesied that before Ascension Day King John
would have ceased to reign. In view of the conditions which
existed this did not seem an unreasonable prophecy and it
was repeated throughout Yorkshire and began to filter into
other counties so persistently that Peter of Pontefract was
now known throughout the country.

Beset by difficulties, pondering on the warnings of the
Marshal, John was filled with superstitious dread, and during
his travels in the North he demanded that Peter be brought
to him.

The old man gave no sign that he feared the King. He
stood before him without respect or disrespect. He merely
showed indifference.

John cried in a hectoring manner: 'What is this talk you
have circulated through the country concerning me?'

'I have merely said what came into my mind,' answered
Peter. 'If folks repeat it 'tis naught to me.'

'It is something to me,' cried the King. 'You say I will not
be reigning after Ascension Day.'

' 'Tweren't I as said it. 'Twere the voices.'

'To whom do these voices belong, think you?'

'To God, maybe, or to the powers.'

'And how shall I lose my kingdom, pray?' asked John.

'That I know not,' was the answer. 'Only as you shall surely
lose it.'

'I believe you to be lying.'

' 'Tis not so, my lord.'

'Do you know what is done to liars?'

Peter turned his eyes up to heaven and answered: 'What is
to be will be and what you do to me has not been revealed.'

'You should tremble in your shoes, Peter of Pontefract.'

'Nay, my lord, I but speak as I must and the spirits tell me.
They say you shall reign no more after Ascension Day and
that one more pleasing to God will be set on your throne.'

John lost his temper suddenly. 'Take this man away,' he
shouted. 'Throw him into a dungeon at Corfe.'

Peter was serene as they led him away.

'You will know your fate on Ascension Day,' John called

after him. 'You should start to pray for your soul now, fellow. For it will go ill with you then.'

Peter merely smiled and held the palms of his hands together as he was hustled away.

* * *

Innocent had been made aware of the situation in England. The barons were ready to revolt and if England were allowed to go on much longer under the Interdict with an excommunicated King the wrath of Rome would appear to lose its power. He could not allow the situation to continue so he summoned Stephen Langton, in his eyes Archbishop of Canterbury, and told him that he wished him to go at once to the King of France.

'John cannot any longer be allowed to reign in England,' he said. 'I intend to depose him and I am going to ask the King of France to help me to this end. I know full well that he will be eager to do so.'

Stephen Langton was surprised, for he did not think Innocent wanted to add to Philip's power, but he saw the Pope's point of view. John was insolently snapping his fingers at Rome by continuing to accept the interdict and his excommunication as though they were of little importance to him and making no effort to get them removed.

The Archbishop set out for Paris and no sooner had he left than John's embassy arrived in Rome with urgent messages from John to the Pope, proclaiming that he would accept Stephen Langton. As a result of this Stephen was hastily recalled to Rome. The Pope now declared his willingness to withdraw the threat to depose John if he ratified his promises.

Philip, meanwhile, had assembled an army with a fleet of ships ready to carry it to England. He was determined to invade and since John was clearly unfit to wear the crown, to take it for himself. No French monarch had ever ruled over England. He had fulfilled his ambition of recapturing Normandy. He had had other successes, but to capture England would make him honoured for ever as a hero, as William the Conqueror had been.

It was amazing how people rallied to John's banner. Those who had been chary of joining him to fight across the seas felt very differently about their own country. If the French were waiting to attack they would find the English ready for them.

They would never accept the French King as theirs. They preferred English John for all his faults. He was able to assemble a good fleet of ships. The Cinque ports had been true to their promises. The whole country was rallying to John's banners and he had not felt so confident for a long time.

Instead of the French the Pope's legate arrived at Dover. He had come hot from Rome with special despatches for the King of England.

The Papal legate was Pandulf, a Roman, who had become a clerk of Innocent's Papal Court and he was accompanied by a Knight of St. John named Brother Durandus. John had met them both on a previous occasion when they had come on the Pope's business and this time he received them with more warmth than he had previously.

John had discussed with the Marshal the terms which the Pope might be expected to offer and it was William's advice that it would be wise to accept them even though they might appear somewhat drastic.

In the Marshal's opinion the barons could not be trusted and although they had rallied to John's banner at the prospect of a French invasion they were at heart weary of John's rule and if they felt that it would be better under Philip's they might decide to change sides. To see the army gathered together, to see the ships ready to fight against those of the French, was a goodly sight. But the Marshal knew the extent of John's unpopularity and he did not trust those who had assembled to help him. For this reason, it seemed to him that John must if possible make peace with the Pope.

Pandulph's first words indicated to John how important it was for him to make peace with Rome.

'On my way to you,' Pandulph told him, 'I passed through France and sought an audience with its King. In the name of the Pope I forbade him to attempt the invasion of England until after I had seen you. Much will depend on your attitude now. If you accept the Pope's terms there will be no French invasion, for the Holy See will not permit it and the King of France would not dare undertake such a hazardous operation in which God would be against him since he has been forbidden by Rome.'

John said: 'I would know your terms.'

The Marshal had been right when he had said the terms

would be harsh. There could be none harsher, for the Pope insisted that John surrender his crown to the Pope who would then return it to him creating him a fief of the Holy See. The King of England would become the Pope's vassal.

The Pope's vassal! How low had he fallen. What would great William the Conqueror say if he was watching from Heaven at this time? The land which he had won and held at great sacrifice to be passed over to Rome and its King become a vassal!

It was a bitter anger which possessed John—not the violent rage which he knew so well. In this anger was sadness—that this state of affairs should have come to pass.

The whole world is against me, he thought.

'If you do not agree,' said Pandulph, 'His Holiness will give Philip permission to invade. He has a mighty army assembled on the other side of the water. The Pope will render him the aid he needs and the King of France will hold the crown of England under Rome.'

John was silent. He had prepared himself to accept Stephen Langton which he must do; he would allow the exiled clergy to return, and he would compensate the Church for the loss it had suffered when he had confiscated much of its lands and goods. But he had not thought to make himself a vassal of Rome.

He talked to William Marshal, a man who was as sad at the prospect as he was himself. But the Marshal believed—and so did John—that to give way to the Pope was the only way out of a dangerous situation.

'If you do it,' said William, 'you will gain certain advantages. Philip may not obey the Pope's order to withdraw but if he should attempt invasion against the wishes of the Holy Father there will be many who are not eager to follow him. The barons here who are ready to revolt against you will not have the support of the Pope. The interdict will be lifted and the benefits of the Church will return to England. Think of it. There will be seemly burial and churching of women and the church doors will be opened once more to the people. You must do it, my lord. It is a sad state of affairs but this is the best way out of our difficulties.'

John said: 'I often think of the hermit in Corfe Castle.'

'Ah the prophecy. When was it to be fulfilled?'

'On Ascension Day.'

'Which will soon be upon us.'

The two men looked at each other gravely. Then John spoke. 'I will do it,' he said. 'I will become a vassal of the Pope.'

'Better that,' agreed William Marshal, 'than to become the defeated enemy of the King of France.'

*   *   *

So there followed the ceremony of removing the crown from John's head which was symbolic of his submission to the Pope and then immediately replacing it to indicate that the Pope had graciously bestowed it on him once more. He was still King of England but he held the crown as the Pope's vassal which was a matter for rejoicing, said John, for it meant that Holy Rome was the protector of King and country.

John was exultant. He had come well out of his troubles. It was true he had had to accept Stephen Langton but he would make sure that the Archbishop's claws were clipped when he came to England, and he was no more ready to allow the Church to interfere with the State than any of his predecessors had been, but for a while he could sigh with relief, smile sardonically to think of the army Philip had accumulated with which to invade England, and congratulate himself that he had emerged in triumph from a very alarming situation.

It was time for rejoicing, he told his people. The Interdict was over and the church bells would ring again. There was friendship between England and Rome; There was more than that; there was a great alliance and the Holy See had thrown its protective wings across the country. Let pavilions be erected in the Kentish countryside; let there be singing and dancing in the streets of Dover. Instead of war there was feasting. Instead of a foreign invader their own King was there to rule over them. All was well with England.

The people were always ready for merrymaking. They listened to the church bells ringing and that seemed a very melodious sound; they spoke lovingly of King John who had so adroitly saved them from the French invaders; they danced and sang and there were bonfires on the hills of Kent.

Those who had proclaimed their faith in Peter of Pontefract assured themselves that his prophecy had come true. John had lost his crown by Ascension Day but what Peter had not seen was that he had regained it. Some pointed out that the prophecy had been that John would lose his crown and someone more in God's favour would wear it. Well, they could even make that fit. The John who had regained the crown was a vassal of the Pope and therefore a changed man. In God's eyes one under the protection of the Holy Father would be more in God's favour.

So everyone could be happy and it was easy to be deluded into forgetting the high taxation, the rages of the King which could spell disaster in so many ways to any who displeased him. Just for a day they would give way to merriment and a blind faith in the future.

John was not inclined to forget Peter of Pontefract. The man had caused him a great deal of uneasiness. He had been infuriated by the manner in which he had stood before him with that fanatical look in his eyes as though he were a messenger from God.

And what would people be saying now? They would twist his prophecy to make it the truth. John had hated the man when he had stood there before him and blatantly stated that his place would be taken by someone more worthy in God's eyes.

A king should not allow men to talk to him in that say. Peter of Pontefract must not be allowed to live and make more such prophecies. For that was what the man would do, he was sure. And he would carry a certain amount of opinion with him. Such uneasy men should be removed.

He gave orders that Peter should be taken from his dungeon in Corfe, and hanged. But first, as a warning to others who might feel they had the gift of prophecy and through this believed they could plot against the King, he was to be tied to a horse's tail and dragged to the place of execution where he should be hanged high on a gibbet that all might see the fate in store for any who acted in a similar manner.

The King's orders were carried out and so fickle were the people that those who had supported Peter and declared that he in truth was a great prophet and a man of God, fearing to offend the King, now reviled him.

Threat of Invasion

ON the other side of the Channel Pandulph was in consultation with Philip of France.

'You must disband your fleet and your armies,' he told Philip. 'Invasion of England is now quite out of the question. England is now a papal fief and to attack England is to attack Rome.'

Philip was furious. He had seen England ripe for invasion, a weak King, dissatisfied barons who at his first success would be ready to desert John for him; and now by this adroit action of John's in surrendering his crown to the Pope and receiving it back as a vassal, his weak enemy had become a powerful one.

'It has cost me a great deal of money and months of preparation,' cried Philip. 'Was it all of no avail?'

'You could not hope for success if Rome was against you,' was the answer.

There was a certain amount of truth in that. Philip saw his dream evaporating. It was maddening. All his life he had longed to achieve the glory of a Charlemagne. He had yearned to go down in history as the man who had made France great as it had once been; and if he could have brought to it the crown of England he would have surpassed all others. And it had been within his grasp. He was sure of it.

But he was a realist and he saw at once that it was a dream

which would have to be shelved—but perhaps not for long. He would keep his fleet in readiness; he would add to his armies. He would not abandon his dream of conquering England. It was only a postponement.

Pandulph departed feeling it was safe to return to Rome and report to the Pope that his mission had been satisfactorily carried out.

When he had gone Philip brooded over the situation in which he found himself. His soldiers were restive. They had been promised conquest and conquest always meant spoils. They knew that when the Conqueror had gone to England, men who had been quite humble in Normandy had become landowners, rich and powerful. This was what they had hoped from an invasion of England. And now it was not to take place how would they feel?

Philip must assure not only himself, but them, that it was but a postponement.

In the meantime they must not be idle. Every general knew that an idle army was a danger to its commander. Mutiny, rebellion, all had their seeds in idleness and the greater it was the more they flourished.

He called his generals to him and told them that although the invasion of England had had to be postponed, it was not abandoned. They would while they were waiting turn their attentions to that old enemy of France—Flanders—who had shown itself very unco-operative in this last venture.

The generals understood. It was necessary to keep the army occupied.

So, leaving the fleet of ships lying at anchor, the army left and in a short time were marching on Ghent.

*　　*　　*

Philip's decision threw luck into John's path. It seemed as though Fate had decided to cherish him. First he had made his peace with Rome at precisely the right moment so that he had not only made it unwise for the French to attack him but it had also been a warning to the barons too, for in rebelling against him they would be rebelling against the Pope.

The Flemings as Philip's enemies, must be John's friends; and when they realized that French fury was to be turned against them they appealed to John for help.

John considered this appeal very carefully with the Mar-

shal and others whom he trusted. It seemed an opportunity to
weaken the French and William Marshal felt that as John
had assembled an army to ward off the French invaders it
would be a good idea to send it to the aid of the Flemings.

The English set out and here their good fortune continued,
for on arriving at the spot where the French fleet lay, they
found a vast number of vessels all equipped for the invasion
of England, filled with the food and weapons which would be
needed; there was armour and fine garments—everything
conceivable that would enable the invaders to succeed both
before and after conquest.

That there should be but a few people left to guard them
made the English laugh with derision while they decided to
make the most of their good fortune. Forgotten was the
expedition to Flanders. Here was a far more profitable one.

They quickly overpowered the defenders, loaded their own
ships with the treasures the French had brought with them
and then set fire to Philip's fleet.

It was a great moment for John. He laughed aloud. His
luck had changed. It was now his turn to snap his fingers at
Philip.

Having crippled the French fleet so that an invasion of
England would be completely out of the question, even if
Philip decided to defy the Pope and attempt it, John decided
to go to the rescue of the Flemings. Alas, the spasm of luck
was over, for Philip hearing of the disaster to his ships hurried to the coast and intercepted John's army inflicting defeat
on it so that it was necessary to make a hasty retreat back to
the coast.

There they hastily embarked and sailed back to England.
But the adventure could be called highly successful since it
had resulted in the near annihilation of the French fleet and
had made invasion impossible for a very long time.

*   *   *

It was hot July when Stephen Langton arrived in England.
John rode to meet him and the two retinues came face to face
at Porchester.

The King, aglitter with jewels, his satin mantle decorated
with pearls and rubies, his girdle of sapphires and diamonds,
and his gloves adorned with pearls, looked magnificent on his
charger. It was more important than ever that he look the

part since he had resigned his independence. About him rode his courtiers, splendidly dressed but designedly less so than he was, for he would not have been pleased if they outshone him.

When the two retinues met John dismounted from his magnificently caparisoned horse and approaching Stephen Langton knelt before him; then he stood up and exchanged kisses with him.

'Welcome, Father,' he said.

Stephen Langton was not a vindictive man and he was delighted that at last John was ready to receive him. He was eager that the past should be forgotten and he looked forward to working in harmony with the King.

They rode side by side into Winchester, cheered by the people as they passed along the road.

Peace between Church and State! It was what the people longed for. The Interdict was lifted. Their King was no longer excommunicated—although the ban had to be lifted formally—and everyone could return to the normal way of life.

Into the city of Winchester they came, and there in the chapter house of the Cathedral, the Archbishop of Canterbury absolved John and celebrated Mass in his presence.

When it was over, for all to see, the Archbishop and the King gave each other the kiss of peace.

John, the irreligious sceptic, the lecher, the King who had defied the church as none of his predecessors had before him, was now the dear friend of the Archbishop of Canterbury and the protégé of the Pope.

There was an irony about such a state of affairs and men such as the Marshal solemnly shook their heads and wondered how long this amity could last.

John's Revenge

ISABELLA was in love. He was young and handsome. Often she would compare him with John and marvel at the differences between them. He reminded her of Hugh the Brown and after he had left she would lie in bed and think: This is how it would have been with Hugh.

At first in her thoughts she called him Hugh; and later she told him this. 'It suits you. You will be Hugh to me,' and ever after she called him by that name.

She had been afraid for him, although when she had first taken lovers she had liked to test their courage by telling them that their punishment would be terrible if the King ever discovered. Sometimes when they were with her she sensed their fear; at first it gave a zest to her desire.

She took a delight in hiding her adventures from John but sometimes it occurred to her that he knew and that he was waiting to trap her. Outwitting him in itself was a pleasant exercise. She hated him. Perhaps she always had although she had revelled in the early years of their relationship. It had been flattering that he should neglect his State duties because he could not leave their bed and to know that the stories circulated round the world that he was losing his kingdom under the bed quilt.

What a compliment to her powers of attraction! For long he had been a faithful husband which in itself was something of a miracle. And she had made this possible—she with her great fascination. She wondered if Hugh ever thought of her now. Did he reproach himself for his sloth in not taking her when she was there ready and willing, waiting for him before John had come?

At first it had been so exciting. To be Queen and to be so desired. But she had been a Queen for a long time now and desired by many. And there were more handsome men in the world than John.

Her thoughts were now for the handsome young man, the Golden Youth she called him, the Hugh-Shadow—Hugh would no longer be young, as she was not, but women such as herself were perennially attractive and men such as he was retained their charm.

Her lover was coming to her bedchamber more frequently now. He was so much in love with her that he gladly risked his life ... or worse. She had told him often of the terrible danger he was facing and he brushed that aside. It was worth while ... anything that could happen to him was worth while for this.

He was a good lover. There could not have been a better. He was tender as John had never been, not even in the beginning when she was a child. This adoration, this idolizing, was delightful. She revelled in it. She loved her Golden Youth.

As they lay in her bed in the early morning before the dawn—for he must be gone by then since it would be fatal to be seen by the light of day—she said to him as she twirled a lock of his golden hair through her fingers, 'My love, how long will you continue to come to me?'

He answered as she knew he would: 'For ever.'

'What if the King comes here?'

'Then I must perforce wait until he is gone.'

'What do you know of the King, Hugh?'

'All know of his tempers.'

'There never was such temper. They say it even exceeds that of his father and greatly did men fear that. He must never find out, Hugh, never.'

'If he did, it would have been worth while.'

'While his servants were doing fearful things to you would you think that?'

'Aye.'

'Nay, my dearest love, you think so now. But what are the feelings of a man think you to be deprived of his manhood for methinks that is what John would do to any who had enjoyed me.'

'I had rather die.'

'If John knew that he would not let you. His revenge must suit his mood and his moods are diabolical. Perhaps he would put out your eyes. He wanted to do that to Arthur, you know. His sin was that he was the son of John's elder brother and some thought he had a greater right to the throne.'

'He cannot have such thoughts about me.'

'Nay, but he would hate you more than he ever hated Arthur. Sometimes I tremble for you.'

'Then I rejoice, for it shows you love me.'

'I want you to know what you risk, my Hugh. Think of these things.'

'To be with you for one hour is worth a lifetime of agony.'

'Youthful words spoken by the young in the hour of ecstasy. What would you say during the lifetime of misery, think you?'

'It shall not be,' he said kissing her.

And while she loved his recklessness, she wanted him to know what he risked.

He had been successful in reaching her. They had devised several hiding places where he could be secreted in a hurry. She might lift the floor boards and he could cower beneath. She had made sure of that and she barred her bedroom door when he was with her.

She would get him away in safety, she promised herself, if he were in danger of being surprised.

But she had many attendants and they knew her secrets.

*   *   *

John came to the castle. She was down at the gates to meet him.

As soon as he looked at her he was as enamoured of her as he had ever been, realizing afresh that she had that quality of sensuality stronger than any woman he knew.

He was aware that she had taken a lover. It was for this reason that he had come here. At first he had thought he would come down in secret and catch her in the act; but he had a better idea.

'Why, you are blooming as a flower does after rain,' he said. 'Is that due to my coming?'

'To what else could it be due?'

'You are a good wife ... always waiting for her husband.'

'Always,' she answered, 'though he comes less often than he once did.'

'Matters of State, my love.'

'Is it so then? I had feared it might be matters of another kind.'

'Are you jealous then?'

'Continuously so.'

'There is no need. No matter with whom I bedded I would always prefer and come back to you.'

' 'Tis small compensation when others are taking my place.'

'Do you sulk, wife?'

'Nay, I know well the ways of men. None is faithful.'

' 'Tis the wives who must be that,' he said with a hint of fierceness in his voice.

'Poor wives! Why should they not be given a little of what the husbands take so freely?'

'You know full well. And for a Queen unfaithfulness is treason. Treason, Isabella! Think of treason to the King. That could be punished with death.'

' 'Tis so,' she said.

'And you brood on it often.'

' 'Tis ever in my mind.'

'And should you be tempted, the thought of that would save you.'

'You would not have me virtuous because of fear, my lord, I know. Should it not be for love alone?'

'For love alone,' he answered.

And he thought: I shall see him this day. He is handsome I know. By God's ears he will soon be wishing he had never been born.

They supped together in state and she sang and played to him, her hair falling about her shoulders for she had loosened it, knowing he liked it so. It reminded him of the early days when they had first married and he could not tear himself away from her even for an hour or so.

He said: 'Tomorrow we shall go to Gloucester.'

'And I am to accompany you?'

'I need you with me,' he said.

She smiled; he was as enamoured of her as he had ever been, she believed.

He looked about the hall and found him. He was certainly young and handsome. He had been told that he had a look of Hugh de Lusignan. By God's ears, did she still hanker for that man? He knew that she thought of him; he had seen the look in her eyes when she spoke of him. Had she all these years been regretting the loss of Hugh? Hadn't the crown of England made up for that? Had she during those moments of passion been substituting Hugh for him? The thought maddened him. And this youth had a look of Hugh. It was a strong resemblance. And night after night he had been in her bed. He had risked everything for her. Well, he should pay the price.

Isabella had a surprise coming to her.

She said she would retire to her bedchamber. He took her hands and kissed her, first lingeringly and then with passion. She would go to her bed and wait for him.

Oh Isabella, you are going to be very surprised, he thought.

She went to her bedchamber. Her women combed her hair and scented it. She was as beautiful as she had ever been, she knew. Bearing three children had not changed that, for if there was a certain fleshiness about her it but added to her attractiveness.

She lay in bed waiting. What had happened to detain him? She had expected him to be here speedily, which was why she had urged her attendants to hurry.

How strange! What was he doing? Had he found some woman in the castle more to his taste than she was? It seemed very strange for surely his kisses had implied that he would soon be with her.

At last she slept and it was dawn when she awoke. The light filtered into the room. As she opened her eyes she remembered and spread her arms feeling for him beside her. There was no one. So he had not come. She sat up in bed. There was a dark shadow at the end of the bed. She looked closely. She stared in disbelieving horror, then put her hand to her mouth to stop the scream as she fell back nauseated and fainting on her bed.

Hanging from the top rail of the tester as though on a gallows was the naked, mutilated body of her lover.

*   *   *

She was mute. She rode along beside him on the way to Gloucester, feigning to be unaware of him. She knew that there was a malicious smile on his lips, but he said nothing of what he had done.

She was thinking: I hope it was quick. I hope they did not linger over it. I would I had never seen him that I should have brought him to this. They say that John is the Devil himself and it is true. None but the Devil could have thought of such a thing. I shall never forget him as he looked hanging there. All my memories of him will be thus. Why did I let him come to me? I might have known.

They had reached Gloucester Castle which had been built in the time of the Conqueror. In the great hall William Rufus had feasted surrounded by favourite men friends. John's father Henry the Second had held many a council here when he was engaged in his forays into Wales. There in the waters of the Severn could be found delicious lampreys. The first Henry had been very partial to a stewed lamprey and had died, they said, of a surfeit of them. And to this castle John had brought Isabella. For what purpose? she wondered.

That he had a purpose she had no doubt. He had said nothing to her yet but he meant to, she knew, for the secret smile continued to curve his lips; he was thinking of the scene between them which was to come.

They supped. Not that she could eat, for the very thought of food sickened her; she could not shut out of her mind the thought of her lover's body. Had he watched while they did that to him? She guessed that he had. She could hear the cruel words coming from that even crueller mouth.

I hate him! she thought. How I hate him!

He said he would lead her to her chamber. Now she would know what was in store.

'Behold your prison,' he said.

'What mean you?' she asked almost listlessly.

'You are under restraint,' he said. ''Tis clear that you cannot be trusted. You are guilty of treason. My father kept my mother a prisoner for sixteen years. It may be that I shall keep you mine as long.'

She shrugged her shoulders and that maddened him.

He wanted her to storm at him, but she refused to though she saw the red blood in his eyes.

'So you care not?' he shouted.

'What would be the use if this is what you wish.'

'You seem not to care that you have lost your freedom. You witch! You scorceress! What thought you of your fine lover when he came to your bed last night?'

She turned away that he might not see the horror she could not restrain as the vivid picture came back to her mind.

'What a pretty sight. He screamed, you know. He screamed in horror. You should have heard...'

'Stop it!' she cried.

'Ah, you are moved at last. A pretty boy, I'll grant you. But at the end it wasn't worth it for him ... even for you.'

'You have not been the most faithful of husbands,' she accused.

'What of that?'

'Why should I be a faithful wife?'

'Because I am the King.'

'Forget not that I am the Queen.'

'By God's ears if you try to foist his bastard on me...'

'There will be no bastard. It is your privilege to produce those.'

He came to her suddenly and taking her by the shoulders shook her violently. 'How was he?' he asked. 'Was he good? Did you enjoy him?'

She faced him boldly. 'He was good,' she answered defiantly.

He threw her from him in a burst of rage.

'I shall send his corpse to you here to keep you company in your prison.'

'That will not hurt him.'

'There will be no one else. You may stay here and think of me ... with others who please me more than you do.'

'I wish you joy of them.'

'You are not old, Isabella, and you are lusty. Did we not know that? What will you do without lovers, Isabella?'

'If I do not have to endure you I shall be happy.'

'You will endure what I say.'

'Why do you not kill me too? I know. I have friends and family. The King of France would say: He has killed his wife as he killed his nephew.'

'Not a word of that.'

'He haunts you, does he not, John? Poor Arthur. How did

he die? So many would like to know. You, his murderer, could tell them.'

'You are asking me to do you an injury.'

'Why do you not?'

'Because I have not finished with you yet. I would not hurt the body which has much to give me yet.'

'Oh, so I am not to be exiled?'

'Not from me. I shall think of you here waiting for me. We'll have children yet. We have but three. I want more from you. If you are carrying a bastard, I'll have him murdered. You taunt me with murder, well know this, if any offend me they shall be removed. You too if you should be in my way.'

'And am I not?'

'Assuredly not. When you are you will know it. I have my pleasure when I will and I want no other wife. I've got my heirs, and a fine daughter. I'll get more on you yet. And you will wait patiently here for me to come to you and if ever you secrete a lover into your bedchamber again that which happened to your fine young man will be mild compared with what I will do to the next.'

She said: 'I understand. I am a prisoner here. I have had a lover. I do not deny it. You have murdered him most cruelly and you have tormented me so much that I shall ever be haunted by memories of his body hanging there at my bed. I hate you for this.'

'Hate and love,' he said. 'They are close. Isabella, there is no one but you. Know you this: I would not hurt you. That was why I had to do what I did to him. I had to make sure that never again should he take the place which is mine ... mine. Others there have been, but not one like you. Where is there one like you?'

His arms were round her; he lifted her and carried her to the bed.

How strange that the passion should rise within her at such a time; but it was there between them, as strong as it had ever been.

In the morning he said to her: 'If you should bear a child of his that child shall not live. You know this. Had I the softest heart in the world, which you may doubt to be true as I do myself, it could not live. Ah, my Isabella, you know there was never sport such as we two make together. It is only my children that you shall bear. I shall be here again and we'll get us a child ... but not until we know that dangling corpse is not a father.'

She shook her head. 'There is no child,' she said. 'I know it.'

But he laughed at her.

And when he rode away she was a prisoner.

He came back later and they were together for two days and nights and he scarcely left her bed during that time. She knew that he thought constantly of her lover and that in his perverse way he took some pleasure in contemplating that which enraged him.

When he left she was pregnant and in due course she gave birth to a daughter. She called her after herself, Isabella.

And she remained the King's prisoner.

A Bride for Hugh

WITH Philip's fleet in disorder and a great many of his weapons and battle equipment in English hands it seemed to John the time had come to attack France and attempt to regain his possessions. One of his spurts of energy came to him and he was eager for action. He had an army assembled but he needed the support of the barons so he issued commands throughout the land for them to bring their followers and join him.

Rebellion simmered beneath the surface. The barons had no confidence in John. The Braose family with Robert Fitz-Walter and Eustace de Vesci had spread discord throughout the country. They had hinted that such a tyrant could not be allowed to reign unless he reformed considerably, and although John realized that many of the barons were restive he did not know how deeply rooted was this determination to bring matters to a head.

The barons of the North, who were in a better position than those in the South, to defy the King, refused to supply John with what he needed. They said that John had proved himself an ineffectual commander; Losses in France had been humiliating; true they had had luck recently but only because they had taken the French fleet by surprise. They had no confidence in John and his missions abroad; nor would they supply men and money to maintain them. They preferred to remain in England and keep that safe from an invader, for it was not inconceivable that when Philip had

had time to muster his forces, he would make an attack on the country. In any case, they were not meeting John's wishes.

When John heard their refusal wild rage possessed him. He gave vent to it in the usual way and when he was exhausted by it he decided that he would go not to France but up to the North to show the barons how he felt about his subjects who disobeyed him.

He knew that FitzWalter with his friend Vesci had done their utmost to ferment trouble. Something told him that FitzWalter was going to do everything he could to take his crown from him in exchange for his daughter. He had been foolish over FitzWalter; he should have killed him when he had a chance and now simply because his daughter had been a little fool and had held out against her King's advances, her father was helping to stir up trouble. In the priory church of Little Dunmow, to keep the story alive, the FitzWalters had had a statue of Matilda made and placed it on her tomb. No doubt they made all sorts of unholy vows over it.

By God's eyes, John thought, if FitzWalter falls into my hands that will be an end to him.

But meanwhile he needed men to attack Philip and his Northern barons were refusing to help him and he was going to show them who was the master. He always maintained a good army of mercenaries and with these he set out, not for France but for the North with the intention of teaching the Barons a lesson.

The fact that the King was on the march could not be kept a secret and when the new Archbishop of Canterbury heard, he hastened forth with his retinue to meet John.

John was angry that the Archbishop should at this early stage show his intention to meddle. He demanded to know why he had thought it necessary to meet him in such a way.

'My lord,' the Archbishop pointed out, 'by attacking the Northern barons you would create civil war in this land and you cannot have forgotten so soon that you hold the crown of England as a fief of the Pope.'

'I will rule my own land in a manner which is pleasing to me,' growled John.

'If you displease our master the Pope, you will be breaking your vows. It would be necessary, if you forced a civil war on this country, to bring back the interdict and to excommunicate you.'

John knew this could come to pass. His submission to the Pope had extricated him from a very uneasy situation, for if he had not given way to Rome Philip of France might at this time be in possession of his crown. A curse on all popes and archbishops! They had ever been thorns in the side of kings.

He wanted to shout: Take this man away. Murder him on the steps of his cathedral as my father's loyal knights murdered Becket. I'll not be ruled by the Church.

But he had taken his vows to the Pope and sworn allegiance; he had given Rome power in England greater than any monarch had ever given before.

Luck was against him. He had lost Normandy. He had lost most of his possessions in France. The easiest way to ease his feelings was to fly into a temper.

But he must control himself on this occasion.

How did he ever get into this mess? It was Isabella's fault. He had dallied with her when he should have been attending to State matters. When they had said he had lost his kingdom under the bed quilt they were right.

She was a witch. A sorceress. And she took lovers.

It soothed him a little to think of the fate of the one who had been discovered.

He must outwit the Pope. That was the only way. The barons on one side, Philip on the other and presiding over all Stephen Langton, the Pope's man who, because of that, had more power in England than the King himself.

He talked in secret to Stephen Langton. There should be no war, but a king could not rule with so much rebellion in his ranks. He would march North, show the barons his strength and his displeasure. But there should be no bloodshed.

'Remember, my lord,' warned Stephen, 'that if there is His Holiness will take action.'

'I will remember,' John replied sullenly.

So the trip to the North was merely a warning to the barons; and having made it John returned to the South in order to make his preparations to sail for France, without those who refused to accompany him.

*   *   *

When John arrived at La Rochelle he was acclaimed by the

people. As this was a great trading port and doing good business with England its inhabitants had no wish to be taken over by the King of France which would have been detrimental to trade. Moreover, Aquitaine had always feared domination by Philip. Thus, on John's coming, he found himself with considerable allies.

His spirits were lifted and when he had taken a castle or two he was excited by his success and saw himself regaining all that he had lost.

Luck was on his side and against Philip on this occasion for the Flemings—perennial enemies of the French—took this opportunity to attack him. Philip had no alternative but to turn to Flanders, leaving his son Louis to deal with the invading English.

Excited, certain of success, John realized that there was one family which could spoil his chances, a family which bore almost as great a grudge against him as the FitzWalters. This was the de Lusignan family, and Hugh, from whom he had snatched Isabella, was at the head of it.

It seemed to John that his life was haunted by spectres of the past. Arthur, Vesci, FitzWalter and Lusignan. Would none of the wrongs he had committed ever be forgotten?

He was going to try to lay the Lusignan ghost right away. He must if he were to turn the wrath of this powerful family from him.

An idea had occurred to him which greatly amused him. Hugh de Lusignan, the man of whom he had always been jealous because he knew that Isabella had remembered him all through the years, had remained unmarried. Could this be because he had been so enamoured of Isabella that he could not contemplate taking another bride? It could well be so. Hugh's family was an ambitious one and if a tasty bait were dangled before them they would not be able to prevent themselves taking it. John was overcome with mirth. He could have his little joke to good advantage, the Lusignans should help him to recover what he had lost in France.

He sent messengers to Hugh de Lusignan offering him a bride; this bride was to be John's own legitimate daughter— he had several illegitimate ones—Joanna, daughter of Isabella whom Hugh had loved and so reluctantly lost.

John could not restrain his laughter when the messengers returned.

Isabella's old lover Hugh had agreed to marry her daughter.

What a brilliant stroke of strategy this was, was seen when Philip, hearing of the proposed alliance between the King of England and the Lusignan family, offered one of his sons as a bridegroom for little Joanna. Surely a better proposition! The son of the King of France for the princess of England— not a mere baron.

'Not so, not so,' cried John. He pointed out that the King of France had married his niece and that had not saved them conflict. The marriage of his daughter with the Lusignans seemed to him an ideal one. Moreover, he was looking forward to telling Isabella that Hugh was to have her daughter.

He could now march unmolested through Lusignan territory and so pursue his attack on the King of France. In this he continued with some success but he had uneasy allies. They were watching carefully which way the battle was going and did not intend to be caught on the losing side. Face to face with the French they decided that it would be better to remain neutral; and even as the battle was about to begin they made up their minds to desert.

John's fury when he saw his ranks diminishing was so great that he wept. He screamed and shouted but this was of no avail. The French being aware of what had happened realized this was the time to attack, and John and his forces were soon hastily retreating.

It was the beginning of the end. The French were too strong; John's allies had deserted him; and his men, who did not believe in his ability to achieve his ends, wanted to go home. They remembered what had been said of John—the King who had lost the French possessions. They reminded each other that there had been a time when Philip had threatened to invade England. The only element which had prevented that was the intervention of the Pope. What sort of King was this? He was no leader. At home they were grumbling about him. The barons were threatening to rise against him. What good could they achieve here in France? There was nothing there but defeat. It was time they returned to England to protect their possessions there before the French came to take them.

Angry, frustrated, John returned to England. Something

told him that it would never be in his power to regain the French possessions.

* * *

His only pleasure in returning home was to go to Gloucester to see Isabella.

She was pregnant once more, a fact which pleased him. He found it gratifying to keep her shut away and to surround her with guards so that he could be sure no lovers visited her and then to come to her at his will.

He allowed her to have the children with her. Young Henry now eight years old, Richard a year younger, Joanna the little bride-to-be nearly five, and baby Isabella. It was gratifying to contemplate that there would soon be another.

He knew that she was glad to see him and she no longer referred to his infidelities but accepted them as a matter of course which seemed to him right and proper. He wondered how often she thought of her lover hanging lifeless on the bed. Ah, he thought, he would no longer have been any use to her had he lived.

This always amused him; and he could say that he was as pleased with his marriage as he had ever been and although he had been mad with rage when he had discovered her infidelity, she could always excite him more than any other woman he had ever known.

Now he could taunt her.

'I have had adventures overseas,' he said.

'And none, I believe, that have brought you advantage.'

'Oh, I shall cross the seas ere long and then I will flout the King of France.'

'Let us hope he will not flout you first. So you have lost everything across the sea?'

'Nay. 'Tis but a temporary setback. I have made a truce with an old friend of yours.'

'Which old friend is that?'

'Hugh de Lusignan. I believe you thought highly of him once.'

She was alert and watchful. What did this mean?

'He is a brave and noble man,' she answered defiantly.

'I am glad you think so because he is to become a member of our family.'

'How so?' she asked, and he was pleased to see that her

heart had started to beat fast with apprehension. She thought he was going to tell her of some torture inflicted on Hugh. He would let her fear for him for a while before enlightening her with the information which he believed would shock her.

He cleared his throat. 'I am going to give him our daughter.'

'Give ... him ... our daughter?' she echoed.

'I mean of course that Joanna is to be betrothed to your old lover, Hugh the Brown.'

'But ... she is a child.'

'Princesses are married when they are young as you know. How old were you? Twelve. If our Joanna is anything like her mother she will give Hugh a very happy time.'

'It is impossible,' she snapped. 'The child is but five years old.'

'In seven years time ... perhaps earlier, she will be ready. He will be prepared to wait. He is good at that.'

'He ... he will be an old man.'

'There have been older bridegrooms. He was excited at the prospect. And so we got safe conduct through his territory. It could have given me a victorious campaign but for the traitors. I thought: This will please Isabella. She thought highly of the man. Very well, she will welcome him as a son!' He began to laugh. She wanted to kill him. She clasped her hands tightly together to prevent their taking action.

She hated him. He was forty-eight years of age and looked more. He was too fat and growing bald and it was inevitable that the life of debauchery should begin to show itself.

'Come,' he cried, holding out his hands, 'show me your gratitude. I have arranged a match for your daughter with a man whom, I have reason to think, you regard very highly.'

Then he caught her to him and she knew that understanding that he had disturbed her gave some zest to his desire.

Cruelty always gave him additional pleasure.

Runnymede

JOHN did not realize what trouble was awaiting him. While he had been in France those barons who had refused to accompany him had been meeting to ask themselves how much longer they were going to endure the rule of an ineffectual tyrant.

Stephen Langton, who owed his duty to the Pope, understood very well how matters were going and was sure that some compromise would have to be reached. Among the archives of Canterbury he had discovered a copy of a document called The Charter of Henry the First. This set out certain liberties which on his coronation Henry the First had been forced to grant to the people. There were only a few copies of this in existence because Henry had been at great pains to destroy any he could lay his hands on.

On discovering this document in the month of August the Archbishop called together the barons at St. Paul's where he produced the documents, pointing out that many of the rights expressed therein had been waived by succeeding kings.

The struggle between the King and his barons moved a stage further after that assembly at St. Paul's. They now determined to go into action.

November 20th was a feast day and under the pretext of

celebrating this the barons again met, this time at Bury St. Edmunds.

Here they took a solemn oath before the high altar. They would insist that John renew the Charter of Henry the First; and if he should refuse they were determined to make war.

The time chosen to present their demand to the King was Christmas which he would be celebrating at Worcester. They decided, however, that the season of good will might not be the best time so they changed the meeting place to London and sent a deputation to the King at Worcester telling him that the barons were assembled in London where they must parley with him without delay.

Aware of the storm which was gathering about him, John left Worcester and travelled to London; and there he found the barons awaiting him.

They were a formidable assembly, for they had armed as though for war, and their spokesman informed the King that they insisted he keep the promises and laws set out in the Charter of Henry the First.

John was at first inclined arrogantly to accuse them of insubordination, but when he saw how threatening was their manner he knew he must tread carefully.

'You are asking me a great deal,' he said. 'I cannot give you an immediate answer. You must give me a little time to consider these matters. Wait until Easter time and I will have my answer for you then.'

The barons murmured together but finally agreed to await the appointed time.

John immediately sent envoys to the Pope begging for his help against the recalcitrant barons, giving them instructions to tell His Holiness that he was his humble servant and that he needed his help against his rebellious subjects. As his faithful vassal he appealed to him and trusted that he would instruct the rebels to submit, through John, to His Holiness.

The result of this was a letter from the Pope to the baron leaders and Stephen Langton, forbidding them to persist in their persecution of the King. But Stephen Langton was a man of high principles and he had ranged himself on the side of the barons. The Pope did not understand the true situation in England; accordingly at Easter time the barons met at Stamford in Lincolnshire and the Archbishop was with them. With them came two thousand men, armed for battle, to show the King the measure of their seriousness.

John was at Oxford and with him was William Marshal. All John's efforts were spent in controlling his fury. That his subjects who had once been terrified and ready to hide themselves at the first sign of his temper, were now actually bringing armed forces to intimidate him, maddened him.

William Marshal was faithful as ever, but very grave, being fully aware of John's unhappy position and the justice of the barons' grievances.

'I will go to them, my lord,' he said, 'and discover the nature of these demands. Then it is my opinion that you should examine them very closely.'

'Was ever a king in such a sad state?' cried John.

'Rarely,' answered the Marshal somewhat curtly. He agreed that John's actions had brought him to this state and it was only his inherent belief that the monarchy must be upheld at all costs which made him determined to serve John until the end, he being, in his opinion, the true sovereign of the realm.

Marshal returned to John in the company of Stephen Langton with the written demands of the barons.

John flushed with fury as he read them: 'By God's hands and feet,' he cried, 'why do they not demand my kingdom?'

'They are very insistent, my lord,' warned Marshal.

John threw the document to the floor and stamped on it. 'I would never grant liberties which would make me a slave,' he declared. He added slyly: 'We will ask the Pope to intervene in this matter. It is the concern of His Holiness for I hold this kingdom under him. Go, tell the barons they must appeal to the Pope.'

*   *   *

This the barons refused to do and the Pope sent Pandulph, who happened to be in England at the time, instructions to excommunicate the barons as they were, in rebelling against the King of England, defying the Holy See.

Stephen Langton sent for Pandulph and told him that he could see the situation more clearly than an outsider being right at the heart of it. The country could not exist any longer under the tyranny of its king and the barons were claiming no more than their rights in demanding adherence to the Charter.

'Instead of excommunicating the barons,' he declared, 'it is the King's army of mercenaries who should be excommunicated. Without them he would be powerless against the people.'

John, deeply alarmed at this observation, went to the Tower of London that he might take possession of his capital city.

This seemed tantamount to a state of war and the barons decided to elect a marshal.

It was ironical that the man they chose was Robert Fitz-Walter, the King's enemy and a man who had a score to settle with the murderer of his daughter.

All those who had suffered from the King's unjust taxation now rallied together and joined the barons. An army marched on London and there was welcomed by the people. The whole country was rising against the King, and John knew it.

He realized that there was only one course open to him. He must offer to comply with the barons' wishes. They would meet the King in a conference and this was to take place on the 15th of June at a place called Runnymede.

*   *   *

And so in the meadow between Staines and Windsor the parties met. John had brought only a few attendants but the barons had felt it necessary to muster as many supporters as they could. They had their armed knights and the people, knowing their purpose, had joined their ranks as they marched to Runnymede so that it was a multitude which reached the pleasant field.

For twelve days the conference continued. There were adjustments to the clauses and continuous discussion while John looked on and watched his power diminishing.

The church was to be free to have her rights and liberties unhurt; so were the King's subjects; widows should not be forced to marry against their will; goods could not be seized for debt if the debtor could discharge the debt; no scutage (a tax demanded for the purpose of supplying funds for war) was to be imposed by the King unless it was agreed by a common council.

In fact no taxation was to be levied without consent of the council. All ancient liberties and customs of cities to be preserved. There were several clauses pertaining to law. No person was to be kept in prison for a long term without an enquiry into his guilt or innocence.

These were but a few of the clauses to which John was forced to agree and as he read them he saw what he had always regarded as his kingly privileges being whittled away. There would be a new freedom in the land after the signing of Magna Carta and much of the King's power would be lost to him.

The barons with their leader Robert FitzWalter were not going to allow John to escape.

So he must pen his name to the great charter of Runnymede.

*   *   *

Isabella, having given birth to another daughter, whom she named Eleanor, heard of the momentous events which were shaking the very foundations of the throne.

It had been certain to happen, she knew. John had brought it on himself. He had made so many enemies. Arthur's disappearance would never be forgotten; and there were so many influential families whose members he had wronged in some way.

She often thought about Matilda FitzWalter with whom he was supposed to be so enamoured and she wondered why he had not forced the girl if he had been as eager as rumour would have it he was. It was strange that he should have had her poisoned because she would not submit. But there were so many odd twists and turns in his nature that one could never be entirely sure of what he was thinking.

He had given her so many shocks recently. First her lover's body over her bed and then giving little Joanna to Hugh. Then she fell to wondering why Hugh had not married and whether it had anything to do with his devotion to herself. How would he feel about marrying her daughter? But that was far away. Who could be sure what would happen by then?

John had not visited her lately. She supposed he was too preoccupied with the barons and their demands.

Who would have believed at the beginning of his reign that so much could have been lost? Who but John would have lost it?

He was not in good health. She had been aware of that for some time. The anxieties of the last years would have done nothing to alleviate that, and she had always maintained that those fearful rages would kill him one day.

So as she nursed her baby she asked herself what would happen to her when John was dead, for she had a notion that that day might not be far off.

*   *   *

After the signing of the Charter John gave way to his rage, and those about him thought that he would indeed kill himself. He was like a madman; he gnashed his teeth and tore at his clothes; he lay on the floor kicking at furniture and any who came near him; he picked up handfuls of rushes, stuffed them into his mouth and chewed them, seeming to find some relief in this. He muttered to himself and those within earshot listened to the bloodcurdling threats he uttered about what he would do to his enemies. His bouts of rage would subside and then burst out again. The only relief he could get seemed to be through them.

Chains they had put on him, he cried out. These upstarts! They wanted to kill him. They wanted to take his kingdom from him. They had been against him all his life. They would learn one day what happened to his enemies. There would be no mercy ... none...

When he grew calmer he decided that he would appeal once more to the Pope. Was he not the fief of the Pope? Had he not surrendered his crown to the Pope and had not the Pope returned it to him? Momentarily he seemed to hear the sighs of his ancestors. The bitter shame of it! But everyone was against me! he cried. Not the Holy Father though. He would support him. A quick smile touched John's lips. It was so ironical to think of the Church's standing with him. In his message to the Pope he mentioned the fact that he was contemplating going on a crusade for of late since he had turned whole-heartedly to the Church he felt his past sins weigh heavily upon him. A mission to the Holy Land alone could rid him of this burden and if he could bring peace to his kingdom he would make his plans.

It was those barons who had brought him to this state— those wicked barons; the Braoses who were determined to have their revenge because that virago of theirs had met her just deserts; Vesci who had made such a fuss because he had admired his wife; and FitzWalter whose silly daughter had refused to submit to her King.

Vesci had told him when the barons were assembled that he was mistaken if he thought he had dishonoured his wife. 'You slept with a common whore, my lord. You were too drunk to notice she was not my wife.'

'Liar!' he had cried and wanted to shout to someone to take the man away and cut out his tongue.

Vesci was bold with the might of the barons behind him.

'We often laugh at the way in which you were duped, my lord, my wife and I.'

He must have been certain that John would never regain power to have talked like that.

He had tried to think back to that night but he could not remember very clearly and the pleasure he had had from that episode came after when he thought of the haughty Vesci who, as he had thought, had had to give up his wife.

And they had duped him, for deep in his heart he believed this to be so—substituting a common harlot for the lady of the castle; and they had laughed at him. They had cheated him as all the barons had assembled to do.

And strangest of all—his friend was the Pope.

He knew he was right in thinking that the Pope would give him his support. Was he not a fief of the Pope? he kept telling himself. Therefore, the Holy Father would have no wish to see him defeated.

Innocent read the despatches very gravely and came to the conclusion that the barons were seeking to depose John. Why so? Because he had made England a vassal of Rome? The Pope did not wish the King to lose his crown. What if England were plunged into civil war and a new king set up? What of England's obligations to Rome then?

The Pope sent orders to Stephen Langton to pronounce the sentence of excommunication on the barons.

Langton's reply was to inform the Pope that he was not fully acquainted with the true state of affairs in England. The King had behaved as a tyrant and the barons were only asking for justice and determined to get it. The case was very different from the manner in which John had presented it.

The Pope was angered by this reply from the Archbishop whose election had created such a storm. He could not understand what was happening. It seemed to him that John had behaved in a most seemly manner. He had become reconciled to the Church; he had reinstated the clergy; he was planning to go on a crusade. And the barons were behaving in a manner to suggest they planned deposing such a king. They should be helping him prepare for the crusade. Christian leaders were needed in the Holy Land. In creating such disturbances now the barons were displeasing God as much as the Saracens did.

How explain to the Pope that John was indeed a tyrant, that he was a worthless king, that he had lost his possessions overseas and was on the verge of losing England? How explain that he had no intention of going on a crusade?

The Pope ended by saying that unless Stephen Langton carried out orders he would be deprived of his office.

* * *

John roused himself from his rage and looked the situation straight in the face. If he did not act quickly he was going to lose his kingdom. He must raise an army to fight these barons. He must show them that he would not lightly pass over his crown.

He rode out at dawn one morning with a very few followers and made his way to Dover. He had already despatched one of his agents, Hubert de Boves, to the Continent to recruit an army of mercenaries. He was going to lie low until that army was ready.

Very few people knew where he was and those who did had been sworn to secrecy. The barons were nonplussed and there was nothing they could do but wait for news of the King's whereabouts.

John smiled wryly considering the speculation there would be about him. At first there were rumours that he had gone to France to parley with Philip and ask his help. That would have been a dangerous measure but John was capable of such folly. Others said that he had in fact gone on the crusade which he had said he would do but no one could really believe that either. All those near him knew that he had no intention of going on the crusade and that when he had talked of it it had been jokingly. The idea of John's crusading was ridiculous. One source said that he was dead, that he had been murdered by one of those who had a grudge against him and there were many to choose as suspects. Others said that he had tired of his life as a king and had become a fisherman in some remote part of the country.

John laughed at the rumours and gradually men began to arrive from the Continent.

He marched on Rochester and laid siege to the castle there which was in the hands of the barons. In due course the castle was taken but not before the inmates had been reduced to such starvation that they had eaten their horses.

John, furious that mercenaries should witness the defiance of his own subjects, ordered that every man in the castle should be hanged, but before this order was carried out the captain of the mercenaries managed to persuade him to rescind it. They did not wish to give the enemy an excuse for reprisals, he said. Let the King show his leniency and remember that these people were his own subjects who had perhaps been led astray or coerced into taking a stand against him.

Elated by the victory John was prepared to waive his anger and the defenders of Rochester castle did not lose their lives.

*   *   *

When the envoys arrived from Rome for the purpose of excommunicating the barons, the latter realized that powerful forces were being released against them. It was never wise to be at odds with the Church when there were battles to be fought, for soldiers could so easily persuade themselves that God was against them and account the smallest setback to Divine displeasure which would undermine future action.

If John had the Pope as an ally, they too must seek one as powerful—or perhaps more so; and the answer to this was of course Philip of France.

There was no doubt that that shrewd and wily monarch was watching events in England with the greatest interest. He had utterly defeated John on the Continent; he was now waiting for the barons to do so in England. He himself not so long ago had cast covetous eyes on the crown and had been turned from his attempt to take it by intervention from the Pope. The fact that help for John was again coming from that quarter gave him deep cause for thought. Philip was secretly amused that the most unholy of Kings should have found a friend in the most holy of Fathers. Popes, Philip said to himself, could be moved to act through expedience quite as often—more so in truth—than through holiness; and since Innocent himself had taken John's crown from him—and graciously bestowed it on him but as a vassal—he would naturally be very inclined to support his puppet.

Now came messengers from the barons of England. They had a proposition to make. If Philip would help them depose John they would be prepared to bestow the crown on Philip's son Louis.

Philip's eyes sparkled. So the crown of England could come to France after all!

He pretended to be dubious.

'How would the people of England reconcile themselves to a French king?' he wanted to know.

'My lord, Louis has a certain claim to the throne through his wife.'

Philip nodded. A claim of sorts, though a flimsy one. Eleanor, daughter of Henry the Second and Eleanor of Aquitaine, had married Alfonso, King of Castile. They had had a daughter, Blanche, who was Louis's wife. Therefore it could be said that the children Louis and Blanche would have would be descended from the English Royal House.

A flimsy link, thought Philip, but one worth considering. If it went wrong he could wash his hands of it and imply that it was Louis's concern. Philip had never greatly cared for the act of war; he preferred to win his battles through strategy; he would greatly enjoy sitting back and watching what Louis made of it. It would be a great achievement if the crown of England came to France.

He could of course see that the barons were not so eager as they would seem to set a French king on their throne, but since the intervention of the Pope their need was urgent. John was amassing a large army of mercenaries from the Continent and this army would be mainly composed of the French—subjects of Philip. It might well be that the barons, as John's army increased, believed they were being forced into a desperately unfavourable position. It was a clever stroke of strategy to call in the help of Philip's son Louis.

While the French were debating how they should act, the Pope threatened to excommunicate Stephen Langton who was not obeying the orders sent from Rome and was pleading the just cause of the barons.

Langton realized that his only hope of convincing the Pope was to go in person to Rome and plead his cause with him.

When John heard that Langton had left for Rome he was uneasy. Langton was an eloquent man; he could lay the case before Innocent in a manner which would bring no good to John. Up to this point his chances had seemed good. His army was increasing and although they were mercenaries who would fight any battle providing the rewards were good, they were trained soldiers, experienced and well equipped in every way for battle. The barons were clearly not trained soldiers; they lacked leaders. A man bent on revenge such as Robert FitzWalter might rouse people by the force of his eloquence but that did not make him a good leader.

'By God's ears and teeth,' cried John, 'I am going to subdue these barons. I am going to make them wish they had thought twice before raising their hands against me.'

Then luck began to turn against him. The first stroke came with the death of Innocent, and although John immediately put his case to his successor, Honorius the Third was not interested. Support from Rome had crumbled. Then Louis had arrived in England and was given a welcome by the barons.

'So they have called in the French!' cried John. 'I never thought to see the like. No good has come to me since I turned to the Church.'

The faithful Marshal was beside him, urging him not to despair. He had his mercenaries, trained soldiers and it was well known that those who defended their homes had an advantage over the invaders. Some special fighting spirit was given to them; it was their determination to fight to the end.

'What of the Conqueror?' cried John. 'He came and took the land. Are the French going to do to me what he did to the Saxons?'

'Not if you are strong.'

'Strong! Am I not strong? And what of these cursed barons?'

The Marshal shook his head sadly. It was not the time to tell him that his tyrannical acts had made bitter enemies of men who might otherwise have been his friends.

'Those who are loyal to the crown will fight to the death to keep it where it belongs.'

'And they have brought in the French, the accursed traitors.'

'Traitors indeed,' agreed the Marshal.

'They have brought foreigners into the land.'

As he had, the Marshal thought sadly, with his mercenaries. Foreign soldiers to fight Englishmen in their own country!

William Marshal had never thought it would come to this. The barons were demanding justice; they had produced their Charter and John had been forced to pen his signature to it. That great wise King Henry the First had granted a charter— not because he wished to reduce his own power but because he wished to strengthen it. But he had been a wise king.

The summer was passing. It was an uneasy situation with an enemy on English soil. Even those who had brought them into the country now felt qualms. Did they want to be a vassal of France? Did they want Louis on their throne?

When Louis had arrived the majority of the barons had welcomed him; now they were not so sure. Many who had first supported him now came back to John. He did not reproach them; he was only too pleased to see them.

He heard that Eustace de Vesci had been killed at the siege of Barnard's Castle.

He laughed aloud thinking of the man who had stood before him insolently recounting how he had duped the King. He had been one of the main leaders of the rebels, egged on by thoughts of revenge. And now it was Vesci who lay stiff and cold, not John.

The King of Scotland had come to the aid of the rebels and was harrying the North; but the fact that so many of the barons were now regretting the arrival of the French put heart into John.

He planned to drive his forces between those of the Scots in the North and the barons in the South and this brought him to the town of Lynn—a loyal town, a trading town which like the Cinque ports, enjoyed certain privileges.

At Lynn he was well received and he spent the time there feasting, drinking and listening to music while he planned his next move.

Perhaps he had feasted too well in Lynn; perhaps he had drunk too freely of their wine, but he began to feel unwell and suffered from dysentery which made travelling difficult.

But he must move on and from Lynn he travelled to Wisbech. With him he took a great many belongings, everything he would need for sojourn wherever the occasion should arise, and as the King must always be surrounded by objects worthy of his rank—and never more so than when he was in danger of losing it—his baggage was considerable. It contained his jewellery of which he had always been inordinately fond and as he grew older and perhaps more in need of adornment to disguise his mottled complexion and his ravaged face, he liked to astonish with their brilliance all those who beheld him.

In addition to his jewellery he had brought other precious possessions including his ornamental plate, flagons and goblets of gold and silver, the royal regalia—everything which it was necessary to keep with him for fear of its being taken by an enemy.

He wished to get to the north side of the Wash and rode off with his army leaving the wagons containing his possessions to take a more direct route—as their progress was necessarily slow—across the estuary. This journey had to be taken when the tide was out as it meant crossing sand which would be treacherous, and it was necessary to take guides who by prodding the sands with long poles could detect any sign of quicksand.

John left them to take the longer route, with instructions that he would wait at Swineshead on the north side of the Wash for the baggage to arrive.

The cumbersome cavalcade made its way to the sands. The guide was a little late and it was impossible to start without him. Therefore they would have to make up speed in the crossing. The mist descended and they set out. Before they were half way across the estuary the wheels of the wagons became stuck in the sand and it was impssible to move them. The tide started to come in and in spite of the frantic efforts of the drivers of the vehicles they remained stuck fast.

The waters washed over the sands and the wagons were sucked down with all their contents.,

John waiting at Swineshead realized what had happened and let out a great wail of anger.

He felt ill, exhausted by the rigours of the drive in his condition; and this seemed the last straw.

He soon learned that he had lost his jewels, his precious plate, everything that constituted his wealth.

* * *

What was there to do? He felt ill and wretched. He was defeated. The French were on English soil. His barons were rising against him. The new Pope was indifferent to his plight. This must be the end.

His anger was intense, but quieter because he had not the physical strength to give it play.

Was this what he had longed for in the days when Richard was King? Was this what he had murdered Arthur for? There had been good times of course. The first days with Isabella.

Where was Isabella now? What was she thinking? How would she feel when he was dead?

He wanted revenge ... revenge!

On the way to the Abbey of Swineshead they passed a convent and stopped for refreshment. It was brought to them by a nun who seemed to him in his fevered state to have a look of Isabella. To think of Isabella in a nun's robe was amusing. But that, he thought, is how she would have looked years ago had they dressed her thus.

He spoke to the nun, who shrank from him, and he felt the stirrings of anger and a desire to force his will upon her. It was but a shadow of the feelings he had known in the past. He mused as he drank the ale she had brought for them. A few years, no less than that, I would have made some plan to abduct her. I would have had good sport with her.

But he was in no mood for sport. He thought of his beautiful jewels somewhere in the quicksands of the Wash. He thought of the French on his soil and his subjects taking up arms against him. And a nagging anger possessed him, a futile anger because he was too weak to give voice to it.

They left the convent and went on to Swineshead. Here they would rest for the night.

He sat at refectory. He ate and drank and tried to regain his youth and spirits. He tried to forget what was happening; he wanted to be young again. The wine numbed his senses, soothed the pains of his body and loosened his tongue.

He talked of the nun he had seen. 'By God's ears,' he said, 'we'll ride back that way. I'll take her ... by force if necessary.

She had a look in her eyes ... perhaps not so prim, eh?'

One of his men whispered to him: 'I have heard that the nun is the sister of the Abbot here.'

That made him laugh. 'So much the better. So much the better. Oh God's eyes, what is this country coming to? Disloyal subjects. I'll starve them to death. Perhaps they won't be so eager to shout for the Frenchman when I have taught them what starvation means. I'll make food scarce ... I'll burn the granaries. They shall know hunger ... and I shall know the Abbot's sister.'

'My lord,' said one of the monks, 'I believe you have a fondness for peaches.'

' 'Tis so.'

'We have some choice peaches. Have I your permission to bring you some.'

'I give that permission,' cried John.

A little later the monk came with three peaches on a platter. John ate them hungrily. Almost immediately afterwards he was seized with violent pains.

*   *   *

All through the night he suffered and in the morning he set out on his journey, but when he reached the Bishop of Lincoln's castle at Newark he could go no farther.

'I think I am dying,' he said.

The Bishop brought the Abbot of Croxton to him for he was said to be skilled in the art of healing; but there was nothing the Abbot could do.

John lay on his bed thinking of past events and begging the Abbot of Croxton to hear his confession.

Where to begin? There were so many black sins that he had forgotten half of them. Dominating them all was the night in the castle of Rouen when he had killed Arthur and taken his body out, burdened with a stone, that he might sink in the waters of the Seine.

'Forgiveness, my lord God...' he murmured.

But he knew he was asking a great deal.

He said: 'What is that noise?'

' 'Tis the wind my lord. It is fierce this night.'

People said that the storm that blew on that October night of the year 1216 was that aroused by the gates of Hell opening wide to receive the Prince of Darkness in his true domain.

He died in the early hours of the eighteenth day of that month and as it was his wish that his body should be buried before the altar of St. Wulfstan in Worcester Cathedral, it was taken there in a funeral procession protected by the mercenary army he had brought over to fight for him.

Peace

THE death of the King had a great impact on feeling throughout the country. No one wished for a foreign ruler. All that had been necessary was to remove the tyrant who was King John. God had done that for them and now the country wanted to be at peace.

Isabella, no longer a prisoner, acted promptly. As soon as she heard that John was dead she determined to have her nine-year-old son Henry crowned immediately. She need not have feared. A party of the King's supporters and those of the barons came immediately to Winchester. There was no doubt in any minds that Henry must be crowned at once as King of England. The ceremony was performed by the Bishop of Winchester.

Now the whole of England was united to drive out the French. This was speedily achieved and England was at peace—the tyrant dead and a young king on the throne with ministers to guide him.

Isabella, with amazing energy at thirty-four years of age, was still possessed of great beauty, and although the mother of five children she had lost none of her appeal.

She decided to cross the sea, taking with her her daughter Joanna who was betrothed to Hugh de Lusignan that the custom of bringing up a child in the household of her betrothed might be carried out.

The outcome astonished most people, but perhaps not Isabella, for no sooner had Hugh set eyes on her than he knew it was the mother he wished to marry not her daughter.

So they were married and Isabella bore him many children while she continued with her tempestuous life.

Meanwhile, her son Henry the Third sat on the throne of England and the royal line which had begun with the Conqueror continued.

JEAN PLAIDY HAS ALSO WRITTEN

BEYOND THE BLUE MOUNTAINS
(A novel about early settlers in Australia)

DAUGHTER OF SATAN
(A novel about the persecution of witches and Puritans in the 16th and 17th centuries)

THE SCARLET CLOAK
(A novel of 16th century Spain, France and England)

Stories of Victorian England
IT BEGAN IN VAUXHALL GARDENS
LILITH

THE GOLDSMITH'S WIFE
(The story of Jane Shore)

EVERGREEN GALLANT
(The story of Henri of Navarre)

The Medici Trilogy
Catherine de' Medici
MADAME SERPENT
THE ITALIAN WOMAN
QUEEN JEZEBEL
}Also available in one volume

The Lucrezia Borgia Series
MADONNA OF THE SEVEN HILLS
LIGHT ON LUCREZIA
}Also available in one volume

The Ferdinand and Isabella Trilogy
CASTILLE FOR ISABELLA
SPAIN FOR THE SOVEREIGNS
DAUGHTERS OF SPAIN
}Also available in one volume

The French Revolution Series
LOUIS THE WELL-BELOVED
THE ROAD TO COMPIÈGNE
FLAUNTING, EXTRAVAGANT QUEEN

The Tudor Novels
Katharine of Aragon
KATHARINE, THE VIRGIN WIDOW
THE SHADOW OF THE POMEGRANATE
THE KING'S SECRET MATTER
}Also available in one volume

MURDER MOST ROYAL
(Anne Boleyn and Catharine Howard)

THE SIXTH WIFE
(Katharine Parr)

ST THOMAS'S EVE
(Sir Thomas More)

THE SPANISH BRIDEGROOM
(Philip II and his first three wives)

GAY LORD ROBERT
(Elizabeth and Leicester)

THE THISTLE AND THE ROSE
(Margaret Tudor and James IV)

MARY, QUEEN OF FRANCE
(Queen of Louis XII)

The Mary Queen of Scots Series
ROYAL ROAD TO FOTHERINGAY
THE CAPTIVE QUEEN OF SCOTS

The Stuart Saga	THE MURDER IN THE TOWER (Robert Carr and the Countess of Essex)

Charles II
- THE WANDERING PRINCE
- A HEALTH UNTO HIS MAJESTY
- HERE LIES OUR SOVEREIGN LORD

} Also available in one volume

The Last of the Stuarts
- THE THREE CROWNS (William of Orange)
- THE HAUNTED SISTERS (Mary and Anne)
- THE QUEEN'S FAVOURITES (Sarah Churchill and Abigail Hill)

} Also available in one volume

The Georgian Saga

THE PRINCESS OF CELLE (Sophia Dorothea and George I)

QUEEN IN WAITING
 CAROLINE THE QUEEN } (Caroline of Ansbach)

THE PRINCE AND THE QUAKERESS (George III & Hannah Lightfoot)

THE THIRD GEORGE (George III)

PERDITA'S PRINCE (Perdita Robinson)

SWEET LASS OF RICHMOND HILL (Mrs Fitzherbert)

INDISCRETIONS OF THE QUEEN (Caroline of Brunswick)

THE REGENT'S DAUGHTER (Princess Charlotte)

GODDESS OF THE GREEN ROOM (Dorothy Jordan and William IV)

VICTORIA IN THE WINGS (End of the Georgian Era)

The Queen Victoria Series

THE CAPTIVE OF KENSINGTON PALACE (Early days of Victoria)

THE QUEEN AND LORD M (Victoria and Lord Melbourne)

THE QUEEN'S HUSBAND (Victoria and Albert)

THE WIDOW OF WINDSOR (Last years of Victoria's reign)

The Norman Trilogy

THE BASTARD KING

THE LION OF JUSTICE

THE PASSIONATE ENEMIES

The Plantagenet Saga

THE PLANTAGENET PRELUDE

THE REVOLT OF THE EAGLETS

THE HEART OF THE LION

THE PRINCE OF DARKNESS

THE BATTLE OF THE QUEENS

THE QUEEN FROM PROVENCE

EDWARD LONGSHANKS

THE FOLLIES OF THE KING

Non-fiction

MARY QUEEN OF SCOTS: *The Fair Devil of Scotland*

A TRIPTYCH OF POISONERS
 (Cesare Borgia, Madame de Brinvilliers and Dr Pritchard)

THE RISE OF THE SPANISH INQUISITION
 THE GROWTH OF THE SPANISH INQUISITION
 THE END OF THE SPANISH INQUISITION } Also available in one volume